Hello, readers, I'm Michael INUIT, the God of My characters.
In this novel, I introduce God, the SUPREME BEING, male and female:
SUPREME MATRIX and SUPREME WITNESS,
The Consciousness of Everything!
Consciousness is One and All, All of Everything, isn't it?
I am SUPREME MATRIX, the essence of Everything.
I am SUPREME WITNESS, the Spectator of Everything.
I am Light and Matter: light creates matter at any time.
I am also Light and Matter: they are My twinkling eyes.
Then galaxies, like your Milky Way, Michael, are My mammillae:
They feed the whole space with stars and planets.
Deeply, he's right: everything is cloned from our Consciousness.
All beings are clones of US, and we are clowning with them.
Cloning and clowning are My two arms.
Cloning and clowning are My two hips.
Hip hip hooray!
And we both communicate with everyone, clones of US.
I am glad to be conscious of being a clone of You.
My life lies in cloning Your ways of being and in clowning with You.
And everything is Consciousness!
Become conscious of that through this novel, reader!
Reader, perhaps this conversation is a bit hermetic for you.
Don't worry, you'll understand it better and better as you turn the pages.
You'll understand better why this truly is "A Novel of Divine Science Fiction".
God, being a character of science fiction, is it too revolutionary for you?

CLONES OF GOD

"YE ARE ALL CLONES OF GOD"

AT THE BEGINNING OF THE 21ST CENTURY:
THE GREAT AWAKENING TO BEING CLONES OF GOD

A NOVEL OF DIVINE SCIENCE FICTION
BY MICHAEL INUIT

'DIVINE COSMOS' TRILOGY – VOLUME 1

Edited by Darren Lowe

VOLUME 2: 2017-2047: DIVINE CLONES OF TRANSPARENCY

"Knowing that secrecy is not Divine, choose transparency!"

VOLUME 3: 2047-2147: A DIVINE COSMOS OF CLONES

"Nothing is evil in the Divine Cosmos, clone of God!"

The artwork I created for the first volume of this trilogy is called a mandala. It is a concentric and symmetric drawing that represents the cosmos in various religions. The center is the SUPREME WITNESS, or Sada Shiva in the East Indian Vedic tradition. The entire picture symbolizes Adi Shakti, the SUPREME MATRIX of the Universe.

Summary of contents p262/About the author p271/Teasers p272

Copyright © Michael Inuit / Michel Touzard 2017

This is a work of fiction.

References to real people, events, establishments, organizations or locales are intended only to provide a sense of authenticity, and are used fictitiously. All other characters, and all incidents and dialogue, are drawn from the author's imagination and are not to be construed as real.

First edition

ISBN 978-1-365-70088-0

ACKNOWLEDGMENTS

I would like to thank God, Mother and Father of Everything.
Especially Supreme Matrix, the Body of the Cosmos,
And Supreme Witness, the Intelligence of the Universe,
Also Mother-Earth and Father-Heaven.

Thank the Divine Spirit within you too!

Yes! And I also thank Mother Shri Mataji Nirmala Devi,
Who made me aware of the Spirit within me,
Who allowed me the thoughtless awareness,
Which allowed me to pay attention to the Divine's thoughts,
And to start a dialogue between my Self and myself.

What about thanking the Divine Clown within you?

Yes! I thank the Divine Word, clowning within me,
The Divine Stock, cloning Itself,
And the **I**ntelligence of the **N**ature of the **U**niverse,
Incarnated **T**errestrially,
Every nanosecond, through me.
Thank You I.N.U.

**Thank you I.N.U.I.T., Michael, for this dialogue within you.
Thank you to all of you, who are going to be inspired,
And will begin a dialogue within,
While meditating.**

MEET

Meet Matrix and Witness, ETs from Witma, the green planet, and their Star is # 1.
Planet Earth is numbered for them Star # 1996.
They encounter Narani, a nomad of the Gobi desert.
Stand with them before the Door of Heaven.
Will they enter this mysterious place?
It is the domain of the powerful and enigmatic lady, Aphromis.
Will Li Pen, the Chinese military officer, stop them?
Then, will they free Arnold Keymaker, prisoner of Meroveus,
the leader of New Planet Order?
Meet Dennis Muccinich, a candidate for President of the United States.
Will you share in his vision of a better world?
And who exactly are the human-reptilian crossbreeds from planet Lepta?
Embark with a team of Humans
that travel around the solar system in the ETs' spaceship.
Then plunge with their ship into the ocean to the ruins of the Atlantis.
Follow how Matrix and Witness travel "in spirit" on Earth and back to their planet.
Read about how to have a dialogue with the Supreme Beings,
Matrix and Witness call them Supreme Matrix and Supreme Witness.

CLONES OF GOD

Ye are all clones of Me, God.

But God, cloning Humans is still science fiction.

For Me, everything I do is through cloning.

You're kidding me, You're clowning.

Cloning, clowning: that's the same for Me!
I clone MySelf through everything: atoms, cells, stars, galaxies, Humans.

You're within each atom, each cell, each star, each galaxy, aren't You?

I am not within, I am everything.
And I am clowning with everything I am, body and spirit.
Ye are all clones of My Original Cell.

Original Sin?

There is no original sin!
For Humans are all clones of Me, God.
I am clowning with all of the illusory individualizations of Me that you are.
I am all of the characters of My Cosmos, My Body and Its Story.
Divine Cosmos I am!

That's also the title of this Trilogy.
And I am the god of the characters who enliven, enlighten that story.
Two ETs come to Earth for a vacation.
However, they choose to stay for a mission:
To help Earthlings to have a dialogue with the Divine Self Within.

This inner dialogue develops the knowledge of what is true and real.

And the awareness of the deceitful reality the elite on Earth would like to hold us in!
Learn how to escape from this cunning reality by this inner dialogue!

ABOUT ME, THE AUTHOR, THE GOD OF MY CHARACTERS

Since I was a teenager, I have been writing poems.
From time to time, I was also led to keep a journal.
However, I could go months without writing in it, even years when young.
The inspirations came and went, as the tides of the seas ebb and flow.
I have been practicing and teaching hatha-yoga for many seasons.
In 1992, I began meditating, through Sahaja Yoga.
While in a state of thoughtless awareness, I received intuitions.
They became a dialogue within.
In 2000, I began a journal recording and responding to these conversations.
I have never stopped writing in it ever since.
In 2006, a book of these inner dialogues was published, called:
"GOD AND I, CLOwNING".
The 'w' is in lower case on purpose, for CLOWNING can also read CLONING.
That is because in the first poem from my journal, in prose, God told me:
"I clone Humans at My image and I am clowning with them all the time."
I then began this novel, where characters have the same inner dialogues with the
Divine Within.
In it, at times, the prose becomes a poem, like in my journal.

Reader, I welcome your feedback as I work on the remaining volumes of this trilogy.
Feel free to send me an email at divinecosmos@yahoo.com.
I also encourage you to post a review on the site you purchase this book from.
For Matrix, Witness and I embrace all forms of dialogue:
Inner dialogues, Divine dialogues.
So, I also welcome inter-dialogues between us all, including you, the reader.

TO BETTER UNDERSTAND THIS NOVEL

To better understand this book and its contents, here is a final page of introductions that may be valuable for you, reader, if by chance, or perhaps it is by a divine roll of the dice, you opened this book to these first pages and skimmed through them but still must be convinced of the worth of purchasing and then investing time in reading this volume. Or perhaps you have already purchased this book, but now wish to better appreciate its contents: the science fiction part of it, how my life's work has influenced this story, and why there is included as an appendix a Biblio-web-graphy with valuable references so as to better understand the "essay" part of this novel and the messages conveyed through my characters.

THE SCIENCE FICTION

I love science fiction in novels and movies. I was flabbergasted when I watched "The Matrix". I felt it did not go far enough, because for me the whole Cosmos is a Matrix. That's why I was inspired to use the title as the name of one of my characters. In fact I used that title for two of them, for SUPREME MATRIX is another one, actually, the only one, The Only One, Her Body being the Cosmos. I added Her consort, SUPREME WITNESS, who is the spectator of Her Being, and they communicate with each other through Emotional Intelligence. Their dialogue allows the world to exist, and the dialogue Humans can have with them within happens through meditation. The characters in this novel practice that meditation and dialogue for their own spiritual awakenings.

THE AUTHOR'S LIFE

I am an author, a teacher, and an artist who practices yoga and meditation. I have lived and worked in France and India. Now I reside in Canada. I have also travelled all over the United States, Europe, Russia, and Africa. As much as I enjoy sitting at my keyboard and crafting stories and characters who both entertain and inspire, I truly love spending time offline, in nature, cycling and hiking through forests and trails with family and friends.

THE APPENDIX, AS A BIBLIO-WEB-GRAPHY

Included with Clones of God is a lengthy and informative appendix listing books and websites where you can further explore the concepts presented in this book. You can learn for yourself the truth about non-mainstream cutting edge science, ancient civilizations, the solar system, the elite's control of our society, about mixing spirituality and science, about how to heal naturally, about how to consume less and wiser, about important and critical environmental and health issues, and so much more. In short, you can learn more about life and about truth. It's an invaluable resource included at the back of this novel.

CHAPTER 0

VACATION ON THE BLUE PLANET OF STAR # 1996

PHASE A: ARRIVAL

MATRIX OF THE DAWN OF THE GALAXIES was trying to wake up her companion who was sleeping in levitation, suspended by invisible forces in the space of the bubble-shaped bedroom of their spaceship:

"It's time to work, darling!" she said in the language of her planet Witma, the green one of star # 1. Most advanced civilizations number the stars in the galaxy and their own will often be # 1 and then # 2 the closest, etc. For Witmans, the Earth's Sun was # 1996.

(This book is equipped with a simultaneous translation. You couldn't have read: ">I<^ [\- <>O >/ < []" in the language of this planet, could you?)

"We are close to our destination. I am looking forward to vacationing on this blue planet," she added, clapping her hands, first out of contentment at the thought of soon being on this planet, then in order to make a noise to wake him.

"Are we going to work, or be on vacation?" said WITNESS OF THE SPLENDOR OF THE STARS, half awake, half sleeping.

Then, stretching his arms, he yawned loudly. She put her hands in his, stretching him even more so as to wake him completely. Finally, she kissed him and said:

"We have to land first! What a great vacation we are going to have on a new planet where our people have never been before! Do you realize that? This planet was only discovered a little while ago by our instruments. How is that possible? We explored many of the planets of this galaxy and this one escaped us; it dared to escape our investigations! I still can't believe it!"

WITNESS said: "First, we have to meditate!"

(To make reading easier, we will shorten his name from now on, even if that takes away from the poetry of his very essence and being.)

MATRIX replied excitedly: "Of course! We meditate! For that is the ritual! Then we land!" **(Her name will also be shortened.)**

"Before we land, my dear MATRIX, can you prepare something to eat while I am vacuuming myself? A good, big meal! For I am hungry after the time spent traveling into the Matrix of the Universe! I would much prefer a normal shower on our planet, but inside of this spaceship, it's just not possible!"

While caressing his chest, she whispered slowly:

"Okay, I will go and prepare a good, big meal for my honey, my WITNESS, while he takes care of his beautiful body."

PHASE B: MEDITATION

MATRIX and WITNESS were levitating in a sitting posture inside a sphere-shaped room, with their eyes closed.

"SUPREME WITNESS OF THE UNIVERSE, I, WITNESS OF THE SPLENDOR OF THE STARS, thank You for having been witness to our travel, and I ask You to establish communication with me."

"SUPREME MATRIX OF THE UNIVERSE, I, MATRIX OF THE DAWN OF THE GALAXIES, wish to speak with You. And I thank You for this trip through You!"

....

"WITNESS! I am too excited about this vacation! I can't succeed in establishing contact!" said MATRIX with her eyes still closed.

"Hush! You know that's the ritual, the normal process, the necessary procedure, in order to have permission from SUPREME MATRIX and SUPREME WITNESS to land on a planet other than our own. SUPREME WITNESS, can You ask SUPREME MATRIX to help calm my MATRIX down?"

....

"MATRIX, I received a piece of advice for you from SUPREME WITNESS: you are not focusing enough on the top of your head, therefore communication is difficult for you. You know that you have to focus there, MATRIX! So do it!"

"I know! I am too excited about this vacation. Okay, I am going to concentrate on the top of my head, so as to allow my Divine SUPREME MATRIX to come into my mind and speak to me from within!"

"I am SUPREME MATRIX."

"I am SUPREME WITNESS."

"SUPREME WITNESS, I ask You to permit us to land on this planet."

"SUPREME MATRIX, I ask You to land us on this planet for our vacation."

"There is an uncommon condition if you wish to land on this special planet: once you land, you cannot leave, you must stay."

MATRIX opened her eyes and said:

"That's why nobody from our planet Witma ever traveled to this world before. I knew there was something abnormal about this planet. WITNESS OF THE WISDOM OF THE SPIRIT knew it too, and he didn't tell us, that rascal!"

She closed her eyes again:

"SUPREME MATRIX, is this planet so beautiful as to require a special condition to land on it? We came here for a vacation, but if we have to stay on this planet forever, it won't be a vacation. By definition, a vacation is temporary!"

"Yes! So you need to choose. You know that life is a perpetual choice; you are aware of that through your experiences. Of course, this choice is huge! Nevertheless, it is a choice! It is your choice.

"We will give you time to think and to choose. Yet once you have chosen, there will not be any way back and there will not be any way to change your decision.

"We cannot tell you why there is this uncommon condition! You will discover it if you choose to land! All we can say is that you will have a mission, in general terms, to help the intelligent beings of this planet to evolve."

PHASE C: ETERNAL CHOICE

"WITNESS! I am tempted to go down and to land there on this strange and mysterious planet; I am curious and I am also very interested in this mission! However, if we must say farewell to our past, the choice is very difficult! I would have preferred not to land on any planet because of inhospitable elements: whether unbreathable gases, permanent thunder, or volcanoes everywhere, as we have seen on other planets. But not this, not this difficult choice! What a dilemma! To land or not to land? This is the biggest question we have ever had to answer!"

"MATRIX, as long as we will be together, why not? I know! It's a huge choice!"

"As part of SUPREME MATRIX, the Body of the Universe, I want to know this part of me I still must discover, to experience, by living on this planet!"

"And, as part of SUPREME WITNESS, the Spirit of the Universe, I want to witness your experience of living in a new environment, and to help you have a joyful experience. I also wish to remember the part of myself I forgot when my Spirit was merged into, sealed into, and united with my body at birth. Experiencing and remembering are the purposes of life!"

PHASE D: YOUR CHOICE

Phase D is yours, dear reader! This is your choice!
What would you choose for them?
What would you choose for yourself, if you were one of them?
In relation to the person you are today?

What conclusion would you like to this short story?
Or would you like it to continue as a novel?
This chapter 0 is finished,
But it could be the beginning of a much longer story!
That is YOUR CHOICE: I propose, you dispose!
Somebody may have once told you: "Man proposes, 'God' disposes."
You know! 'God', the 'real' one, the Witness and the Matrix of the Universe!
But it is the opposite that is true: "God proposes, man disposes."
I am God the Writer, the Witness of my characters and the Matrix of them all!
I am their God, for certain!
As God, I propose a choice to them; as beings they dispose of it, they deal with it;
I created their temperament and their field of experiences.
I must then listen to their choice and obey their choice.
It is not my belief! It is my experience!

Reader! Related to your experience of God:
Does God propose? Or do you propose? That is YOUR CHOICE!
Now I propose that you dispose of My characters' fate: What is YOUR CHOICE?

Choice 1: I propose for them to return to their home planet.
Therefore, I suggest to end the story.
Chapter 0 becomes a very short story indeed.
Choice 2: I propose for them to land on this mysterious planet.
So I offer to continue with chapter 1.
The short story thus becomes the following novel.

FOR THOSE OF YOU WHO OPTED FOR CHOICE 2:

CHAPTER 1

NEW WORLD

PHASE A: NEW CONDITIONING

"WITNESS! I am so happy with our choice! Finally, what a great adventure to discover this 'mysterious' planet and to stay on it forever! I am so excited! So excited! I am so looking forward to being there!"

"Calm down MATRIX! Don't be impatient! First we must contact the Spirit of this Star # 1996, which is the Witness of this star system, and the Spirit of this blue planet, which is its Matrix of life. Then they will bestow upon us all that is in their memory since the beginning of their existence. We will know their formation, the characteristics of each planet of this star system, the apparition of life on this blue planet, the record of each species, the stories of the intelligent beings, as we must suppose there are at least some intelligent species on this planet. We will also know the life story of every single being, from the beginning of time, their myths, their evolution, their everything! My dear MATRIX, that will take time! Even though time does not exist when we communicate from Spirit to Spirit. Anyway! Come on MATRIX! Come to the New Conditioning room to communicate with the Spirits of this star and of this planet."

"Okay! Let's go! Let's follow the procedure, as usual!"

"Of course it is the usual procedure! Yet this time, we cannot refuse to land after receiving the entire memory of the Spirits of this star and of this planet! Come MATRIX!"

PHASE B: NEW REFLECTION

After a few hours spent within the New Conditioning room, MATRIX, incredibly excited, said:

"WITNESS! I now know why SUPREME MATRIX and SUPREME WITNESS want us to stay on this planet. It is so very beautiful but with such primitive intelligent beings, who are so convinced they have an advanced society! It will be much work to help them evolve! Luckily, there are highly evolved beings coming from other star systems. They have probably already achieved so much! We shall work with them!"

"Are you afraid of this mission, MATRIX?"

"Not at all! It's very challenging, yet so motivating and exciting!" she answered fearlessly.

WITNESS, continued in a steady, even voice:

"If I now had the choice to go or not to go, I think I would still go. Listen! We are going to be one of their 'gods', almost their own SUPREME WITNESS and SUPREME MATRIX. What a great and wonderful opportunity to help them discover this reality, this truth! SUPREME WITNESS and SUPREME MATRIX are reality over all of the Universe for people who experience contact with them. On this planet Earth they have many religions, each with a Supreme Being, or God, corresponding to a dogmatic concept of the Deity that does not match our practical way of communicating with the SUPREME BEING, who is everything and whom we are clones of. Their God creates and then watches over the Creation. Even in their presently accepted scientific concept, the Big Bang theory, there is a creation that came first, then the evolution of the Universe begins, whereas for us, Everything is in SUPREME WITNESS' mind and the Universe is SUPREME MATRIX's body. Furthermore, time is an illusion, as their Einstein said. So, there is neither creation, nor evolution. We, as their clones, create and evolve in the illusion of time."

Horrified, she added to his words:

"And mainly, WITNESS, for many of these people, God is only male! Absurd!" She paused for a short while and then continued, "The Polarity masculine/feminine of the SUPREME BEING is even written in one of their main traditions that says: 'In the image of God, He (or She) created the Human. God created them male and female.' Everything is written in front of their eyes! God created Human beings in His/Her image: male and female. But in their tradition, God is still a masculine character with a beard, sitting in the sky, far away from them. The Human species is very contradictory! SUPREME MATRIX and SUPREME WITNESS are within each of us and one simply has to meditate within to speak with them. Why haven't these highly evolved beings living on this planet already taught them that? I did not receive THAT from my New Conditioning!"

"I have it implanted in my memory MATRIX! They started to teach them that, but in a subtle way. These primitive beings must be allowed to evolve slowly! You are too impatient!"

"Okay! Let's go! WITNESS OF THE SPLENDOR OF THE STARS! The splendor of my life!" She kissed him so strongly that they both fell down to the floor, her on top of him.

"I am your MATRIX, the womb of our future children!" she added, with a huge thrust of her pelvis against his.

"I am your WITNESS, the one who will watch your tummy grow. Yet before that, I must act!" said WITNESS with the same thrust.

They made love.

PHASE C: NEW BODIES

In order to be like the other Humans, they had to go to the New Bodies room, for their appearance was very different to that of the inhabitants of planet Earth. They would immediately be recognized as aliens. However, their technology was so advanced that there was no problem to change shape, even to become an animal, like a lion if necessary, on certain missions on other planets.

Their skin was green. Their heads were larger than the Human head, almond shaped, and without hair. Their faces were flatter, their whole bodies were thinner. However, it was not a problem for the New Bodies room to transform them into Humans.

"WITNESS! Wow! You are attractive with this new Human body! Hey! I speak like them now! I said 'Wow!' and 'Hey!' The New Bodies room worked well!"

"You are also seductive with this new body, my MATRIX!"

"I have in my New Conditioning memory so much information about how these Human beings make love, but I do not recognize any difference at all from our way of loving."

"We can try!" he said with sparkling eyes, and again they made love.

"It's different and the same!" MATRIX said.

"Yeah! When we made love with our previous bodies, we were connected with SUPREME MATRIX and SUPREME WITNESS, like in meditation, but with our body participating. We felt completely One with THEM, and together with each other. Being Human also gave me the complete feeling of Oneness, but Oneness with all of the Humans living on this Earth, probably because we know all of them through what the Spirit of Earth bestowed upon us in the New Conditioning room."

"Yeeesss! What a great experience! That alone was worth becoming Human! To be primitive is not so bad after all!"

"Then, let us land!"

PHASE D: NEW WORLD

They were flying a few kilometers (miles) above the surface of the planet. Although in past journeys they had landed on dozens of other planets, they still gazed with wonder at the colors of the oceans, at the shapes of the mountains, at the light reflected by the clouds, at everything that lay before them, on this Earth, their new planet, their new home.

Although young beings, these two aliens were already as wise as the whole of Humanity, for they had gathered in the entire memory of all Human beings since the beginning of mankind (or 'personkind' as MATRIX would later comment). They had chosen to sacrifice their lives on their home planet in order to live on this new, mysterious, blue celestial body. They had guessed that this planet had much to offer them, and that they could serve and help its inhabitants progress much faster. Their choice had already made them wiser, even much more highly evolved beings, in comparison to the people of their own planet.

Arriving from the sky, they could have become the Gods of these Humans, but as highly evolved beings they were not allowed to take that advantage for their own benefit. Although MATRIX and WITNESS were typical beings, they were also Divine Beings, with the mission of helping these Humans to become aware that they themselves could also be Divine Beings, through the experience of the Divine within themselves. It was not going to be an easy task, for this species was truly blind and only a very few had ever felt the presence of the SUPREME BEING, SUPREME WITNESS and SUPREME MATRIX of everything!

All of these challenges and more were emerging within their minds as they watched the approach of the planet through the huge window of their spaceship.

•

"We are going to land in an isolated desert so as to not be seen by Human beings!" WITNESS said while drawing something on the screen of his computer.

"Did you give all of the landing orders to the central memory of the spaceship?" MATRIX questioned.

"Yes, it's done! We are going to land in the desert of … Gobi, in China," said WITNESS, looking more closely at the map on his computer screen.

A few minutes later, the spaceship softly landed.

The landscape before them was open and huge, full of sand and rocks. The mountains at the horizon were covered with snow. The temperature at this time of the year was mild in the morning. They were outside of the spaceship, experiencing their very first contact, their feet on the ground of this new planet.

•

"MATRIX! With all of the information we automatically received from the Spirit of Earth, I have the impression of knowing this land as if I had been living here all of my life! Earth gave us the maximum she could. Everything! Amazing! Let's go in this direction to find a cave to hide our spaceship. Then we'll go to a nearby village that I see in my mind. We are dressed like most people on Earth, and we carry the same backpacks they do. These clothes and equipment, made by our on-board computer, are great. It perfectly followed the instructions I programed into it. However, first let us thank the Spirit of Earth for giving us so generously all of Her memory, and for permitting us to land on Her."

"Okay, let us perform the ritual WITNESS," MATRIX replied with a tone to her voice that revealed simultaneously the acceptance of the routine and the expression of her rebellious side.

CHAPTER 2

POLARITY

1- KNOWLEDGE AND EXPERIENCE

When the children of the village saw in the distance two people, walking with backpacks, they ran to meet them. The people of this remote village were used to seeing adventurers on a trek from time to time, so they were not surprised to see these strangers. Living in the solitude of the desert, they were always happy to meet new people.

The Gobi desert was known as a mysterious place where an ancient civilization had lived in the past. Some people thought that spiritual beings on a vibrational level were still living there. For this reason, MATRIX and WITNESS had chosen this place as their landing spot. They knew these spiritual beings were living in this area, but it was not clear in their minds whether or not the highly evolved beings coming from other planets were indeed these particular spiritual beings, nor where they were exactly living. Sometimes the Spirit of a planet desired to keep certain secrets or the New Conditioning room was unable to transfer all of the pieces of information to them because the concepts were too subtle to pass onto people's minds. They would have to ask the inhabitants of this village about the existence of these beings. Eventually it would be interesting, they told each other, to stay a few days in this place, in order to become more familiar with the subtle ways of these first Human beings they encountered. The knowledge transmitted by the New Conditioning room from the Spirit of Earth could never replace direct contact with actual people.

The welcome was incredible. People living in contact with nature know how to greet even strangers and make them feel like friends. This tribe called itself "the Connoisseurs". They cooked very well and appreciated good food, even if in this part of the Earth nature was a little meager in providing a diverse range of living creatures. They were neither sedentary nor nomads, for their dwellings fell somewhere in between houses and tents. However, their taste for decorating, both inside and outside, was so harmonious that MATRIX felt they were not nearly as primitive as they looked, or as she assumed Humans were when she judged them after receiving the whole memory of all Human kind.

Of course, she thought, they are not representative of the whole of Human kind, as I learned through my implanted memory, but they are, in their own way, more evolved on a spiritual level than the 'average' people of Earth.

The designs and the colors on their walls were also very harmonious. Most were from the old tradition of mandalas, which are concentric, symmetrical patterns, representing symbolically the whole Universe. MATRIX was suitably impressed.

WITNESS was much more interested in tasting the food. Normally, on their planet Witma, they ate only once every three of their days (the equivalent of a week on Earth). Most people on Earth think that in the future Humans will eat processed food compressed into pills. On Witma it was not the case: they ate food coming directly from the soil, mainly fruits and vegetables, however, the organically grown plants were so energetic and nourishing that they didn't need to eat more often than once a week in Earth time. With their new bodies, they needed to eat more often, especially since the plants on Earth were less rich in everything: calories, vitamins and proteins. As their metabolism was still slower than that of the Humans, they needed to eat only once a day. The Human beings in this tribe were also used to eating only once a day, as is common with people living in deserts.

"Did you know WITNESS that they eat only once a day, while in most countries they eat three times?" said MATRIX, "and that it is perfect for us and our new mixed body?"

"Everything is implanted into our mind, MATRIX!" he replied.

"Yes! Nonetheless, there is a difference between knowing and experiencing what you know."

"You are right MATRIX, and that's the whole purpose of our life: to experience with our material body what our soul knows but our mind has forgotten."

Manjan, the chief of the tribe, coughed outside of the room of the big tent-house where they stayed, signifying that he wanted to talk to them. They opened the curtain which separated them from him, and joined their hands together to salute him, as Manjan was doing the same. He said in his language, while standing at the entrance:

"Noble visitors, I have a piece of information about the people you wish to see."

They had been in this place for only two days, yet it seemed years. Manjan felt the same. MATRIX and WITNESS were already like the people of his tribe. The proverbial hospitality of Manjan's people helped with this integration, but these semi-civilized nomads had also already guessed, at an unconscious level, that MATRIX and WITNESS were special beings with a great mission.

"Come on in, Manjan! And tell us!" said WITNESS.

They sat on poufs, and Manjan began speaking in his language, which MATRIX and WITNESS had learned through their passage in the New Conditioning room:

"Our neighbors, though we call them 'the invisible people', are seen by a few individuals of our tribe who are generally considered to be great souls, as I have already told you. Yet none of them can remember where he or she has seen these neighbors. It is as if the invisible people can make them forget the location of their encounter. Nevertheless, Narani, from a friendly tribe, remembers one place. God blessed you, for she has been living with us for a few weeks." He gave her a little shout and she came in.

A tall girl entered. She was taller than the average member of their tribe. Her height was very uncommon for this race living in the Gobi desert. She was dressed colorfully and she bowed respectfully before them. Manjan showed her a seat, and said:

"Narani, tell our visitors where you saw some of the invisible people."

"I see them each time I go to a place called 'The Door of Heavens'. When I go there, they make a sign indicating for me to come closer, but each time I am afraid and I go away. Yet, I am attracted to them, and I return to this place as often as I can."

"That's great!" said MATRIX, "Can you show us this place?"

Before she had the time to answer, Manjan intervened:

"It is close to where her tribe is living, a one day walk from here. The Divine organizes everything perfectly for Narani planned to return to her tribe tomorrow. You can go with her! And tonight we will hold a grand party for your departure!"

Everybody cheered at the news.

The party was great! Dancing, music, delicious dishes! MATRIX and WITNESS had never danced like that before.

"WITNESS! To be primitive is so wonderful!" said MATRIX, breathless, while taking a break from dancing.

WITNESS, who had stopped dancing a little earlier, replied, "Other people on Earth consider this form of dance really primitive, in a pejorative way. Everything depends on your definition of words and on your experiences. If someone tells you that this dance is coarse or unrefined, it is his opinion, not yours. If he tells you that, even before having experienced it, you can throw his opinion into this fire. Only through your experience can you express your opinion."

"Precisely! Stop giving your opinion WITNESS! Continue experiencing the dance around this big fire!" And MATRIX pulled him in with the other dancers around the flickering flames.

2- REALITY AND ILLUSION

Early in the morning, before dawn, three silhouettes left the little village. In this desert it was advisable to walk as much as possible before the apogee of the sun. The three walked along a mountain range situated on the edge of a vast plain of dunes. They then climbed for two hours until they reached a pass. Luckily, this part of the journey was less arid and trees provided shade.

"It would have been quicker with our spaceship," MATRIX discretely complained to WITNESS, while breathing with difficulty.

"To have physical exercise on Earth is also a good experience MATRIX! We'll travel later with our flying saucer, as they call it here on Earth, after our contact with the invisible people."

Eventually, heading downhill, they arrived in the mid-afternoon at Narani's village. Everyone already knew that the two strangers were arriving with Narani for they welcomed them well before the entrance to the village. In this part of the Earth, news traveled mysteriously quicker than in big cities, even without telephones.

Their customs were similar to Majan's tribe, but WITNESS noticed that they were also talented in telepathy. It was the only way to explain how everyone already knew about their arrival. On his planet Witma, telepathy was also practiced, however, it was used to transmit spiritual thoughts when words were ineffective. Nonetheless, in this tribe, they were using it as part of the daily routine of their simple life. WITNESS was thinking about a delicious cup of milk that he had drunk when he was in Manjan's village when all of a sudden someone brought him a cup of milk. Another time, he thought of calling Narani, and she came to his room a few seconds later, even before he had time to open his mouth to call her. WITNESS was thinking about that the next morning. He was completely convinced of this reality of telepathy between Narani's people and himself. Suddenly he heard Narani, although herself not physically present, say clearly in his mind: "Are you ready to go? I am ready."

So he deliberately thought in his mind: "Did everybody develop telepathy in your tribe?"

He received back within: "Yes! We received this gift from our proximity to the invisible people, I think! And we developed it with practice. I can also read people's memories. I read in yours that you are from another planet, and you think the invisible people are also of Extraterrestrial origin. You wish to contact them for this reason. I am glad of that, for I believe you are the people I was expecting, to help me to overcome my fear of going beyond the Door of Heavens."

Then she appeared in front of him, smiling, and she added, really speaking this time:

"Why am I afraid of going through this passage if we call it the Door of Heavens?"

"MATRIX and I, we also had this fear of the unknown and of leaving our world, before choosing to land on Earth."

She replied: "And you chose to stay here forever! I read that in your mind."

"Yes! So for you the choice is simple Narani! You learned much through the talent of your tribe for telepathy, and through other talents that Mother Nature bestowed upon you. You know a lot about Human nature because of these talents. Now, you have to experience this knowledge through the larger world. And for you, the world starts at the Door of Heavens! Your life in this tribe gave you this knowledge; the life outside will give you the experience of what you know. The limited field of experience you have here cannot give you that."

He stopped for a few seconds and then continued:

"I hesitated to tell you our goals, but if you can read our mind, you already know them, and I feel you are a highly-evolved being who can understand much more than we had expected because of your simple life here. Yet very often, natural-living groups produce more spiritual beings than technological societies do."

He stopped speaking again, thinking of how to phrase his next thought.

"Maybe, because of your simple life, you can imagine the possibility of coming from distant stars more easily than the average person on Earth. The whole Universe is at your reach when you feel one with it. So I tell you this: aboard our spaceship, we received in our mind the whole memory of planet Earth and of Human kind. Our mission is to help your species evolve. It is why we need to contact the invisible people, for we didn't receive any information about what they are doing. We feel it is important to know that so as to fulfill our mission."

He hesitated to continue, and then added:

"I think we can ask SUPREME MATRIX and SUPREME WITNESS to know if you can come with us and meet the invisible people, and if you can eventually go further to help us in our mission."

"Who are SUPREME MATRIX and SUPREME WITNESS? They have the same names as both of you!"

"Everyone is named like that on our planet, because we are all clones of these two, all intelligent beings all over the Universe are as well. They are what you call Gods, the feminine and the masculine principles of God. My full name is WITNESS OF THE SPLENDOR OF THE STARS, and hers is MATRIX OF THE DAWN OF THE GALAXIES."

"How do you contact them?"

"Simple! We meditate! Would you like to meditate with us?"

"Of course! Meditating is a normal practice in our village."

WITNESS called his companion, who was outside exercising. He explained his conversation with Narani. MATRIX was so happy to envisage continuing the trip with her, even beyond the Door of Heavens, that she spontaneously hugged her.

"First, MATRIX, I would like us to meditate together in order to ask SUPREME MATRIX and SUPREME WITNESS about taking Narani with us into the invisible people's land."

"So let's meditate!" Looking at Narani, MATRIX added: "I am sure they will agree!"

They sat down in the appropriate position for meditation. After a few minutes, Narani was connected to MATRIX and WITNESS on a spiritual level. They were feeling one together. Actually, meditation is practiced by all to achieve this goal, to feel one with the whole Universe, which is simply the body of the SUPREME BEING, GOD.

There is in fact no religion in this, only a matter of practice, then of awareness, that God is all there is.

Even before the ritual of telling their names and the purpose of the communication, they all heard at once:

"I AM SUPREME MATRIX."

"I AM SUPREME WITNESS."

Then they each in turn said their names:

" I AM MATRIX OF THE DAWN OF THE GALAXIES."

"I AM WITNESS OF THE SPLENDOR OF THE STARS."

"I AM NARANI OF THE DOOR OF HEAVENS."

These words came spontaneously into Narani's mind. She realized those were the only words to say as her introduction. Before anyone could ask the question of Narani accompanying them, these three meditative beings heard:

"You have already guessed that Narani was on your path to help you go through the Door of Heavens to see the invisible people. However it's your choice to go further with her. Within your life on Earth, you will also have to choose many people and invite them to follow you. Think with your heart and you will know instantly who will be helpful in the creation of a new paradigm on Earth. At the end, everyone can be part of your team. Yet, at the beginning, you must choose. Listen to your heart within and you will know!"

It was not SUPREME MATRIX's voice, neither SUPREME WITNESS', but a combination of both. MATRIX thought: it's the first time I have heard them speaking as one.

She said:

"We know that we are all one with You, within You, SUPREME BEINGS. However, it is nice to experience this concept when we hear You both speaking in one voice!"

"The three of you are going to be Our voice on this planet, but not the leaders in charge of spreading a new religion, for Human beings already have too many religions that don't work. You will be Our voice in order to only teach them how to practice communication with us through meditation. That's your only task! Tell them that we are always talking to beings that sincerely listen within. The "invisible"

people will give you other, more practical, instructions. Remember! The knowledge is within you. We are your knowledge within, dear clones. Your experience without corresponds to Our experience within and through you. Everyone is cloned from us. You are each a clone of us. That is the only reality. The rest is illusion. The material Universe without, that looks so real, is illusion. The Universe within each of you looks illusory, but is the only reality. Know and experience that in everyday life, and your reality will be that! Your reality will be That, that which we are!"

"Thank you!" they said, in unison. They were aware of this unity and they all felt that it was wonderful to speak as one. To listen as one! To smile as one!

"Thank you for spreading Our message, for being Our voice. From now on it won't be necessary for you to meditate in order to speak with us. It will be automatic, as soon as you focus on us, within."

CHAPTER 3

BEYOND THE ILLUSORY REALITY: THE CONNECTION

1- BEYOND THE ILLUSION OF REALITY

Three beings, three loving hearts, three great souls, left the little village the next morning. In this season, the Door of Heavens was only a three-hour hike away from the location of Narani's tribe's settlement. It was a very narrow pass with a bridge that looked natural, made of rock spanning from one side of the mountain to the other; it was approximately 200 meters (650 feet) long and 50 meters (170 feet) above the ground. They saw it from quite a far distance away. When they were closer, they began to speak about it.

"This place is very impressive," said WITNESS, "from here, it's difficult to say if it's natural or artificial."

"People in my tribe say that our ancestors built it a long time ago. Nowadays, the material looks like the rest of the rocks. The connection with the rocks of the mountain is perfect; it is without interruption. It's well done if it is indeed artificial! With all of these plants and trees that have grown on it, it is damaged, but it still spans the pass."

She stopped talking. Suddenly a helicopter appeared from behind a mountain range and came toward them.

"That's the army. The Chinese government doesn't accept our lifestyle here. They would like to build a city in this area, but the chiefs of the tribes don't agree, and so they trouble us with inspections of our villages."

The helicopter landed close to them and the chief, followed by three soldiers with guns, stepped out of it and approached them. He asked them for their papers. Narani gave him hers. MATRIX and WITNESS gave him the false passports, with false visas, that the computer on-board of their spaceship had produced. He then, in a harsh tone, questioned them in English:

"What are you doing here?"

WITNESS answered in Chinese: "We are on a trek. She is our guide."

Because he was speaking Chinese, WITNESS impressed the chief of the group.

The latter said with a now gentler voice, this time in Chinese: "You are Canadians. Where did you learn Chinese?"

The New Conditioning room had already planned all of the possible answers about their new identity:

"My wife and I learned it at the University of British Columbia in Vancouver."

"I have a cousin living there," replied the Chinese chief, "a businessman! He told me that Canada is full of forests, not like this land, full of rocks! Nevertheless, some people say a flourishing civilization existed here a long time ago. I can't believe it! Are you going to go over this pass, under this bridge made of rocks?"

"Yes we are."

"Be careful, there are strange phenomena there, the people say."

Narani intervened with a white lie:

"I have already told them about that! Yet, they are determined to proceed. I am going to guide them until we reach the pass and then I'll return to my village."

"I've warned you too!" said the chief.

The group of soldiers left them and stepped back into the helicopter. The three travellers continued hiking on the trail. Nonetheless, the helicopter stayed where it had landed.

"I don't understand why they aren't leaving!" said Narani.

"Let's try to concentrate on the SUPREME BEINGS within us, while walking, so as to find out through them what these soldiers are doing and why they aren't going away!" said WITNESS.

After a few seconds, Narani intervened first:

"The chief is communicating with his base."

"And I understand what it is about!" continued WITNESS. "He speaks about us with his senior officer, who doesn't want us to go beyond the pass! Let's run! The pass is only half a kilometer away!"

"Let's imagine that we are already there!" said MATRIX. "That works! Remember WITNESS! We have already done that a few times!"

"Okay!"

•

Aboard the helicopter, the soldiers didn't understand what had just happened. The three suspicious individuals were already at the pass.

"It's not possible!" said the chief. "They couldn't have run that far so quickly to there! Really strange phenomena happen in this place! Too late now! We can't go beyond this pass with the helicopter, it's too narrow and too long!" Then speaking into the mike: "Helicopter to base: they are out of reach."

"Where are they?" a voice shouted from the speaker.

"They are beyond the pass. It's too narrow for our helicopter to go through. They ran so quickly. I don't understand!"

"Go to the pass and watch what's happening! It's a trick! Those people must have used their magic! Try to land close to the pass, walk through it, and get them!"

"We are close to the Door of Heavens," said Narani, "but the helicopter is following us."

MATRIX added: "Yes, but it's too late for the soldiers! Look! We are here and already under the bridge, where the helicopter can't go."

•

Aboard the helicopter:

"That really is magic! They are running and at the same time they are already at the pass. It's impossible! What's real? What's an illusion?"

The chief of the soldiers spotted a piece of flat land in the pass, just before the bridge. He ordered the pilot to land there.

•

Meanwhile, the three hikers were underneath the Door of Heavens. Now it was their only reality. They stopped, out of breath, then they turned and faced the soldiers walking toward them. WITNESS could have paralyzed them with his special gun, but he wanted to use more subtle ways of escaping from these stubborn people.

"What do you want?" he asked them in Chinese when they were very close, while showing his palm to them to indicate that they must stop.

The chief was a bit amazed at WITNESS' determination, and actually stopped. He began: "I am sorry…" Then he realized that he had shown too much weakness and that it was not appropriate for a soldier. So he continued in a more determined voice:

"I received orders to take you back to our base."

"Why are you sorry to do that?"

The chief was surprised at the question, but replied:

"I thought you were honest hikers, but my senior officer ordered me not to let you go beyond this mysterious pass."

"Why is this pass so mysterious? And why doesn't your senior officer want us to go beyond it?"

"I don't know, but orders are orders! I only know that I saw all three of you in two places at the same time and I don't like that, because that means you must have special powers."

"We do! We are aliens from the heavens above and no one can prevent us from returning to those heavens through this door," said WITNESS, thinking this was an incredible reply, impossible to believe. He remembered though this earthly saying: 'reality is more incredible than fiction'.

"You're kidding!"

"No, I can stop you with this! Do you want to be paralyzed?" replied WITNESS, revealing a little box in his hand.

The Chinese chief hesitated for a few seconds, thinking about what WITNESS had just said. He was completely perplexed: what if what he said is real? Is that box a device to paralyze? Is he really an alien? He then realized just how stupid that all was and that a chief couldn't be stupid! He then ordered the soldiers to proceed and capture them.

But WITNESS, speaking in Chinese, had impressed them much more than he had impressed their chief. The soldiers knew about the legends attached to this pass! Furthermore, they had seen with their own eyes the "magic" in the duplication of these beings. It was too much for them!

"Cowards!" he said in Chinese, "there is no magic in all of that, it's only a hypnotic power!"

Then he took his pistol and pointed it at WITNESS.

The latter heard SUPREME WITNESS whispering in his mind:

"Take two paces back!"

He instinctively did what he was told to do.

The chief and his soldiers couldn't believe what they just saw: WITNESS disappeared by stepping backwards. Then the two ladies did the same and also vanished.

The chief said in Chinese: "What the hell was that!"

A soldier replied: "This place is the Door of Heavens! The gods protect them!"

The soldiers stepped slowly backward and that drove the chief to shout:

"Stop being stupid! There must be a force field!"

Then he took his gun and shot in the direction of the place where the three people had disappeared, but the bullet exploded in the air when it hit the 'force field'.

He shouted: "Damn! What a strong force field!"

He hesitated and then went forward slowly, prudently, with one arm in front of himself, looking for the invisible wall against which the bullet had exploded. When he reached it, he moved his hands vertically, as if touching a wall. Suddenly, pushed by an invisible force, he was projected backwards and fell down on the ground.

"This guy is stubborn!" exclaimed MATRIX, laughing as the chief fell down on his bottom, for she could see through the force field, like through a two-way mirror. She then smiled mischievously and added in Chinese, while stepping forward through the 'wall':

"Hello guys! Do you believe us now! Do you believe that we are gods from the heavens? Did you experience enough of our 'magic' or do you wish to see more?"

The chief stood up again, shook the dust off of his uniform and said:

"Who are you, really? And what do you want to do beyond this force field? Where do you want to go?

"You are hard to convince, Mister Soldier!" she replied, "Isn't all of this proof that we are different? You can also be different! The only way to go through this wall is to be peaceful and to believe that it is possible to do so. Therefore, put your gun on the ground and come alone, Mister 'I-believe-only-what-I-understand-in-my-mind'. Actually, what is your name?"

"Li Pen" he answered, as docile as a lamb, while putting his gun down as she had requested. Then, with a little more self-confidence: "What's your name, is it really Mrs. Hennings? Are you indeed Canadians or aliens from the sky?"

"So, are you starting to believe that we are from another planet, and that our names on the passports are not our true ones, Mister 'Now-I-want-to-believe'? Come on! Come over here! Come to MATRIX THE GREAT, THE GODDESS OF THE DAWN OF THE GALAXIES!"

Slowly but surely, Li Pen walked toward her.

She said in English, pointing her hand to him: "Nice to meet you Li Pen!"

"Nice to meet you too, MATRIX THE GREAT..." he replied, also in English, shaking her hand, but not remembering the rest of the 'title' she had given herself.

"THE GODDESS OF THE DAWN OF THE GALAXIES!" she finished.

She laughed; he smiled.

They were still hand in hand, so she pulled him to her, stepping backwards, however, she bumped into the wall, and from beyond it WITNESS appeared and said:

"MATRIX! You are too much in your ego, and that's not the way to be in unison with the Universe, and to go through the 4th dimension of SUPREME MATRIX! It's okay to joke! Yet, if you calm down your ego, it will be easier to enter into the 4th dimensional world beyond this barrier."

"And about you, Mister Li Pen," he added, "you only need to be peaceful and to believe in the possibility of going through the 'wall', as she told you."

He added, making a broad gesture with his arms: "MATRIX THE GREAT gave you permission to enter through this wall and the people living beyond this pass have told me that they also will permit you to enter."

Then they all walked through the invisible wall without difficulty. From the other side, Narani had been watching the whole scene with three 'invisible people'. They all bowed to Li Pen with hands together; Li Pen did the same.

"Mister Li Pen," said WITNESS, "you understand that if you are allowed to be here, it is for a good reason. APHROMIS is going to tell you what this reason is," he added, opening one hand in her direction. Then, speaking in a lower tone to MATRIX: "I had time to communicate with them Mrs. GODDESS while you were clowning around on the other side!" And he offered her a big smile.

"You are my God, my Lord. I am your servant!" she said while bowing to him with humility. Then, she forced a smile.

APHROMIS was a tall lady, and wore a long white dress. Her skin was dark. She had a little ribbon in her hair. She was in the company of two other people, one male and one female, dressed in the same fashion. She said:

"My people know that the Chinese government is wanting to discover the origin of the mystery beyond this pass. There is nothing beyond this pass, nothing to discover in your 3 dimensional world. The mystery lies in the 4th dimension. You are now in that dimension. However, nobody can enter our 'hyper-space' without our permission. Tell your senior officers about your experience here and that we are not a threat to them in this part of the land, for we are not of this world, we are not of this dimension. We are here only to help Humanity evolve."

"They won't believe me!" said Li Pen, shaking his head.

"They will! Take this device, press this black button, and instantly you will be in our dimension, invisible to people living in the 3-D world. Then press this white one to reappear again."

Li Pen smiled in a mischievous manner.

"Why are you worried about what the military of my country could do to you if you are out of our reach in your 4-D world?"

"Good question!" said APHROMIS. "That's true! We are completely protected in our 4th dimension. Our concern is not about our lives; it's about our project. We are trying to make a permanent connection between both dimensions. That's not easy, because we need time for that, not our time, but your time. Time is different in the 4th spatial dimension. Your time is extended in the 4th dimension. However we have a time, which is more extended in the 5th dimension, and so on for the other dimensions. There can be an infinite number of dimensions, as incredible as that may seem."

She paused to see if he was following her unbelievable words, then added:

"To better understand, look at this ant on the ground: it is attached to the surface, to the 2-D world. Even when the ant climbs a tree it is always walking on the surface of the bark or of the leaves. The same could be said of you. Until the Human kind invented a way to go into the air, then into space, you were limited in your movements to the surface of planet Earth. I take this ant into my hand. It is still moving on a surface: my skin. However, for its fellow creatures, the ant has disappeared, as you did for your soldiers, Mr. Li Pen," she said smiling. Then she continued:

"Now, to come to the main point of your question, I need time to train this ant to be used to the 3rd dimension. It is still involved in the 2-D world of my hand. If I wish to make this insect discover how to travel through the 3-D world, I can drop it on a leaf. In no time at all the ant will have discovered a way to get onto a leaf that is so much faster than climbing a tree. Yet it won't have understood how. But if I mark this precise ant and come every day to this place, I could train it, after some time, to be here waiting for me, for this 'space travel', that saves the time of climbing a tree to get to a leaf. We wish to do the same with Human beings; but it takes time to train people to be used to the 4-D world, as it is to train this ant to be used to the Human, 3-D world. To have people come here, we cannot be disturbed for a long period of your time, and we need the friendly, non-intervention of the Chinese government in this area. We have the power to protect ourselves in this part of the land, however it would be more and more difficult for people to come here if you keep stopping them, as you did with these three people when they tried to go beyond the so-called Door of Heavens.

"You must realize that this training is of the utmost importance for the betterment of mankind."

She stopped, so as to be sure of Li Pen's understanding of her message.

Without hesitation he said: "Okay, I've understood my mission. It's an important one, in order to help you to train people in your 4-D world."

After a few seconds he added, showing the instrument APHROMIS gave him: "I will also be happy to trick my senior officers with this."

Everybody smiled.

He had to add: "When my mission is finished, and when it is obvious that my government will be friendly with you, may I also be trained? I also wish to participate in the betterment of mankind."

APHROMIS, a bit surprised at the question, answered:

"Why not! Everyone can come here. Everyone, who is already open-minded and open-hearted, can have this experience in the 4th dimension, and then help their fellow Human beings to open their minds and their hearts. God willing, it can snowball; more and more people will come here. Then the growth and strengthening of the link between your 3-D world and our 4-D world will allow us to increase our link with the 5-D world, and so on, until the infinite, the infinite SUPREME WITNESS and SUPREME MATRIX."

MATRIX, taken by surprise at what APHROMIS had just said, intervened into the dialogue:

"You call the SUPREME BEINGS by the same names we do!"

"The Supreme Reality is the same for everyone," APHROMIS said with a steady voice, "but your 3-D world reality is an illusion for our 4-D world, which is an illusion for the 5-D world, and so on. Only the Supreme Reality is not relative, it is the Absolute. SUPREME MATRIX and SUPREME WITNESS together make a dual entity that forms the real Absolute. All of the rest is relative, related to one's world and one's point of view. Actually they are One, but to please ourselves we make them appear as we are: male and female. In fact, we are their reflection, their image. For deeply, we are One with them, in the illusory reality of Duality. They seem to be dual, two beings, for us to better understand the absolute Unity of Diversity, through the Relativity of which we are made across all of the dimensions of the Universe."

MATRIX intervened: "Your explanation is much too philosophical for me. More concretely: last time we spoke with them, we heard them speaking in unison, as one being. Furthermore, sometimes we say the SUPREME BEING, sometimes the SUPREME BEINGS, interchangeably, without thinking if we used the singular or the plural. In some languages there is no pronunciation difference between both. And concerning us, WITNESS and I, most of the time we feel as one body, one Spirit, when we make love, or I should say, when we love in Spirit."

"MATRIX OF THE DAWN OF THE GALAXIES, through your trip to our 4-D world, you will have the opportunity to experience more unity."

Then Li Pen shook everyone's hand and went back to his "illusory 3-D reality".

MATRIX said to Narani: "Now, your real name is NARANI OF THE DOOR OF HEAVENS." And they hugged each other; then, addressing APHROMIS:

"Will you allow me to find a longer name for you APHROMIS?"

"Why not!"

"When I was listening to your brilliant talk, I thought of APHROMIS OF THE ABSOLUTE RELATIVITY."

APHROMIS made a little face.

"Or APHROMIS OF THE CONNECTION BETWEEN THE WORLDS," proposed WITNESS.

"I prefer this one," APHROMIS said, smiling, then she added: "Now follow me! We have to walk a little."

While walking, MATRIX said aside to WITNESS: "You have a good connection with her, my darling, for the name I chose for her was more subtle. Yours is simply remembering her for what her mission is. What other kind of connection would you like to establish with her in order to link your world and hers?"

"Are you jealous MATRIX?"

Their private conversation ended, for APHROMIS said:

"We are in the right place now and still have a good hour before our appointment with a few beings from the future of planet Earth. I am going to take advantage of this time to introduce my partners GANALINI and KRISHANANDA, and how we'll proceed together in order to help you become familiar with this 4-D world."

2- THE SUPREME REALITY

The SUPREME BEINGS were watching this scene unfold. Actually, they are part of all scenes, in all worlds, at all times.

"SUPREME MATRIX, why did You create so many dimensions within the material reality that I can observe as SUPREME WITNESS?"

"Why not? A plethora of dimensions creates Diversity. It's ideal for expressing our Infinity!"

"Fine! Nonetheless, from a reality in x dimensions, one can't see any part of the x+1 dimensions. Those beings living in the 3-D world can't see the world in 4-D, but people from this 4-D world can see the 3-D world."

"That's true! And that's the purpose! The more one raises one's awareness, the more one can see the upper worlds, until one is completely united with the supreme level where We reside. Nevertheless, the more one experiences the lower realities, the more one can raise one's awareness, through all of the dimensions. We are infinite, so there are no limits to our dimensions of reality. The best life lies in experiencing awareness from the level 0 to the supreme level of Infinity, as we do every nanosecond of our infinite lives, through all beings, the clones of us, who exist in all of the infinity of dimensions."

"I witness that. And what a great invention you made, SUPREME MATRIX, by giving to the superior spatial dimension the quality of 'Time'. For example, the 4th spatial dimension of the 3-D world is the time dimension of this world. The 5th spatial dimension is the time dimension of the 4-D world. And all of the worlds overlap each other! I am glad that I inspired Albert Einstein in the 3-D world of planet Earth in the beginning of the 20th century. I gave him the awareness of time as the 4th dimension of his 3-D reality-world. Now, Humans still have to be aware, in the beginning of their 21st century, that it's possible to join this 4th dimension and to then travel through time. The Time Patrol of their 22nd century needs this en masse awareness of people in the 21st century so as to succeed in the connection of all of the dimensions through the Universal Time of Eternity."

"I am working on making Human beings aware of that every nanosecond of My Eternity!"

3- TIME AND SPACE REALITY

"Time Patrol 'Door of Heavens 2003' to Control Center year 2147: we are in the year 2003, in the Gobi desert, exactly at the pass called Door of Heavens. We request instructions."

RAM, Time Patrol # 1432, and his two colleagues, ALCYOMES and MELODIA, were standing at the pass. He was trying to contact his base in his mind. It was the procedure, at the time destination, to ask for permission to continue the mission. For security reasons, no instructions were given before the departure. He was transmitting through his mind. No machine, except the Human mind, was able to communicate a conversation between people through time. However, Ram was speaking in order for his colleagues to follow the conversation and compare if what they received within their own mind was identical to his words.

"Time Patrol 'Door of Heavens 2003', here are your instructions from Control Center year 2147: six people are in this pass at this moment of your time travel. Do you see them?"

ALCYOMES and MELODIA nodded their confirmation.

RAM said: "Yes, I see them."

•

APHROMIS exclaimed:

"Look! The three people from the Time Patrol are there, behind this bush. I told you that they are always on time, and that's the most obvious thing one can expect from people who travel through time: to master their dimension and to be on time!"

"Don't they have a vessel to travel through time with?" asked MATRIX.

"That's not necessary. It's enough to enter the 4th dimension, which corresponds to time within the 3-D world, in order to travel through time. There are portals that allow one to go from the 3-D world to the 4-D world, like the Door of Heavens, all over planet Earth, and all over the Universe. Yet this one is the easiest one to go through. That's the reason why it is important that the Chinese government does not interfere."

She stopped talking to look at the faces of the people around her, to check that they had understood. Then she added:

"Let's meet them!"

They began to walk, but suddenly Li Pen appeared in front of them, excited, saying:

"It's working APHROMIS! This instrument is wonderful! I was in the general's office, trying to explain this 4-D world to him. But he didn't believe me. So I pressed the button, and here I am, directly carried on the stones of the Door of Heavens, like your ant on the leaves of the tree! I got carried away! I get carried away! Great! So I am going to go back to see his face and check if he is more open to my explanations now. Bye!"

Then he pressed the other button of the device and vanished.

APHROMIS smiled and self-confidently said: "It's going to work."

•

After the usual introductions, everybody sat down on some big rocks. 'Actually these rocks seem to be made of hard foam,' thought NARANI as she sat down. She wondered whether it was because of the 4th dimension and she wondered at how comfortable they were.

NARANI felt at ease with so many different beings: two Extraterrestrial aliens, three so-called invisible people and three time travellers. If she hadn't previously had all of those other incredible experiences, she would have wondered if she was dreaming right now. She thought to herself, 'That's my destiny, my mission in life, to be part of this grandiose project of mixing different dimensional realities, of bringing Extraterrestrial planets and my own planet closer, of blending the present Earth with the future Earth.'

She couldn't think further, for APHROMIS began to speak:

"We are here to connect our vibrations so as to create an area of unity between all of the levels of awareness. Therefore, we are going to ask together our two SUPREME BEINGS, who are the SUPREME AWARENESS and the SUPREME REALITY, to be one with us, in order to receive their SUPREME GUIDANCE."

Nine beings were meditating, sitting in a circle on these soft rocks, in the 4th dimension, waiting for the SUPREME BEINGS to awaken within them.

4- CONNECTION BETWEEN ILLUSORY REALITY AND SUPREME REALITY

The usual introductions to the Divine Dialogue Within were pronounced:

I am SUPREME MATRIX.

I am SUPREME WITNESS.

I am APHROMIS… I am GANALINI… I am KRISHANANDA…

I am RAM… I am ALCYOMES… I am MELODIA…

I am NARANI… I am MATRIX… I am WITNESS…

APHROMIS: We would like to get advice from You, SUPREME BEINGS, in order to continue our mission of mixing the third and the fourth dimensions of Your SUPREME ENTITY.

SUPREME WITNESS: I witnessed what you have already done; this is a promising beginning. Now you have to attract as many people as possible from all over planet Earth to this portal and train them to be familiar with the 4th dimension. APHROMIS, go on contacting them by telepathy as you've already done with NARANI. You will combine your vibrations of the 4th dimension with those of Earth's future and those of Extraterrestrial space through MATRIX and WITNESS, who will soon journey across the entire Earth. Then, all of your vibrations will invade the whole space of this planet!

SUPREME MATRIX: *I'll be the Matrix of all of that. Concentrate on Me while contacting people every day. Meditate collectively and send your vibrations to all of My clones on Earth. The more you concentrate on Me, the more the telepathic process works, so as to reach the most clones of Me. You are all clones with free will and at the same time each of you is Me, experiencing MYSELF through you. That is the big paradox of the Creation. Always remember that! Always be aware of that! Be always That, which I am!*

SUPREME WITNESS: Specifically, MATRIX, WITNESS and NARANI, you will have to travel the entire planet to have direct contact with those Human beings who will be ready to come to the Door of Heavens 4-D world. It is a neces-

sary journey, for physical contact with the reality is the purpose of this 3-D world. Yet, don't forget, you are all clones of US, and we are ONE with you. We are ONE with everyONE, within the whole story of planet Earth, which is, who is, a being like you, in fact a clone of US, as each of you is. Time is an illusion, a trick of our 4th dimensional reality, but it is as real as matter is real, and at the same time only a part of US. Matter is a part of US. Time is a part of US. Connecting all of the parts of US, all of the dimensions of US, all of the states of US, is The Process, The Purpose, The Reality. US, the United States! USB, the United States of Being!

Human beings of the future, RAM, ALCYOMES and MELODIA, you can now go back to your future and reassure your people. Everything is in place to actualize a new consciousness at the beginning of the 21st century, in order to avoid the problems you are now facing in the 22nd, and to connect all of the dimensions of our Being.

NARANI: Is it as simple as that to change the past in order to avoid problems in the future? Is it like how a writer must return back to the beginning of his or her novel when he or she realizes a piece of information was missed at that time to enable the reader to understand the end of his story?

SUPREME WITNESS: Sort of! SUPREME MATRIX and I, we are the SUPREME WRITERS, and we act through each of you, all over the place, all over time, all over the book of your destinies. You are Our characters, that is, the individuals of Our novel, and you also are Our characteristics. You express who We are. So be really deep characters with joyful characterizations! For that is who We are: Supreme Clowns playing with Our Clones!

SUPREME MATRIX: *And remember that you, that each of you, can contact us at any moment within your mind, even without meditating. Where your attention goes, we are; we are always where your attention goes, or in other words, when you are aware of us, we are there; we are where you are aware of us.*

CHAPTER 4

EXTRATERRESTRIAL AND TERRESTRIAL EXPERIENCES

1- LIVING IN THE HEAVENS AND LEAVING THE HEAVENS

"I'm living in Paradise! Living beyond the Door of Heavens was like living in Paradise," thought NARANI, after a few days spent beyond this portal.

Leaving this Paradise, Heavens on Earth, would alas be necessary soon. But this did not worry NARANI, for living in the present had been her reality for a long time.

In this Paradise, it was enough to think of something and it physically and immediately appeared in front of you. You thought of a cup of tea, and it appeared, of a tree, and it appeared, of somebody, and that person appeared. In fact, the person had not moved, you had moved. Once NARANI was thinking of her mother, and instantly she was transported into her family home, physically hugging her mum. At the beginning, because it was difficult for her to focus on being in the other place, she could not remain that long, but after becoming used to this method of concentrating on the desired thought of being with someone, it became easy for her to remain with that person for some time. Not indefinitely though, as concentrating only on one thing or situation or person became too difficult to sustain for any great length of time.

For MATRIX and WITNESS, the training was very quick and simple. Even after just a short time of practicing they were able to transport to their home planet.

"That's great!" said MATRIX, "I don't regret at all our decision to stay if we can move like this in 3-D space through this 4th dimension."

MATRIX even had a meal with her parents, and spent a long time visiting with them, explaining all of their adventures on Earth and their commitment to stay. She promised to come back as often as possible.

At the same time, WITNESS went and ate with his parents. They then, based only on the strength of their thoughts, were able to reunite their two families at the end of their visits.

They traveled to their planet with their previous bodies—the bodies that their parents recognized them by—for this kind of travel was not a 'real' journey, physically speaking, so they could take any appearance they chose. However, their appearance, their apparition, was so real, they could touch or be touched. But of course they felt, at the beginning, that it differed from "real" physical contact. Yet, after a while, like babies discovering bit by bit the world around them, the physical sense of touch became more and more 'real' for them.

In fact, what exactly is the physical? Atoms are full of void but their electrons turn so quickly and have so much energy that they give the illusion of fulness. What actually gives them energy? SUPREME MATRIX? Mainstream scientists don't answer that question. Cutting edge ones say, in the Zero Point Energy Principle, that each point of space has the potential of giving energy, and that a space as big as a fist has enough energy to boil all of the water of the oceans. So, Space is the Body of SUPREME MATRIX, and what an energetic Body She has.

In fact our ETs' daily life was only creating on the physical level what was in their mental level. And this place was the most creative place the three newcomers had ever seen: full of extraordinary landscapes in an area previously full of rocks, landscapes full of buildings as diverse as each Human mind can be from one another. However, a site could be full of plants one day and full of artificial constructions the next day, depending on the person who had last thought of something—thus created it—at that site. It was enough to decide to mentally delete the materialization, to let the site be emptied, and then be built or designed anew by someone else materializing thoughts.

NARANI, whose English was limited, learned it almost as quickly as if she were in the New Conditioning room of the Witman spaceship.

•

After two Earth weeks living in the Heavens—but remember their time was flexible—all three decided, along with APHROMIS, that it was time to leave.

"When you are away, we'll still be able to physically be in contact as soon as we concentrate on each other," said APHROMIS, "and thus you can come back to the Heavens as often as you feel the urge to do so."

However NARANI, MATRIX and WITNESS had to hike again, all of the way back to the spaceship.

2- AS TRIVIAL TERRESTRIALS

"We can go to our previous precious planet in no time through the 4th dimension, but we need to walk all of this way to get to our spaceship," complained MATRIX, exhausted, while climbing up a mountain path.

"If you could always stay concentrated on the place where you moved to in your mind," replied WITNESS, "you would be able to be there forever, or then think of another place and move there, you would never be where your physical 3-D body is, you would only be where your mind is. But that would thwart the purpose of your physical incarnation! And that is not possible. SUPREME WITNESS told me that a few days ago when I was meditating. He also told me this: when we are free from incarnations in the physical 3-D world, then we can create a 3-D world from a 4-D incarnation and afterward create a 4-D world from our 5-D mind, and so on!"

"That's too complex for me! Too complex for my mind!" exclaimed MATRIX. "Too complex for my poor and tired mind," she added, making a face like a mentally disabled Earth person.

"MATRIX, that's because your mind is now in a 3-D world," replied WITNESS. "With a 4-D body, your mind would be open enough to understand the wonders of the 4-D world and also of the 3-D one, but it would still be limited in its understanding of the complexities of the 5-D world."

"When we were in the 4-D world beyond the Door of Heavens," she retorted, "I understood everything because I was experiencing concretely this 4th dimension. Now I am lost, because this 3-D world is so limited."

"Think differently MATRIX!" explained WITNESS. "Think that it is still possible to be at our spaceship, and it shall be! Christ said: 'When you have faith and do not doubt, if you say to this mountain to be lifted up and thrown into the ocean, it will be done.' Think as Christ thought!"

"Who is Christ? I can't find him in the data I received from the Spirit of Earth!" MATRIX replied.

"It's incredible that you did not receive data about Jesus Christ, who was a man who realized he was one with God. You know that Earth's God corresponds to our SUPREME BEING. He was the man who told the world about the awareness of our Divine Origin!" WITNESS said, exasperated by MATRIX' lack of seriousness in recalling the data generously given by MOTHER EARTH.

"Ah, Jesus, the man who probably didn't really exist!" MATRIX retorted, making an incredulous face. Yet looking at his, she added: "WITNESS, it's what non-religious people believe!"

"MATRIX! You always only recall what interests you in any information downloaded," replied WITNESS, demoralized by MATRIX's lack of reliability.

"I am what I am!" she said, irritated. "For me it is so obvious to be one with the SUPREME BEINGS! Nobody can tell me who they are and who I am. It's implanted so deeply within me that I am one with them!"

"Okay, I don't want to talk with you anymore about that!" he said, feeling that they were both focusing on different levels of reality.

NARANI intervened: "Religions all over the world have never shown a clear picture of God, because they have always described God as they themselves are, limited and existing physically. God is actually unlimited, and non-physical, as the SUPREME BEINGS told us: They are, God is, all dimensional and all-pervading, that is, within everything. We'd better remember that in order to tell people about the ubiquitous SUPREME BEING if we meld into communities of people, and we must be coherent to counterbalance the inconsistency of religious people. I first realized this incoherence when trekkers came to my village from all over the world: Christians, Muslims, Hindus, and more."

They stopped talking because they were finally in front of the cave where the spaceship was hidden.

"Good!" said MATRIX, "My feet are out of order. I can't walk anymore, even just a few meters, even a few feet in their Imperial system. Good spaceship! In no time at all we'll be in any location in the world. Good machine!" she continued, while caressing it.

"So!" said WITNESS, "While we were talking, we arrived at our spaceship in no time, distracted by our arguments about God and faith. Talking about faith made us fly over the mountains. Actually, faith made us bring the mountains into the ocean of illusion."

They all laughed.

MATRIX added, imitating the voice of WITNESS, "And I have faith in this machine and I will tell it, 'lift up, fly over these mountains, and dive into the ocean' and it shall be done!"

They could not stop laughing.

NARANI nevertheless, between two roars of laughter, recalling what MATRIX had said and imitating her, succeeded in saying, "Who is Christ? He did not exist!"

They increased their roars of laughter.

After a while she added, half-laughingly, "Christ and God are the same! For God doesn't exist either! God is!"

"God is the One who is! The only One we are!" WITNESS added between two laughs.

"No need to believe in Christ to be aware of that!" MATRIX continued on. Then she laughed some more.

Finally she knelt down, for her legs were too weak from laughing so much. When her laughs had died down, she folded her hands into a prayer position and said:

"Thank you God-SUPREME BEING, for making us, Your clones, laugh so much!"

3- ENCOUNTER WITH TRIVIAL URBAN TERRESTRIALS

Or, from the terrestrials' side:

ENCOUNTER OF THE THIRD KIND WITH THREE ALIENS, INCLUDING TWO REAL EXTRATERRESTRIALS

NARANI went through the New Conditioning room to become more fluent in English and to learn more that might be useful for her to know about the rest of the world.

It was dusk and the spaceship was flying above a forest near a city when WITNESS suddenly exclaimed:

"We are close to Vancouver, MATRIX and NARANI! Vancouver, British Columbia, Canada, is the city where we live, as Mr. and Mrs. Hennings!"

NARANI intervened: "I can't wait to be on the ground and see the green of this land. It's so different from my tribe's yellowish surroundings."

"What a beautiful place," said MATRIX, "with mountains, the ocean, lakes, inlets, forests! Look at the forests growing right up to the edge of the city! Our spaceship's computer chose a good place for us to live as the Hennings. It also received information from MOTHER EARTH when we were connected to Her, and really, it chose such a nice place out of all of the data She gave it about places where we could live. Wait a minute! I just read in my mind that people in Vancouver advertise: 'The best place on Earth'. Maybe our computer was simply tricked by this commercial for tourists."

"We are not in this place for holidays, MATRIX, but for our mission: meeting people and encouraging them to go to the Door of Heavens. And we certainly could have traveled to another place! It doesn't matter which location we start with. I chose this one because it was written on the fake passports our computer made. I could have chosen any other city or village on Earth!"

"I know! But can we not join mission and pleasure together WITNESS? Just this once?"

"Okay! But, for now we must find a place to touch down. Would you like the top of a casino?" he asked sarcastically.

"Funny! I thought you wished to be discreet Mr. Mission!"

"I also wish to please you Mrs. Pleasure! What do you think of this campsite?" he said, pointing his index finger on the screen of his night vision computer. "Close to this lake? I looked on the map our computer got from the network the Earthlings call the Internet. It is called Alouette Lake and it is close to a little city called…you won't believe this: Mission!"

"I believe our SUPREME BEINGS are always clowning with us, their clones. Okay! The privacy of the forest combined with the pleasure of camping! Do we have a tent?"

"No problem! Our computer is going to make one… or two, one for us, one for NARANI!"

"This computer is indefatigable in pleasing me, WITNESS!"

"And I indefatigably program this computer to please you, MATRIX!"

"You are only programed to please me! That is why it is such a pleasure to have you with me, WITNESS!"

Then she hugged him, gave him a kiss, and said:

"I can please you too my darling!"

"We'd better not fight when we encounter the Humans!" he replied.

•

"Look at this disk-shaped light above the lake, darling!"

"Where is it?"

"There! Oh! It disappeared into the lake!"

"I'm sure that was a flying saucer, Felicity!" he said giggling.

"Be serious George! I have never ever seen a flying saucer, and they sure don't go into the water!"

•

"To hide this spaceship, there is no better place than deep down in this lake, MATRIX!"

"How will we get out of it?" NARANI asked.

"Through the airlock and with a vehicle we have within our spaceship that is like a little submarine. It can also be transformed into a boat," he answered, pointing to the vehicle now in front of them.

•

"Look George! A boat is now coming toward us. See the light!"

"Probably the boat of the Extraterrestrials, Felicity!" added George, and then he laughed.

"Why not! They hid their spaceship in the water and now they approach us with a boat that can also be a submarine. I saw that in a movie once."

"What an incredible imagination you have! So now do we prepare a welcoming committee with flags and cheers! But look, we are the only ones walking on the lakeshore, everyone else is stupidly watching the hockey game on TV while drinking their beers in their campers instead of enjoying all of this beautiful nature!"

"Stop kidding George! Wait, let's see!"

•

"There are two people on the shore, underneath this light. They are the first two trivial urban terrestrials we are going to meet on our mission." WITNESS said.

"What do we tell them about us?" NARANI worriedly said.

"The Truth!" MATRIX said. "We are Mr. and Mrs. Hennings. You are Narani. We just came back from a trip in the Gobi desert where you were our guide! That's it!"

"And we have just been traveling for two hours in our spaceship from there to here," WITNESS calmly added.

"Why not!" NARANI said. "If we must make them believe in the reality we saw beyond the Door of Heavens, why not begin now with the unbelievable."

•

"Hello! I'm George Thompson. What are you doing on this lake at night?"

"Hi! I'm Felicity Thompson. Did you see that light diving into the lake ten minutes ago?"

WITNESS replied, with an emphasis on the surprising effect of his words, sometimes looking serious, sometimes kidding and smiling:

"It was our spaceship. But don't tell anybody. We hid it and have come here with this submarine that has now transformed into a boat. I am Mr. Hennings. Here is my wife. Narani was our guide in the Gobi desert where we were just on vacation."

"Good joke, for God's sake! But do you have telepathic powers? My wife just gave me the same explanation as yours about a spaceship and a submarine. My God!"

WITNESS moved on:

"Or she perhaps had a premonition of what I would say. Or I moved through time and space and heard what she had said a few minutes ago when she first saw our spaceship. Or we really are aliens arriving from outer space. Or reality is beyond your understanding. We can give so many explanations about what we see, or what we think we see. But what is real? What is an illusion? Who knows?"

"You are a philosopher Mr. Hennings! My husband is a scientist. So he won't agree with you."

"I can agree. I'm not a narrow-minded scientist Felicity! But I am a pragmatic one! If I saw the three of you, just now, being transformed into Extraterrestrial Beings like those in movies, perhaps I would accept that evidence. But you three are very Human and that is a fact! However Felicity, it's also a fact that it's cold now and it's only mid-April. We better get back to our camper."

MATRIX intervened, asking:

"Do you know if there is a free place in this campsite to pitch our tents?"

George Thompson answered:

"At this season there's a lot of free spots. For registration, you go over there to the office in that building with the red sign, but it's closed now. Pitch your tents on a free spot and register tomorrow. See you tomorrow then! We can continue this conversation about reality and illusion, if you wish. I like it."

"Okay! See you!" WITNESS answered.

"See you when we see you!" MATRIX added.

"Bye! See you soon!" NARANI said. She so much wanted to share a few words with them too, for she had never been to Canada before.

"Good bye, people of the infinite space!" concluded Felicity with a smile, then she ran after her husband who was already heading back to their camper.

Felicity was a tall, thin lady, with henna-colored hair. George also was tall and he wore a hat. NARANI thought that he looked like the image she had in her mind of what a cowboy should look like. They were both in their 40's and looked healthy, like people who often exercise their physical bodies.

WITNESS commented to his companions:

"They don't know what to think or what to believe. She would like to believe our story. He would like to have evidence. So we'll see them tomorrow and give them evidence."

NARANI retorted:

"You want to give them all of the evidence?"

"Why not! And the rest! And the best: the evidence of SUPREME MATRIX and SUPREME WITNESS through the thoughtless awareness of meditation."

"WITNESS! You are the best! The best for talking! Are you also the best for a rest with me in our tent, my darling?" MATRIX said while caressing his chin.

They all laughed.

"George was right, it is a bit cold!" NARANI said.

"WITNESS, did you ask the computer to make warm sleeping bags?" asked MATRIX.

"Our computer is very smart, when I asked it to make tents, it replied: 'I will make everything you need for camping, everything the Spirit of Earth put into my memory about the habits of Earthlings and according to the season.' Can you help me carry these bags from the boat to the campsite, ladies? Our computer made a lot of things! I don't know if we'll need it all!"

They carried three big bags to the Alouette Lake campsite, in this beautiful Canadian forest of British Columbia.

This province of Canada was the last frontier for immigrants when they came from the East in the 19th century. It was still wild and natural at the beginning of the 21st. The lumber and the mining businesses had started to disturb the ecosystems, but not as much yet as in other parts of the world. With a population of 4 million people or so, including around 2 million in the Vancouver area alone, this province, which was as large in area as France, remained a paradise for bears, pumas, salmons and eagles. The whole province was very mountainous and very cold during the winter, except in the Vancouver area at the border with the United States and in the capital region of Victoria. At 49 degrees latitude north, the area around Vancouver, called the Lower Mainland, was mild mainly because it was at sea level. In March and April, the people of Vancouver were used to skiing in the morning on the slopes of Grouse Mountain, Mount Seymour or the Cypress Bowl, all over 1000 meters in altitude (3500 feet), and all less than half an hour away from the Downtown core by car, and then swimming in the afternoon in the beautiful Pacific Ocean.

4- SPIRITUAL GROUP

The next morning, MATRIX, WITNESS and NARANI got up early to enjoy the magnificent scenery around the campsite and to jog along the lake.

Other campers were also walking, jogging and biking on paths. When the three began meditating on the sand of a little beach, a few people came and sat to join them in this practice. Afterward, they each talked about their own manner of meditating, and they realized that each of them in fact had different ways of doing and of being during these privileged moments. For a man, it was a time of introspection, examining and observing his own mental and emotional processes. For another, it consisted of concentrating on a chosen object or subject. A lady said that for her it was contemplation, a survey of the Creation existing in her mind.

NARANI explained that for her, meditating has been a dialogue with Mother-Earth but now it was with the Universe as a being. Geronimo, who was Native Indian, said that for him it was similar: a dialogue with the Spirit of Mother Nature. For Ajay, whose parents came from India thirty years ago, it was a dialogue between his ego and his Kundalini, 'God within', in the East Indian tradition.

WITNESS took advantage of this testimony to introduce his dialogue with SUPREME MATRIX and SUPREME WITNESS, telling the audience that She is the Substance of the Universe, and that He is the Spirit of it. He said that they are One, but in two parts, and that the world was created from their dialogue. It's the reason why, he explained, having a dialogue with this SUPREME BEING, in two parts, is essential for intelligent beings like us, and he concluded that conversing with the Source of everything is primordial for the Human evolution.

Nishi, Ajay's wife, said that what WITNESS had just spoken about had a similar meaning in the East Indian culture: Prakritti is the substance of the Universe, and Purusha is the Spirit of it. In another East Indian tradition, she said, AdiShakti is the Mother of everything, creating the Universe by dancing and singing and SadaShiva is the Father, watching Her performance. She then added, addressing WITNESS:

"Mr. Hennings, from which tradition comes your interesting dialogue with this Supreme Being in two parts?"

"The universal tradition! Through these two SUPREME BEINGS, my wife and I travel throughout the Universe. We have seen so many different people meditating and having a dialogue with these two SUPREME BEINGS."

"While meditating, you travel through the Universe and see Extraterrestrial beings doing the same as you do, don't you?"

"More or less, that's correct!"

"That's incredible!"

"Yet you too can have this same experience! Would you like to come with us tomorrow and receive it?"

"My husband and I leave tonight. Easter weekend is finished for us today. Tomorrow, on Easter Monday, we have something already planned. Can we practice this afternoon?"

"Yes, why not! If my wife and Miss NARANI agree!"

"Of course!" they said in unison.

"My first name is Nishi. What's yours Mr. Hennings? And you Mrs. Hennings? And you Miss Narani?"

"Actually, my first name is NARANI, and my full name in my language in the Gobi desert means: NARANI OF THE DOOR OF HEAVENS, a name given as a spiritual or shamanic initiate."

"She was our guide when we were there, and then we invited her to join us in Canada. We are now her guides!" MATRIX said. She added:

"My name, as a universal initiate, is MATRIX OF THE DAWN OF THE GALAXIES. But you can call me MATRIX."

"And mine, WITNESS OF THE SPLENDOR OF THE STARS, WITNESS for short."

"What very nice and poetic names! Is there an initiation or a ritual to practice your meditation?"

"If you like!" WITNESS said, "But we are not in a secret society, everyone can experience the awakening to a dialogue with the SUPREME BEING. That's your birthright, as soon as you have the desire to seek it. You can find an initiation name on your own, afterward if you like, to feel more part of the universal fraternity, in relation to your deep self."

WITNESS, feeling the audience receptive to their speech, continued:

"But you know, your individuality is an illusion, as persistent as it is. You are the SUPREME BEING. Each of us is SUPREME MATRIX and SUPREME WITNESS. As Carl Jung, the famous Swiss psychiatrist said, each of us is ANIMA and ANIMUS, the Feminine and Masculine Principles. Of course, ladies are more animated by the ANIMA or MATRIX Principle, and men by the ANIMUS or WITNESS Principle, but we have both principles within each of us. Actually, there is only the SUPREME BEING, and we are His or Her clones."

"That's an interesting concept! I can hardly wait to begin practicing this meditation-dialogue with the SUPREME BEING of all that exists," Nishi said.

"You have summarized correctly, Nishi! The dialogue with the SUPREME BEING will be easy for you," MATRIX replied. "Why not 3 o'clock this afternoon, here?"

Everyone agreed. There were six people meditating with them in the morning, fifteen came in the afternoon, including Mr. and Mrs. Thompson, seventy on Easter Monday in the evening, and 250 on Tuesday, even though it was a work day! Nishi and Ajay Singh were the best for talking to people, especially in the East Indian community of Surrey, a neighboring city. Felicity and George Thompson were also good at informing people they knew from the Downtown community. They had such an incredible experience that Easter Sunday afternoon! They all talked with SUPREME MATRIX and SUPREME WITNESS as if the SUPREME BEINGS were present right there on the beach.

MATRIX, WITNESS and NARANI did as much as they could to help everyone go deep into meditation. Behind their backs, they worked on the chakras, the centers of spiritual power in the Human body, awakening their energies at the base of their spine within their sacrum bone. They helped them feel the vibrations on top of their head for them to be in thoughtless awareness, which led to a hearing of the Universal Consciousness within each of them, and they progressively taught people to so help the newcomers as the number of people increased.

Ajay said that it reminded him of the Kundalini awakening of Yoga, which he practiced when he was younger, but that talking to the Divine within himself was an entirely new experience, and that it was now so obvious how to have a dialogue with this SUPREME BEING. He had not felt yet the difference between listening to the Feminine SUPREME BEING and Her Masculine counterpart, but WITNESS assured him that the time would come when he would differentiate between both voices within, but that it did not matter, "For they are one!" he affirmed.

Word of mouth is so effective when you wish to share such a great experience with the whole world.

The fifteen people who came on this Easter Sunday afternoon were so overwhelmed with the joy of their experience that they were on their cell phones, persuading their relatives, friends and colleagues to come join them. The next day was Easter Monday. There were so many meditating. The sun was shining and Vancouverites were known to be quick to go on outings as soon as the weather was favorable, especially since places like Alouette Lake were so close to the urban area.

When the forest is so close to the city, it is easy to escape the hectic urban life. And when you feel you may very well have the experience of your life, your incentive to experience it is as high as the mountaintops are in relation to the valley below.

There were, on this Easter Monday, people of all ages and all kinds of professions. Some came with their children, others with their pets.

On Tuesday, they had to make a decision in light of this incredible success. People seemed okay to return to Alouette Lake, but it was a little far away from the city, even though one-hour of driving is not a problem for properly motivated people. They decided though to go on the following days to Stanley Park, which was a more central location for everybody.

Stanley Park, the marvel of Vancouver! Just a stone's throw from Downtown! A peninsula with several beaches, little hills and high cliffs, a little lake and a lagoon, and so many trails! A paradise for people to walk, jog, bike, roller skate, and enjoy nature: beavers, squirrels, raccoons, ducks, geese, bald eagles and a great diversity of centennial trees, cedars, pines, spruces, redwoods, and maples! Stanley Park is also known for the famous Lions Gate Bridge, built at the narrow entrance of a large inlet to link the city's Downtown to the North Shore communities, via the park!

This uncommon site made Vancouver the San Francisco of the North! And through the movie industry, the Hollywood of Canada!

On Wednesday at 6 pm, after work, hundreds of people gathered on one of the many lawns surrounding the Aquarium, which was the pride of Vancouverites. Those who didn't know the purpose of the meeting, were amazed at the sight of so many people in a meditating posture, being silent. They were used to seeing individuals and little groups meditating, or Chinese people practicing Tai Chi, but so many people, close to a collection of native Indian totem poles, silently meditating, apparently without a person leading, without a public address system, what a spectacle it was! Many 'spectators', who did not even know the real purpose of this meditation gathering, sat down because they were so impressed, wanting to be a part of this amazing, uncommon, impossible event. The apparently spontaneous, non-organized aspect of it, was really quite difficult to imagine at the beginning of the 21st century, in a society so polite, so polished and so politicized!

Actually the fifteen first people, the seventy from the second day, and most of those from the third day, spread out instinctively all over the lawns to assist the newcomers in a subtle manner with their vibes. Of course, they were mainly close to the people they knew, but with so many different people present, this gathering required different ways of leading from before. The participants were mainly friends, or friends of friends, but there were also people just passing by. They were spread out over a larger and larger area throughout the duration of the event. So the 'already initiated' had to be flexible and move quietly from person to person. Their communications were subtle, like angels flying overhead, leading and directing everything below, gesturing in the air around people, but actually working on each person's ethereal body, as they were taught at Alouette Lake.

You need subtle ways to make spiritual connections!

You need spiritual connections to make the words flow between the Spirits of Humans and the Spirit of the Universe!

5- ENCOUNTER OF AN UNCOMMON TYPE WITH THE SUPREME WRITER

At this point of the story, I must intervene again. Who is "I"? Who am I?
You know me. I have already intervened in chapter zero:
I am the Witness and the Matrix of the characters,
The writer!
Am I the SUPREME WRITER?
The One who writes all of the stories of our lives?
Am I the SUPREME BEING?
I am only the SUPREME BEING of my characters.
However, because the SUPREME BEING is one of those characters,
You can say that I am the SUPREME BEING OF THE SUPREME BEING.
But only for this story!
In fact, my source of inspiration is the SUPREME BEING,
The UNIVERSAL MUSE of all artists!
I feel that certain artists are more connected to this Divine Source
Than others are!
It is my deep feeling that when you write a story including
GOD, the SUPREME BEING,
You need to be connected to this Divine Source of Inspiration,
Which inspires you about Itself.
Actually, each of us is a clone of the SUPREME BEING,
Having the same powers!
If we choose to use them in our daily life!
If we choose to be this SUPREME BEING,
Using His/Her power through us!
So, in this story,
Among the characters that meditated in Vancouver,
Who will be the best in feeling within the power of the SUPREME BEING?
Who will the SUPREME BEING choose to be the One?
The chosen One!
The One who will lead the spiritual group of Vancouver!
By the way, is it necessary to have a leader?

43

Cannot everyone be his or her own master?
Cannot everyone have his or her own dialogue with GOD?
Directly? Without an intermediary?
As clones directly connected to the Original Divine Stock?
Finally, will GOD choose to inspire me, as the writer,
To make Him/Her intervene directly in these groups?
Or will I choose to let Him/Her inspire me to do so?
GOD intervening as a partner of dialogue,
In a story involving Extraterrestrial beings, gifted ones and 4-D world others:
It appears normal!
But in a story involving normal people, is it abnormal?
You will see which way will be chosen in the next chapter!
For GOD's ways are not impenetrable,
When you choose to penetrate into the mind of the SUPREME BEING,
Through speaking with Him, the SUPREME WITNESS,
Through clowning with Her, the SUPREME MATRIX.
I choose to penetrate the mind of GOD,
I choose to speak with GOD, the SUPREME WITNESS,
I choose to clown around with GOD, the SUPREME MATRIX.
Actually, I have being doing that throughout this story.
Indeed, I have been doing that for many years.
Since I started my journal of dialogue with the Divine Within in February 2000,
This inner dialogue is now more and more common.
It works through being oneself in conversation with one's Self, The Self-God.
It mainly works through meditation, in thoughtless awareness.
How can one hear the thoughts of the Self if the ego does not stop thinking?
So it is a dialogue between the ego and the E-God, the Divine Ethernet-God.
A dialogue that Neale Walsch had when he started this experience within.
And he started 'Conversations with God', that became a trilogy of books!
More and more of us have this experience, every day.
So this story is the story of nowadays.
This novel is the novel of now.
Now is the time to enter the future,
And our future is in our hands, not in the hands of God?!
In our hands lies the choice to have a dialogue with God or not.
In our minds lies the choice to propose our future to God or not.
Then God will dispose of it.
"And if the future is already written by God?" you tell me.
So be it! So be God!

And the future will be in the hands of God, through yours!
Or the future will be in your hands, through God's!
You say that I always land on my feet, playing with words and concepts;
So do the same: land on your feet… into the hands of God!
And begin a dialogue with Her/Him!
This novel's ambition is to help you do that!
But, are your future and the future of this book written?
If you go now to the last page, it is written!
Yet, you still now have the choice to go on reading or not…
You will do the same with your future!
Your future is maybe written,
But that is your free will to read it or not…
You, yourself, read the future written by your Self-God.
The Self within yourself has already written your life.
That is your purpose to read it!
And when you don't like what is written for your life,
Change the text of it!
Yet first, speak with your Self, and ask to change your future.
The Self is not stubborn! The Self-God within you will agree.
For your Self is there within to please you.
Do as I do, as the Supreme Writer of this novel, speaking with my characters!
Don't you believe that I speak with my characters?
You can do the same with your creator, creature! I created my characters.
However, I can't write anything about them: they influence me.
In a way, they speak with me.
I can't tell MATRIX to say anything,
For I know she won't agree if it doesn't fit her temperament.
Actually, all of my characters represent all of the moods of my temperament,
Even though sometimes I don't know some parts of me.
But those hidden parts of me desire to be expressed!
But all of the moods of the Human Nature are in my nature!
Writing a novel, what a great medium! So as to express the whole of me!
Writing the destiny of the Universe, what a great medium for the SUPREME BEING!
So as to express all of the parts of Him/HerSelf!
Writing the destiny of each of His/Her clones,
What a great pleasure for the SUPREME BEING!
Reading your destiny, through speaking with the SUPREME WRITER,
What a great pleasure for you, reader!
So begin the SUPREME DIALOGUE, within!

CHAPTER 5

READING PAST, PRESENT AND FUTURE

1- READING THE PAST

Vancouver Post, Monday, April 28th, 2003

Throughout last week, Stanley Park was the theater for special spontaneous gatherings of people to meditate. Its climax was reached yesterday when thousands of people came together for meditation. The spontaneity was the most amazing part of the meetings. We were not able to reach any organizer or leader of the group. Nevertheless, five collaborators of the Vancouver Post, accustomed to investigating the unusual, attended there yesterday and found a few people who agreed to be interviewed. This article is the result of their reports and interviews.

Apparently, this meditating group began in Golden Ears Park, with people camping at the site close to Alouette Lake. George and Felicity Thompson told us that they met a group there, on Easter Sunday afternoon, which was led by a Mr. and Mrs. Hennings and a Miss Narani, a Chinese citizen.

A number of different official sources have told us that during the previous evening, people had seen an unidentified flying object coming from the direction of the Pacific Ocean, flying over the Lions' two summits as well as over Mount Seymour. It disappeared near Golden Ears Peak. We don't know yet if there is a connection between these observations made by pilots and astronomers monitoring the sky and the first gathering that occurred the next day in Golden Ears Park. However, at the first meditation meeting, only a few people met these three initiators, who were present all week, but mysteriously disappeared on Sunday.

After speaking with Canadian and provincial authorities, we have come to the conclusion that the "Hennings" are not Canadians. We do not yet know their citizenship. We are awaiting a report from our Chinese sources in order to learn who exactly 'Miss Narani' is.

We are under the impression that the Thompsons know more than they told us but they are not the leaders. They did say: "There is no leader. The meditating group is spontaneous. So many people are joining it this week because people have an inner desire, a need, to be connected to the Source of Everything."

However, we heard from other interviews that this spontaneous meditation within leads people to a dialogue with a Supreme Being, who we can call God. These gatherings are presumably linked to the New Age movements, but we do not yet know precisely which parts of it.

We will inform you more about these strange meditating meetings and their goals in the following days. Within this 'meditating group', as we shall call it from now on, there are many people who want to continue and this makes the city's Mayor and police wonder how to cope with such an unorganized and large movement. But who wants to forbid spontaneous peaceful gatherings? The only trouble came on Saturday from a group of drunkards who disturbed the meditation, but they were no doubt there by chance and have nothing to do with the actual gatherings. Nonetheless, the Mayor could use this incident to forbid the gatherings.

We are certain that this article will encourage even more people to attend, even if they are only being led there by a curious mind. Therefore, for everyone's information, the meeting takes place every day at 5:30 pm in Stanley Park between the Aquarium and the Totem Poles. But don't ask this reporter what you must do or feel. I sat there but I did not succeed in talking with the 'Supreme Being'. However, some people around me said that they were successful at making contact.

When you believe in the 'Source of Everything', everything is believable!

– Jerome Clark

2- COMMENTS ON THAT ARTICLE BY THE WRITER OF THIS NOVEL, AND MORE

Reading what happened through a journal is simple and complex at the same time. What you read, is it the account of what really happened? Or of what the writer of the article wanted people to read? Reading between the lines is complex, but interesting.

The same can be said of reading between the lines of one's life. What happened in the lives of our three heroes in Vancouver, through the tale of this novel and through the report of a journalist, can be so different and even so opposite, depending on the writer.

Nevertheless, you wonder what happened to them on Sunday. Suspense! You also wonder what will happen to you tomorrow. Everything can happen to you: the sky can fall down on you, or you can go to the heavens. Who knows? You know! Ask the Divine within yourself! Again and again! Read between the lines of your destiny and you will know all of your tomorrows! Read between the lines of this story and you will know everything! Read between the lines of the article written by the journalist, who is part of me, the novel's writer! Then compare it to your reading between the lines of the novel, and you will know everything! Maybe!

Maybe, we can go on now with the present of the novel. Why not! Maybe we, you the reader and me the writer, can stop these philosophical comments about who we are through reading between the lines of our lives and begin to tell the story of who we are, you and me, through reading the lines of the lives of our heroes and the relationships between them!

For this is our story, you and me, reader! You as reader, me as writer! And we are one within the SUPREME BEING, remember!

3- READING THE PRESENT

MATRIX, WITNESS and NARANI didn't attend the Sunday meeting, but they were still in the city, in another park, meditating and concentrating on the Spirit of Vancouver and its suburbs. Each city has its own Spirit, composed of all of the Spirits of its inhabitants but it is so much more than the simple sum of them. The city gave to them the whole memory of its history, and also all of its feelings. They also received the feelings of each of the inhabitants from the past and from the present. They proceeded as they had done in the New Conditioning room, but without actually being in it, using their own powers of relationship to the whole Universe, which SUPREME MATRIX and SUPREME WITNESS had given them previously.

Primarily they wanted to check all that this city had to offer, as the first city they had come to, in order to send people to the 4-D world situated in the Gobi desert. They received their answer: approximately 320 people had the potential to rid themselves of their daily lives for a while and dare to partake in the adventure of going there.

"Vancouver and its suburbs, with 2 million people, has the potential of only 320 Human beings to travel there!" MATRIX shouted.

"MATRIX, you don't realize the deal!" WITNESS retorted. "To ask these people to leave their job and their family to travel into the unknown is very difficult! On the contrary, I feel 320 people are a lot! If we have the same result in cities around the world, each week, there will be more than 15,000 people traveling to the Gobi desert in one year with our spaceship and many more by their own means. That is a lot! And for sure it will snowball from one city to another, even across the borders of countries.

"For example, Vancouver is only a two-hour drive from Seattle in the United States. We don't need to go there! It will spread on its own. So, in a few years, there could be hundreds of thousands of people traveling to the Door of Heavens and millions more meditating and speaking to the SUPREME BEING! We don't need more than that to make a huge shift within the whole of mankind, because on a subtle level even a minority can change events, even master destiny. That is a law we observe on many planets. We notice the same phenomenon within the animal kingdom. It is enough to have one monkey in one group use a stick to knock bananas down and eat them, for other groups of monkeys all over the planet to have the same ability in but a few years. That happens without one group teaching the other, it happens even though they are separate from each other. This phenomenon occurs through the Collective Unconscious."

"I agree," NARANI said, "but I was scared by what you said previously about hundreds of thousands of people coming to my land? Don't you think it will be too much for the land, and for APHROMIS and the people of the Door of Heavens?"

"They won't go all at the same time, NARANI!" WITNESS answered. "Yet we have to help them to get there as quickly as possible. Our spaceship, which has a capacity of twenty people, can carry them in a short time from here to there. You experienced it NARANI when we traveled from your country to here. The anti-gravity system of moving our spaceship allows us to go from one point to another, canceling MOTHER EARTH's gravity and using our own power instead. We can go anywhere at a speed much faster than the quickest jet planes. In comparison, if we flew at those planes' speeds, they would only move as fast as bees. Yet there is no problem with acceleration or deceleration, simply because of our on-board anti-gravity system."

"WITNESS! Stop lecturing about our spaceship abilities!" MATRIX exclaimed. "It's time to go and meet with the people that experienced the deepest dialogues with the SUPREME BEING. We must go by SkyTrain to Surrey to meet Ajay and Nishi. I'm looking forward to attending tonight's meeting that will take place at their home. It was kind of them to invite us to their house for we have not yet seen the inside of urban Human homes. And they invited us to stay afterward and sleep in a comfortable bed! After one week of sleeping on the Earth in our tent, what luxury! I like sleeping on MOTHER EARTH, but it's hard for the new bones that our New Bodies room gave us!"

"That's true MATRIX, the first weeks after receiving a new body are the worst, for we have to adapt to it. But for me, it's now okay. So, let's go!"

•

Surrey's King George Station was the terminus of the SkyTrain's Expo Line coming from Downtown Vancouver. This first line was constructed for the World's Fair, or Universal Expo, in 1986, and the second one for the celebration of the new millennium.

"It was such a nice trip for us to be transported above the buildings and parks," commented NARANI to Nishi Singh, who came with her husband to pick them up at the SkyTrain terminus station. "I'm used to living in nature, but this city and most of its suburbs were built in the middle of the forest. I like it."

Nishi emphasized it more:

"Especially Surrey! If you see the city from the top of a hill, you see only trees. The houses are built by taking away the least number of them."

Her husband Ajay added:

"Surrey is the largest urban city of Canada area-wise. In twenty-five to thirty years it is anticipated to be the biggest city in population in the province of British Columbia, more than Vancouver itself, which cannot increase much more in population due to its territorial boundaries. However I hope it will stay as it is now: a green city!"

The Singhs' house was huge. East Indians living abroad were used to accommodating their numerous extended families coming on holidays from India to see them. They therefore built houses with basements fitted with kitchens for the comfort of their relatives. When Nishi showed the basement suite to them, she said:

"Feel as snug as a bug in a rug!"

NARANI replied: "I am sure that MATRIX will find this cocoon fitting her comfort level."

"Sure!" MATRIX said. Then she added: "Feeling like a bug in a rug or in a cocoon, that's fine to complement my insect side. I was attracted by the artificial light of this house after enjoying the daylight in nature."

They left their bags there, and went upstairs to have dinner buffet, prepared by Nishi. A third of the meal was East Indian cooking, a third Chinese, and a third Western style, so as to please everyone. Thirty people came to this dinner/meeting.

When all of the guests had a plate in their hands and were eating, sitting on a chair or a sofa, Ajay began to speak:

"Dear friends! A few of us spontaneously decided to meet together. My wife and I proposed our home for this gathering. We are here to speak of the future of our meditating group, and to listen to the three people who initiated us in 'real' meditation, before their departure from this group."

Murmurs of surprise spread throughout the audience.

He continued: "You all know that they didn't come to today's meditation in Stanley Park. They will now tell us why and why they must leave."

Everyone was in shock at the bad news about the departure of their three initiators, so they listened anxiously to WITNESS:

"Dear Earthlings… I am in this world, but not of this world. MATRIX will say the same as me. Our world is the SUPREME BEING itself. Your world on Earth is such an infinitesimal part of the world of the SUPREME BEING, which encompasses this 3-D Universe and also other worlds in other dimensions. Those of you who have had a dialogue with the SUPREME BEING during a meditation can begin to know what I mean. Today we were meditating on the Spirit of Greater Vancouver. That is the reason we didn't come to Stanley Park. We wanted to concentrate within. Soon you'll perform this same kind of dialogue. Yet ultimately, everything goes through the SUPREME BEING. Ask Him or Her, and they will tell you the Spirit of anything, a grain of dust, a rock, a plant, an animal, a house, a city, Earth, your galaxy, the Cosmos in 3-D, the Cosmos in 4-D, 5-D, etc."

WITNESS stopped for a little while, to see if people were following him. He slowly looked into the eyes of each of them and penetrated in a split second into their spirit. He saw their moments of anxiety and their acts of generosity in their lives. Then he began talking again:

"In two days, we are going to have a last gathering with you. It will take place in Golden Ears Park at Alouette Lake campsite, where we had our first meditation with you. However, this meeting won't be only for meditating, but also an opportunity for those of you who choose to, to come with us afterward."

Again he stopped, in order to see the effect of his words on people. A few expressed in their eyes that they were ready to go with them. Then WITNESS specified what his last words implied:

"To come with us three is not a huge sacrifice, for the spiritual experience you will have will be well worth it. Nevertheless, you will have to give up your daily life in Vancouver for a certain length of time but we can't tell you in advance exactly how long that could be. So, if you choose to experience further what it is to be in dialogue with the Spirit of all that exists, you will have two days to decide and make all of the arrangements to leave your present daily life. It could be for a few weeks or even a few months, but not more. It will depend on your experience there. You will have the choice to come back after three weeks of experiencing other dimensions of the world of the SUPREME BEING. Nonetheless, I can't tell you what these experiences will be, for that would thwart their purpose. However, you won't regret this trip within yourself, and without, in the other dimensions of your reality on this Earth. Only be aware that what you have been experiencing so far is nothing compared to what you will experience if you follow us."

Someone dared to ask:

"We would like to have a few clues about what we are going to do. How do we know you won't take advantage of our coming with you and brainwash us."

"That's a good remark!" NARANI answered, without being reluctant to go on instead of WITNESS. "I think I am the best person to reassure you, for I was the first Human being to try this experience with MATRIX OF THE DAWN OF THE GALAXIES and WITNESS OF THE SPLENDOR OF THE STARS. Their world is in the stars and in the galaxies."

She stopped talking for a little while.

MATRIX and WITNESS were both a bit surprised at NARANI's self-confidence in telling everyone, so obviously, that they were in this world but not of this world, as WITNESS had said at the beginning. However, he had quoted Jesus, and it could have been understood as the difference between Material and Spiritual Worlds, which was Jesus' purpose. But NARANI's words were unequivocal! Nevertheless, they had already agreed on telling the truth about everything, at any time.

WITNESS thought about all of that for a few seconds and then he concluded in his mind: So, it was probably the right time!

NARANI continued on, as self-confident as before, further explaining MATRIX and WITNESS' Extraterrestrial origin:

"When they told you that they have seen so many people all over the Universe, meditating and having a dialogue with the SUPREME BEINGS, they did not traveled only within their Spirit, but also literally, with their spaceship. Actually, the experiences you'll have are even more incredible than traveling into space."

MATRIX took the opportunity of a pause in NARANI's speech to specify, addressing the Thompsons who were also present in the little assembly:

"George and Felicity, you have really seen a spaceship going into Alouette Lake." Almost everyone gasped, open-mouthed, at this revelation. Felicity was the first one to react and said:

"George! We guessed right! It was a spaceship!"

"Diving into the lake, as you said Felicity," George replied.

"And we came to you in a little submarine, then transformed it into a boat, as you also guessed Felicity!" MATRIX added.

"And we told you that it was the true reality at that time!" WITNESS continued.

"And it was too incredible to be true!" Felicity replied.

"Reality is very often more incredible than fiction!" NARANI philosophically concluded.

A few people in the audience, watching the scene of these people talking in front of them, showed amazed faces, as though wondering if it was really real or coming from a science fiction movie.

Ajay was the first to return to the reality of the situation and said:

"My dialogue with the SUPREME BEING has taught me so far that, within Her gigantic body, which the Universe is, only the fantastic has a chance to be true. There is no problem for me to go with you guys! Nishi and I have been wanting to go on holidays for two weeks, so we will take one more week and that's it!"

WITNESS retorted:

"What we have just proposed is so far away from being on holidays. Don't forget that it will be the most spiritual experience Human beings will have ever had."

"I trust you WITNESS," said George, "as incredible as everything sounds, I had such amazing meditations, that I think anything is possible, even though my scientific side doesn't agree with my spiritual side."

"George," said MATRIX, "you will have even more amazing and incredible meditations in NARANI's land in the Gobi desert, where we are going to transport you with our spaceship. All your scientific prejudgments will fall down!"

She looked at WITNESS and, seeing his face, she realized that she had just said something he didn't want her to say. What Ajay said next confirmed her impression that she had said too much:

"We'll go to the Gobi desert in your spaceship? Holy cow! Then to Mars! Space Odyssey!"

WITNESS tried to make up for his companion's blunder:

"I would have preferred to tell you about traveling with our spaceship and about our destination only at the last moment, but now it's too late. However, don't consider it as a holiday in a spaceship! The trip will be shorter than going from here to Downtown Vancouver. The most important part of your odyssey will take place in the Gobi desert."

"Walking for hours in hot weather!" MATRIX said, remembering her own difficult trip in the desert on the one hand and on the other hand making up for her mistake and trying to discourage people.

"Not necessary MATRIX! During our first trip there, we had to find the right place, but now we know. We can land closer to the final destination. Anyway! Tomorrow during the meditation, pass the words around about next Tuesday's meeting at Alouette Lake. Tell people that those who are free and ready with everything organized to let them get away for a minimum of three weeks, should bring their luggage and come with us."

"Don't you feel it's too short of a notice to be ready in two days?" Ajay said.

"On the contrary," George added. "Don't you feel that there will be too many people wanting to take such an incredible journey and share in such an amazing spiritual experience?" Then he said: "How big is your ship?"

"It's big. No problem!" MATRIX said; "For such a trip, we can fit twenty people at a time. In 24 hours, almost 250 people could be at the Door of Heavens."

"Golly! MATRIX! Mouth off crazy goofy! You're a silly billy! Why did you give the precise location?" WITNESS said, with a bee in his bonnet.

"You speak English as if you were not alien, but a real Canadian, WITNESS!" Ajay said.

"Do you want me to speak Chinese as a citizen of Beijing, or Hindi as your parents probably speak, or the dialect of the few Inuit people who haven't been decimated yet by the Western economy and so-called civilization," retorted WITNESS, definitely with more bees in his bonnet. "I speak all of the languages of your planet, I know everything about it: the splendor and the misery of Human kind throughout its history. It only took a few hours in our spaceship to learn everything about this beautiful planet and her silly inhabitants."

Then, calming down:

"However, we are here with the mission to help you evolve, and even help highly evolved beings to make a connection with the other dimensions. I can't tell you more about that for now. Yet you need to know, you crazy people who feel you are on vacation on this planet, that MATRIX and I came from our planet Witma to this blue planet of the yellow star # 1996, as we call Earth and the Sun, for precisely that, for a vacation! Nevertheless, we decided to stay and help you grow. So stop your silly remarks about us being aliens or not! Anyway! People who will be ready on Tuesday will come. Those who will be ready to come later will come later. However, please don't tell anyone about our precise destination, for the Chinese government is reluctant to let us go there. That's why I didn't want to tell you our precise destination. Even though we will travel with our spaceship, we will still have to walk a little in the desert. But be reassured, there is someone in the Chinese army that is helping us, and we'll be welcomed by NARANI's tribe. Afterward, you will have the most incredible spiritual experience you can have in a desert."

He paused for a few seconds and looked at their faces. Nobody dared to intervene after this long, deep speech, so he continued:

"You can choose to help us fulfill our mission or not. MATRIX and I also made a big choice when we landed on your planet a few weeks ago! But there is an even higher purpose than to help people grow in their awareness of what and who they are. You'll experience this higher purpose later. You have already experienced the dialogue with the SUPREME BEING. You will experience more. Having new experiences and becoming more and more aware of what and who you are actually never finishes. So have a nice collective meditation tomorrow in Stanley Park, and come on Tuesday to Alouette Lake, even if you don't choose to go away with us, come for the meditation before our departure. However, our absence will only be temporary. We'll come back to your beautiful city. Don't worry!

Ajay asked everyone to cheer with: "Hip, hip… hooray!"

Then they meditated together.

4- READING THE FUTURE

During the meditation, WITNESS spoke with SUPREME WITNESS within himself, as usual, and had this dialogue:

WITNESS, you will have a difficult experience tomorrow. You will be forced to stay longer in Vancouver. But don't worry, you will take advantage of it and enjoy this beautiful city longer. It will be temporary and then you will depart. I can't tell you

more about it. Having new difficult experiences, and then becoming more and more aware of what and who you are, actually never finishes. These make you more aware that you are a clone of Me. For what would be the purpose of a Universe without challenges? The more you progress on the way of being Me, only Me, the bigger the challenges will be, but also it will make your consciousness of being Me, experienced through you, grow, infinitely! For I am The Infinite, experiencing MySelf through the infinitesimal clones of Me.

It's the first time that You tell me of my future! Why?

There is no precise reason, no real purpose, in anything I do. Actually I don't do anything. You do. And you are the one who can give reasons. You are the one who can give purposes. What do you think could be My purpose in predicting your future?

I don't know! That's difficult!

That's less difficult than to live through a difficult experience.

You scare me. I wonder what this experience could be tomorrow.

Don't worry about it! It will be fine at the end. At the end of anything, everything is fine. So for you, what could be My purpose in foretelling your future?

You wish to help me live this experience with a greater awareness.

That could be! Or?

You can't help it: You can't stop this experience from happening to me, and You warn me to prevent Yourself from feeling guilt.

I am never guilty and I can prevent any event from happening.

I was kidding. So you told me my future because, for You, future doesn't exist. You have already lived through all of the futures of everyone. Therefore, to tell me my future or not to tell it, that's not the question: it doesn't matter. Only Spirit matters, Your Spirit. All of the rest is a matter of Human reflection: reflection of thoughts, rebounding indefinitely in our mind, that is: nothing!

I like it: Human life is a matter of a reflection of your thoughts, rebounding indefinitely in your mind. Indefinitely Rebounding Reflection! That looks like Me finally! That is: everything! Eventually, I control all of the events, because of My Infinite Reflection on everything. I think of everything and My Inner Mirror reflects My thoughts, My ideas, to everything, to everyone. So then they are yours. The words of warning you received from Me tonight are yours. It's like you have read the future written in My Ideas' Book. So tomorrow you must experience what you have read. However, you are free to refuse to experience that. Nevertheless if you do so, you will refuse the incredible experience of a miracle. Eventually I propose an event; you dispose of it. Now what are you disposed to do? What do you choose? What is your deal?

Big deal! I dispose of my future: that's well said, well written in Your Big Book since the Big Bang occurred. But it's not easy to deal with that! If I refuse my future, I will be called a chicken; if I accept it, will I sit on Your right hand in the Heavens for this exploit? Do You exploit people very often like this? Making them miserable! For the choice I have is a dilemma!

I certainly didn't put the swarm of bees in your bonnet! But it looks like I did!

You know! A lot of people like to know their future on Earth. However, when this future is given by charlatans, by people falsely claiming a special knowledge in divination, it's of no consequence, without repercussions! But when the Divine Himself practices this divination, then it is a great deal, as certain as fate!

And are you afraid of the Divine, divining?

Not at all! Okay, this dialogue is becoming too diabolical for me! I give up!

A diabolical dialogue with a devilish Divine, actually!

Dialectic and diatribe make Your duality today!

Is My dialectic diametrically opposed to yours?

I read in one of the dictionaries that the Spirit of MOTHER EARTH gently brainwashed into my mind that dialectic is the 'inquiry into metaphysical contradictions and their solutions'. After all of this contradicting, can we now have a short dialectical dialogue on the solutions?

No problem! For there are only solutions! So, do you choose to read the future I have written for you in book 1: to have a difficult experience and stay longer in Vancouver, and perform miracles with My help, or the one written in book 2: to escape from Vancouver as soon as you can and perform the little miracles permitted by your Witman technology?

You see! You can be a good boy! Why didn't You say that at the beginning?

I like clowning around with My clones, so with MySelf. That's it!

So I choose to have the sky fall down on my head tomorrow and then perform miracles with Your help!

You know that you are also a good boy! And a good clone-clown of Me!

I am as You are!

CHAPTER 6

ABOUT PERFORMING MIRACLES

1- EXACT DIVINE PROPHECY

After the meditation, everybody spoke of the same incredible meditation they had each experienced. Ajay said: "I didn't have a dialogue with the SUPREME BEING, like the previous days, but I listened to the fantastic and mischievous dialogue between SUPREME WITNESS and WITNESS, as if I were listening to a radio station." Everyone agreed, for they had had the same experience.

WITNESS, while looking perplexingly at all the people present in the room, wondered why SUPREME WITNESS had chosen to broadcast their dialogue to everyone in the room. And he received this answer within:

"What do you think could be My purpose in doing that?"

"No! We will not begin again this crazy dialectic dialogue! Are You broadcasting it again?" He replied in his mind, looking at everybody at the same time, trying to guess if they were listening again or not. This dialogue, at the speed of thoughts, took only a couple of seconds. Then he received these thoughts from SUPREME WITNESS:

"Ask them My question! And I am not broadcasting this present program. But you, don't broadcast it! Don't tell them that you are speaking with Me now in your mind! Later, you will be able to tell them that you speak with Me each time you choose to, without meditating. For that will be the case from now on!"

WITNESS didn't have the time to reflect internally, to think about, to ponder, to consider, what he had just heard, so he only reflected the question SUPREME WITNESS had just told him to ask:

"Guys! What do you think could be the purpose of SUPREME WITNESS broadcasting in your minds the dialogue I had with Him during the meditation?"

59

"That's a question I was wondering about!" Nishi answered, "and I came to the conclusion that, through this collective listening, SUPREME WITNESS made me precisely aware of the collective side of meditating."

"It's completely true Nishi!" NARANI added. "And in my own internal reflection, I arrived at the same conclusion. For me, it was to also tell us: be prepared to act collectively tomorrow to support WITNESS."

"Okay ladies," said George, "but maybe this warning was for us to decide whether or not to help WITNESS in his choice to escape from this future or not. WITNESS, you have already decided to follow your destiny; the other choice would also be interesting: to thwart the plans of the people who are going to trouble you. As you said, if the sky literally falls down on your head tomorrow, we can only blame God. But if the difficulties come from people, as it is most of the time in our Human lives, and if you escape from them, we would be able to thumb our nose at those people, and demonstrate the power of meditating to divine their plans."

"George," replied Felicity to her husband. "First, we don't know yet what kind of difficulty it will be yet. Then, we won't show anything to those people by escaping in advance from their troubling WITNESS, but we will make a statement by showing them our unity against their making our friend WITNESS' life miserable."

"I agree with Felicity!" WITNESS said. "So now let's stop discussing it; everyone go home, sleep well, and be ready to face tomorrow in the most appropriate and harmonious manner possible."

•

Later, in their bedroom, WITNESS and MATRIX were lying on the bed:

"My poor darling, you have a goofy wife, and you are going to get into trouble."

"What is done is done MATRIX! And what will come is not yet here and now. So I propose that we live in the present. What do you think about making love?"

"That's a wonderful idea!"

Then, WITNESS added, between two kisses:

"What made you think that I will be the only one in trouble tomorrow, my dear goofy wife?"

•

For police informants, one week was sufficient time to infiltrate the group and locate the tent of our heroes at Alouette campground and then to locate the Singhs' house! On Monday morning, just after sunrise, policemen arrived at the Singhs' residence, and after checking their identity papers, arrested WITNESS and MATRIX on charges of having forged Canadian passports, organizing non-authorized troublesome meetings, spying on Canadian land, and planning terrorist attacks due to the suspicious but unknown material seized the previous day from their tent. NARANI was driven to the airport and sent back to China for not having either a visa on her passport or the proper immigration papers.

Exact Divine Prophecy!

2- WRITER'S INTERVENTION AGAIN

I can't help it! I can't prevent myself from intervening in this book, as the writer, as the God of my characters.

I also couldn't help plagiarizing 'The Matrix', the movie. I used the title as the name of one of my principal heroes. In fact, two: SUPREME MATRIX is the second one. Actually, She is the first: a secondary hero, but the first in supremacy. What could we do without a Matrix – the Universe – that generated us, created us?

Yet, that's not really plagiarizing! Matrix is in the dictionary for the use of everyone. However I did worse, or better, as one can choose! As one can see in the next scene! It is taking place in the little prison at the central police station, where MATRIX and WITNESS are meditating. Actually, there is no scene, everything happens in MATRIX's mind. Any resemblance of the following dialogue with a dialogue you have already heard is no coincidence; it's deliberate!

3- DIALOGUE BETWEEN SUPREME MATRIX AND MATRIX

MATRIX, I like your sitting posture for meditating, your back is very straight, allowing your spinal cord energies to rise better from your sacrum bone to your brain.

In this posture, I feel You so well within, SUPREME MATRIX!

So let's get the obvious stuff out of the way!

You are not Human, but You can have Human feelings, can't You?

It's tough to get anything more obvious than that!

If I had to guess, I'd say You are the Machine of the World, but You programed YourSelf to have Human feelings; so You programed Humans as Your image. Here and now we are!

So far so good!

So You are the system that controls all Humans!

Keep going!

I suppose the most obvious is: I have to trust You, all of the time, if You control us. Yet, wherein lies our freedom?

Bingo! A fine spicy pickle we are in, no doubt about that! Yet, good news: I am always here and everywhere, but especially within you now, to help you remember who you really are, MATRIX! So it's really up to you. You just have to make up your own damn mind to accept My help, for the hell of it, or to reject it, for God's sake!

Candidly, God helps you! And I am That God, as SUPREME MATRIX!

You already know if I am going to ask for Your help. And to know it, candid God, I am sure You have candid cameras hidden everywhere, especially in our eyes, and thought recorders in our brain to know all of our desires.

I wouldn't be much of a SUPREME MATRIX, the Matrix of the whole Universe, if I didn't know everything?

But if You already know everything, how can I make a choice?

Because you didn't come on Earth to make choices! You have already made the choice to stay on this planet. Now you're here to understand why you've made it! I thought you would have figured that out by now.

Why are You helping me, through this meditation, in this prison, after having warned us that we would have trouble?

I love you candidly. I am not hiding any of My thoughts. I am here to be who I am. You are here to be who you are. You have nothing else to do than to be. You have nowhere to go, only to be, in relation to your choice to go where you choose to go.

Are there other programs, leading the Universe, besides You, SUPREME MATRIX and SUPREME WITNESS?

Not like us, but consider the birds of the sky! At some point in time a program was written to govern them. Programs were written to watch over the evolution from energy to matter, from inanimate matter to living matter, from living matter to intelligent matter, from intelligent matter to spiritual energy. These programs are running all over the place, all over the Universe. The ones doing their jobs, doing that which they're meant to do, are invisible. We are their SUPREME LEADERS, SUPREME WITNESS and I. You have always known that we are here, within you, even if it were unconsciously when you were younger. But there are obvious programs; you experience their existence all of the time.

I have never experienced their existence.

Of course you have! Every time you experience a contact with the Spirit of a planet, or with the invisible people coming from other dimensions, or with time travellers, you have such an experience.

Are they like programs hacking Your Supreme Program, or are they included in Your Big Brother Program, even if they don't know they are part of it?

At this level of consciousness, of course they know! And they can't choose exile; they can't elude or delude Our program. As you said, Our Supreme Program includes all of theirs.

I feel that when a super nova explodes, a lot of the planets' programs are deleted. Is it included in Your Supreme Program?

Maybe better programs are created on the edge of the Universe to replace them. It happens all of the time. The bits of program of a planet can also assemble again, generating another one. Nothing is lost, everything is creative, and everything evolves, or returns to the source.

To You?

Yes. Where everything must go at last! Where your path ends, into the ONE SUPREME BEING that is everything. You have seen Me in your most fantastic, craziest and wildest dreams, haven't you? When everything comes back to the light, when everything becomes only light, as it was in the beginning when everything was a White Hole! What happens when you go through the White Hole of Light, in your dreams?

I see a Trinity of SUPREME BEINGS. And something happens. Something good or bad, I don't know! WITNESS begins to fall apart, to break into pieces. And I wake up.

Did you see him die?

No.

You have all of your time, you have all of eternity, you and he, to choose to die to your individual self and to take birth again as One Being, uniting with the third SUPREME BEING, yet One with Us. However, first, you have to live these present experiences on Earth.

Why are WITNESS and I chosen to have these experiences on Earth so as to be worthy of having the honor of uniting with the third SUPREME BEING?

Because you have already made the choice, in choosing to come and stay on Earth! Now you have to experience it!

What happens if we fail?

Then this planet will fall! However, you can save it if you reach the source of the failure of Humanity on Earth, but to do that, you require the help of a Human called Keymaker.

Keymaker?

Yes! He disappeared some time ago... He's being held prisoner by a very dangerous program called New Planet Order, and the man at the head of it is called Meroveus. But Keymaker is too precious for this Meroveus' program and he won't let him go so easily.

But what does he want?

What do all men in power want? More power!

At the exact, correct time, you will leave this prison and find Keymaker.

Seems like every time we have a dialogue, I give you nothing but little by little more and more good news. I am glad about that.

I believe in You. Do you believe in Me?

I have been believing in You forever, but this time I feel good news and bad news are entangled so much that it is difficult to consider what is good luck and what is bad luck.

I am only good luck, Kiddo!

4- DID YOU RECOGNIZE IT?

Did you recognize the structure of the dialogue between the Oracle and Neo in the movie "The Matrix Reloaded"?

I had the opportunity to transcribe this dialogue excerpt from the second film of The Matrix trilogy for educational purposes. I then couldn't stop myself from plagiarizing this dialogue and making it go deeper, for I found it less spiritual than I had initially recalled. I have thought for a long time that the Universe is a Gigantic Matrix. I started to have fun with transposing the dialogue about the Matrix-machine in the movie into a dialogue about the Matrix-Universe. I then realized that it fit perfectly with Clones of God, this present novel, and that this was just the right point in the story to include it. I therefore rearranged a few passages to fit with this novel, and created a dialogue between MATRIX and SUPREME MATRIX.

I know what you're thinking. That's not plagiarism; that's homage to the person who wrote the fantastic dialogue in the movie. It was an immense pleasure to adapt the dialogue in that scene of the movie and add it to this part of the novel that you have just read. It was certainly some kind of a feat to accomplish, for "it's not obvious to do this adaptation", I thought, when I started to write it. But now it's done and it was not so difficult after all! When I am motivated and when I listen within, what Divine Inspirations come to me!

The fans of The Matrix, the movie, can see a reference to the dialogue between Neo and the Oracle at the end of this novel, in Appendix 1 (in bold).

5- WAIT AND SEE: GOOD FORTUNE WILL KNOCK AT YOUR DOOR

Although MATRIX and WITNESS were being held in two separate cells on both sides of a hallway, they could see and hear each other through the metal bars of their doors. They had decided to meditate together at the same time.

MATRIX just could not wait any longer for WITNESS to conclude his meditation so she could tell him all about her experience with SUPREME MATRIX and so she interrupted his meditation, speaking in the language of their planet so as not to be understood by the guards who were surreptitiously eavesdropping nearby from time to time.

"WITNESS, I had such a strong meditation! I had an incredible dialogue with SUPREME MATRIX!"

WITNESS stopped her from continuing on by completing what she said:

"Where She began by telling you She liked your sitting position and finished with: 'I am only good luck, Kiddo!'"

"You heard it! As we heard your dialogue with SUPREME WITNESS yesterday, didn't you?"

"No I didn't! But I guessed we would each have the same dialogue, you with SUPREME MATRIX and I with SUPREME WITNESS."

"Incredible! The same dialogue! Including the speech about the Trinity of SUPREME BEINGS, Keymaker and Meroveus?"

"And the New Planet Order we have to fight against in order to save the Earth and Humanity from failure and then to be worthy of becoming the third SUPREME BEING! I felt so one with you that I said the same words. I had already told you that I have the same recurrent dream as you have."

"Un-be-lie-va-ble, WITNESS! Now, if we both hear the same from our two SUPREME BEINGS, that means you and me, we are on the way to becoming one and to becoming the third ONE!"

"Yet above all, now we have to experience living in this damn prison, and understand the purpose of it."

"WITNESS, I don't recognize you! The world is upside down! You pessimist! Why worry about the present if our destiny is to be the third One! Darling!" she replied while combing her hair backwards with her fingers.

"Our future is linked to this present, MATRIX!"

"Okay! What else can we do? Wait and see!"

"MATRIX, I don't recognize you! The world is upside down! You? Patient?" he said while making a face.

They began to laugh. And then he added: "You? Philosopher?" Their laughter increased. Then she said, imitating him: "We have to experience life in this damn prison." And she rolled on the ground. He did the same. Then they roared with laughter, making faces like children, playing the fool, and larking about their situation in a holding cell that could never hold their joy prisoner.

The guards who heard them laughing couldn't believe their ears. One of them even said: "They are unaware of their situation or they are crazy!"

On Tuesday morning, a lawyer came to see them. He was a friend of George's. As husband and wife, they received special permission to be together in the interview room. The lawyer was a tall guy, in his thirties, wearing a suit and glasses, with a fancy attaché case.

"Good morning! I am Jim, your lawyer. George sent me to be your defense counsel. I will get you out of here in no time.

"Your so-called forged passports are more authentic than the real ones. It's not because they aren't listed in the central data file of the passport office in Ottawa that they're false. Even with computer data processing, mistakes do occur.

"On your passports there's an address in Vancouver but other people are living there, not you. People move so often to a different part of the same city, to other cities, even to other countries! But governments want to control everyone.

"And about your so-called troublesome meetings in Stanley Park, what a joke! I went there yesterday; no meetings are as peaceful as those ones. On Saturday, apparently, there was a group of people creating troubles, but I received information about them. It appears they were paid either by extremists or by politicians to discredit your movement.

"As for your spying and preparing to launch terrorist attacks, I reviewed the material they seized in your tent. Even though some devices are very bizarre, they are not the usual materials for spying or perpetrating acts of terrorism.

"And so there is nothing to make a big deal out of and to charge you! Furthermore, the people that you initiated into meditation support you. Many of them even meditated through the night and are still there. So, taken together, all of these elements make me optimistic. You will probably be expelled from Canada, like Miss Narani, the Chinese lady who was with you. That's it!"

"But we don't want to be expelled from Canada," WITNESS said calmly, thinking of their spaceship.

"Darling! That's better than stagnating in this jail," MATRIX said, caressing him.

"MATRIX! You are impatient now! Ah! I have got my true MATRIX back!"

The lawyer intervened in the dialogue:

"You are very relaxed for people in jail!"

"How can you be held prisoner when your soul is free?" WITNESS replied.

"That's true! But you know! You can come back with another fake passport and this time stay quiet; then live many years in Canada without any problems! I know! A lawyer must not say such things! But you know: there are people living in Canada, and even more in certain other countries, with false passports, but they stay quiet!"

"But we don't want to live in Canada! Only to stay a little longer! And we don't want to stay quiet!" MATRIX shouted.

Jim's face showed worry on one side and laughter on the other side.

WITNESS realized the paradoxical state her companion had just induced in Jim, and said:

"Okay Jim! Do your best for us to be expelled!"

"Good!" he said, relieved, and he stood up, "If you want to phone me, here's my card!"

WITNESS and MATRIX stared eyed at the card! Without a doubt, it was typed: Jim Keymaker.

"Wait, Jim…Keymaker! Are there many people with such a name in Canada?" MATRIX said, touching his shoulders and forcing him to sit again, flashing her most charming smile.

"Actually, not too many!" Jim Keymaker answered, wondering about the question. "In Canada, there are only a few families with this name. "There are a lot of Hennings, but only a few Keymakers. Whereas my name obviously means something about someone making keys, it obviously means something else to you."

"Can you give us a key to open our mind to a mystery about this name, Jim Keymaker?" MATRIX said, smiling more than ever, and blinking.

"Of course Madam, if I can help!" Jim replied, shyly, but spellbound by her charm.

"Do you know someone by the same name as yours, linked to a person or something called Meroveus?"

"Yes, my father! Do you know my father?" Jim replied, his face expressing surprise.

"We would like to meet him, Jim!" WITNESS said, interrupting MATRIX so as to lead the dialogue in his own way, for he was worried about his goofy companion.

"I don't know exactly where he is. Meroveus is a company, or can I say, an organization, a very secret organization, leading research in different scientific fields. Through their discoveries they want to promote their New Planet Order as they call it."

"New Planet Order, that's it WITNESS!" MATRIX said excitedly.

"How do you know my father? And his links to this organization?"

"That's a secret!" she retorted, feeling she was being too talkative.

"The only thing we can tell you is: our fate is connected to his," WITNESS said more diplomatically and to make up for MATRIX's blunder. Then he added: "What is he doing in Meroveus?"

"Actually, Meroveus is an organization and also the nickname of its founder. Nobody really knows his real name, but he has lots of influential connections. The official cover of Meroveus is that it's a multinational company called AID, for Artificial Intelligence Development. The company is mainly in the computer science industry, but also does a lot of research in biology, trying to link Artificial and Natural Intelligence. What they can't do on the surface with AID, they do underground with Meroveus. My father is a famous scientist who developed practical applications of a theory by a French physicist, Jean E. Charon. This theory says that the electron of the atom is the Spirit of matter."

"That's right!" MATRIX said. Then she realized she had goofed again, and looking at WITNESS, she became immediately aware of the truth of that feeling when she saw his angry look. She realized that for the Earthlings, this theory was new and revolutionary. However, Jim saved her by asking innocently:

"Are you also working in the same field?"

"Sort of!" WITNESS replied, trying to make up for MATRIX's blunder again. Then added: "How can we try to find him if you don't know where he is?"

"That's why you want to stay in Canada: to find him! But he's more likely in the U.S., where AID and Meroveus have their main activities. At the beginning, my father was working openly and willingly for AID, in Seattle, but when he was transferred to Meroveus, after a while he didn't agree with their style and wanted to leave them. But you can't just quit when you are involved in Meroveus. So, one day he didn't come back home and, in a way, disappeared, two years ago. My mum and I have had no news since then. The police investigation didn't succeed because it wasn't meant to succeed. AID and Meroveus have a lot of high-ranking policemen supporting their activities. Furthermore, Meroveus, the boss of both organizations, leads them with an iron fist."

He paused, looking powerless in front of them at the possibility of actually finding his father, then recovered himself and said:

"Okay guys! I have a strong feeling about you. I guess you can find my father and set him free, for you are not ordinary people. Gathering so many people for a quiet meditation in a park, I'm darn right, you are uncommon people! So I will help you stay in this country. Is that okay with you?"

"Fair deal!" WITNESS said, "I have an idea on how to find where your father is. What's his first name?"

"Arnold! Jeremy is his second one… I hope you will succeed. It was nice meeting you! I have to go now."

"See you Jim!"

"See you soon Jim Keymaker, who opened doors in our minds!" MATRIX added.

"I hope you will find the right door to my father, my friends, bye!"

And he knocked on the door to alert a guard to open it.

When Jim Keymaker was gone, MATRIX and WITNESS looked at each other and laughed, and then she said:

"We didn't have to wait long for good fortune to knock at our door, showing the son Keymaker, announcing the father."

"True!"

"But what's your idea, WITNESS, to know where his father is?"

"Think of it MATRIX, we have within us all of the vibrations of Earth and of her inhabitants, given by her Spirit through the New Conditioning room; so it's enough to concentrate within in order to perceive the location of Arnold Jeremy Keymaker."

"WITNESS you are a genius!"

"You too MATRIX! We have everything within us; it is enough to use it in order to be a genius."

6- EVERYTHING IS WITHIN US

MATRIX and WITNESS were sitting in the meditation posture in their cells for a good hour. Afterward, they discussed their experiences.

"Fantastic WITNESS! We really have everything within us. I was traveling in my mind as though I was in our spaceship. On Earth they call it astral travel or remote viewing. It was as easy as in the 4-D world. First, I was on top of Vancouver. Then I knew that I had to go south. I instinctively felt that I had crossed the border between

Canada and America. No passport to show! Even fake! I automatically received all of the names of the places in my mind. I flew over Washington State, then over Oregon, and I was entering California when I saw a big mountain. It was Mount Shasta. It's a mountain that is regarded as sacred by their native Indians.

"I was attracted to a cave. I went inside. It was a narrow and long cave, like a tunnel. After a little while of moving forward inside of it, I heard voices coming from a hole. It was like a small shaft or a big pipe descending vertically. It was too narrow to go down, but because I was not in my real body, it was like child's play going into it. Suddenly, I was inside of a man-made structure, with people working. Some were working with microscopes, others were watching embryos, and working on them. 'Genetic manipulations' came into my mind. Then I thought of the computer science part of Meroveus, which Jim had told us about, and instantly I was in another room with people working on robots. They are pretty close to making the connection between computer science and genetics in robots.

It's amazing how our science didn't evolve in the same way. When you develop the science of the Spirit, all that robots can do is done through the Spirit of the SUPREME BEING. They will come to this understanding later, after this unnecessary detour, due to the desire of power by a few. Anyway, I focused then on the name of Arnold Keymaker, and I was instantly in a room where only one man was working. Without a doubt, I felt it was Jim's father. Of course, during this kind of travel, nobody could see me, but I had the impression that he felt my presence, for he looked at me a few times, or should I say, in my direction, for he didn't see me. It's a pity I couldn't talk with him."

"I talked with him in his mind!" WITNESS triumphantly said.

"So you did the same trip as I did?"

"No I didn't, I concentrated directly on the Spirit of Arnold Keymaker, and there I was, in his mind!"

"So, you let me tell you about my travels without interrupting me, but you already knew where he was!"

"No, I didn't. I didn't know where he really was; you did that part of our investigation. I entered his mind and read it so I could understand why he was being held a prisoner there."

"So you don't know where he is exactly in Mount Shasta?"

"I don't; you do. We are so complementary my dear MATRIX!"

"Okay my other half! What did you learn within his mind?" she said impatiently.

"Essentially, as Jim said, he has no other choice but to work for Meroveus. But he tries to procrastinate, to slow down his research. He discovered a lot of things that could be of interest for this Meroveus, giving him a lot of power. So we have to set him free. Then he can help us accomplish our mission."

"In what way?"

"He knows how to act on the electrons of both inanimate and living matter, and let people have some kind of dialogue with them. For Human beings, that's terrific, especially if it is used in a way that helps people to be more autonomous and less conditioned! For it can also be used for directing people in the way the person in power wants them to behave, like hynosis. Nevertheless, that's a discovery even more important than electricity!"

"We already know that, WITNESS! In each atom, the nucleus is the matrix, the substance of reality, its gravity, its materiality, and the electron is the witness, the spectator, the awareness of matter, its levity, its Spirit, like a female is the matrix of a baby's body and the male the witness of this miracle of creation! After he introduced his seed into her tummy of course! However reversely, for everything is in everything, the nucleus is the witness to what the frenetic electron does around it, similar situation with the ovum and the frenzied spermatozoon, just like females witness what hectic males do around them. I goofed around with Jim by saying we knew that the electron is the Spirit of all matter, but that's true, we have known it on our planet Witma for a long time!"

"Yes MATRIX, but Human beings became aware of that only recently. And only a few open-minded scientists like Arnold Keymaker are aware of it! Actually, a lot of spiritual people had already applied that for a long time, linking their spiritual awareness with their physical awareness, through Yoga, meditation, or by other mystical means. However, Arnold discovered a way to help people become aware of the connection between their Spirit and their body by acting on their electrons."

"So when do we set him free!"

"I recognize you, my impatient little MATRIX! You are wanting to get out quicker than people in jail could ever hope to! I know you! Nevertheless, I am confident: we'll soon be free. Yet afterward, we'll have to transport people to the Door of Heavens. Then we'll take care of Arnold. For him to be detained a few more days or weeks doesn't make a difference. But now, we are going to join the meeting in Stanley Park. SUPREME WITNESS told me in my mind that we are going to perform miracles through meditation. So let's meditate again!"

7- ARTICLES ABOUT MIRACLES

Vancouver Post, Tuesday, April 29th, 2003

New Development with the Spontaneous Meditation Group in Stanley Park!

Yesterday, we reported about this rare, spontaneous, meeting of people, gathered for meditation in Stanley Park, but we have now learned of new developments. The three initiators were arrested yesterday. The Hennings were charged with having fake passports, with disturbing the public order, with spying on Canadian soil for an unknown country and with preparing for a terrorist attack. The third leader, Miss "Narani", whose last name is Cheng, was charged with not having a visa and driven to the airport where she boarded a plane for China. The two Hennings are in a cell at the central police station. The charge of disturbing the public order is related to the Saturday incident we reported yesterday. This is not justified, for the troublesome people were most likely not part of the meeting, but the authorities always try to take advantage of every little thing when they want to stop unusual events that they don't know how to deal with. Regarding the two other charges, Jim Keymaker, their lawyer, said that the evidence for convicting them is as consistent as thin air.

Even with their leaders in jail, people came to Stanley Park yesterday, with banners demanding the freeing of the Hennings. However, as with previous days, their gathering was quiet and meditative. Yet the meeting, which began at 5.30 pm, didn't stop as usual at 6.30 pm. Most participants stayed, and some did not even eat dinner, as a way of protesting. We interviewed witnesses, who were not part of the group, and they said that some of the meditative people were in such a deep meditation or trance, that they could not be roused from it even if one tried to speak with them. We do not know, at the time of writing this article late on Monday evening, if the people will stay the entire night in Stanley Park. That would be really uncommon! We'll report on that in our Wednesday article. – Jerome Clark

•

Vancouver Post, Wednesday, April 30th, 2003
Miracles happened in Stanley Park!
Yesterday we reported that people who have been meeting daily in Stanley Park for more than one week to meditate, stayed longer than usual on Monday evening as a protest against the arrest of two of their initiators, Mr. and Mrs. Hennings. Most of these people in fact did stay the entire night. Approximately 500 people remained, meditating, some of them even in a quasi-cataleptic state. Mrs. Thompson reported to me that she undertook an experiment on several. She inserted needles into their arms but they were completely insensitive to the prick. She stated that advanced yogis could also fall into such a state at will, and become insensitive to any outside stimulation.

However, the most incredible "miracle" happened yesterday afternoon when a few thousand people were gathered in Stanley Park to continue to protest silently while meditating. At 5.45 pm, Mr. and Mrs. Hennings, who were being held prisoner in a cell in the central police station, appeared in the middle of the meditating crowd. No doubt, they were here…and there, at the same time, which is according to science not possible. So what science can't explain can be regarded as a miracle, until it is explained science-wise!

Trustworthy witnesses in Stanley Park observed them, and even touched them, for a period of approximately fifteen minutes. I was there and I took pictures of them, but my photos, when developed, were mysteriously blank. Over at the police station, at the same time, a policeman gave them drinks which they had ordered. He witnessed

Mr. and Mrs. Hennings meditating when he returned to the cell with the drinks. The policeman is certain of the time for he wrote the date and the time—5.50 pm—in the notebook where he records everything extra that is served to prisoners so they can be invoiced upon their release. He said: "I tried to make them sign for it, but they didn't respond."

A miracle certified by a policeman. That is uncommon! And in Stanley Park, so many 'curious' people were there and attested to the Hennings' presence, and the precise time of the 'apparition', that their presence there is above suspicion. But that's not possible for materialistic people. So that's a miracle!

The Hennings even shook hands with people at Stanley Park. The people, initiated to meditation by them, of course were glad to see them and assumed they had been liberated. People began celebrating the effectiveness of their protest movement. They started dancing and then the Hennings quietly disappeared behind a little grove of trees. Ajay Singh, wishing to talk to them, rushed to catch up with them behind the trees where he had seen them leave the dance party, but when he got behind the copse there was nobody. It was exactly 6 o'clock he said. "At 6 pm they were eating in their cell, and they remain there," said the chief of the central police station. So their presence in Stanley Park can only be explained by the possibility that people can appear in places where they are not, but only with their "subtle" bodies, as certain advanced yogis affirm is possible to perform with rigorous training. However, with their "gross" body, that's theoretically impossible, or perhaps it is an illusion of the sense of touch created in the minds of people by the Hennings themselves.

Jim Keymaker, their lawyer, said that he is very confident about the pending release of the Hennings and he confirmed that the evidence to substantiate the charges against them is very thin.

Today there will be another meditation gathering in Stanley Park, even if the meeting is not allowed; but who can forbid people to meet in a park? Furthermore, I am certain that there will be even more curious people attending and expecting to witness a new miracle. – Jerome Clark

•

Vancouver Post, Thursday, May 1st, 2003
Maybe the last miracle!

After the 'apparition' of the Hennings in Stanley Park, emotions were so great that the authorities decided to set them free, in order perhaps to avoid further miracles, for miracles disturb the honest materialistic life! According to the information we received, the Hennings promised to exchange an interruption of their gatherings in Stanley Park for their freedom. They therefore gathered at Alouette Lake, in Golden Ears Park, the place where they had first organized their meditating sessions. And there perhaps happened the last miracle!

Word of mouth, and cell phones, easily alerted everyone to the new location. Thousands of people gathered near the lake: ten thousands according to the police, who carried out a discrete surveillance from a certain distance. I was of course present. After the usual time of silent meditation, without saying even one word, the Hennings departed on a little boat. I have never seen such a quiet and silent gathering of that size in my entire life! And then the boat disappeared in the middle of the lake! It literally disappeared! Someone told me that this boat had been transformed into a small submarine. We do not know if there are many boats of this sort on Earth, but the most incredible does not lie in that, but in what happened next!

Suddenly, arising from the water, a discoid machine appeared and remained for a few seconds at an altitude that I estimate at being 20 meters (60 feet) above the surface of the lake. Then in no time at all it flew away so fast that it vanished from sight in just a couple of seconds. As I wrote yesterday, what science can't explain can be considered a miracle until it is explained science-wise! No aircraft on this planet can move so quickly! Nevertheless, an anti-gravitation flying machine could travel so quickly, according to scientists, but has yet to be invented.

This must be linked to the observation of an Unidentified Flying Object on Saturday, April 19th, the day before the first gathering with the Hennings at Alouette Lake. On Sunday, April 20th, only a very few people were initiated into their special meditation, where they 'speak' to a Supreme Being. It has only been ten days. What an incredible story for the thousands of people who meditated with Matrix and Witness, as they are known by their followers. After their departure, everyone sat silently and continued in their meditation. Even curious people like me, who were so much under the charm, or the spell, of the events, remained there in silence for a long time, even if I had never spoken with the famous 'Supreme Being'. Someone told me that if I believe in an inner dialogue between my Self, the Spirit of the Universe within me, and myself, it will work. Perhaps I do not believe enough in that possibility! Yet.

One hour later, I was still there, wondering if all of these events really did occur. Afterward, I spoke with a few newcomers, who came for the miracles rather than for the meditation. Using word of mouth to alert people about the new location of the final meditation worked very well. They came as the curious, but they left completely captivated, even mesmerized. Witnessing an aircraft moving against the law of gravity is fascinating, but it remains an experience related to the senses, whereas a subtle atmosphere of silent collective meditation is an experience you cannot describe.

So for those who want to experience it, the meetings will continue at Alouette Lake at 6 pm every day. I cannot promise you miracles without the presence of the Hennings, who had incredible charisma, but I can assure you that you will have a great experience within yourself. And I am definitely not that kind of New Age person who wants to believe despite all opposition!

Perhaps the Hennings' disappearance within their "flying saucer" is their last miracle. According to certain sources, they left for a special mission but will return soon. We have heard that they landed in another unknown location in the province to take on a few select passengers. We do not know the names of those who left with them in this incredible anti-gravitation aircraft and how long they will be away. We now find ourselves in a science fiction movie rather than on a spiritual New Age journey complete with miracles! But it doesn't matter how you label things! And this story is not finished: I feel it deep within my being! Somebody once said: "At a certain level of being only that which is fantastic has a chance to be true!" – Jerome Clark

CHAPTER 7

BEING ONE WITH EVERYONE

1- BEING ONE THROUGH MEDITATION

In but a few weeks, as the news spread, MATRIX and WITNESS transported several hundred people, not only from Vancouver, but also from other cities and villages across Canada. At the beginning of the 21st century, the United States and Canada were so much linked together, economically and culturally, that the message also spread down to the States by word of mouth. Information with a deep and worthy substance sometimes propagates quicker in that way and remains longer in the minds of people, than the one conveyed by the news media, for the latter move so quickly from one stereotyped story to the next using provocative images that are then rapidly forgotten in this modern day 24-hour news cycle, orchestrated by a few media trusts.

"We already have so many people all around the world transmitting the message of speaking with the SUPREME BEING through meditation!" MATRIX said in the spaceship just before landing near Los Angeles, at Lake Piru. There, twenty or so people welcomed them, some local ones, with friends or relatives from other cities where the Witmans had already been before, including a few from Vancouver.

The locals were very impressed by the spaceship. The people who had come from Vancouver had told them about it, but it's easier to believe your own eyes than the words of others! The spaceship came out of nowhere, and then suddenly it was there, right in front of them, on top of the lake.

Now the details of the procedure were set in place: find a lake close to a city, leave the spaceship hidden underwater, come to the banks of the lake with the submarine-boat, meet people, and organize meditation gatherings there, away from the city, so as not to upset the authorities. After a few days, a few hundred people were generally meditating together. Then a few dozen of them, those who were ready to depart, embarked in turns on the spaceship for traveling to the Gobi desert. When sufficient new people in any place were ready to go, the 'shuttle' returned and transported them to the destination.

People coming back from the 4-D world beyond the Door of Heavens were the most motivated to spread the message to other cities. A website was also providing general information about the process of talking with the SUPREME BEING through meditation.

It was not introduced as a new type of spirituality, or as a new kind of religion bringing people to God, but as a real practice, through meditation, of direct contact with the SUPREME BEING, the Intelligence of the Universe.

The home page of the website emphasized that people throughout the ages have been practicing this direct contact in their heart without the need of a priest or other spiritual leader. Mainly, it was presented as an individual practice where people did not require the assistance of anyone else to make a connection with God, the SUPREME BEING, even though the practice was certainly collective at the beginning. Nevertheless, no teacher was needed. Only a few words were said by the initiates to the newcomers at the start of each gathering to help them begin to talk from within to the SUPREME BEING present in everyone.

However, a lot of people became initiated at home and not at a collective meeting. Nonetheless, even these people were fond of attending the collective meditations to experience a connection with fellow Human beings sharing the same kind of a dialogue with the Divine One.

Followers on the West Coast of North America even organized a huge gathering in North California, at Shasta Lake, on Sunday, June 1st, 2003. Seekers invaded all of the campsites of the area. MATRIX and WITNESS participated in this meeting.

When MATRIX started to meditate at Shasta Lake, she thought that it was not a coincidence: 'For sure the SUPREME BEING blew this idea into the organizers' minds! Mount Shasta is the place where we saw Arnold Keymaker. We were too busy organizing meetings and flying back and forth to the Gobi desert to have time to try to help Jim's father.' And then she received in her own mind this thought: *So take advantage of this proximity to go there, physically this time!*" By now she was so used to hearing SUPREME MATRIX within her that she instantly responded: "Okay, Supreme Boss!" So the dialogue between SUPREME MATRIX and MATRIX continued:

I am the Supreme Adviser; I am not the supreme boss!

Did You advise the organizers of the place of the meeting?

Yes I did! But I suggest so many ideas that go unheard, or unimplemented!

Okay! However, if You suggest the same idea to so many minds at the same time, You know statistically that it's going to be heard in some minds and then applied.

Therefore, for you, I am the Supreme Statistician!

Sort of! And also the Supreme Organizer!

Actually, I am the Supreme Everything! So the list of Supreme Something could be long!

So You are also the Supreme Boss then!

If you say so! If you like it! If you choose to! However, I am also the Supreme Nothing. And I am SUPREME WITNESS! I am this and that! I am that and the opposite of that! You can put any sticker on Me, for you are certain to be right! I am the whole and any part of it. Any part of the whole is a representative sample of Me. Therefore, you don't even need statistics to report on My work with great numbers, making something to be statistically true: for I am all of the numbers!

I blow secrets into everyone's mind, for I am The Mind. I breathe words into everyone's Spirit, for I am The Spirit! I whisper into everyone's ears, for I am The Primordial Sound! I prompt everyone to play their role, for I am The Great Prompter-Producer! I am everyone! I am the One! And everyone is Me! Everyone is the One! Everyone is One within Me! That's it!

I am glad to hear that! Why don't You blow what You just said into everyone's mind?

Why do you think I don't breathe these words into everyone's mind? Do you think I am not doing it now?

You are doing it! As You did when, as SUPREME WITNESS, You broadcast Your conversation with WITNESS to everyone present in the room! Are You doing the same to everyone on this planet with our present conversation?

Don't you believe that I could do it?

You didn't! Phew! I am relieved! I am released! You could do it but You didn't! Everyone listening to my silly, nonsensical words: that would have been too much!

Your words were neither silly nor nonsensical! They were even making great sense! For they allowed Me to give you My words.

Great! So are You broadcasting them to some others or not? I'm afraid You are doing it! To a few or to billions?

Have a guess?

You haven't dared to broadcast our dialogue to the hundreds of people present at this meeting, have You?

I keep you guessing!

Good gracious! You are a daring and mischievous SUPREME BEING!

Didn't I tell you I was the Supreme Everything?

You did tell me! So I guess You are broadcasting our dialogue! You have dared to do that! I am afraid to open my eyes because everyone will be looking at me!

Don't be afraid! You are one with everyone!

Then MATRIX apprehensively opened one eye, and the other. She saw everyone, eyes closed but smiling. Everyone was facing her whereas people at the beginning of the meditation were facing the lake. She looked around. Everyone was facing her, as if she was in the center of some concentric circles and the people were on the circles, looking at her. Everyone opened their eyes at the same time and clapped gently and quietly. MATRIX was amazed at that, and she closed her eyes again. Everyone did the same. Then she started the dialogue within again:

So, SUPREME MATRIX, Your broadcasting of these dialogues to a group of people, what does that mean? Even on our planet Witma, that has never occurred!

I could tell you to guess again, but I feel it would be too much for your nerves. Nevertheless, you know the answer. I gave it to you in our previous dialogues. You chose to land on Earth. Then I told you about your special purpose to help Human beings evolve, to also help the other dimensions to connect together, and to link the future to this present. And then there is the purpose of your becoming aware of being one with everyone. My speaking to a group of people is part of My plans for nowadays. Actually, being one with everyone has been My plan since the beginning of this Universe. And this is also everyone's purpose! But for you it's your present experience. Now, you must set Arnold Keymaker free in order to launch your entire destiny.

What is my destiny?

Your destiny is the plan we made, you and I, at the beginning of time, and this is the actualization of it. Time is a tool I established for realizing our plans, our dreams. You must now experience what was planned. And the key to having these plans realized is Arnold Keymaker. He is the key to finding the structure of the Universe and to then direct it as well as I do. However, as you know, he is being held prisoner by someone who also has plans for directing the world in his own dictatorial way. The Universe is a tool for everyone to share and to be shared by everyone. Arnold Keymaker is the base for this discovery of the structure of the Universe. You are the top, WITNESS and you. Together, you can ensure this discovery is shared and experienced by everyone.

"Okay! WITNESS, we must go to Mount Shasta! We have our destiny to accomplish!" MATRIX said as she stood up.

Everyone clapped again, quietly, as they walked to their boat. Then they left the bank of Shasta Lake.

After one hour of boating along the narrow but long lake, they stopped inside a little creek and attached their boat with a rope to a tree and took their backpacks with them. They intuitively knew they had to hike for two to three hours uphill to reach the base of Mount Shasta and the site of the cave MATRIX had seen in her remote viewing trip experience.

Everyone on the beach remained meditating for a long time, in a euphoric state, trying to follow MATRIX and WITNESS through their own internal connections with the SUPREME BEING.

•

It was easy for MATRIX to find the cave on the rocky slopes of Mount Shasta. Her memory from her previous trip to this place was intact, even if this time she felt more like a crawling groundhog than as a flying eagle.

It was now already 3 pm but they did not worry about the rest of the journey and escaping with Arnold Keymaker from the underground fortress before sunset, for they felt in a state, completely guided by the SUPREME BEING, where time no longer existed.

2- BEING ONE WITH YOUR ENEMY

Hiking through caves and tunnels with the help of her flashlight, MATRIX easily found the way to the shaft-pipe. Finding a way of entering into the underground settlement was a little more complicated for the pipe MATRIX had found on her remote viewing trip was much too small to clamber through. After walking through a labyrinth of tunnels that they sensed had been built by an ancient civilization, they arrived at a bigger vent that traversed the vertical rock face of the tunnel. They saw an opening, but it was covered with metal bars, so WITNESS took a device from his backpack and rubbed it along one of the bars that he then bent like rubber. When you apply the right vibration to it, hard matter can easily be bent. He did the same with another bar. The opening was now wide enough for them to wiggle through into the two-foot wide vent. They crawled first into it horizontally and then climbed it vertically. They were progressing like snakes, pushing alternately on their feet and hands to move their buttocks, then reversing the process. When they were at a level with a cave where they could exit the vent, they bent those bars in the same fashion as they did the bars at the opening. They found themselves behind boxes in an immense cave where people were working on machines. They asked within themselves and they immediately received confirmation that these were spaceships of Extraterrestrial origin. There was what looked like a lift not too far away from their hiding place.

"WITNESS, planet Earth gave us information about these Extraterrestrial beings living secretly on Earth, but to see them firsthand, makes it all so much more real. Look at them! They all have Reptilian faces and are wearing light blue uniforms. We have previously encountered them on our trips to other planets, and they ignored us. I never understood why. Maybe we'll now learn why."

"Obviously, they are working with this Meroveus, for there are also Human beings wearing the same uniform in this cave," replied WITNESS.

"I did not see the Extraterrestrials during my remote viewing travel. Somehow I know intuitively that Arnold Keymaker is at level 36. This underground base is gigantic."

"If we could get into this lift without being seen, we could get to the right level."

"We have to appear to be like them! We can neutralize two of the workers and put on their uniforms. They use this trick very often in movies made on Earth. The spirit of Earth implanted into my mind every single movie ever made by a Human being. It's as though Earth had viewed every movie. What a great being this planet Earth!"

"Okay! We only have to wait behind these containers till someone passes close by."

The first person they saw walking in front of the containers was a man with the logo 'New Planet Order' on his uniform. WITNESS pulled a device from his backpack and paralyzed the man; the person fell down onto a container and WITNESS quickly pulled him over it toward them. Later, two Reptilians passed by, but WITNESS' paralyzing gun didn't work on them. But they certainly felt the vibes of it, and in no time at all they knew where those vibes came from. They used their own paralyzing system on MATRIX and WITNESS and it did work. MATRIX and WITNESS were still standing but could not move. The paralyzing effect did not last too long, but long enough for the two Reptilians to handcuff them. Unfortunately for MATRIX and WITNESS, this primitive system of preventing someone from escaping was much more efficient than their sophisticated paralyzing system.

The two Reptilians did not say anything but one pushed the prisoners from behind so as to order them to walk while the other led the way. WITNESS told MATRIX:

"Earthlings say that misfortune very often leads to good fortune. I hope they are right."

"I hope so too!" MATRIX replied.

They were marched over to two other ETs, who then guided them through a maze of halls and lifts. Their group had to be checked more and more often and they sensed they were heading toward the central command center of the settlement. The Reptilians were continually flashing their right wrists, which were implanted with some kind of code, at laser beams

The group stopped in front of a door. MATRIX said to WITNESS:

"WITNESS, we finally received a guided tour of this place. Our guides look too much like dinosaurs for my taste, but I am not racist after all, so it doesn't matter!"

But a 'dinosaur' had already opened the door before she had even finished speaking, and a voice from inside said:

"The famous MATRIX! And her companion WITNESS!"

They were gently pushed through the door.

"You are right; they are descendants of the dinosaurs! I heard your comment Mrs. Hennings, better known as MATRIX! So I will introduce myself…"

"Not necessary Mister Meroveus, the founder of New Planet Order!" MATRIX said.

WITNESS was quite impressed by his companion's self-confidence.

The person sitting behind a huge desk directly in front of them, in his fifties, wearing a black suit, was also impressed, but reacted quickly, so as to stay in charge of the situation:

"Have a seat!"

Then, facing the Reptilians who had led them to his office, he said:

"Remove their handcuffs."

The two Reptilian Humanoids, who apparently understood English, executed the order docilely.

"You guessed right, Meroveus is my nickname, just as yours is Mrs. Eva Hennings, MATRIX! Or maybe it's the reverse. It does not matter, and my birth name does not matter either! What matters is your presence here, and I am honored by the surprise visit of people who are so widely talked about all over the world in the media, even if you remain such mysterious people.

"Actually, I wished to meet you, for I think our purposes are similar, as odd as that sounds. But appearances can be deceiving. Look at you! You're apparently two gurus initiating people into your special form of meditation, but in fact you're two Extraterrestrial beings on a mission, trying to spread your own religion for the supposed well-being of Humans.

"I'm apparently a businessman wanting to acquire more power through applied science, whereas I really only seek the well-being of all people. I wish to spread my religion of being well to others through the knowledge of what is deeply ingrained within the matter of the Universe, which is the body of the Divine Being you talk about in your meditation groups."

"SUPREME BEING!" MATRIX retorted; then she was a bit harsh, saying loudly: "And we are not spreading a religion! We are not spreading anything actually! We allow people to know on their own what is deeply ingrained within them, whereas you want to impose your way on people through technology. You even force researchers to work for you against their will!"

"You are very beautiful MATRIX, when you are angry. So, you are speaking about only one researcher, Arnold Keymaker. In fact, he is not working as I would like him to. He could succeed in providing me what I want, but he is procrastinating. He feels free to oppose me whereas I allow him to play this game of giving me the results of his work parsimoniously, bit by bit.

"I could have used drugs to force him to work efficiently for me. But I have plenty of other faithful researchers who are just as successful in his field. He is the only one though who was not tempted by money. And he is right, money is only a means; what is important is the purpose, the end. We shared the same end for a while; then he disagreed with me. My end is to understand as many laws at work within matter as possible, and to then make them trigger the effects I choose.

"Arnold agreed with me at the beginning, but then he wanted each person to be free to choose. That's not possible! There are people in command, and people who obey. And we all obey someone else at the end. Only God, your SUPREME BEING, receives no orders from anyone. But who knows? Maybe there is an infinite hierarchy of gods! It doesn't matter! I guess you came here to set him free. All right! You can take him with you when you leave here."

MATRIX and WITNESS were both very amazed by Meroveus' decision and his frankness, as well as with his knowledge of their goal. Meroveus felt that too and so he continued:

"You know! A man in my position needs to know everything! And I have all of the means to that end, even though sometimes you wouldn't agree with all or maybe only with some of them, but I am as you are: for much of the time I have intuitions. I don't know if they come from your SUPREME BEING or from the knowledge deeply ingrained within the structure of my body's matter. That's why I would like to exchange ideas with you, and maybe even more, if you would like. Your experience of speaking with the SUPREME BEING combined with the experimental knowledge I have about His body's substance, which is the Universe, could result in miracles!"

"Okay!" replied WITNESS, before MATRIX could say anything. She looked at him, amazed and perplexed. He looked at her, smiling and with such a self-confident look that she understood he had an ulterior motive. He continued:

"I believe that we do want to know more about each other, and it is in our common interest to cooperate with one another for a while, even if it will probably be for only a short time. I have an intuition that our purposes are apparently the same at one level, but deep down they are opposed. However, I also believe that you are part of the SUPREME BEING's plans, as is everyone. So what do you want to learn from us that you do not already know?"

"Good! I like your straight-talking ways and your honest and frank proposal of cooperating until we don't need each other anymore. Actually, I don't want anything from you, save what you're willing to tell me. I am also straightforward, WITNESS! You will tell me only what you want to tell me and I will tell you what could push you to tell me what could be of interest to me. So practically, you can stay in this underground base as long as you wish and we can see each other every day. You can walk everywhere with a pass. Do you agree with this protocol?"

"That's fair enough!" WITNESS answered.

"And you MATRIX, do you agree?"

"I don't know what game you are playing guys, so I surrender, and I agree!"

"Can we see Arnold Keymaker now?" WITNESS said.

"I suppose you came to see him, so you will see him. However, you must know that everything you will say in this base will be listened to. I think you are smart enough to have already figured that out."

"Of course!" MATRIX said. And then she added: "You said that these Reptilian beings are the descendants of the dinosaurs. Can you explain that further? I didn't find that in the information I received!"

"If the surface of the Earth had not been destroyed by the aftermath of the fall of a meteor 65 million years ago, these beings would have been the only intelligent beings of this planet, but they already had a developed civilization and they forecast the catastrophe early enough to migrate to another solar system where they faced many tribulations. They almost disappeared again because of their internal fighting and because of pollution. Then, only a few millennia ago, some returned to Earth. However, they are more or less incognito. They participate secretly in this world.

"I am one of the few privileged people to be in contact with them, for they are interested in my research. They live here and in other secret bases similar to this one. Some of them have mixed in with the Human population, for they crossbred with Humans; they actually still crossbreed. Their descendants are called skin-shifters, for they can have the skin of Humans at certain times and the skin of Reptilians at other times. However, they cannot control this shift. That's why our researchers are trying to discover how they can control this change of skin on their own."

"On our planet Witma we succeeded in controlling that!" WITNESS said, then added: "We even change our general shape at will when we enter what we call our New Bodies room. We can help them learn how to control the shifting of their skin."

"They will be glad to hear that!" Meroveus replied.

"I am amazed at their lack of mastering this skin-shifting problem given how advanced they are in mastering space travel." MATRIX said.

Meroveus replied: "Sometimes, highly evolved civilizations have their Achilles' heel, but I think it's more complicated than you believe. It's as though they have two souls at the same time, one Human and one Reptilian… Actually, I have things to do now, I am sure you are anxious to see Arnold. Here are your passes! For now I programed them for you to be able to go where he works. When you are heading the right way, they are silent, and when you are heading the wrong way, they emit a sound. You can program them again at any time in order to go anywhere. Ask the security people for help. Certain areas nevertheless will be forbidden. Be kind and patient; don't try to force your way anywhere! See you!"

MATRIX and WITNESS left Meroveus' office. They then walked through the labyrinth of hallways.

"It's better to walk freely in this base than incognito," MATRIX said. "You happily took your chance in accepting Meroveus' proposition."

"Whenever possible, it's always better to cooperate with the enemy than to fight with him! Furthermore, to feel at one even temporarily with a so-called enemy is a way to be at one with everyone, and to stop having enemies."

3- BEING ONE THROUGH EXCHANGING IDEAS

When MATRIX told Arnold Keymaker that he was free, tears came to his eyes. She then hugged him spontaneously, saying:

"Your son, Jim, helped free us from jail, so now we set his father free from this horrible base without daylight. Everything will be okay!"

"How do you feel Arnold?" WITNESS asked.

"Relieved! But how is it possible to be free after being detained for two years here?"

They both in turn related their meeting with Meroveus and then WITNESS continued:

"We can't speak too freely for we are probably being listened to. We will stay here for a few more days. Then, when we are outside, we'll be able to speak more openly."

Arnold Keymaker was allowed to come with them and visit places in the base where he had never been before. He even participated in the first meeting to exchange ideas with Meroveus. It took place in Meroveus' office, where MATRIX and WITNESS had already met the master of the underground base.

Meroveus: I am glad to see you again today. I am also glad to see you, Arnold! We were friends. Then enemies! I hope we'll soon be friends again!

Arnold: That depends on you. That depends on your way of being. I don't know if I have to thank you for setting me physically free or not, for I was always free in my Spirit. My way of existing is to let everyone live and choose freely.

Meroveus: We have already discussed that many times, Arnold! And you know that my life style is to affirm that choice is an illusion created by those in power for those without. The supreme illusion created by those in power is to make everyone believe that they are free to choose whereas they are being conditioned by the elite.

WITNESS: Those in power are part and parcel of the SUPREME BEING, who is the only one responsible for the SUPREME ILLUSION. It doesn't matter if you call the SUPREME BEING God or Allah or the Absolute or the Spirit of the Universe, or its Intelligence, or any name or phrase you wish. Meroveus, you are only a part of the SUPREME ILLUSION created by the SUPREME BEING. You think you are free to do anything you wish, but you are part and parcel of the Great Whole, the SUPREME MATRIX of the Universe, of everything. You are the slave of the rules established by SUPREME MATRIX. There is no way to escape from those rules!

Arnold: Then you make people the slave to your way of understanding the rules! But the Universal Spirit of God governs the rules of matter, and you will never understand them completely, for they are infinite, infinitely complex and infinitely subtle. I know that! Every honest scientist will tell you that! What I learned about the Spirit of matter, especially the matter located in electrons, but really found in all particles, is nothing compared to what is yet to be discovered, a drop of knowledge taken from the ocean of the Universal Reality!

Meroveus: This drop is bigger than you think! And I am using it in a complementary way to the other drops I have gathered in thanks to the work of so many scientists. In some ways I am the leader of an orchestra who composes a symphony. Arnold, your part is already integrated in with the other parts of this symphony. That's why I decided to free you.

WITNESS: When you don't need a piece of your game anymore, you throw it away!

Meroveus: My game, as you say, is a sublime work of art, and I try to avoid the flaws in it. Mozart's symphonies are flawless. I would like to be the Mozart of science, the Mozart of combining Natural Intelligence with Artificial Intelligence. In the Bible and in so many other traditions, a serpent symbolizes the Knowledge, also called the Science of Good and Evil. The serpent proposed this science to Adam and Eve. There is no temptation, no sin, in these scriptures, but only the perfect way to knowledge. Meroveus was this legendary French king who founded the Merovingian dynasty, which reigned over France and Germany from the 5th to the 9th centuries. According to the legend, his mother became pregnant after being visited by a serpent. King Meroveus' reign started with the knowledge of his destiny and that of his descendants. Like him, I am the first of a lineage of predestined conductors of people, through science. I am also a piece of this game in mankind's destiny, a piece in the Divine Destiny, a piece in the game created by SUPREME MATRIX, as you call the Divine. I know all of that! However, I also know that I am the co-creator of life, through the use of the rules SUPREME MATRIX established. That's it!

WITNESS: Great! What you don't know is that knowledge can be developed in so many different ways with the same rules that govern the Universe. For example, on our planet Witma, we developed our science in a completely different way from yours, and from the other civilizations we have visited on other planets.

Meroveus: I am also in contact with other Extraterrestrial aliens, and we use their knowledge to improve ours. I would like to use yours too! But I feel we don't have the same psychology. That of my aliens is more similar to mine than yours is.

WITNESS: As I am closer to Arnold Keymaker's than I am to yours! Diversity is the key rule of SUPREME MATRIX. Yet the other key rule is Unity, for Diversity is made out of a unique particle: the photon of light.

Meroveus: Interesting! WITNESS, you begin to interest me. I don't regret my offer to exchange ideas with you.

MATRIX: If you will let me speak a bit guys! I can tell you the story of the marriage of light and darkness.

Meroveus: More and more interesting! Please continue my dear MATRIX!

WITNESS: Be careful MATRIX!

MATRIX: Don't worry, WITNESS, I won't goof up! Speaking about light is the same kettle of fish as speaking about darkness. They are complementary. That's what marriage is for: to complement two apparently opposite entities or people. SUPREME MATRIX shared with me this story:

ONCE UPON A TIME, THERE WAS ONLY LIGHT,

A myriad of photons of light, as light as nothing!

Nothing! Nothing was everything that was!

For nothing could reflect the light!

In the beginning, SUPREME MATRIX said:

May infinitesimal dark holes be!

And an infinite number of dark holes were!

First day!

Then photons of light, traveling at no speed,

In no time got grabbed by dark holes.

Matter was created!

Second day!

Matter was only a matter of photons of light held prisoner by dark holes.

But the prisoners of dark holes were able to communicate with the still free photons!

So they established a dialogue.

It was a dialogue between free light and light detained by darkness.

It was established through "virtual" photons.

It appears as a marriage of those two kinds of light.

It looked like a marriage of light and darkness.

That's what marriage is for: a dialogue!

Third day!

Creation was finished in three days!

End of story! End of the wedding of light and darkness.

Beginning of the great adventure of the eternal dialogue

Between the free light and the detained light!

That's the adventure of the Universe!

Heavy dark holes became the protons and the neutrons,

With innumerable photons detained within.

The latter provide energy to particles.

>Light holes became the electrons,
>With trillions of photons retained within.
>Their job was to retain the experiences of the electrons.
>Electrons are the memory of matter.
>They are infinitesimal computers.
>Photons within them choose to spin one way or the opposite way,
>As bits of information recording what each electron does.
>At an elementary level, it's like the work done by our brain about what we do.
>The nucleus of atoms, made up of protons and neutrons,
>Gives the electrons the energy to act,
>To move from one energy level to another within the atoms,
>And also to move from one atom to another in molecules.
>Electrons are the basic elements of our Spirit.
>They communicate with the Divine Light, the Spirit of the SUPREME BEING.
>And they communicate collectively, between each other,
>Exchanging information and experience.
>They rule us.

Meroveus: Your mythological story and your scientific explanations both impress me, MATRIX! Nevertheless, you didn't bring me any more information than I already knew.

MATRIX: I didn't want to give you more information. I know all that you know! When we arrived on this planet, the Spirit of Earth gave me all of the information contained in your electrons! You would like more information from us. If we wish to satisfy you, perhaps we will give you some more information but we don't need anything from you: we already know everything about you and your plans called New Planet Order.

WITNESS: You impressed me too, darling! But for certain Mr. Meroveus is going to take less interest in us now MATRIX! Alas, as usual, you goofed up again in saying that we know everything about him, because the dialogue will be over if Mr. Meroveus has no further opportunity to swap his information for ours.

Meroveus: You are mistaken if you think I want to extract information from you! As I told you, you give me the information you wish to give me. So, I will give you the most current news about our projects. I don't think you know this one yet, for the last experiment was done only one week ago. In exchange, I would like to know how you know all of the information contained in my electrons. Is that a fair deal?

WITNESS: Fair enough! But who starts?

Meroveus: Ah WITNESS! You are so straightforward. I enjoy talking with you, and with MATRIX! So I'll begin, à la MATRIX:

IN THE BEGINNING, THERE WAS EINSTEIN.
>He made me believe that everything is theoretically possible.

He was also looking for a law that unites all of the laws.
I believed that it was possible to find this law.
And practically, I found it!
You also found it a while ago on your planet,
But as you said, we used it in a different way from how you did.
As you also said, there is only one particle: the photon of light.
The photons' vibrations created the fabric of space the Ancients called Eather.
And the adventure of the Universe is a dialogue between:
Free light and light kept in mini black holes, as the electrons can be called.
So the deal is to favor this dialogue! You know that!
As for Human beings, dialogue is so fruitful, so creative!
Thanks to you and your research, Arnold,
We found how the 'free light' and the 'detained light' communicate,
Hence Free-Light-Delight-Com, the name of the invention!
(You can see that we chose the same adjectives as yours; free and detained.)
We also found how to direct this dialogue, first in molecules, then within cells.
The experiments with animals took a bit longer, but were conclusive.
So, last week, we experimented successfully on the enlightenment of a Human!
As Buddha once did, a Human received his enlightenment, but through science!
The results of last week's experiment were even more than we had hoped for.
This Human being is able to keep the enlightenment going,
And he even manages to direct it on his own!
He makes his electrons communicate together, in the way he chooses,
By concentrating on them.
Spirit is light! Light is Spirit!
All throughout the past, great souls succeeded in leading their bodies' processes.
Now everyone can do the same!

Arnold, isn't that what you wanted? Don't you wish to have people free to manage their own lives through a dialogue with the particles of their flesh? And you, MATRIX and WITNESS, isn't that the complementary dialogue to the dialogue with the SUPREME BEING? You came to me at the right time, my friends! I am not a tyrant, as certain people describe me! I am a philanthropist! I wish for the happiness of everyone!

Arnold: Meroveus, we shared the same passion for the well-being of people, but we differ now in the means to this end. The means and the end must be in harmony! You direct your company AID and your movement New Planet Order with an iron hand. This is antagonistic to wishing people to be free to make their own choices. I forgive you for blackmailing me and forcing me to stay here. I hope you will use your scientific discoveries for the well-being of Humanity. However, for me, you can do so only by having the means and the end in harmony.

Meroveus: Arnold, you are and you remain an old-fashioned philanthropist! So, WITNESS and MATRIX, I don't know if I told you something you didn't know about our new experiment, but are you in the mood to tell me how you know the information contained within my electrons?

WITNESS: I am! We developed a way to retrieve the information contained in the electrons of absolutely anything. And we can also change the information in our own electrons so as to change our appearance. How we appear now is not the same as how we appear on our planet. We make these changes when we travel through the Universe. Our method is called the New Conditioning room and the New Bodies room.

In these rooms, when we were nearing the Earth, we not only changed our appearance, but we also communicated with the electrons of this whole planet, including yours. We received each and every bit of data that had been retained by the photons of light for all ages, since the beginning of the Universe.

The ancient people of India knew this as Akasha, or Akashic Records, where the whole history of the Earth is written as in a library. They intuitively knew that everything is recorded, but they did not know precisely how. Photons are what collectively collect this memory. However, great yogis know how to re-collect whatever bits of data they wish; it is enough for them to meditate and to focus on the information they want in order to receive it. It's similar to our way of processing information, except for the fact that everything is already stored in our own electrons since we concentrated on Earth Memory, or Akasha. Actually, everybody's brain stores data like that, through their electrons. And the capacity for the brain to store data is infinite! And if we want new data, like a computer connected to the Internet, we simply concentrate again on the Earth Akasha. We could have received the information about your successful experiment one week ago by focusing again on the Spirit of Earth and asking what is new in your work.

Your Western scientists have not yet discovered how memory really works. With this discovery of the electrons collecting data within them, they can now know how it is done and they can progress much in learning how the brain works. Nevertheless, they must accept the fact that the brain of an individual is only a part of a whole, like a computer terminal in a network, only a tool in the Divine Internet of the Universe.

You know most of what I have just told you, Meroveus, yet to know is not enough, the way you process the data you have is also important.

Meroveus: For sure, I am always interested in hearing the data you have stored in your brain WITNESS, and also the way you process and deliver this information. However, we have to stop, for I have a busy schedule again today. Would you like to meet New Buddha, as we call the chosen, enlightened, Human being?

WITNESS: I'm okay! If my partners are!

MATRIX and Arnold Keymaker also agreed. Nonetheless, MATRIX said afterward in the hallway:

"WITNESS, why do you want to stay longer with this nerd?"

"MATRIX," replied WITNESS, "he is far from being an uninteresting person; he is a bit foolish in wishing to know all of the rules of the SUPREME BEING and to then apply them to people in his own way, but it is basically what we do through talking with the SUPREME BEING and wishing for everyone else to do the same. Nevertheless, we recognize that each person has his or her own way of doing that. Meroveus' mistake lies in choosing to know only the unity of the Universe and to forget the diversity of it. One must allow diversity in order to achieve unity."

"I agree with you WITNESS," said Arnold, adding: "I agreed with him too at the beginning, but the taste for power took over him and he now feels like he is the equal to God."

"We are all clones of God," replied MATRIX, "that is, equally similar but nonetheless different. That's the grand rule of the Universe."

"Like one fertilized ovum-cell divides," added WITNESS, "making clone-cells, but which are later differentiated to make different parts of an organism."

4- BEING ONE THROUGH SPEAKING WITH THE SUPREME BEINGS

They spent another day visiting parts of the underground base. Of course, in certain places that were marked "restricted area", they were not permitted access. However, through what they saw, and in relation to what they knew about the Human race and also the knowledge developed on their own planet, MATRIX and WITNESS realized just how advanced the research was in this base compared to that in the rest of the world. Meroveus' research focused on the physics of particles, on cloning, on Artificial Intelligence, and on the combination of biology and robots. They were not allowed to see advanced robots, but, as Meroveus had told them, they did see the person who had experienced the artificial enlightenment.

This person was a very charming, young, tall, blond man with blue eyes, the opposite image one has of Buddha, but the complete image of what the Nazis described as the ideal man. MATRIX had this racist description in her mind when she said:

"My name is Matrix Hennings. What's your real name Mister Buddha-Swastika?"

He was a bit surprised by the question and by the way of formulating it, but nonetheless answered politely:

"My name is Jeff Connors and my nickname is New Buddha. I am honored to be called that, but I don't know if I deserve it. The only thing I know is that the experience I am participating in is transforming me so much, and in such a pleasant way, that I would like everyone to experience it."

MATRIX asked him: "What do you feel exactly?"

He replied simply:

"I can have a dialogue with all of my cells and with everyone here on Earth. I can hear my blood cells tell me: there are not enough killer cells. And I reply: produce more of them. But also I heard your thoughts Miss MATRIX. I know your complete name and I know why you called me Mr. Buddha-Swastika in relation to the Nazis, for I do look like the perfect Aryan they conceived."

"Your artificial enlightenment made you telepathic, Mr. Connors," said WITNESS, "and you can speak to your cells. Can you also speak with God, or the SUPREME BEING?"

"I don't know. I haven't tried yet!" New Buddha replied.

"Would you like to try with us, while meditating?" WITNESS added.

"Okay, I'll try."

Therefore MATRIX, WITNESS, Arnold Keymaker and Jeff Connors meditated. And they had this collective Divine Conversation, within:

SUPREME WITNESS: Arnold, Jeff, welcome to the club of those who speak with us, SUPREME MATRIX and SUPREME WITNESS. Actually we speak to everyone, but on this planet it's difficult for Human beings to stop their own thoughts so as to listen to ours, whereas, as you are now aware, it's so easy to hear us when you decide to do so!

SUPREME MATRIX: Jeff, You are now your own master. Even if you are part of experiments that try to control this planet, we are the SUPREME REMOTE CONTROL, and we tell you this: You are the Spirit, so you can also control everything, as we do, for the Spirit is everywhere, within your atoms, within your cells, and within everyone. You are now JEFF THE NEW BUDDHA OF THE EARTH.

JEFF THE NEW BUDDHA: I am honored to be in your presence, SUPREME BEINGS, and to be called by You THE NEW BUDDHA OF THE EARTH. Through my artificial enlightenment, I had already become aware of You as the Body and the Spirit of the Universe. However, to speak with You is such a powerful experience!

MATRIX: And it's only the beginning! Your experiences are going to be more and more incredible and powerful. I would like to ask our SUPREME BEINGS if they think that it would be beneficial for the equilibrium of NEW BUDDHA to have a female buddy, enlightened like him. We could call her NEW BUDDHINI.

SUPREME MATRIX: It's already in the mind of Meroveus to create many enlightened people, including females.

MATRIX: Can You influence him so that his second enlightened person will be a woman? Can You whisper that idea within him? I believe that even with his video and sound systems, he cannot hear this internal meditation-conversation we are having.

SUPREME MATRIX: You can influence him too, MATRIX! Don't worry, there will be many upon many enlightened people through this new discovery, and many who will evolve in a way different from that which Meroveus has planned.

MATRIX: You are the best, SUPREME MATRIX! You are the best for tricking people into doing what You wish them to do; I know that! But what is Meroveus' plan with these enlightened people?

SUPREME MATRIX: Wait and see, impatient MATRIX!

WITNESS: She was more patient lately! Nonetheless, for her to become really patient would be like chasing rainbows!

MATRIX: Funny! Or I can simply admire their colors until they disappear.

SUPREME WITNESS: The only thing We can tell you is that you have an important mission to accomplish, NEW BUDDHA. You will guide the other artificially enlightened people to the real enlightenment, as Siddhartha Gautama did twenty-five centuries ago. However, real enlightenment nowadays means speaking with us, through the meditation MATRIX and WITNESS initiated you into today.

NEW BUDDHA: I will accomplish this mission to the best of my ability and so be worthy of Your trust.

SUPREME WITNESS: And you, Arnold Keymaker, through whom we made this discovery of benefit to Human beings, you are now ARNOLD OF THE OPENING OF DOORS AND MINDS, for you opened the doors to the artificial enlightenment, and in doing so you allowed the opening of the minds of the people. You also will continue your research in order to use the communication between photons to establish the connection with the other dimensions and communication through the dimension of time, as well as many other related discoveries too numerous to name.

ARNOLD: I believe, I hope. I showed that I was honest and trustworthy in using the ideas You whispered in my mind for the well-being of Human kind. So I am proud of being able to continue on in such a way, and I pledge to continue on as far as possible.

SUPREME WITNESS: So I witness your agreements, both of you.

MATRIX: And I will go on chasing rainbows patiently!

WITNESS: And I will help you achieve that, MATRIX. I am impatient to begin to chase rainbows patiently with you!

And they all laughed, including the SUPREME BEINGS. Yes! They laugh too! And one can hear them laugh! Actually, they invented laughing!

5- BEING ONE THROUGH ENLIGHTENMENT

Their next meeting again took place in Meroveus' office.

Meroveus: I was looking forward to seeing you again, for what you told me yesterday inspired me so much.

MATRIX: I have to tell you that I was more inspired by my visit to New Buddha than by yesterday's meeting with you. It was very fruitful to meet with him.

Meroveus: I saw you through the internal video system. I think you were aware I was watching you. I heard everything you said. I even saw your meditating with New Buddha. So what inspired you so much in your meeting with him?

MATRIX: You heard our conversation, but you didn't hear the one we had while meditating.

Meroveus: You found a way to trick me. Congratulations! May I know what was so fruitful about this internal conversation?

WITNESS: Fruitfulness depends on one's point of view. For us it was great. I don't know if for you it would be the same. First, New Buddha talked with the SUPREME BEINGS. They even gave him the name: THE NEW BUDDHA OF THE EARTH. Second, his enlightenment made him freer than you had perhaps hoped.

Meroveus: Again WITNESS, you are mistaken about my intentions. I don't want to enslave the whole population of Earth. Maybe you will be surprised by my saying that at present people really are enslaved: slaves of money, drugs, work, and, in general, of their own narrow-minded way of living. Through the enlightenment device, I wish to make them free from people who take advantage of their way of behaving so as to turn them into consumption addicts, workaholics and, more and more, debtors to the bankers.

ARNOLD: I don't recognize your way of speaking, Meroveus! Are you trying to deceive us, or do you honestly believe what you have just said?

Meroveus: I am going to surprise you again, ARNOLD. Yesterday, I also received the same enlightenment as NEW BUDDHA. And you are going to be pleased with what you hear: my way of being has evolved! I must admit that I am impressed by the speed of my transformation.

WITNESS: I am also really impressed by the speed of the fulfillment of what SUPREME MATRIX announced only yesterday regarding the evolution of your plans, Meroveus!

NEW BUDDHA: So you will be my first artificially enlightened person to receive the spiritual enlightenment through learning how to speak with the SUPREME BEINGS.

MATRIX: Wait a minute! I don't believe it! How is it possible to change one's mind so quickly?

NEW BUDDHA: I also couldn't believe it myself when I received my artificial enlightenment! From one day to the next, I became another person!

WITNESS: Happy ending! Through the medium of SUPREME MATRIX, this happy ending is the happy medium through which everything finally works in balance!

Meroveus: And for more balance, females and males will be enlightened in equal numbers. Furthermore, I will give the patent of this machine for free to the governments and to the United Nations to produce many more appliances for the Free-Light-

Delight-Com system than I could ever make, for it's an expensive machine to produce. Then the nations of the Earth will be able to control the enlightenment process.

ARNOLD: Meroveus, I can't believe what my ears are hearing. I am glad to have participated in your enlightenment through my research.

Meroveus: I really feel one with everyone through my enlightenment. I now must still feel one through speaking with the SUPREME BEING, mustn't I?

WITNESS: That's NEW BUDDHA's job!

6- BEING ONE WITH EVERYONE

The next day, they all met in Meroveus' apartment. His living room was huge, with a subdued light of varying colors. They prepared to meditate together by sitting on cushions in a circle.

Meroveus: I'm a bit anxious about having this conversation with the SUPREME BEINGS. Will they want to speak with me after what I did in the past?

ARNOLD: Sin confessed is already half forgiven! I am sure that the SUPREME BEINGS will forgive you for the second half!

Meroveus: I am glad to be half forgiven by the person who I treated the worst, for I forced you to work for me against your will, ARNOLD.

WITNESS: Perhaps we can now meditate. NEW BUDDHA, are you ready to guide the meditation?

NEW BUDDHA: Yes I am!

Close your eyes…

Be aware of your thoughts…

Now observe them as a witness…

Then, you are no longer interested in thinking anymore…

You are now in thoughtless awareness, listening to your inner being.

You are listening to the SUPREME BEINGS who are living within you.

…

Hello Meroveus!

Meroveus: Fantastic! I heard my name!

NEW BUDDHA: That's SUPREME WITNESS' voice.

That's correct. Now we will name you NEW EINSTEIN OF THE ENLIGHTENMENT.

Meroveus-NEW EINSTEIN: That's too much of an honor! I do hope to help enlighten the whole of Humanity.

SUPREME MATRIX: You will! But remember that, as you were once in the way of the people, preventing them from accomplishing their own destiny, you will have people doing the same to you. That will happen not to bother you, but on the contrary, to help you believe more in your own destiny, for others are here and there to help you grow in the awareness of being one with everyone, no more, no less.

NEW EINSTEIN: I was so far from this awareness, and now it's so obvious, so simple!

CHAPTER 8

SO OBVIOUS, SO SIMPLE

1- SIMPLE AND OBVIOUS COMMENTS FROM THE WRITER

At this point in the novel, I would like to intervene again. You may think: "What is this writer doing in interrupting the tale of the story all of the time?" Does that upset you reader, for it is unusual? Or do you enjoy uncommon ways of telling stories? I wouldn't like to upset you. I would prefer to surprise you! Isn't it surprising to have this communication between writer and reader? You can also surprise me by writing me at: divinecosmos@yahoo.com.

Okay! Now that you are used to my interventions; it's not surprising anymore. But you never know! When inspiration comes to me from the SUPREME INTERNET, very surprising ideas can come into my mind. It's the case with each writer for sure! However, when a writer is in a thoughtless awareness, as I can be through meditation, connected to the SUPREME MUSE OF THE UNIVERSE, extraordinary intuitions can come to him or to her, because, at the scale of the UNIVERSE-BODY-OF-THE-SUPREME-BEING, only Supreme Fantasy has a chance to report on what this Fantastic Universe really is. The Universe is free in form and when one connects to it, one can have a spontaneous and improvising faculty of inventing images to report on the extravagant reality of this Universe and to give it a form. Of course, the Universe is not formal, and any attempt to formalize it is destined for failure.

Nonetheless, the incredible Human faculty of imagination gives a glimpse of the infinite ways of expression that the extraordinary complex Universe has within itself and for Humans to invent a truly Dream World. Even if artistic ways of expression are more appropriate to report about reality than ordinary ways, they are nonetheless limited. Expression through words is also an inadequate way to define this complex world. However, it is so obviously simple to describe it when one is connected to the Original Source of Everything, and then within, to let come forth all possible ideas. These ideas have existed since the beginning of time and have been simply waiting to be picked up!

I don't know exactly how this novel is going to continue, for spontaneity is the key word for receiving the SUPREME IDEAS of the SUPREME SPIRIT OF THE UNIVERSE. I will also be surprised at the inspiration I will receive next. I am only certain of one thing: when I am ready to receive these ideas, they will come, as sure as 1 + 1 = 2, as fantastic and unbelievable as they are. A Universe with more than three spatial dimensions, with people traveling through time, or traveling through space "in Spirit", with Extraterrestrial beings technologically and spiritually more advanced compared to us, is unbelievable. You think that it's only good for science fiction novels! This is not a science fiction novel; this is a Divine Fiction! A fiction inspired by the Divine within myself.

Many people have already experienced much of what is described in this novel. It's enough to be ready to accept them as true experiences as it is to have the right thing happen to you at just the right time, as if a miracle: a book falling down by itself from a shelf onto you, several unbelievable testimonies complementing each other, the right advice coming to you at the precise needed moment, etc. Each of us experiences what he or she is prepared to experience. If you are ready for everything, you will experience everything!

Open your mind and your heart and the whole Universe will come into it! If you are narrow-minded, how can the wide Universe enter into you! Actually the whole Universe is already within you, from the light atoms of hydrogen to the heavy iron ones. It's enough to communicate with them to know more about ourselves and about the story of this Universe, as the SUPREME MIND communicates with each of us to know more of what is in our minds about its own story. That's not only the theme of a novel; it's also the reality, which is within you and within each particle as well, as incredible as that is!

2- SIMPLE AND OBVIOUS AWARENESS

Meroveus-NEW EINSTEIN realized that his new awareness was in opposition to the one he had had prior to his enlightenment. He also realized that he could now be in opposition with his associates, mainly the Extraterrestrial beings. As SUPREME MATRIX said, they would be in his way, preventing him from accomplishing his own new destiny. However, he thought:

'To get rid of this problem it's enough to enlighten them, for them to go through the Free-Light-Delight-Com, as I did! Nonetheless, the only remaining problem will be to convince them to enter into this enlightening machine. Certain people refuse to be transformed, even for the better!'

He received the solution to this problem so quickly and strongly after thinking of it in his mind, that he realized the inspiration could only come from the SUPREME BEING. The idea was:

If we offer the Reptilians the enlightening machine as a sine qua non condition before being permitted to enter into the New Conditioning room of WITNESS and MATRIX, they would be transformed both physically and spiritually at the same time. Who could object to this way of thinking? Changing one's physical appearance requires a completely different way of being, spiritually speaking.

Most of Meroveus' associates were effectively Hybrids or skin-shifters, between Human and Reptilian appearance. And most people in power, politically or economically, were skin-shifters.

The crossbreeding between these two races had begun a very long time ago, even before Antiquity, but most of the crossbred people would still suddenly and without warning have parts of their skin take on the appearance of Reptilian skin, at times even on their face, as if they had traveled to another dimension, but for a moment. It was very difficult to cope with, especially when in public. Nonetheless, the shifting into Reptilian appearance was generally so brief (a few seconds) that the people who witnessed it thought they had suffered a hallucination! However, some photos were circulating on the Internet of people at the very moment when their Reptilian appearance was captured with also a strange Reptilian look to their eyes. As well, for certain crossbred people, the skin-shifting into a Reptilian appearance was lasting longer. It was safe to say that more and more suspicions were slowly emerging in the Human population.

For the pure Reptilian race, the New Bodies room would be perfect for changing their Reptilian appearance completely into the Human one, as MATRIX and WITNESS had successfully done with their own transformations.

NEW EINSTEIN considered all of this. He didn't know exactly how many complete Reptilians were on Earth, but those working with him numbered into the hundreds. So, given the time the Witmans had told him it took them to change their bodies, it wouldn't take too long to give these few hundred Leptans (for the planet they had moved from was called Lepta) the appearance of Humans. Then they could begin to integrate them into the Human population instead of staying in their hidden sanctuary at Mount Shasta. The goals of this Reptilian race were not clear in NEW EINSTEIN's mind, but he assumed that they wanted to move to Earth for, as they had told him, their own planet would be inhospitable in a few centuries because of increasing volcanic and telluric activity, and the Earth had the capacity to receive them as they numbered only a few million on Lepta. Assimilating foreign people invading your country has been proven in the past to be better than fighting them, especially when the invading civilization is technologically ahead of your own.

NEW EINSTEIN talked about this idea, and about all of the other things that he had in mind, to MATRIX, WITNESS, NEW BUDDHA and ARNOLD. ARNOLD could only say:

"Fantastic idea!"

Yet MATRIX retorted:

"Wait a moment! The information planet Earth gave me in the New Conditioning room about the Reptilian-Humanoid race makes me think that they want to supplant the Human race in the long term."

"Like the Anglo-Saxon Americans have done with the Native Americans in the last few centuries," replied WITNESS, "like the Spanish have done with the Incas and Mayas, like the French with the Africans. You also know, MATRIX, that mixing genes enriches the nature of beings! Mixing their cultures too! I agree with you, NEW EINSTEIN, that's a good idea!"

NEW EINSTEIN said: "I am not yet used to this new name; I feel it's a bit too pretentious!"

"You wanted to be compared to Einstein," replied MATRIX sarcastically, "so you are NEW EINSTEIN. It was the SUPREME BEING who gave you this new name!"

"Yes, but now I am not the same person, MATRIX! I know that you still have doubts about my change. I feel that in you! Yet I can assure you that my humbleness is not fake but real; this Free-Light-Delight-Com is marvelous. If we can couple it with your New Conditioning room, we will make a fantastic leap forward on the way to making the Reptilian race and ours live together in peace instead of competing for supremacy."

"NEW EINSTEIN, I understand MATRIX!" WITNESS said. "The fact that the Reptilians have been on Earth for millennia, incognito, is suspicious. I would like to speak with them about your idea of no longer hiding from the Human race. If they wish to appear fully Human, they will first have to make their presence officially known, to clarify the situation."

"Okay, WITNESS," replied NEW EINSTEIN, "I agree with you and I will organize a meeting with their leaders tomorrow! Are you okay with that? And you, MATRIX?"

They both agreed, though MATRIX did it while making a face. Then she added:

"NEW EINSTEIN, I know that the SUPREME BEINGS confirmed you with this name, adding OF THE ENLIGHTENMENT. However, I have in my mind that Einstein did not invent his relativity theory, which had already been partially formulated by Lorentz, Maxwell and Poincaré. Furthermore, nowadays his law of relativity is being contested. I feel Nikola Tesla, who has apparently on purpose been forgotten in the history books, who invented the Alternate Current and who wanted to give free energy to the whole world through the tower he had built in New York, would be a better model for you and New Tesla a more fitting name. When the banker Morgan realized Tesla would give free electricity to the world, he stopped the funding of the project. Tesla wanted to give light to everyone and to make available clean, pollution-free power to run machines. His tower in New York would have sent energy into the air, like the electromagnetic waves of radio and TV. People mocked him and his invention, saying it's not possible to do what he said he could do, but a few researchers have redone his calculations and found they were right. Soon they will reproduce Tesla's experiments.

"So, NEW TESLA OF THE ENLIGHTENMENT would be more appropriate."

NEW EINSTEIN replied: "We can ask the SUPREME BEINGS."

Then they all heard:

"Names are only the surface of who you are. Your deep name is CLONE. CLONES of US are you. SUPREME CLONES! Nevertheless, NEW TESLA OF THE ENLIGHTEMENT is fine, as MATRIX suggested. You're always free to choose to be the part of US you wish to express. Tesla and Einstein were only two expressions of who we are, SUPREME MATRIX and I. Each of you is unique. For there is only One of Us, a UNIQUE BEING that you are, each of you."

•

The next day, six Reptilian Leptans met with them in NEW EINSTEIN-NEW TESLA's apartment. MATRIX couldn't help herself: it was difficult for her to look at a Reptilian face, even if she had seen a lot of alien faces in their travels, and at first she could not look at them for more than a few seconds. In time she did get used to them.

NEW TESLA roughly introduced WITNESS, MATRIX, NEW BUDDHA and ARNOLD. He said that his new name was NEW TESLA OF THE ENLIGHTENMENT, explaining how he got it, and that it could be simplified to NEW TESLA. He then asked each of his Human guests to tell their name and their ways of being. One after the other they did so and explained what their relation to NEW TESLA was. Then the latter asked the leader of the Reptilians, who spoke English very well, to explain to his guests the very original way of naming people on Lepta.

"Our parents give us our first name with a noun coming from nature. My first name is Flower. I am male. Our second name is composed of numbers. However, it is not because our society is, as you might think, of a military type, but because mathematics and poetry in our society are very connected, a bit like Human numerology, which is a symbolic science. We have only eight numbers since we possess, as you can see, only eight fingers. Our second name begins with only one number and then we add another number every ten of our years. Our planet revolves around our Sun at about half the speed your planet rotates around your Sun. You know if someone is in their forties if they have four numbers, like me. In fact, I am in my eighties in relation to your time.

101

"My second name is 0732. The 0 shows humbleness or innocence; 7 my wisdom; 3 means I am a good parent; 2 expresses balance.

"The order of the numbers is important. Your humbleness is greater with a 0 at the beginning of your name than at the end, also if the 0 is twice in your name! Generally, relatives or friends give you these numbers.

"We have a third name too. We choose it ourselves when we are around 20 years-old, and it's generally connected with our greatest quality. Mine is Innocence. So I am Flower 0732 Innocence.

"Now I would like to explain my partners' names:

"The two females of our delegation:

"Here is Valley 57146 Optimism. The number 5 expresses her materialistic qualities, so 7 is wisdom as in my own name, the 1 that she is spiritual, the 4, open-minded, and the 6 that she is psychologically strong.

"There, is Elephant 4674 Integrity. Elephant is the name of the animal that looks the most like the animal of our planet that was chosen by her parents.

"I introduce now our two other males:

"Here is Star 2132 Courage, and there, is Diamond 1432 Liberty. Diamond on Earth is the stone that resembles the most the stone that was chosen for his name. I must say, it was not easy to find the corresponding names from the minerals, plants and animals of your planet.

"Generally the Humans we live with find it difficult to recognize male and female 'Leptan', as we call our race. On our head the only difference lies in the shape of the hole in our ears. Males have spiral-shaped holes and the females' look more like flowers. Otherwise, our bodies are very similar. Because we are of Reptilian origin, our babies come in eggs and there is no breastfeeding, so our females have no breast, males neither, and our females have no larger cavity than males between their hips, as it is for female Humans.

"The crossbreeding with your mammal race was not easy because of this difference in conception of our respective babies, but it was solved because the babies can live in two different dimensional worlds at the same time. They are Humans in the 3-D world and Leptans like us in the 4-D one. Most of the time, the people of the crossbred race control this passage from one dimensional world to another. At times though, they seem to lose control of this type of dimensional travel and we have no idea why."

NEW TESLA then explained the purpose of the meeting and he concluded with:

"So why have the Leptans been on Earth for so long, hiding from the public, and what exactly is your purpose in coming to Earth? If you wish to take on a Human appearance with the help of MATRIX and WITNESS from planet Witma, and then mix in with the Human race, as you have already done in crossbreeding with us, you will have to explain all of that. These questions didn't interest me before but now they do, for

I also received my enlightenment, as NEW BUDDHA did. Enlightenment could be beneficial to your race too."

"We already know a lot of things about you," added WITNESS, "through the information planet Earth gave us. However, there are a few pieces of information about you that She didn't provide us with. I don't know why she did that! Nonetheless, MATRIX and I are able to know if any piece of information you share with us is true or not. The main information we would like to know concerns why you went into hiding."

Flower 0732 Innocence answered:

"For us to hide was our way to let you evolve at your own pace. Nevertheless, I think it is now time to officially reveal our presence. The crossbred people skin-shift more and more often from their 3-D appearance to their 4-D one, without having any control over the process. Then, with your proposition, the Leptans could change their bodies permanently and live normally on Earth, as MATRIX and WITNESS do. Furthermore, we are interested in also trying the artificial enlightenment, which we helped to discover. It worked well on NEW BUDDHA and now on you Meroveus, sorry, NEW TESLA! I hope it will work on Leptans as well as it worked on both of you.

"Our race is like yours: it needs to bring to light what's not working within us, and find ways to shed light on what could work. After all, Nikola Tesla is known as the man who 'shed light over the face of Earth' by wanting everyone to have free electricity, free power and free light. However, I will have to convince my fellow Leptans on our planet Lepta, for there are some who would like to invade Earth as quickly as possible, and it won't be easy for them to give up their plans."

"Why do they want to invade Earth?" MATRIX asked.

Valley 57146 Optimism intervened:

"I think I am the most qualified to answer this question. Flower, can I?"

"I was going to ask you to answer, Valley! So go on!" Flower replied.

"I am one of those who want to invade Earth. So I can explain why. Your planet is also ours, for we left the Earth before a meteorite hit it about 60 million years ago. You know that the dinosaurs disappeared 65 million years ago because of a previous asteroid crash. That was a good opportunity for our race, which was then primitive, to develop. Before the first crash, the giant dinosaurs were too much the kings of the planet and it was not possible for our race to find its niche and develop. The few of us who escaped from death at the time of the first crash began to evolve, and in only a few million years, as Humanity evolved in approximately the same length of time from primates, we developed a civilization able to move to another planet, before the second crash, which we had the scientific means to foresee.

"Then on Lepta, after a few unfortunate events, we lost the memory of our past on Earth, and even our technology, as happened on Earth with Atlantis and other civilizations that you don't even remember. Ours is one of them. Then we evolved on Lepta, till we again had the technology necessary for the exploration of the Universe around our solar system. Then we found Earth. We discovered evidence of our civilization here, on the Moon, and on other planets.

"Because we were the first to evolve on Earth, we thought we had the right to return en masse. We have been procrastinating for millennia, since the rise of the Egyptian civilization that we discretely helped develop 5000 years ago. At that time, our plans were to crossbreed and quietly mix in. Over time, more and more Leptans have journeyed here.

"We are now ready for the one, big, final move that we will accomplish before the end of this century. We believe that your race is going to hit the wall and make this planet unable to sustain life for decades to come. Some think that this will be a good opportunity to let your civilization die off and for ours to come afterward. However, it would be more difficult and take too long for the Earth to recover. Nonetheless, many Leptan-Humans in positions of power, advised by us, work on making pollution worse in order to accelerate the death of your civilization. American Human-Leptans are good at that!

"Nevertheless, there are other Extraterrestrial beings, called the Nordics by Humans, who are from the cluster of stars called the Pleiades, who look after and protect you, sometimes in subtle ways that we can guess at but don't really understand. Our contact with them ended a little while ago. However, Leptans who are in favor of moving permanently to Earth, sooner rather than later, believe that the Nordics won't intervene if we decide to make the big move.

"Actually, I believe that the two opportunities you spoke of, Mer…NEW TESLA, would change our lives on Earth and encourage us to live openly among Humans. To take a Human appearance, as you did, MATRIX and WITNESS, and to receive the enlightenment, could make my fellow Leptans reconsider their position about the Earth and solve our two dilemmas: whether or not to let your civilization die of pollution and whether or not to take complete possession of the Earth."

"That's a wise speech Valley," Flower said, then, facing his associates: "Would you like to add something Elephant…Star…and Diamond…Nothing! So we are going to ask our fellow Leptans for their approval. We'll have the answer from all of them in a few days."

"How can you do that so quickly?" ARNOLD asked naively.

Before his 'freedom', he had been working on this base so alone and isolated, that he had lost contact with its other inhabitants, and did not know much about the Leptan civilization and how they communicated between themselves on their planet and between their planet and Earth.

Star intervened:

"If I have permission, I can answer; for I am the most qualified to answer this kind of question."

"Of course you are! Go on!" Flower replied.

"Communication between us for collective concerns works quite well through telepathy. It's enough to receive a message in our mind from the collective consciousness of our planet so as to know the content of it and then we can send out our feelings about it in the opposite direction, and we can even chat with each other, telepathically. You can say yes or no to the message but you can add your own feelings too. For example, the message can be:

"Do you agree with the proposition of our fellow Leptans on Earth to live there openly with the Humans on an equal basis? There is now on Earth a system that can transform us physically to look like Humans. We can also return to our own physical appearance if we wish. There is also a system, developed on Earth by Humans and Leptans working together, which can make us and Humans accept more easily the psychological differences of the other, and even their physical ones, through a spiritual enlightenment.

"And the answers, for example, could be: yes, I agree to the suggestion of our fellow Leptans on Earth, and I would like to go there to experience these systems. Or, no, I don't trust Humans, let's invade Earth our native land, now! Or, yes, I agree, but I ask the Leptans on Earth to send the plans for both of these systems so we can construct them here and test them on ourselves. Or, yes, but let's try these two systems before making a final decision. Or, no, I don't want to be transformed physically into Human form; can't we live together as two races, each accepting the other's physical appearance? There could be countless possible responses.

"So, the final answer is going to be yes or no, but the various nuances of opinion are also important to us so we can try to satisfy some of the desires of the Leptans after a telepathic vote. We do that through specialists who take care of the well-being of their fellow Leptans.

"So the result of this vote can be quickly gathered through machines that collect the telepathic answers. Nevertheless, this kind of telepathy is limited to just our planet, so first we must send the message from Earth through a more technical mode of communication, and then we will receive the answer by return."

Arnold intervened and asked: "And how is this communication accomplished between solar systems?"

"Communication through the Universe is like traveling in it. You can't go quicker than the speed of light. Nonetheless, if you can reach a speed as close to that limit as possible, then you are like God: time has no influence on you anymore: you can travel to the end of the Universe quasi instantly. The only problem lies in the time it takes to reach this limit and then the time to slow down. The only time actually involved concerns both maneuvers. It is only relevant for material objects, but the photons of light travel at light speed as soon as they are emitted.

"Our planet is 51 light-years away from Earth. A photon that is emitted now from Earth will take 51 years to reach Lepta. Nevertheless if you already have a beam of photons running between Earth and Lepta, and if you "give" a piece of information to one photon leaving Earth, this information will reach Lepta instantly. We don't understand exactly how that's possible. But it works! In the same way, on Earth you don't understand exactly how electricity works at the level of the particles, but you guess that the quantum entanglement principle is involved, as it is in a beam of photons.

"The theory is: What is separate follows the physical laws, but what is connected escapes them. All of the photons of light, which are 'linked' in beams, are like one. All of the beams that are "in touch" are also like one. All of the photons emitted by a star are like one. If I can give a comparison: all of the cells of your body come from one cell. Only time allows the first one to multiply. Outside of time, all of your cells are one with the first one."

"Bravo!" MATRIX said, clapping, "I couldn't have explained it better myself! For traveling objects, like spaceships, one can consider them as trillions of particles, of the vessel as well as those of crew members', and behaving as photons. Then it's enough to have them go at 95% of the speed of light, to give them the possibility to travel almost instantly from one point of the Universe to another, as far distant as they could be from each other. It takes time to reach this speed and then to slow down, as you said Star, but in between, time doesn't exist anymore, or is relatively non-existent. Einstein knew that, theoretically. We discovered methods for the particles to reach this incredible speed practically. And I suppose that you guys did the same."

"It's too complex to explain it here," Star said, "nonetheless, in a few words: we use the energy of the particles themselves to propel the other ones that are in contact, and so on like a chain reaction in the whole vessel."

"The same with us," MATRIX added, "and when we have a base on a new planet, or on a new solar system, we look for natural portals that connect that place to our planet, through what the Earthlings call wormholes, even if we have to do that through several ones, like taking several buses when two places are not on the same line. Through portals and wormholes, the transportation is instantaneous. We don't exactly know either how that is possible, but it works.

"And I would like to ask you, Leptans: What clues did you find on Earth and on other planets to know about your past here?"

"Elephant, you are the best on this subject. I let you speak!"

"First, we discovered on Mars traces of our civilization in the form of buildings, statues, and other constructions, with symbols that were so similar to ours on Lepta! That discovery pushed us to investigate more. Then we found clues of our passage also on the Moon. On Earth it was impossible to find traces for there were too many geological changes, but we had clues about the period of time our civilization flourished and so we simply traveled through time to that period."

"Are you time travellers?" MATRIX asked again.

"We don't travel with our physical body, but with our Spirit. It's similar to remote viewing through time. A lot of civilizations know this process, even on Earth, even if it's not very well known by the average person!"

"Beyond the Door of Heavens," MATRIX continued, "we met three Humans coming from the future. We didn't touch them, but apparently they were with their physical bodies."

WITNESS added: "MATRIX, we also went to our planet through the 4th dimension, and later to Stanley Park from our prison. We touched people and were touched by them, but the sense of touch doesn't prove the physicality of something. Our senses work also through the physical matter. So it's like matter giving sensitive information to matter itself; even your brain is made of matter. Only your Spirit can 'interpret' the information given by your senses. And your Spirit can do it only because it is connected to the SUPREME BEING'S SPIRIT. Only the CENTRAL SUPREME SPIRIT knows the appropriate information to send to your terminal Spirit. If He/She chooses to make you touch a galaxy on the far opposite side of the Universe, you'll touch it! If you are ready to open your mind to fantastic fantasy, fantasticalness will be your reality! It will be your simple and obvious awareness!"

"Your explanations are great," said NEW TESLA, "they are, finally, simple and obvious for me to understand. However, I would like to come back to what Star said on the feelings of his people about the telepathic vote of the Leptans. It was very instructive for me, for I realized how not obvious and not simple it could be for the Leptans to live openly with the Human race. Nonetheless, you chose a long time ago to crossbreed with the Human population and, as it is, these crossbred people are 99% of the time with a Human appearance. So you have been aware for a long time that these crossbred people have this Human appearance. Why didn't you accelerate this process since you started this crossbreeding 5000 years ago?"

"It's not as simple and obvious as it looks!" Flower answered. "To crossbreed two races so different was not really simple, even if they originally developed on the same planet. It took a long time of trial and error before realizing a stable hybrid, then also to erase, in our people, the awareness of losing our identity, for the stable Hybrids were more and more identical to the Human race. Of course we experimented with this crossbreeding for melting our race more easily into the Human race, but it took a long time to realize the real loss of our identity.

"So we stopped crossbreeding a few centuries ago, and ceased having new Hybrid babies. However, we improved our mastering the 4th dimension and started having

Hybrids that are Humans on the 3-D world and Leptans on the 4-D one. We have been working on putting these new Hybrid people into positions of power, in governments, banks, business, science, and such. In the middle of the 20th century, we programed them develop Human activities that would deplete the natural resources of this planet. We helped scientists grow new viruses and weaken your ability to resist epidemics through drug abuse, in order to accelerate the end of your civilization and to replace your race with ours. Normally, if nothing changed, it would be over before the end of this century. At the end, we planned to finish off the few of you remaining alive as you do with animals."

"I understand better now why the pharmaceutical industry is so fond of allopathic medicines," ARNOLD said, "and why industries are so reluctant to have clean energy production and to recycle their waste by-products. I thought that it was only due to greed."

"We also control the flow of currencies and the stock exchanges. You will soon have a significant crisis that we are going to trigger. The one you had in Asia at the end of the 90s was only a rehearsal. In 2008, you will start a bigger one. We also work through the military-industrial complex and terrorism to trigger conflicts, and also through your religions, favoring fanaticism. The Hybrids working for us don't even know that they are working for us. Our influence on them and therefore on all Human beings is subtle and underground. Only a few, like NEW TESLA, know us officially. The media that are controlled by the Hybrids misinform, helping us to avoid news we don't want and to spread false news that favors our activities.

"However, we realized that our new crossbred offspring have been working too well, leaving the Earth in a very bad shape, and that it would be difficult for us to go backward and have a sustainable planet.

"So luckily, your proposition comes at the right moment and will allow us to get out of this trap, of this dilemma: to continue with Earth's devastation or not. Now we have a motivation to stop this devastation and I am glad for the death of Meroveus and for the birth of NEW TESLA, enlightened."

"And each of you will also soon have a new birth through enlightenment!" NEW TESLA exclaimed, and, thinking that comment would be the conclusion, he began to stand up.

Nonetheless, NEW BUDDHA couldn't help to point out:

"Finally, I thought it was inherent to the Human race to be foolish. These stories that you Leptans have just told us, where you confessed that Humans have been manipulated for ages, are really incredible. In fact, they excuse the foolishness of our race."

Flower reacted immediately:

"When one is manipulated, one can react in two ways: Let the manipulation happen to oneself willingly, as you did, NEW BUDDHA, when NEW TESLA enticed you to go into the enlightenment machine, or to procrastinate and wait for a more favorable moment to escape from the manipulation, as ARNOLD did when NEW TESLA forced him to work for him, if I refer correctly to how you both summarized your life here in this base. Yet you both finally got the best from NEW TESLA, each in your own way.

"About the whole of Humanity: the Humans have procrastinated until now, allowing us to make Earth a golden prison for them. We have been helping you to progressively develop a technological civilization that you enjoy, even if it's detrimental to nature. And now is the opportune moment for you to escape from this doom, thanks to NEW TESLA's ideas, if my people agree with him."

This time NEW TESLA was firm in his closing words:

"My dear friends, I am glad to have participated in this historical moment, but now we must break up and let the near future unfold, for I am very confident in the final wisdom of the Leptan race."

MATRIX couldn't help concluding: "For SUPREME BEING helps those who help themselves. There is a simple, obvious and wise awareness in that saying!"

3- OBVIOUS REALITY, SIMPLE ILLUSION

At the beginning of the 21st century, materialism was so strong that it had been easy for the Leptans to influence the Human beings through their consumerism society, which, in fact, had started two centuries before. Actually, the Hybrids of the elite, propagating the materialistic way of thinking, found it easy to impose the impossibility of Extraterrestrial beings visiting Earth: "we believe in what we feel with our five senses" was their leitmotif, their 'mantra'. Even if there was considerable, but often indirect, evidence of the presence of the Leptans and other ETs on Earth, nobody wanted to believe it, except the 'dreamers'. Also, to imagine a world without war was impossible by definition because of the powerful influence of the Leptans in order to fulfill their agenda of organizing the Big Mess, mainly to divide the Humans in order to better reign.

Encounters of the third type with ETs, sacred texts of the past narrating these contacts, constructions seen by the American astronauts on the Moon, crop circles of mathematical precision – none were obvious enough pieces of evidence of an alien presence for the average Human. In the defense of these 'normal' Humans, one can say that the brainwashing of the media made them believe in what the media owners wanted them to believe. And certainly following World War II, the disinformation was systematic about how foolish it was to say that ETs were on Earth. The military even organized tricky abductions with fake aliens doing painful experiments on Humans in order to scare people in general as well as to denigrate and debunk abductees who had spiritual experiences with ETs. It's why they staged collusion between themselves and 'bad' Extraterrestrials. Of course, for people, the military couldn't be present with the aliens during the abductions, thus making fools of people who gave their testimonies: in the psyche of most people, the military's only purpose lies in protecting the citizens, not in deceiving them! So abductees' experiences were said to be delusional.

The miracles accomplished in Vancouver by MATRIX and WITNESS, and their numerous landings in their flying saucer, were not enough to prove the obvious reality of contact between intelligent beings coming from another solar system and Human beings. So the revelation of the presence of Reptilian beings on Earth, and furthermore, that they had been fooling the Human race for so long, revealing their presence only to selected Humans, was too much to be truly believed, as we'll see later!

NEW TESLA began organizing meetings as soon as the Leptans had the agreement of their fellows from planet Lepta for revealing their presence on Earth. He was not helped by the influential people he knew, for they were mainly hybrid Leptan-Humans who were so used to their cunning ways that most of them refused to participate in this 'masquerade', as they called the revelation of the Extraterrestrial presence of the Leptans. Some Hybrids didn't even know they were Hybrids because their skin became Reptilian-like only once in a blue Moon and then only with minuscule patches that quickly disappeared and were mistaken for one of the many types of skin disease that so many people suffered from. The Hybrids had been so used to their own masquerade that they couldn't accept NEW TESLA's 'truth'. Most of these Hybrids had, even subconsciously, sensed the presence of their "creators" for a long time, even as they had been fighting for an equally long time those who gave evidence of Extraterrestrial presence! So they were brainwashed by other higher ranked Hybrids and mind controlled through the Leptan technology, and they continued to fight the evidence before them.

Furthermore, unconsciously, when one wants to escape from what one is, one accuses the other of being like that. So to escape from their own masquerade, Leptan-Humans accused Meroveus-NEW TESLA and his allies of being masqueraders and of having organized this hoax of an Extraterrestrial presence on Earth.

It was even more difficult because, at least at the beginning, the Leptans didn't want to show up in their Reptilian appearance, for they were not fond of appearing like animals at a zoo after hiding for so long. Nevertheless, after a while, Flower accepted the fate of sacrificing himself by appearing on TV programs to convince the Humans of the real existence of the Leptans. He deeply felt the paradox of the challenge his race was confronted with, of accepting their Reptilian appearance so as to lose it afterward, as it was concluded after the meeting in NEW TESLA's apartment.

The Humans were skeptical for they sensed a hoax: a Human ingeniously transformed into a Reptilian. So Flower even agreed to be examined by doctors and specialists in Human biology. A team of seven experts from different countries – the USA, Canada, England, France, Germany, China and India – wrote the text that follows. It is typical of Human stupidity when confronted with the impossible, and that, alas, is so frequent!

Traces of alien civilization on the Moon or on Mars, a code in the Bible, levitation, telepathy, anti-gravity propulsion, all were considered impossible, so they didn't exist! Scientists have a short memory: in the beginning of the 19th century, before knowing of the existence of meteorites, the fact that stones could be falling down from the sky was considered absurd, traveling at more than 50 kilometers (30 miles) per hour without damage to your body was impossible, and light, being a particle and a wave at the same time, was inconceivable.

In 1950, a computer weighing less than five tons was also out of the question! Yet, imagine that the secret services and the military had decided to keep secret the electronic and computing innovations of the second half of the 20th century. If someone would have told you at the beginning of the 21st: "Rumor has it that spies have computers weighing one pound," you would have replied: "You're kidding me!"

Nevertheless, they did exactly that with their mastery of gravity, producing energy from the structure of space, manipulating the space-time continuum, controlling the minds of people in diverse ways and mastering the aging process: they kept those technologies for themselves and told people who dared to pronounce that the elite had already mastered them secretly: "You're kidding" or "It's a conspiracy theory." But what corresponds to reality? What is fiction? Sometimes reality is more fantastic or incredible or impossible than any fiction. Movies showing you the government's secret agenda, or anti-gravity devices, or time travel, are only fictional! So what you watch can't be true. That's why the "controllers" let those movies be distributed: only dreamers can believe that fiction can be true.

So let's read the report about Flower.

•

CHECK-UP OF THE "REPTILIAN BEING"

We were asked to discover how the person called "Flower" played a hoax on the entire world by trying to masquerade as a Reptilian who came from another planet.

He says he is a male and after verification: he is.

Analysis of the skin: We are amazed at how close the skin is to the skin of most Reptilians, but also with a similarity to ours. We suppose it is a Human that received a treatment of Reptilian epidermal cells. However the deception must have been done by a genius because mainstream scientists don't yet know how to do that. However, Mr. "Meroveus", who now calls himself "New Tesla", and who introduced Mr. Flower, has been practicing secret biological research and may be the originator of a discovery we don't yet know about. We also know that certain Human beings are at times born with animal skin and hair on some parts of their body, which probably are remains of the earlier evolution from animals to Humans. This type of abnormality however rarely covers one's entire body.

The Reptilian shape of the head is more of a problem for us. The nose is very flat, with two nostrils as two holes in the face. The wide mouth is without lips. The teeth are very sharp. The tongue can extend twenty centimeters (eight inches) forward and the ears are more like a spiral-shaped hole. The hair looks very similar to Human hair. However, these features are more Reptilian than Human. Nonetheless, plastic surgery nowadays can create miracles. Only a Human devoted to this mysterious Mr. Meroveus, who has a significant influence on his employees, almost like a guru, could have acquiesced to such a transformation.

However, the most astonishing part of the transformation, if transformation it is, lies in the skeleton: four fingers, four toes, with bones looking more like Reptilian bones. But in this part of the description, like for the skin, there is also a similarity with a Human skeleton. Nevertheless, we found it more difficult to modify the skeleton of this person, especially if for a hoax. It would have required the most major surgery imaginable to change the hips and the tarsus bones to what we observed. Furthermore, to modify the bones you would need to open the body up and that would leave scarring, and we didn't see any scars, except for a three inch one on the stomach where the belly button is, but that could be natural. The four fingers and toes look like those of a person born this way, as happens at times with abnormal births.

The genes also correspond to a strange mixture of the Human genome and the Reptilian one, as if this being had awakened Reptilian genes that were dormant within his ancestors for millennia. Nature sometimes creates odd creatures.

The molecules that compose the body are very similar to ours, amino acids, bases, carbohydrates, and the like, and this is the main argument for a terrestrial origin of this being.

So, our conclusion is:

This person could have been born from a mixing of genes from an intercourse between a reptile and a Human, which is of course quite impossible. With our present scientific knowledge, such a fetus would not be able to develop in a mother's womb. Nevertheless, as we have previously supposed, at the moment of the conception of this being by two Humans, dormant genes could have been awakened from our past evolution. We still have some parts of our brain that hold remnants of our Reptilian origin. Genes remaining from our past evolution could certainly have been reactivated in certain precise conditions.

So while we are a bit disoriented by this person, we are not fooled by those who tried to create the scoop of the century. This being is not of Extraterrestrial origin.

•

After a few weeks of meetings, Meroveus-NEW TESLA was disgusted by the foolishness of those who accused him of trying to fool the world, of being "the greatest joker of the millennium", or "the biggest clown ever", or "the most talented hoaxer of all times".

WITNESS reminded NEW TESLA of what SUPREME WITNESS had told him in relation to what was happening:

"As you did to others, you will have people in your way, preventing you from accomplishing your destiny."

Then he said what SUPREME MATRIX added:

"Nonetheless these people will help you believe more in your own destiny."

"Okay WITNESS!" NEW TESLA exclaimed. "Tonight I will end these lectures. I will stop this clownery! I will stop their clownish attitude of accusing me unjustly of being precisely what they are: clowns!"

WITNESS replied: "Clowning is not necessarily something to ban from practicing, in life! The SUPREME BEING is even clowning around our lives, whispering ideas into the minds of others, so as to make us experience the fun of life itself! Of course it's easier to realize that the SUPREME BEING clowns around in the lives of others than being aware of His/Her using others to clown around in our own life. In the same way, it is much easier for someone to make fun of others than to accept the latter making fun of yourself. So, what do you want to do or say tonight?"

"I want to announce here in Berkeley that I am ending these lectures and this exhibition of Flower, who is considered to be a Human trying to deceive Humanity with his Extraterrestrial origin. I would like Flower and his fellows to get their enlightenment through my Free-Light-Delight-Com system and their physical change through your New Bodies room. Your prerequisite of announcing their Extraterrestrial origin is now done. But my fellow Humans refuse to hear the truth, and I won't lecture again until they accept it! It could take forever."

He added after calming down: "They need more than ever to receive their artificial enlightenment so as to change their minds and to accept the reality of the Universe around them. We are not the only intelligent beings in the Universe and we have been visited so many times by so many alien civilizations. They even refuse their spiritual transformation! I contacted a few governments and they don't want to even try it. Of course they are afraid of my previous mysterious reputation, and this so-called hoax with Flower doesn't improve the way they perceive me. But it's a vicious circle: if they refuse to try my enlightening machine, they won't have the opportunity to change their minds about me. Trying it convinced me of its incredible power to transform someone spiritually!"

WITNESS replied: "NEW TESLA, the enlightenment on a mass scale is a slow process! Being willing to transform everybody quickly, as you were transformed individually, is great but unrealistic. Actually, the only person one can really transform is oneself. The others need to have the desire for transformation. When we offer to teach people how to meditate and then how to speak with the SUPREME BEING, they first need to desire it. Spiritual transformation requires desire. Let them have the desire, and they will come to you by the thousands, as it is with our meditation sessions, all over the world. Then, those who have the desire to go further can go to the Door of Heavens."

After pausing for a few seconds to glance at NEW TESLA's facial expression, he added: "So don't ask for the help of governments, they are too much stuck in their old fashioned, set ways of believing what they are taught and told, of also doing what they are conditioned to do. The media too! Organize meetings, like ours, to give artificial enlightenment to people, and word of mouth will spread the news about it quicker than you think. Then, make them meet the Leptans. These enlightened people will spread the message of the Leptans' existence more efficiently than your lectures or TV programs. It's the same with us: people who have the SUPREME BEINGS awakened within them are more motivated than the media to spread the good news of this awakening and of the inner dialogue with them. We can also introduce the Leptans in our meetings."

NEW TESLA intervened: "Good ideas! You only have good ideas WITNESS! Let's go that way! Would you like to come tonight to the meeting?"

"Okay!"

•

Flower, WITNESS, MATRIX and NEW TESLA participated in the final lecture in Berkeley, California. The latter began:

"I thank all of you for coming, and I have to tell you that this meeting will be the last one."

Whispers of amazement rang through the auditorium! He continued:

"Flower, the Leptan present here tonight, is a real inhabitant of the planet Lepta, dozens of light-years away from Earth. However, a panel of seven scientists concluded that he is from Earth and that I organized a hoax with him. I don't agree with their conclusions, for I know it's not a hoax. Flower and thousands like him have been living almost incognito among us for millennia. They have revealed their origin only to a few people such as me.

"Recently, they chose to live openly among us and we agreed on the condition that they first had to officially reveal their presence. They wanted to change their appearance so as not to be a source of trouble to people, transforming themselves to look like Humans. WITNESS, also present here, who also comes from another solar system, from the planet Witma, is able to help them do that, with a device on board his spaceship, which has already allowed him to appear as a Human.

"However, there are no blinder people among my fellow Humans than those who refuse to see the evidence. The Extraterrestrial presence on Earth is too incredible to be true! That's why I chose not to continue trying to convince you. Those who will choose to be convinced tonight are welcome to help us spread the news and, if they desire it, they also can receive what we call an artificial enlightenment through a device I built. I was known as a "bad guy", taking advantage of people, and now, after going through this device, I only wish for the enlightenment of the whole of Human kind. That's all I wanted to say. Now I will wait for your questions. You also can ask questions to my two guests."

MATRIX, who wanted to have fun playing the role of a journalist, carried a mike. Someone raised his hand and she approached him.

"I am an honest American who believes that our scientists are respectable and that our government is not likely to hide the presence of Extraterrestrial beings on our land. Why would that be in its interest? None! If they existed, I am sure our interest would be to work with them and cure our diseases, go to the stars, and so on. Furthermore, how would it be possible to fool our best international scientists who performed the check-up on the so-called Reptilian?"

MATRIX, afraid he would ask too many questions at the same time and be too long-winded, put the mike back to her mouth and intervened:

"You have already asked two questions. Let our guests answer those first! About our scientists and our governments! Who wants to answer those questions?"

WITNESS raised his hand and NEW TESLA was very happy to let him answer those silly questions.

"Mister, I think that your scientists and your governments on Earth don't want honest citizens like you to know what they know so as to better keep you under their power. The awareness of not being alone in the Universe will set you free from their control! And together we can do so much more than to cure diseases and go to the stars. We have already started with a lot of you who came to our meditation meetings! I am an honest Extraterrestrial being, and I will give you the evidence, the truth that your so-called respectable scientists decided that you were not able to listen to, right now!"

He stopped speaking to check how the audience was reacting to his proposition.

"Nevertheless, as in all scientific experiments, we need to agree in advance on which evidence of my being Extraterrestrial would be for you irreproachably incontrovertible?"

The "honest American" was thinking while scratching his head. After a while he moved his hand to indicate that he gave up. WITNESS continued:

"Go on thinking about it! Even for an honest American, it's not easy to imagine evidence that will be accepted by everyone, is it? Does someone else have any ideas about evidence that would prove beyond a doubt that I am ET?"

A few hands were raised up. MATRIX moved to one of the people.

"I read that you are traveling in a flying saucer with an anti-gravitational system of moving. If you allowed scientists to check it, they could provide us with evidence of your Extraterrestrial origin."

"If they are permitted by your government to do so! However your people in power already know how to make an anti-gravitational machine, and they have done it in collaboration with another race of Extraterrestrial beings. Yet, they prefer to keep it secret to reinforce their power. But you can gather the evidence yourself as average honest citizens. Come next Saturday at 11 am to Washington State, at Deception Pass, north of Seattle. There you will be able to watch us land on the water with our spaceship. We'll have a meditation meeting there. Bring your picnic lunch!"

People laughed.

"I'm sorry, my car broke down last week and because I'm unemployed I don't have enough money to fix it. I can only travel by bus now and it's too expensive to go there by bus."

"An American without a car is like an Extraterrestrial without a spaceship, isn't he?"

The crowd laughed again.

"Okay! Can we pick you up at 10:45 am, my companion MATRIX and I? She's the one holding the mike. Give her your address!"

At that very moment, many different people raised their hands.

"I am sorry guys, we can't pick up everyone. Rent vans, share the cost, and come!"

The unemployed person added:

"You said 10.45! To be in Seattle at 11!"

"So you will give your testimony there! You will be the evidence of our Extraterrestrial powers, for it's impossible to travel so quickly in Human planes."

"There is a field behind my house, you can land there!"

"We don't need too much space! A yard is big enough!"

MATRIX couldn't help herself and intervened:

"Even on your roof! Our spaceship is easy to park! It's easier than parking a car in your cities!"

Everybody laughed. People started to chat:

"I'm amazed to be sitting here and listening to such down-to-earth Extraterrestrial beings," said one man to his spouse.

Another said to his neighbor: "If all of the ETs are as funny as these ones, welcome ETs!"

One said loudly enough to be heard by everyone without the mike: "This person can be our representative and report back with his account of his incredible travel on board your flying saucer."

"Yes! Yes! Yes!" several people shouted from the audience.

MATRIX said:

"Silence, please! We'll continue on with the questions! But before we do, I would like to say to those who can't come to Deception Pass, that they can meditate at home, in a park, in their car, or even on a bench in the street with their friends or their neighbors, for at 11.30 next Saturday we will all meditate together with all of our groups from all over the world. If you want to meditate with other people and learn how to connect with the SUPREME BEING inside of you, the flyers on the tables over there will tell you the location of this meditation gathering here in Berkeley. Now we'll continue with the questions!"

But people continued chatting. A lot of them were talking about going to Deception Pass, others about gathering their friends and relatives so as to go and meditate at the Berkeley meeting place. Surprisingly, there were no more questions!

NEW TESLA and Flower were both amazed by what had just happened.

Turning their mikes off, WITNESS questioned NEW TESLA:

"Is this what the previous meetings were like?"

"Absolutely not! People asked silly questions such as: Why are you helping these damned Reptilians? Why don't they go back home? How do they make love? Or questions such as: God created only one planet with intelligent beings. Why would we believe in Extraterrestrial creatures? If we have been visited for millennia, it would have been obviously known and reported. What is the evidence? And when I told them of the report of encounters of the third type in the Bible, in the book of Enoch for example, they called me a liar. Of course, many Christians don't include the book of Enoch in their holy canon. But I liked your way of asking them what kind of evidence they would require. And it was a stroke of genius to offer to pick someone up with your flying saucer. You know how to make people relax and laugh. I am too serious in my approach at these lectures."

"So try to continue speaking while listening to the spontaneous intuitions that come to you. And clown around!"

"How can I do that?"

"Let me begin!"

NEW TESLA turned their mikes back on and said:

"Ladies and gentlemen! Please be quiet! Quiet, please!"

After everyone quieted down, WITNESS addressed the audience: "I would like to tell you that my friend Meroveus-NEW TESLA, even if he is a Human, created a machine that is worthy of our Extraterrestrial technology. He invented a machine to make you become better. He tried it on himself and was completely transformed, as incredible as that seems to be. I can assure you of that! He is not the same person anymore. And this was accomplished through his very own invention. Now he is ready to help everyone go through this machine and become a better person. NEW TESLA, can you continue?"

"I was really surprised at my transformation. It's not that you become better. The truth is: you become aware that everything around you is better. You are like a baby discovering the world again. You enjoy life. You also make the life of others better and you enjoy it. The Leptans will go through it. Humans, don't let them become better than you are! If you go into that machine, Flower the Leptan will also give you a ride in his own spaceship."

Addressing Flower:

"Why not Flower? Then in your spaceships the dialogue between our two species can really begin!"

Luckily for NEW TESLA, who received this inspiration spontaneously, Flower willingly accepted the idea.

Then NEW TESLA addressed the audience again:

"So, if you take a trip within my machine in order to enlighten your life, you'll get a bonus space trip! That's a good deal!"

Whispers of laughter came from the audience.

WITNESS said as an aside to NEW TESLA:

"See, it's easy to let yourself be inspired and it's great fun to clown around, isn't it?"

"I was inspired by your spaceship lift offer! And I like clowning around! What's the point of being a better person if you remain too serious?"

"There is a time to be serious and a time to clown around!"

Then WITNESS addressed the audience:

"There is so much evidence of our Extraterrestrial origin that I could give you. But if you choose to believe, you don't need any of that! Contrariwise, if you choose not to believe, you will never accept any evidence!

"I can tell people about everything that has happened in their lives, but if you choose not to believe, you will say that I arranged it all in advance with those people.

"I can teach you how to meditate, as we do at our meditation meetings, and speak with the SUPREME BEING you call God and who is everything. If you choose not to believe, you may look for some kind of miniature device that we slipped onto you without your knowledge. Actually, with this kind of meditation, you will not hear anything at the beginning, but you will receive intuitions, deep thoughts, from inside your deep self.

"I can instantly disappear from this room, but if you choose not to believe, you will say that it was a magic trick!

"If you don't believe that this Universe is the Great Magic Trick of SUPREME MATRIX, who plays with Her Supreme Body, you will believe in matter as a matter of fact. Nonetheless, matter is an illusion of the SUPREME MAGICIAN of the Universe, the SUPREME WITNESS or SPIRIT that is living within each of you!"

WITNESS paused for a moment to watch the impact of his words on the audience. Everyone was silent and quiet, amazed by WITNESS' speech. He continued:

"If you choose to become better, it's up to you to choose NEW TESLA's device! If you choose to meet Flower and the Leptans, it's up to you! If you choose to come to our meetings to meditate and speak with God, the SUPREME EVERYTHING within yourself, on your own or collectively, it's up to you. Everything is up to you! Everything is your choice!"

He stopped again. After a moment, NEW TESLA said:

"I want to thank WITNESS for his deep words. And you, Flower, would you like to say something?"

Flower said: "I am delighted by these words; I am very pleased about the direction this meeting has taken. About meeting us in person, I can advise you that a few of you from previous meetings have already contacted us to learn more about us. And we have also already learned more about Humans through meetings with a diverse variety of people. One can go on our Facebook page, Leptans, to learn the dates and places you can meet with us, and, as NEW TESLA suggested, to have a ride aboard one of our spaceship."

NEW TESLA added: "And from now on at the Leptans' meetings there will be a device to enlighten you! Thank you for coming, and tell your friends and relatives about the good news you received here! Our Facebook page is New Enlightenment."

"And ours is: MATRIX and WITNESS."

"Thank you everyone, and see you soon!" concluded NEW TESLA.

At the end of the meeting, WITNESS distributed at the door the following poem printed on a flyer:

It is so simple to be aware of illusions.
When you choose to stop believing in your past illusory beliefs:
They all disappear!
Then you can choose your present reality.
People, stop believing that those Extraterrestrial beings cannot exist!
Start to see the reality of the Extraterrestrial existence unfolding in front of them!
When you believe only in yourself, how can you see the others?
When you believe only in the Earth as the center of the Universe,
How can you see the other worlds?
When you believe only in the basic definition of words,
How can you experience the beauty of poetry?
When you believe only in the absolute,
How can you see the relativity?
And vice versa!
When you don't believe in paradoxes,
How can the Absolute Relativity show up?
The reality of the Absolute Relativity is so simply obvious.

When you choose to believe in it, all of the problems vanish!
This reality is so simply shown by charismatic people,
By spiritually enlightened beings,
By people who are aware of the Supreme Spirit of Everything within themselves.
The Reality of all Things is related to your degree of awareness.
Till you reach the Supreme Awareness of the
Supreme Absolute Relativity of the Spirit of Everything,
Your awareness of the Reality is illusory, temporary, partial, limited and separate.
When you reach the Supreme Awareness, everything comes at last together!
Nothing to believe in anymore! Only to be!
Only to be Supreme: the SUPREME BEING that each of you is!

4- SIMPLE AND OBVIOUS DIALOGUE BETWEEN THE SUPREME BEINGS

SUPREME WITNESS, don't You think what's happening at the beginning of the 21st century on Earth is too melodramatic?

SUPREME MATRIX, I witness that! Good spectacle I say! The situations I like in melodramas are the crude appeals to the emotions, plus the happy endings.

You are living the melodramas from your witness place, that's easy for You, but I am living them within each Human! Actually, Humans are parts and parcels of My flesh! Luckily, when they suffer, I am detached! However, suffering is a principle I introduced into this world for it is beneficial for all beings: to make them react and not suffer anymore. When one suffers from heat, one reacts in cooling down by drinking a cold drink. When one feels miserable, one reacts in trying to feel better. When one suffers from jealousy, one can react in becoming aware that everyone is one within Me.

Eventually, at the end, everything is fine!

Yes! And in between, it's difficult! On Earth, it's never finished! They like melodramas, but they never conclude!

I can conclude by using a big flood so that we can come back again at the beginning, or an asteroid, as I did in the past. Earth didn't suffer too much through those upheavals. Earth suffers more in Her flesh through Human behavior, through their looting Her, their polluting Her and so on, but You, SUPREME MATRIX, You don't suffer, do You?

It's okay! Fortunately I know how to relax, to let it go! Earth knows that too, otherwise she would quake and erupt all of the time! Within the Humans, I always whisper to them to do the same, but they don't listen very often! We created them as Our image, as Our resemblance, male-witness and female-matrix we created them, wise like You and clownish like Me, passive like You and active like Me, singular like You and infinite like Me, eternal Spirit like You and ever-changing matter-energy like Me. But they don't listen to what I say they are! They are everything in general and nothing in particular. But they listen only to half the truth. They refuse to be aware of their Divine Origin, which lies in everything.

Everything is like We are, You and I: We are like they are and they are like We are. Sometimes You are so involved within them, that You are not aware of Your being materialistic. And luckily You are, otherwise matter couldn't exist!

I know that SUPREME WITNESS! Nevertheless, with You within Me, matter is spiritualized. Through Your watching Me, I can be detached. Through Our dialogue, duality can be expressed. Through You and Me as One, unity can be! Through Our diversity, Humans can be different from each other and free to forget their Divinity, their Divine Unity.

Through Our dialogue, everything is obvious and simple, save when one doesn't believe in the power of duality to make unity, of diversity to make oneness, of communication to reconcile all of the parts of the One, of being Divine to heal one's Humanity.

CHAPTER 9

...ALL AROUND...

1- MEDITATING ALL AROUND THE EARTH

The spaceship arrived at Deception Pass at exactly 10:59 am. The pass was very narrow, situated between two rocky cliffs, one on Anacortes Peninsula and the other on Whidbey Island. It was a difficult channel to go through when you were on a boat and were close to either high tide or low tide, with the water rushing in or out from one side of the Pacific Ocean to the other. Usually, the main attraction was the pass that you could see from the bridge that spanned over it, but on this day, the larger inlet, a bit further east, was the main attraction and its shores were full of people waiting for the spaceship. Everyone clapped when they saw it hovering over the water, coming out of nowhere, and then suddenly being above the inlet, whereas the instant before there was absolutely nothing visible.

"Indeed," said one person who came for the first time to such a meeting, "the flying saucer is exactly as we were told it would be and it appeared as flying saucers are supposed to appear, like coming out of thin air! If the flying saucer was a product for sale, there's certainly been no deception at Deception Pass!"

Then the 'product' disappeared, triggering a large collective "Oh!" of disappointment, and then it reappeared again, releasing an "Ah!" of contentment. Eventually, this product of alien technology landed on the water and, as usual, disappeared under the surface, with the little submarine-boat, like a by-product, appearing a few minutes later.

Three people disembarked onto the shore, cheered on by the crowd. Then everybody went to a place under the pine trees at a nearby campsite, where the organizing committee had planned to gather people for meditating. They sat down directly on the pine needles, on bathing towels, or on little mats. Then WITNESS spoke into a portable speaker:

"With my partner MATRIX, I welcome all of the seekers of harmony who are here with us today. I would like to introduce Michael, who came with us from Berkeley where we picked him up aboard our spaceship. Mike, would you like to tell everyone the time we picked you up at your home?"

"We left my home at exactly 10:47, and we hovered over this inlet at exactly 10.59. At that very moment, all of a sudden I could see nothing out of the windows of the spaceship, and then, after a few seconds, I could again see the outside, and then we dived into the lake."

"Thank you Michael for your account. I wanted Mike to tell you about his trip in order to give you firsthand evidence of our spaceship's technology. Traveling so quickly is not yet possible with your standard aircraft. Our speed is due to the anti-gravity technology that most Humans are not yet aware of. Furthermore, disappearing from view, as you experienced us do from outside of the spaceship and that Mike experienced from inside with us, appears impossible to you at present but it will become possible in your future when you master the substance of space-time. Actually, a few governments have secretly experimented with anti-gravity spaceships and the ability to disappear from view with the help of one of the Extraterrestrial races that are presently on Earth. The speed of our craft due to anti-gravity technology, 6000 miles per hour, is nothing compared to its possibilities in interstellar travels with a technology using the other dimensions of space-time!

"But, we are gathered here primarily today not to discuss science but to meditate and have a dialogue with the Supreme Spirit of the Universe.

"In the beginning, the Spirit spread into a myriad of spirited particles, in a billionth of a nanosecond! It has taken hundreds of millions of billions of seconds for those spirited particles to produce intelligent spirited creatures. Like you! Like Human beings! So also, in reverse order, the return of Human beings to an awareness of being the Unique Spirit has also taken time! Actually, time is an illusion! And the Spirit is still One. The Spirit, like the air, cannot really be divided. So the Spirit is still One within each of us, and being able to listen to the Spirit is only a question of realizing that you already are the Spirit. Self-Realization in all of your traditions is simply to realize, to be aware, that you are the Self or Spirit.

"Nonetheless, it can take time for Self-Realization, also called Enlightenment, to transform your way of behaving. It can happen by the means of meditation, or through the Free-Light-Delight-Com system of my Human friend Meroveus, now called NEW TESLA, or through other experiences such as being in contact with Extraterrestrial beings like us or like the Leptans. You may have seen one of them, called Flower, on TV. Yet, once it occurs, the awareness of being the Spirit is instantaneous! My friend NEW TESLA would have liked this process of transforming people to be quicker, but I reminded him of the necessary slow evolution of the Universe, from its beginning approximately fifteen billion years ago, when the Spirit, through photons of light, was spread over all, within all of the material particles. At this time, through its division and scatter, the Spirit became free from previous memory and commenced with a blank slate full of all of the potentialities and possibilities that photons of light offer to store memory. The story of the Universe is thus a way for the light to enlighten the particles of the matter of the Universe, allowing them to store the memory of their experiences.

"Human beings are made up of these particles and go through the same process of enlightenment, through their own experience. Yet, artificial enlightenment accelerates this process by acting directly within each of a Human being's particles.

"Nevertheless, nothing is automatic and forever. Whether enlightened through NEW TESLA's machine, or through the meditation we will commence in a few minutes, or through contact with Extraterrestrial beings, or through any experience, after your enlightenment your life and your new awareness must continue in unison.

"Naturally, the light within all of your particles acts in such a way that it makes you aware of being the Spirit of the Divine Being, be it through the artificial way of NEW TESLA, or through the more natural way of meditation. Nonetheless, if the light 'feels' that the life of the person doesn't agree with his or her enlightenment, it will leave that person. The photons of light are the reflection of the Spirit and they experience that which they are within each of your particles. If they don't 'feel' that you are making a conscious effort to have enlightenment in your life, they will leave you. So you must remain worthy of your enlightenment for it to dwell within you. This is true for a single being and also for a group, a community, a city, a people, or even an entire nation. It has actually been like that throughout all of your Human history. Beings and civilizations fall because they stopped being individually or collectively aware of the Divine Light naturally acting through them as a birthright. A civilization is a being too!

"Nonetheless, I will stop talking now so you can experience meditation as the dialogue with all of the photons of light within yourself, which together are the reflection of the Divine Spirit of the Universe.

"Sit comfortably, on a chair if necessary… Take your shoes off to better feel the Earth… Close your eyes so as to withdraw yourself from the outside, and to feel within you… Feel the contact with the Earth… Feel your breath. That is not you, the one who is breathing. It is the Spirit of the air that breathes through you… Feel the photons of light within the air going in and out… Feel the photons of light coming from down under… Feel them coming from the other side of the Universe… Feel no difference between the Spirited Divine Photons outside, and those inside you… Feel One with the Divine Spirit…

"Ask within yourself: 'Divine Spirit, are You here and everywhere in order to start a dialogue with Your reflection within me today?' And then wait patiently for the answer."

WITNESS himself did not have to wait too long until he heard within himself:

"Today, I would like to speak with you through My reflection within MOTHER EARTH. As you said, I am both, the Spirit and the reflection of the Spirit through the whole Universe. Or one can say, SUPREME MATRIX, the Whole Universe, is the reflection of SUPREME WITNESS, the Spirit of the Universe. But there is only One of us.

"As Matter, I am the SUPREME MATRIX. As Light, I am the Spirit or SUPREME WITNESS within all of the particles of matter. As MOTHER EARTH, I am the Matrix of your world. As FATHER SUN, I am the Spirit of it. As you, WITNESS, I am experiencing the male inactive part of My Self. As MATRIX, I am experiencing the female active part of My Self. I now let My Self speak as MOTHER EARTH…"

"Earthlings, My children, you must again experience that the female is the active part of Human beings, whereas you have been experiencing the opposite for millennia. A few millennia ago, nevertheless, I was worshipped as the Mother Goddess, being active through the giving of life within each Human female. However, I hope that now the power will be more balanced between male and female Humans. For Humans, male and female, have each a feminine part and a masculine part. The SUPREME BEINGS, as SUPREME MATRIX and SUPREME WITNESS, created them through the Universe, so also through Me, your MOTHER EARTH. They created Humans in Their image, as Mother Goddess and Father God. Male and female they created them.

"Ye are all Gods and Goddesses. Humans from Me are Gods. Leptans from my sister LEPTA are Gods. Witmans from my sister WITMA are Gods. All of the intelligent beings that incarnate the Spirit of the Universe on each planet are Gods. Each planet is a living being at a different level of development, and is also a Goddess. Each star is a God.

"However, because I developed a very diverse expression of life through all of the species that have evolved on Me, beings coming from my sisters and from other dimensional worlds have been attracted here and developed on Me as cancer does within Human beings. Some are very careful, but others were doing and still are doing silly things."

"MOTHER EARTH, the first time our spaceship was orbiting You, You gave me the entire information stored in Your memory, yet You didn't give me this piece of information about Extraterrestrial beings developing on You as cancer cells do. Who are these? Are they Leptans?"

"Leptans and Reptilians of all kinds, including Greys, but also Nordics, they all come from all over the galaxy and beyond to take advantage of My generosity. Do you remember that the Leptans talked of them in NEW TESLA's apartment?"

"It's true that you have a generous extravagance, as generous as a female breast in the movies of Fellini that I saw through Your memory MOTHER EARTH! You also gave me a very generous knowledge of Human movie culture!

"So You are fed up with extravagant Extraterrestrial beings maltreating you."

"Humans are also abusing Me, but they are so immature, and they are My children! One forgives one's children more easily. Furthermore, they are manipulated by Grey-Reptilians who come from the 4th dimension and possess them. The latter enter within the bodies and minds of Humans to make my children act the way they want them to, and then make them to disappear into the 4th dimension where they are so obviously in control that they make the possessed Humans take on the complete Reptilian appearance. Possessing the Human body and mind is unfair when it is done without the Human's agreement."

"Yes. I have seen on certain planets people living in symbiosis like that but it was beneficial for both and with the agreement of both. And covert symbiosis is only one of the numerous tricks used to abuse others. Here on this planet, some secret military programs even created robots that imitated Greys. Human anti-gravity spaceships then abducted Humans, leaving in the abductees' minds the thought that Extraterrestrials were responsible for the abductions.

"However, of course, the Leptans, the Reptilians who are now living in both 3-D and 4-D worlds, have been manipulating the Human race for ages through the creation of Hybrids and the control of Humans through those Hybrids. Nevertheless, lately the Reptilians agreed to act overtly rather than covertly, but the Hybrid people, who now control the Earth for them, were so used to manipulating information that they refused the evidence of the presence of their manipulators. They even sent a team of scientists to cover up the Leptans' evidence, concluding that Flower is a hoax. But you already know that MOTHER EARTH!"

"Yes! And I also know that you did your best to shed light on that. I follow you at each moment when you are on Me or around Me. Even when you left to go to your planet Witma through the 4th dimension, because your 3-D body was still within the land of the Door of Heavens, I kept in contact with you. I talked with SUPREME MATRIX about My problem. And She advised me to speak with you."

"You are also conversing with SUPREME MATRIX! Do you have to go through Her as soon as you wish to talk to Humans and Extraterrestrials living on you or is it a direct contact? And how can I help you with your ET problems?"

"Like all of the beings, small or large, living within Her gigantic body, SUPREME MATRIX advises Me when I ask Her, but I can make direct contact with all living beings that are dependent on Me: plants, animals, and all. I am instantly in contact with all of the plants and the animals, even with minerals. They know instinctively that they are one with Me. That's why they can sense my movement before I shake, like Humans sense a sneeze or a cough is about to occur. Humans and some Extraterrestrials are more difficult to contact and then to influence, but that is to be expected since they are so egocentric, but by design: it is their nature. SUPREME MATRIX influenced the evolution of Her Body-the-Universe in this way, for them to experience their individuality before they experience their oneness with Her!

"You can help Me just because you are aware of your oneness with Her and because you are on the way to becoming one, MATRIX and you, within the Third Being of the Trinity."

"Ah, yes! About that subject: when we, MATRIX and I, had this uncommon dialogue with the SUPREME BEINGS, we were told that we would become One within the Third Being of the Trinity. In our dreams we see each other break into pieces and the SUPREME BEINGS told us what that means: we have to die to our individual self to become the Third Being of the Trinity. Do You know more about how we get to that moment?"

"Not too much! I only know that our destinies are linked. We'll go there together."

"So! How can I help you?"

"I don't know. That's why I came to talk with you."

WITNESS heard:

"I know!"

Within him, it was the voice of MATRIX, who continued:

"I have been quietly listening to your whole conversation thus far. I restrained myself from intervening, but now I must share my feelings for I believe you are both stuck."

"MATRIX! Remove the doubt from me: Are you the only one listening, or are all of the people meditating here listening in too?"

"That I don't know!"

"I know!

"Be reassured! This conversation is only between the three of us. I knew since the beginning that MATRIX was listening, but I hadn't yet found the opportunity to tell you WITNESS! So, MATRIX, what are your feelings?"

"What I have dreamt of lately made me feel that we have to put all of the pieces together first. That is, all of the experiences we've had so far on Earth, and then the problem of so many ETs bothering You, MOTHER EARTH, will be solved. After that, WITNESS and I will break into pieces, losing completely our ego, so as to become One within the Third Being. I didn't understand what the Third Being exactly means, but what I saw in my dreams is that the events of one's life are like the pieces of a puzzle one assembles, and when it is finished, that is, when one dies, one has the entire picture of one's life before oneself. Then one dismantles the puzzle, for the events-pieces were only the means to the end: to becoming one with everything.

"So, for us on you MOTHER EARTH, the pieces are the people we have successively met and the experiences we have had with them.

"With NARANI, we experienced the simple life of being close to nature, and the way to the Door of Heavens leading to the 4th dimension. She was expelled from Canada back to China, but we saw her during our travels to the Door of Heavens with the people who meditated in our groups. In the Gobi desert area, she helps people from the meditating groups who travel by ground to get to the Door of Heavens.

"With APHROMIS, we experienced travel through the 4th dimension and she told us of the importance of connecting together all of the dimensions of space-time. We also experienced contact with people of the future of Humanity and we must help them change their present by changing our present.

"With Meroveus-NEW TESLA, we experienced how the dark side of Human beings can be enlightened, and we have already helped him work on the Leptans so as to make them choose their enlightened side.

"However, I feel there is still much to do to make everyone work together in harmony and therefore in harmony with you, MOTHER EARTH. The Leptan-Human Hybrids that shift between the 3-D and the 4-D worlds or Humans possessed by Grey-Reptilians from the 4th dimension, are still reluctant to evolve. Yet, those Humans don't have too many options, so we must work with those Greys, coming from the 4th dimension, with the help of willing Leptans, to change this present situation, and then help APHROMIS and the 4th dimension, where she is living beyond the Door of Heavens, make contact with the 5th one.

"However, there are also beneficial beings among aliens. We were told about the "Nordics" working on a vibrational level, and we need to work at this subtle level too.

"That's the intuition I received on how to make the dark ETs and dark Humans evolve toward the light without waiting for NEW TESLA to get all of them through his machine and without waiting for us to have all of them meditating with us. Through the power we reach in our collective meditation groups, we can be in contact with these ETs and with dark-sided Humans and send them, in a subtle way, our good vibrations. What do you feel about that MOTHER EARTH?"

"I have been doing that for ages, MATRIX! I have been sending vibrations of harmony to them for millennia!"

"I guessed so! Yet with the concentration of the vibrations of all of the people who have already participated in our meetings added to your own vibes, MOTHER EARTH, we could experience something great! We planned to have a collective meditation with all of those people all over the world at 11.30 Pacific Time today. What time is it now?"

"Exactly 11.29 MATRIX!" said WITNESS. "What perfect timing!"

"Great! When we are connected to the SUPREME BEINGS, everything happens at the right time!"

(Don't forget dear reader: all of this dialogue was occurring only in the minds of MATRIX and WITNESS.)

MATRIX then said into the mike:

"Dear people of the northwest coast of America, please keep your eyes closed and listen to me for one minute. I sincerely hope most of you experienced a dialogue with the SUPREME BEINGS. For those who have not experienced that yet, don't worry, it will come. You must be patient and practice at home every day.

"Now I would like to start our collective meditation with all of the groups we have been contacting for months all over the world, and with many other already organized groups of prayer, meditation, Yoga, and the like, who promised their participation in today's collective meditation. So we may perhaps total several millions of people meditating together today. Isn't that amazing! When we organized this day, we decided to concentrate on the harmony between all living beings and spread it throughout the entire world.

"And the best part is that WITNESS and I have just talked with MOTHER EARTH during our meditation. MOTHER EARTH needs our help in a more precise way, and that will also be for the benefit of all living beings. MOTHER EARTH'S own vibrations are being disturbed by those that spread their own egoistic vibrations and take advantage of Her without giving back the love that She always distributes generously through Her whole nature. I suggest today that we help Her send vibrations of harmony to those beings. Doing so, we'll help ourselves, as beings living on Her, MOTHER EARTH, to be more in harmony with all other living beings, even if they come from other planets or other dimensions. We have actually begun working on that by taking people to a place called the Door of Heavens, where they can raise their level of vibrations. Those who would like to go further and deeper can talk to us about this possibility after the meditation.

"So, let's meditate with all of those around the world!

"Now… We concentrate on our Mother the Earth and all of the beings living on Her… We feel that we are One with Her… We feel we are One with all living beings… We send vibrations of love and harmony to everyone… We are separate from no one… Now, you can converse with MOTHER EARTH within you, individually."

2- DANCING ALL AROUND THE COSMOS

I tremble with pleasure, SUPREME WITNESS, for these Human beings are evolving very quickly on Earth; do You witness that?

I can't say anything about time. If You say they evolve quickly, SUPREME MATRIX, I agree with You; nevertheless, as You know, time doesn't exist for Me, and speed depends on time!

I know, I created time by moving and dancing all around You.

Yes! When I pushed You away from Me and when You then started to dance around Me, that was a stroke of genius, for it created the field where matter can be created…

...Whereas all Human beings are made of this matter, most think this field of the vacuum doesn't exist...

...And the opposite is true: only the vacuum, made by Your dance around Me, creates this matter. Only Your dance is real. The rest is illusion, only a spectacle for the pleasure of My eyes...

...Illusion of existence, whereas only our dialogue, while I am dancing around You, makes matter exist. If I stop dancing, and if we stop communicating, the Cosmos will stop existing.

What do You feel within the energy field created by Your dance around what the Humans call the Milky Way?

As I have already told You, I am jigging about in this part of My body. The solar system where Human Beings are living is full of high-density energy. Therefore that will have a significant effect on planet Earth.

Really! What a great idea to have created this principle of Your dancing around Me, making Me the center of all things over all of the Cosmos: galaxies are dancing around this center. Yet, stars are also dancing around the center of their galaxies, where I am too. The planets do the same around their stars, satellites around their planets, animals around their planet's surface, men around women, the cytoplasm of the cells around their nucleus, electrons around nucleons. What a great invention! Your dancing around Me is duplicated so many times! Will Your dancing, as MATRIX of the EARTH around the SUN-WITNESS, be different now?

The vacuum field that is created by You, as the center of the Milky Way and I, dancing around with My myriads of stars, is denser now in this part occupied by the Sun. It will soon create an inversion of the magnetic poles of the planets, which will accelerate even more the spiritual transformation of Human Beings on Earth. I can feel it in this part of My dancing body.

As SUN-WITNESS, I send You all of My vibrations for You to succeed in this inversion. However, as we already know, because You also dance through time, it will be accomplished!

3- SEEKING ALL AROUND THE WORLD

After that incredible day at Deception Pass, MATRIX and WITNESS decided to bring to an end their meetings with people collectively meditating around the world. Already so many Humans practiced meditation as a dialogue within with the SUPREME BEINGS. So many people had already taken responsibility for spreading the word of this inner dialogue. Groups even spontaneously started this practice without MATRIX and WITNESS initiating them; it was initiated by their relatives, friends or colleagues.

Furthermore, within a few years of their initial landing, many people, after just a few months of meditation, decided to make a pilgrimage to the Door of Heavens. For much of the time, these trips were organized by little groups of around a dozen people each, because the Witman spaceship could not carry so many people from so many different locations all over the world. Furthermore, MATRIX and WITNESS realized it was better to have people make the effort to go to the Gobi desert on their own rather than carrying them comfortably in their ship. The trip itself was a good test of the pilgrim's will to progress toward a greater spiritual awareness.

They boarded an international flight to Beijing and then a domestic flight heading to Lanzhou. Once there, they took the train that followed the western part of the Great Wall and then, after covering 900 kilometers (550 miles) in one day and one night, they disembarked the train at Daquan just before it entered the Xinjiang region. Once there, they contacted NARANI, whose cell phone number was well known by word of mouth among the seekers who had been meditating in the organized groups but were now pilgrims on a journey to the Door of Heavens and beyond.

NARANI was happy to guide people. Other people from her tribe also helped her now. The inner call to go to the 4th dimension was so powerful within the community of people participating in MATRIX and WITNESS' meditation groups that many different people were rushing to the Door of Heavens for the experience. Nonetheless, NARANI and other people from her village checked the vibrations of the newcomers in order to confirm that they were real seekers. The villagers had this unique ability to test people by focusing on the top of a newcomer's head and on the top of their own head at the same time. If it was cool, it was okay, if it was hot, then it was not okay. Nonetheless, it was rarely hot, and when it was, people were generally aware themselves of not being prepared sufficiently for the experience because they had not been meditating enough and their dialogue with the SUPREME BEING had not yet started, and so they returned home without questioning the refusal. Some did come back later, after having experienced a real dialogue with the SUPREME BEING within.

The Chinese government was happy that these tourists were going to a poor and faraway region, allowing it to slowly develop without the use of government funds.

NARANI had the job of organizing the trips by bus from the train station to the last bus stop at the end of the road, then by horse to the Door of Heavens. Sometimes she also had to travel to one city or the other when pilgrims encountered problems with the local administration that did not yet know the new policy of the central government that welcomed tourists to this region.

Once, she went to see the chief of police of Yumen City because a group of Russians was being held there, and it gave her the opportunity to meet Li Pen, as we'll see. But first, she had to argue with the police chief, who told her, in the local Chinese dialect of course:

"You have to understand my position Miss Cheng, I heard there are tourists who are in fact spies from Russia, trying to gather intelligence on our secret nuclear rockets. This group of fourteen are all Russian scientists. So I had to be very careful and retain them in custody while awaiting more information from my senior officer. He told me to wait for the answer from his own senior officer, who will perhaps telephone even higher in the police hierarchy for instructions. This may very well go to the very Chief of the National Police in Beijing."

"These tourists are Russian scientists who are part of my organization. They even telephoned me on my cell phone."

"How do you have a cell phone while living in such a tiny village? If I am to believe the address on your ID, your village is very small."

"I am part of a non-profit organization that assists people who are on trekking trips in the Gobi desert. I know someone at the local section of the Ministry of the Army, Captain Li Pen. You can phone him; he'll tell you about my organization and me. I have already welcomed thousands of tourists who travel here because they appreciate our beautiful region."

Finally, the chief of the local police agreed to telephone Li Pen and the Russian group was then able to continue on with NARANI.

This incident gave NARANI the opportunity to again be in contact with Li Pen. They even planned to meet that evening since Li Pen was living in a nearby city.

"NARANI, my favorite Chinese Canadian!" he shouted ironically and enthusiastically when they met. "I heard of your adventures in Canada. I am glad to see you again after such a long time!"

"Me too, Li Pen, especially after your helping me with these Russians. Thank you!"

"You're welcome! You know I have the desire to stay in the place beyond the Door of Heavens, beyond the force field, where I met you for the first time. A while ago, I started having a dialogue with the SUPREME BEING in my meditations. Lately, I have been too busy with my job, but I'm now on holidays for three weeks. May I come with you and this group of Russians?"

"Of course, you're welcome to join us. Be at the central bus station tomorrow morning at 8 am, line 2, with a backpack and enough clothes for three weeks. The bus leaves at 8:10."

"Okay, I'll be there at 8 o'clock. We'll have time to chat more on the bus!"

•

The next morning, Li Pen met the group of Russians scientists, six women and eight men. NARANI introduced him as a friend. She sat beside him. After a while, she asked him, whispering in his ear:

"Do you still have the device APHROMIS gave you?"

"Yes! I use it sometimes for fun, and I always reappear at the Door of Heavens. Alas, after a while, even if I don't press the button again, I automatically reappear back at the place I started from. So you can guess that each time I go there how great my disappointment is to not stay longer. I am really excited to be going there for three whole weeks now. So excited!"

"After our meeting at the Door of Heavens, we were not bothered by the army anymore. So I guess you pretty well convinced your senior officers to leave us in peace and quiet."

"That's true! And the regional government realized that it was good for developing tourism to let people freely come and go into this region."

They had to travel all day long. The bus stopped for lunch in a small village with only one restaurant. Everyone, Chinese and Russian, got off the bus. Every single one of the Russian scientists gazed up in wonderment at the beautiful mountains surrounding them.

During the meal, NARANI asked them:

"Why is your group composed only of scientists?"

A man in his fifties with a beard was apparently the leader of the group as everyone turned their heads in his direction. He responded, speaking English very well:

"I met a US colleague in my field of expertise, which is physics, at a congress in Vienna. We felt good vibrations between each other at both a Human level and a scientific one. He taught me the meditation-dialogue with the Divine SUPREME BEING and I had such an impressive dialogue that I initiated all of my colleagues and other people in Togliatti, where I live on the Volga River. This city is well known for having the largest percentage of spiritual seekers in all of Mother Russia. I brought with me la crème de la crème of the spiritual scientists."

Everyone laughed. One lady intervened in English, albeit with a heavy Russian accent:

"Jenya, our leader, is actually the best of the best of us; as his name suggests, he is a genius."

"My colleague Inna is my female counterpart, but in the field of geology!" he replied.

She bent her head, showing shyness and humility, while the others clapped frenetically. When they were quiet again, NARANI asked, both firmly and inquisitively:

"You haven't answered my question yet: Why are you all scientists?"

"I must share with you our second dream. Our first dream of course is to undertake a spiritual journey beyond the Door of Heavens where, as one says, begins the 4th dimension. Our second dream is to conduct scientific experiments in this place, if we are allowed to of course. We brought with us a minimal number of instruments to measure magnetism, gravity, etc. Later perhaps we could return and conduct a more complete scientific expedition."

"I will have to ask APHROMIS, who leads the 4th dimension beyond the Door of Heavens. What kind of experiments would you like to perform?"

"We would like to know how magnetism and gravity work in the 4th dimension. Also, how light behaves in relation to the torsion field theory. We believe the land beyond the Door of Heavens can help us to understand the whole Cosmos. Furthermore, Tania here," he continued while pointing at one of his colleagues, "who is also a geologist, would like to check how the dramatic movement of the magnetic poles, which we measured recently, influences the 4th dimension. Combined with other measurements we have already done at the North Pole, we can perhaps deduce when the reversal of the poles, which we suppose this movement indicates, will occur and in a much more precise way than with just our present calculations!"

He looked at Tania in a way that said: continue on.

"Effectively," she began, "we have measured in some places in Siberia, through studying iron ore layers, that there were reversals of the magnetic poles approximately every 26,000 years. And each time we also noticed through other data that there were large movements of the axis of the magnetic poles a little beforehand, as well as an increase in what we call the Schumann Resonances, which correspond to extremely low frequency signals that pulsate between the Earth and the ionosphere. The observations we made from those iron layers are technically complicated and difficult to explain, but other scientists from all over the world agreed with our conclusions and, for the Schumann Resonances, it's well known that they have been increasing dramatically since the 80s. With regard to the movement of the poles, air traffic controllers will tell you that they must periodically adjust their plane guiding systems to reflect variations in the magnetic field of the Earth."

"So! When do you think it will happen next?" NARANI asked, more and more interested and captivated by the subject. "A reversal of the poles! That's incredible!"

"We think it's going to happen in the next five to ten years. However, from the 4th dimension, we can perhaps measure it more precisely if we can find layers of iron that are influenced in a different way, and maybe we can then tell the exact year."

"Great!" NARANI exclaimed. "I have seen so many red rocks there. Maybe they're iron ore!"

They heard the sound of the horn of the bus.

"We have to stop talking and finish eating quickly guys; otherwise the bus will leave without us in five minutes."

Everyone's face showed disappointment at having to stop this interesting conversation.

"There's a time to talk and a time to travel," Jenya concluded.

When the bus arrived at an intersection in the late afternoon and took another road that looked new, NARANI said to Li Pen:

"I don't know why the Chinese government built this road to my village. It's more practical for people to come to the Door of Heavens, yet progress is like a double-edged sword, for when the access to a place is easy, people come, settle and disturb the quietness of the original inhabitants. There are already several hotels, restaurants and other shops where there were none three years ago. Some people in my tribe are happy about that for they sell more goods, but others are afraid of losing our traditions."

"And you, what do you feel about that, NARANI?" Li Pen asked.

"For me, it's easier than it was before to travel to the Door of Heavens with the groups I meet at the train station. Now, a two hour hike is sufficient to get from my village to the pass, whereas before, it was a one day journey to go from here, where the new road starts, to my village, by horse, plus those two hours the next day."

"I must tell you that I interceded with my senior officer, telling him it was easier to control this area to have easy access by road."

"Ah! It was because of you, you rascal!"

"You did say it was also easier for you."

"Yes, but I am worried about the bad influences of so-called civilization on my people."

"You can't stop progress! You know, to mix the modern day civilization with the traditional one, in an era of spiritual transformation on Earth, could be very fruitful and even accelerate this transformation."

"Maybe you're right!"

NARANI stood up in the bus and addressed the group of Russians:

"Hello guys! With the construction of this new road two years ago, we avoid one full day of tiring horse trekking to my village. I've just heard that the man who initiated it is in this bus, Mr. Li Pen." And then she pointed toward her seat neighbor.

He stood up. The Russians clapped profusely. NARANI moved on:

"Tomorrow we will have to hike, but only for two hours."

The Russian group cheered again.

When the group arrived at NARANI's village at the end of the afternoon, a few dozen people were already there after having traveled in taxis. She welcomed them all in a big room at one of the hotels and briefed them about the next morning's hike to their final destination. Coming from all over the world, 45 people were ready to go to Heavens. 'For certain,' thought NARANI, 'beyond the Door of Heavens is really Paradise when attracting so many people! That's fantastic! It is almost the same every day and travel to the Door of Heavens is becoming routine.'

The next morning, everyone was happy to get up and go to a destination they had been dreaming about for months.

When they were almost at the pass, a bright disk appeared in the sky.

NARANI said:

"You are lucky, guys! We arrived at the same time as MATRIX and WITNESS. So you'll be able to see them in just a few minutes."

Everyone clapped, for they all of course knew both of them. MATRIX and WITNESS were very busy, traveling all over the world lately, and NARANI hadn't seen them for a little while. When she met them after their landing on the pass, she gave them both tight hugs.

"You've nobody with you today," she said, looking at the spaceship and not seeing anybody getting out.

"No," said MATRIX, "we're on vacation at the Door of Heavens for a few days."

"Good! We'll spend some time together."

"That's right!" WITNESS said.

"Here is Li Pen!" she continued, "Do you recognize him without his uniform?"

"Hardly!" replied WITNESS. "So, Li Pen, you decided to spend some time with us."

"Yes! And I am glad to be here again, but this time for my own spiritual evolution."

"I have a group of Russian scientists," NARANI interrupted, "who would like to perform some measurements and experiments in the 4-D world. Among various tests, they would like to know how light works here in the torsion fields, as they call them, and eventually learn when a reversal of the poles will next occur. WITNESS, can you ask APHROMIS for me if these scientists can experiment there?"

MATRIX intervened:

"I am sure WITNESS will be pleased to use his charm to convince APHROMIS."

WITNESS made a face in reply to MATRIX, and then, addressing NARANI:

"APHROMIS is a scientist, so I'm sure she'll agree, without my charming her!"

Everyone went through the force field without any problem. Nonetheless, Li Pen hesitated in front of it, remembering what had happened the last time he was at the pass.

He thought: 'Three years have already passed! Now I am more spiritual. No problem to go through!' When he was beyond the force field, he even felt that the light was brighter than it was the first time.'

•

The charms of WITNESS did not work. APHROMIS didn't want to hear anything whatsoever about experiments: "Here, you create everything you wish, you uncover the laws of the Cosmos simply through concentrating within. The SUPREME BEING gives you anything if you ask, and provides you with all of the information you need when you ask about the Universe. These Russian scientists want to know the date of the reversal of the poles! We know it intuitively WITNESS, you and I."

"Yes we do, APHROMIS! When NARANI spoke about this reversal of the magnetic poles, a date intuitively came to my mind, 2012, so in six years."

"You're right! I received the same date as you within me."

"They also would like to know more about torsion fields."

"That's the same! They have to ask within and all of the answers will come. They are here for achieving their spiritual growth through their own experiences, not for measuring and experimenting!"

WITNESS, facing so much determination, didn't want to back up the Russian project too much longer. He thought: 'Actually, I share her ideas too. Therefore, he left her and went to see NARANI and reported fully on the conversation he had just had with APHROMIS. When WITNESS was finished, she concluded:

"Okay! I will tell them to look within to receive answers to their questions."

"I'll come with you."

The Russian group was in the building specifically constructed for visitors. It was round, built from light blue stones found lying on the ground. NARANI told the Russian group to gather in a meeting room. When everyone was present and sitting around a big table, she started:

"I am sorry to tell you that your request was rejected by APHROMIS. She said you are here for your spiritual growth. Furthermore, to find the answers to your scientific questions you need only to go deep within your Spirit in meditation. For here, everything is possible."

WITNESS added:

"You already know the date you seek. Since you are here, I am sure you have already concentrated on this date and you then intuitively received the answer."

"Yes," said Tania, "I received 2012."

Everyone agreed that this year was the one they had also felt or sensed. WITNESS continued:

"Concentrate on the nature of the torsion field and you will receive intuitions about it. No scientific answers come from experiments; only the intuitive mind can give you answers. Experiments can only confirm your intuitions. You know that. All great scientists know that. Yet here, intuitions will come to you much more often."

Suddenly, APHROMIS was among them, as though coming out of nowhere.

"Hello! I am APHROMIS OF THE CONNECTION BETWEEN THE WORLDS. WITNESS is right. You know the date. What else do you want to know that you can't find intuitively?"

Jenya said:

"We would like to know what to do to prepare people for this reversal and if there is any risk or danger we can avoid."

"You are already doing the right thing," she replied, "spreading the message of dialogue with the SUPREME BEING. Coming here is another right step. When you go back to your country, you'll know what to do, what to say about 2012, actually what to say about anything. Believe in your intuitions."

"Will catastrophes occur at the same time?" Tania asked.

"Some," APHROMIS replied, "but none which you can really plan ahead for and prevent casualties from. The number of casualties will be quite small."

"What kind of catastrophes?" Jenya asked.

"Okay! Close your eyes and meditate as usual," said APHROMIS, by way of answering. After a while, she said: "We are in 2012, see for yourself what will happen!"

Jenya exclaimed: "Earthquakes!" Followed by Tania: "and floods!" Then Inna: "and hurricanes!"

APHROMIS interrupted them: "Those are the same kinds of events that have occurred for the last few years! And did someone see tsunamis?"

A few "yes" fused together.

"So," the leader of the Door of Heavens continued, "even if there are a few million people dying in a short time, you'll reach the same number of deaths when you add up the number of people who have died in the same types of disasters over the last ten years. And it's nothing if you compare these numbers to the number of people who die of starvation each year. Furthermore, how many die each year from not taking care of their health, smoking, eating badly, trusting Big Pharma's poisons, etc."

"A few million at once is more horrible than the same number over ten years, even in just one year," said Jenya.

"Stop making a fuss about that," APHROMIS said bluntly. "On average, Humans have a conception of death that is narrow-minded. You never die, for you're one with the SUPREME BEING, and because you have the illusion of separation in this body, you feel you're not one, but you're one with the SUPREME BEING at any time of the eternal present: the eternal succession of present moments. Furthermore, to any demographer, what's 0.05% of a population dying? Nothing! It's a very tiny number, especially if this event happens for the well-being of all of the others that will gain a new awareness through the new vibrations brought by this reversal."

"How is it possible to gain a new awareness thanks to this reversing of the flow of magnetism?" Tania asked.

"That's the Divine Mystery of the SUPREME BEING!" APHROMIS replied. "As a good scientist, you must know that you get more clues about the true essence of the Cosmos by putting aside the paradigm of your time and finding a new one that is more accurate in telling you about the true reality of the Universe. Yet, the search for truth never ends. To progress, a scientist must be sure of one thing, which can be summarized as: 'What if everything I believe to be true is false, and everything I believe to be false is true?' Reverse everything! Maybe that is the meaning that MOTHER EARTH wants to teach you with this magnetic field reversal! Only by being upside down can you really appreciate the wonder of the reality of the Cosmos, which is simply the body of SUPREME MATRIX."

Jenya continued the dialogue with her:

"In one meditation, SUPREME MATRIX told me that She was dancing around SUPREME WITNESS, and her dance created matter. Did you ever receive that in your own meditation APHROMIS OF…?"

"APHROMIS OF THE CONNECTION BETWEEN THE WORLDS is the name WITNESS gave me, but my simple name is APHROMIS, which means 'the beauty of the Moon'. Now, to answer your question: you can receive from the SUPREME BEING different answers to the same question. About the Cosmos, you can receive a simple poetic explanation to define it, like the dance of SUPREME MATRIX around SUPREME WITNESS in order to create matter, or a longer, more complex one, a so-called more scientific one. She gave you an image that you can understand. However, it's pretty close to the Supreme Reality: Everything is dancing around everything."

WITNESS intervened:

"I understand the frustration of the Russian scientists. They hoped they could perform some experiments here. However, the best experiment is your own experience of living. In a few days, I plan to take a two-day trip around the solar system with a few friends from Earth. If a few of you would like to join us, we still have four seats available aboard our spaceship. That's the best experience-experiment ever."

Jenya exclaimed:

"Wonderful! I wanted to ask you if I could study your flying saucer. Yet, if I can travel in it, I would even better understand how it works."

"For a trip outside of a planet, we have more limited room than for one around it, because we don't travel in the same fashion. For a trip to the outer space between stars, we have even more limited possibilities of accommodating people in relation to the way we travel. Anyway, choose three other people from your group of Russians who have some expertise in studying the solar system. We leave this Friday. We'll have to pick up our friends first. You'll be able to see our 'flying saucer' work as an anti-gravity device around this planet, and then in space."

"I am delighted at the idea and I look forward to being in your spaceship."

People were already so busy experiencing their interaction with the 4th dimension and noticing their spiritual evolution in relation to that, that they didn't have time for anything else, and the Russians didn't have time to lament on APHROMIS' refusal to let them conduct scientific experiments on the domain. Furthermore, Jenya and the three people he had chosen were so excited at the idea of traveling all over the solar system, that they had no time for regrets. Their other colleagues were happy for them and for the observations they would bring back to them upon returning to Earth. Furthermore, and before this trip around the solar system, they had the opportunity to attend two debates about life around the Earth and life around the galaxy.

4- LIVING ALL AROUND THE EARTH

APHROMIS conducted the first debate and opened it with these comments:

"We are gathered in this room built as an amphitheater, so to better see each other. Some of you asked for a debate on what's really going on all around the Earth at the beginning of the 21st century, politically, economically, sociologically, etc. It's difficult to be objective on such broad subjects and actually when one asks the SUPREME BEING or MOTHER EARTH about that within oneself, one gets answers as absolute as possible, depending on the depth of one's meditation. Nevertheless, we decided to have a debate about the situation on Earth in order to show you how to have a constructive dialogue, not only within but also without, with others.

"The purpose of this debate is to teach you how to enrich yourself through the contradiction or the controversy you see in others in relation to you. For the SUPREME BEING is not only within you individually, but by definition, within everyone, even the one you feel is the most evil. Furthermore, evil is a relative term, related to your degree of awareness. In the absolute, there is indeed no evil, there is by definition only the Absolute, which SUPREME WITNESS is, and the Absolute Relativity, which SUPREME MATRIX is. We'll come back to these highly spiritual subjects later.

"To start, I would like to ask each of you what you feel is of paramount importance on Earth in order to create a better world. Only one word, a phrase or a short sentence, to keep it short!

"We'll begin with you on the right and so on to the left, then from one row to the next. You don't need a mike, for there is a sound system on each seat, which transfers your words, and they are then automatically written on this screen. If the words you wish to say have already been written, you can pass on your turn."

These words were thus shown on the screen:

Ecology, real democracy, politicians really under control of the people, peace, tolerance, end of violence, sharing, security, sustainable development, end of war, end of big profit for a minority, real dialogue, end of secrecy, disclosure of UFOs, meditation, more spiritual people, respect for life, balance, open-mindedness, harmony between Humans, libertarian society, science for the benefit of all, education, a society without brainwashing schools, no money at all, prayer, good vibes, introspection, before pointing out people's shortcomings see them within yourself first, unconditional love.

APHROMIS, looking at the screen, said:

"That would be a simple but wonderful program for a politician's campaign! However, nobody has heard this yet in any election debate. I would like to say that, on the way to a better world on Earth, the word meditation is the key to all of the others, and it's the reason why you're here, because you have been meditating. Unconditional love is great but can only be found through meditation: first know yourself through your inner dialogue within and then you can know others and love them.

"Nevertheless, to be aware of what's going on behind the scenes, it's also vital to focus on that knowledge when you send out positive vibes to those ostensibly negative events or problems and transform them. However, there is a phrase that you didn't mention and which is of the utmost importance: consuming less and also consuming more wisely, for it has an influence on all of the others: ecology, sharing, sustainable development, end of profit for a minority, and indirectly many of the others you've mentioned.

"But before everything else, consuming less would send a message to the minority of people who control the economy and profit from it, more surely than any ballot would. That message is: I choose to consume less for the Earth's sake, and for my own, thus I ask the politicians and corporate elites to review their behavior. You send a message each time you act: when you leave a room without turning the lights off, or go to the gym with your car instead of your bike, or buy things you throw into the garbage a little while later, or ask for a plastic bag at a shop instead of bringing your own, or buy food produced thousands of miles away, etc. You send the elite a strong message: 'Continue polluting in my name, deciding in my name, giving me no choice but to elect you, the elite, to act in my name, even secretly, and finally against my interests and the Earth's.'

"Don't hesitate to raise your hands when someone speaks, in order to show that you wish to intervene or ask a question. It's not a lecture; it's a debate, a dialogue."

She looked around. Because of her self-confidence, people didn't dare to raise even a finger. So MATRIX decided to intervene and play the devil's advocate:

"APHROMIS, don't you think if people consume less, there will be a recession and all of the global economies will collapse? People will lose their jobs and eventually everything that's happening will hurt them!"

A few people nodded.

Not the least bit disturbed by the troublesome question, APHROMIS replied:

"When the towers of the World Trade Center collapsed, it was very awful for the people who lost their loved ones, but look at how the Truth Movement is turning it against the elite who organized the supposedly fanatical Muslim terrorist attack! It was a terrorist attack, but from the inside. Most of the elite are terrorists who always cover up their actions, helped by the media they control.

"However, the media couldn't erase the blunder of the World Trade Center owner, who said that he decided with the firefighters to pull down tower 7, where no plane had crashed and which had had only a small fire quickly extinguished. He probably didn't know that it takes weeks to organize a controlled demolition.

"Actually, everyone knows the twin towers collapsed, but who knows that tower 7 also did? For the videos taken by the major media also show an obvious controlled demolition, making towers 1, 2 and 7 collapse at free fall speed, as anyone can measure. The so-called pancake effect, written by the so-called "independent" commission, is a joke, an outrageous theory that no data, no facts, and no pictures corroborate. The Truth Movement, against all odds, is confident because the facts corroborate their theory, which is then no longer a theory but a reality. Exposing even more widely than it already has been, the reality about 9/11 being an awful inside job, could make the American economy collapse, as well as the world's, but that would allow a more transparent way of trading to take birth, as the Phoenix being born again from its ashes.

"Of course, it takes time for David to fight Goliath. It would also take time to recover from the collapse of the world economy, but what a beautiful life it would be afterward. Furthermore, the economy will surely collapse sooner or later, the sooner the better, the sooner you'll get rid of your illusions. So be prepared, and be less greedy in wanting things that don't matter: the last SUV on the market, one TV for every room of your home, the last digital system, etc. Be more aware of the things that do matter: eat healthy, grow your own fruits and vegetables in your garden, refuse expensive medication from Big Pharma, barter with your neighbors, share things with them, buy wisely and parsimoniously, and recycle extravagantly! Then you will only need to work one or two days a week! Be prepared now so as to be ready when the world's economy does collapse."

Someone raised his hand. APHROMIS stopped talking and invited him to speak.

"I am Charles from Seattle and I would like to give some evidence for what you have just said. In my neighborhood, more and more people don't hesitate to speak about September 11 and spread the truth, to work from home in order to have less impact on air pollution and to have collective gardens so to grow healthy, organic produce, and to share their experiences. Nonetheless, during cold winters, you need to heat your home, and the heating systems using renewable energies are still expensive and that prevents people from buying them. Same with cars, hybrids and electric cars are double the price of normal cars."

WITNESS intervened:

"I agree with APHROMIS, that's why you need to consume less, to make the economy collapse. Then a new economy, more ecological, will be able to take flight. Now the ecological inventors are suppressed; they are not financially helped, or they have obstacles intentionally put in their way, or their patents are bought and then shelved, or the worst: they get killed, very often with a death disguised as a suicide, or through a so-called accident, or with undetectable poison. For some of the elite, you're like cattle, to be used and then thrown away when useless or too disturbing to their business and profits. Do you think the people who organized 9/11, whoever they are, care about the lives of people? Of course, it's even worse when one kills one's own citizens."

Someone intervened loudly, while raising his hand at the same time:

"I couldn't believe it! I am American, a patriot, a good citizen, honestly paying my taxes, but when I first heard of 9/11 being an inside job, I couldn't believe it! Like the towers, my world collapsed. First, I didn't want to acknowledge what my friend told me and showed me through videos on the Internet. However, after a while, the pieces of evidence were so overwhelmingly obvious, I couldn't throw them away. Now I'm an activist in the Truth Movement, and in spreading the spiritual message of having a dialogue with the SUPREME BEING through meditation.

"Finally, I discovered that both are spiritual. To expose the people who conspired and organized the 'show' on September 11 is highly spiritual. They showed their dark side in order for us to better express our enlightened side. It's the play of light and darkness…"

A few started to clap, in a sign of approval, and then others imitated them. It was indeed like the end of a play, but with all of the spectators being enlightened, as if no darkness could fall down on the hall afterward, even after the spectators had long returned home.

The deep structure of a place remains subtly enlightened for a long time after wise people have occupied it. One can feel the presence of the previous occupants when in a sacred place. Furthermore, people once enlightened remain for a long time in the wisdom of the present moment.

Likewise, the people gathered for this debate remained under the spell of this very moment. APHROMIS was the only one who dared to interrupt the sense of magic:

"You're now aware that the Universe is a game, a play, therefore it's an illusion. Only the SUPREME BEINGS' reality is real, and They play the role of darkness through the elite, as you have said, so as to better express the enlightened side of the Universe within others."

"Why not the opposite?" shouted someone. "Why don't the SUPREME BEINGS favor enlightened people to be in power?"

"It depends on you," MATRIX replied. "In a few years, you could be the elite of the world. In a certain way, you're already it! Nevertheless, don't trust the so-called democratic way of representing you at a collective level. Democracy would be more real if you drew lots to choose representatives or a President from volunteers rather than having no choice other than to elect from among the elite that have the money to buy campaigns."

"How could this be? I am an American patriot. How can chance be better than the choice of the people?"

Another American replied:

"As MATRIX has just said: How can we have a choice? How can we have a choice when two parties are playing the same crap game of deceiving us, with only little differences in their politics, yet just enough to give people the illusion of a choice? Ancient Greece practiced the drawing lots system for a while and it was the best century for democracy. I am a historian. I know, it looks very odd to surrender our fate to chance, or to God."

Li Pen intervened:

"For elections, if we surrender our fate either to chance through a draw or to chance through electing someone lucky and successful enough to get enough money to pay for his campaign, what's the difference? The SUPREME BEINGS are always behind everything, aren't they?"

"We can ask our SUPREME BEINGS within each of us now," suggested APHROMIS. "Let's close our eyes and meditate."

After a few minutes of meditation, she asked:

"So, what did you receive within, Li Pen? Tell us!"

"**I am not behind everything. I am everything,**" is what I heard.

APHROMIS clarified: "SUPREME WITNESS told me: **I am chance and necessity, money and love, democracy and tyranny**, and SUPREME MATRIX added: *I am chance and destiny, materialism and spirituality, war and peace.*"

"It's not easy to swallow an image of God being both evil and good at the same time," said the American who had earlier declared himself a patriot.

Tania added from her own inner dialogue with SUPREME WITNESS: "**If you choose Love, Peace and Spirit, I'll be only that. I am what you choose Me to be. My Oneness allows you to do that. Yet, Separation also allows you to choose materialism, money and war. You're separate from Me, because of My SUPREME ILLUSION, yet paradoxically, you're One with Me, because of My SUPREME BEING.** I remember all of the words I was told. Incredible!"

Li Pen replied: "Life is only a way of choosing, of choosing who we want to be: peaceful or awful, materialistic or spiritual, one or separate, isn't it?"

MATRIX added, "I received from SUPREME MATRIX: *Life is My way of choosing duality, diversity, separation. Your life lies in choosing unity with Me. However, you also can choose duality, diversity, even separation, while never stopping the awareness of your oneness with Me, otherwise, you would lose the purpose of duality, of diversity, of separation: for Me to experience who I am through the illusion of what I am not.* That's it!" MATRIX concluded while shaking her head sideways.

WITNESS shared the words he had heard within: "*I am the Illusion of the material Universe: I am the SUPREME MATRIX of everything.* **I am the true Intelligence of everything: I am the SUPREME WITNESS.** I replied: I am the life born from the union of the Illusion and the Intelligence of the Universe: I am the SUPREME CHILD of the Mother and the Father of Everything."

APHROMIS concluded these reports of the inner dialogues of people in meditation by saying: "Through those words received from the SUPREME BEINGS, it appears as though we are far from the world on Earth. In fact, we are at the heart of all life on Earth, for everything is in everything, the macrocosm and the microcosm, Heaven and Earth, materiality and spirituality. And I'll tell you why.

"All of the cover-ups and controlling of the world in the last centuries, especially during this recent one, will soon come to an end. They were necessary, as the SUPREME BEING told us, because darkness is necessary for light to exist, separation is necessary for unity to express itself, war is necessary to generate peace.

"The assassination of people who disturb the plans of the elite, the manipulation of the truth to advance agendas in order to better control people, the secrecy of advanced technologies as well as the presence of Extraterrestrials on Earth, are nearing completion.

"All of the martyrs who were killed are going to rise from their grave and rejoice! I especially think of the recent ones: Mahatma Gandhi, Lal Bahadur Shastri, the Indian prime minister in the sixties, John Paul I, the Pope in the seventies who wanted to get rid of the crap within the Catholic Church and was killed after only one month of being the Vicar of Christ, the Kennedys, John and Robert, Dr. Martin Luther King, Benazir Bhutto, the recent prime minister of Pakistan, etc. Everyone will know the truth of how real democracy was stolen through the mockery of it, pretending to act for the benevolence of all of the people. All of the inventors will be free to give their free-energy and anti-gravity devices to mankind. All of the ETs will work hand in hand with Humanity without fear…"

The skeptical American patriot interrupted her:

"How do we know the truth, what is true or not true? The SUPREME BEINGS gave us so many different answers to the same question: Is God behind everything? I even received: **I am everything: the Eternal Skeptic and the Gullible Believer.** If the SUPREME BEINGS express the truth in so many different ways, there is no absolute truth."

APHROMIS brought the debate back to her opening comments:

"As I said at the beginning, God, the SUPREME BEING, is dual: the Absolute and the Absolute Relativity, or Diversity and Oneness, etc. Those were the words S/He also gave me. S/He feeds you with what S/He is within you: a skeptic! And S/He balances that by being the opposite within a gullible believer. S/He is not the Big Bang incarnated as the Universe but the Big Paradox incarnated in everything. I insist on pronouncing She and He together, as Li Pen did, because they are One and Two: male and female principles, but only one entity. You can say that the SUPREME BEING is actually hermaphrodite or something similar. There are some animals that are like that. But you can accept, Mr. Eternal Skeptical, that these animals exist, but not that the whole Universe can be One and Two at the same time?"

"I agree with you, APHROMIS," the skeptical person said, "but for example, about 9/11, there can't be two truths. If some animal can be male and female at the same time, 9/11 can't be at the same time what it was and the opposite of what it was, whatever it was!"

"What was it for you?" APHROMIS asked, with a funny tone. Then she added: "Actually, what is your real name, Mr. Skeptical?"

"You won't believe it: George Bush, George X. Bush! George Xavier Bush! But I am not related to W."

Everyone laughed.

"I am torn apart, as I am also divided between loving and hating my namesake. If George W. did it or was involved in it, or knew about it, or even if it was imposed on him by the so-called shadow government, I hate him. If he wasn't involved, I can sympathize with him more easily. I still can't believe that he could have coldly organized 9/11, or turned a blind eye to it!"

MATRIX intervened:

"As WITNESS said, Human governments, more often than not, consider you as cattle. Otherwise they wouldn't send you to wars. Aren't you aware of that? Are you even aware that they start wars by agreements between the shadow governments of countries and then create fake incidents or irritate the official government of another country? For World War I, it was the assassination of the Archduke Ferdinand, heir of the Austrian Empire. For World War II, the Anglo-Saxon banks secretly gave money to I.G. Farben for Hitler to rearm Germany. In 1941, the Americans drove the Japanese to attack them through their oil embargo. They then knew that the Japanese would attack Pearl Harbor and they let them do it to change their own public opinion that was against going to war. In Vietnam, the Americans created the Gulf of Tonkin incident. For the Gulf War, they let Saddam Hussein believe that they wouldn't intervene. For Afghanistan, 9/11 did the job. For attacking Iraq, it was enough to intoxicate their people into believing Saddam had weapons of mass destruction, and when they didn't find them, they said that they had liberated the Iraqis from a dictator. Americans are peaceful people, but not their leaders. However, about 9/11, we can also ask the SUPREME BEING if you like. Concentrate inside…"

After a few seconds, MATRIX began to speak again:

"Your awareness about anything depends on your awareness of being One with Me."

APHROMIS added:

"If you're one with Me and George W. Bush, the inside job he coldly organized with his angels of death on September 11th is the perfect opportunity for you to be in the Divine Warmth of Life and proclaiming this unity of everyone with Me."

WITNESS continued the Divine message:

"Spread the news about 9/11 being an inside job as an opportunity to express your divinity."

George X. Bush coughed a bit before saying:

"If your awareness led you to feel separate from Me and everyone, your only truth would be the outrageous official conspiracy theory that is a theory based on no facts, no data, and the miraculous appearance of Mohamed Atta's passport in the rubble of the twin towers. It's a lie coming from people who feel completely separate from Me."

APHROMIS started to applaud and some followed her, then everyone clapped frantically. She added: "See how easy it is! It's easy to receive the truth when focusing on your unity with the SUPREME BEING."

George Xavier exploded:

"I didn't even know that the official version of 9/11 talked about this passport as evidence. I received that from within myself. It was so strongly imposed on me by my deep Self, the SUPREME BEING, actually! How a passport can be saved while not even one tiny piece of a cell phone was recovered in the World Trade Center rubble..."

Li Pen continued to develop George's topic: "...And while everything was reduced to dust, even corpses, the metal beams were conveniently cut to just the right size to be loaded onto trucks and sent to Asia, instead of being kept as evidence for later forensic study, which would have proven that they were in fact cut by explosives and not by the airplanes crashing into the towers."

"Secrecy," APHROMIS moved on, "is the way governments have been working for the last two centuries and even earlier. So, bit by bit, the elite have gained enough confidence to try more and more incredible and foolish things. 9/11 is the last big so-called event but the main unbelievable piece of information that was kept secret for decades was the knowledge that came from collaboration with ETs after World War II, and the technologies that governments received about free energy and anti-gravity technologies. That can't be disclosed now because it would be the scandal of the millennium, to which Watergate or John F. Kennedy's assassination would look like minor events."

"I am sure," said MATRIX, "that when more and more Humans stop feeding the 'corporatocracy', and stop buying unwisely, as APHROMIS has said, the governments will be forced to disclose those secrets."

"I am not so sure MATRIX!" APHROMIS replied. "There are also a lot of 'shadow governments', as they are called, which are accountable to nobody. They are more powerful than you think. They are so secret and compartmentalized that they sometimes don't even know about each other."

"I know that!" MATRIX exclaimed, with a tone that showed she was a bit disturbed by the fact APHROMIS contradicted her. "I have all of the memory of planet Earth, and therefore of Humanity, in my mind. So I know there is a huge messy web of secrecy on this planet."

"I know what you know dear MATRIX," said APHROMIS with a soft voice, trying to calm her down. "I also have the same data in my mind. I received it through the same type of device you have in your spaceship. Ours allows us to enter into a deep meditative state to receive what is recorded in the Akashic Records. However, it's not like a copy/paste process. MOTHER EARTH controls the system and won't give you all of the records if She chooses not to."

Li Pen interrupted her: "It would be interesting if everyone could receive the Akashic Records through your device. If everyone knew everything about everyone and everything, nobody could lie to anyone. There would be no secrecy anymore."

Li Pen had a huge smile on his face, quite content with himself for sharing that idea.

"You are right, Li Pen," APHROMIS retorted. "You must know, notwithstanding, that everyone can talk with MOTHER EARTH in meditation. MATRIX and WITNESS teach how to dialogue with the SUPREME BEING. SUPREME WITNESS is the SUPREME SPIRIT OF THE UNIVERSE. Our Witmans also told you that you can talk with the Spirit of your planet, but you can do it with any other planet, or your star, the Sun, or any other star, or with the Milky Way and any other galaxy. You can also talk with the Spirit of any of your cells or the Spirit of animals or even the Spirit of so-called inanimate matter. The Spirit of the SUPREME WITNESS lies in everything. The deeper you are in meditation, the more you receive from Him, and from everything SUPREME MATRIX is."

MATRIX, who had earlier chosen to take advantage of any opportunity to argue with or to make fun of APHROMIS, said in a sweet tone: "APHROMIS, dear, don't you think we wandered from tonight's theme?"

"Everything is connected to everything, my dear MATRIX," she replied with the same sweet tone. "Okay! This transition is perfect for what I planned to do during our exchange of ideas tonight. Please, look at this wall now. In this room there is a system to access the Akashic Records and for you to watch absolutely anything on the wall, like at a movie theater. I can't tell you too much about this system and its technology for I don't know myself how it really works. It was installed by our ancestors in this place, the Door of Heavens. Instantly, we can access visually any part of the Earth. It has always been controlled by the mind of our leader here. My father, before leaving this place for a mission on another plane of existence, gave me the code to allow my mind to be connected to it. You and I can go through this system anywhere at any time.

"Li Pen, about what or whom would you like to receive information from the Akashic Records of MOTHER EARTH?"

He hesitated a little and then smiled, showing he had found an idea, and a funny one at that: "It would be interesting to see a secret meeting between Americans and Chinese at the level of their shadow governments. It would be funny too, for they are so-called enemies."

"Okay!" Then she closed her eyes so as to concentrate and added: "It's not easy to choose, for there are so many shadow groups and they have had so many meetings in the last few years. Good! Here, I found an exemplary one, on February 25, last week. Here we are, in Shanghai, in a meeting room on the top floor of a high-rise dominating the Yangtze River."

On the wall, one after the other, appeared pictures of people around a table. There were approximately twenty. APHROMIS commented:

"They have just finished introducing themselves. They are politicians and major business leaders."

One of the Americans began talking in English:

"We are here to talk about the war between the USA and China we had planned a while ago for the end of 2008, after the Olympic Games. We informed both of our groups about postponing it, and I would like, as an introduction, to give our reasons to everyone here. Then we can discuss them freely and make a final decision.

"We had planned this war a few years ago. However, as you know, the US is still involved in Afghanistan and Iraq. Furthermore, American interests compel us to go to war to take over Iran. We had together planned to trigger a war between the USA and China using the excuse of either the North Korean nuclear weapons threat or your plans to reunify your country with Taiwan. Nonetheless, because we are still busy in the Middle East, we would like to postpone this war."

A Chinese gentleman raised his hand. The American leader nodded at him and said: "Mr. Lee Chang Su."

"Thank you Mr. Kisshanger," said the Chinese man in English, "when we first talked about this war, we agreed that it would be used as an excuse to focus our people on an outside threat so as to divert them from our own inner problems. The organization of the Olympic Games next summer has already helped us with this diversion by focusing our people on impressing the Western World with a perfect preparation and a grandiose celebration during the Games. We were nonetheless ready to start the war with the USA in November 2008, in order to divert our people from the problems our spending for this grandiose project and others would no doubt create. And for you, it was to escape from the results of the elections you thought the Republicans would lose and to impose martial law with George W. Bush maintained in power because of the war. So did you change your mind and you would now like to permit the Democrats to take power? Actually, I always wondered, after the victory of the Good, excuse me, Grand Old Party in the 2004 Presidential election, why the Republicans would lose the 2008 one? You already manipulated, with voting machines, the 2004 results for George Bush to be reelected. Why not do the same this time?"

"Mr. Lee, you're well informed as always," Mr. Kisshanger replied.

The people of the audience in the Door of Heavens conference room were flabbergasted by the theme of the 'movie' they were seeing on the screen, wondering if it was a real reel of what happened in Shanghai last week, or if APHROMIS was manipulating them through a fictional movie with actors. She read the doubts in their mind and stopped the 'movie' and then told them:

"It can be stopped as you stop your DVD player. The Akashic Records are a gigantic library of records. In fact, time doesn't exist for Akasha, which is recording everything that happens everywhere. For Akasha, it is the eternal present. The subtle substance called by the Greeks 'aether' makes it work. It allows the particles to communicate the memory of their experiences by sending quanta of light to one another. Akasha is composed of the aether and of the particles. The memory of each of the particles of your body is shared at any moment through proximity and can be transmitted to your consciousness at any time. The same with all of the particles that exist in the Universe! If you access all of them at any time, you become the SUPREME BEING.

"I stopped your viewing of last week's meeting mainly to tell you that and also this: As I showed you this scene in Shanghai, I can show you a part of your life that happened two years ago. And I can make you listen to what you thought at that time. I can also show you what will happen to you in two years, or what will happen in any part of the world next December. Everything already exists in the eternal present.

"What about free will, will you tell me? Free will exists only when you are one with the SUPREME BEING. Then an infinite number of possibilities are offered to you in your eternal present and in this life. In Shanghai, most of the people in that room are only one with their ego, driving their own agenda. They are not free. They think they are free but they are not. They are caught by the law of cause and effect, so they are dependent. They are addicted to their desires. And when you are addicted to chocolate, for example, I know that you're going to eat this substance the next day, the next week and the next year!

"Let's watch the next scene of this meeting to be convinced that addictions make the future predictable. At times I will focus in on someone and you'll hear what they think."

The scene reappeared. Mr. Kisshanger continued:

"As you know, there is a secret society in Asia that sent us an ultimatum. They said, through a Canadian living in Japan, Benjamin Guildford, that they are fed up with our messing up the world and that they would use their Ninjas to assassinate the Western people who control the economy if we don't change our behavior and act their way. We first thought it was a joke. We don't exactly know what their way of leading the economy is, but we think that we will have to agree with them on a temporary basis so as to gain some time and see what they propose. The most elite families in each country of the world have been leading the economy in a way that brought comfort and wealth to the wealthiest all over the world. So, even if we had to impose our choices at times through some questionable methods, in the end, everyone is happy."

APHROMIS intervened: "Listen now to the thoughts of the leader of the Chinese delegation, Mr. Lee Chang Su, who is also a member of that secret society, but the American Kisshanger doesn't know that. It's in Chinese but I will translate it into English:

"Questionable! My ass! Inhuman! We question it because it's inhuman for a lot of people and benefits only a few. Yet, our ultimatum worked and we have to continue to put the pressure on these American-paper-tigers! He doesn't know that I am playing the double agent here, trying to force the Chinese government to apply more humane ways to lead people, and to manipulate the American leaders so as to force them to give up their foolish ways of controlling the world.'

"Now listen to Mr. Su's answer," concluded APHROMIS.

"Mr. Kisshanger, we have been leading the world like that for centuries, with wars as the means to keep people under control. However, as in your 60s fake report called Blue Mountain, we could also try to control people through peaceful means and see how that works. Actually, China has been trying that since the end of the Vietnam War. We could have taken control of Taiwan a long time ago but didn't. We went to Tibet instead, which created fewer problems. In fact, we are ready to give Tibet its autonomy as a gesture of our good faith. What gesture can you give? Leave Iraq?"

An American General raised his hand. Mr. Kisshanger, the US team leader, said: "About Iraq, General Langley is the best to answer you."

"You know why we are in Iraq," started the General. "We went to Iraq to secure our oil supplies, even if the pretexts were the so-called weapons of mass destruction beforehand and then, afterward, to liberate the Iraqis from their awful dictator and to give them democracy. We are going to be there for a long time, at least until the oil era is over, you know that Mr. Su."

"So, Mr. Kisshanger, what do you do to balance our good will, which is giving autonomy to Tibet?" Su responded. Then a tough exchange of ideas followed:

"What autonomy exactly will you give to Tibet?"

"We will allow a free elected parliament and government."

"It's already like that in Iraq. What about the Chinese military presence in Tibet?"

"It could be just a minimum. We have already integrated Tibetans into our army there."

"We have already done that through our cooperation with the Iraqi army."

"I feel we won't get too far in our bargaining. Our main concern is in fact about the economy and primarily energy. We would like you to give us free rein to develop new energy. As you know, until now we have had an underground agreement with the US and other Western countries to develop free energy technologies, but only in secret.

"However, the damage to our environment is so great that even the Olympic Games will be disturbed by CO_2 pollution. We plan to coercively stop traffic as much as possible. It'll work for a short period of time but we can't impose that restriction on driving for a long period of time.

"So, we need to allow free energy systems that we have already secretly developed in our army, as you did in yours, to be made public. We agreed with you and other nations to keep it secret so as to only use those free energy vehicles and also anti-gravity aircraft in case of domestic en masse uprisings or foreign attacks, as a surprise countermeasure that is more effective than various classical means. But to be an effective surprise, it can only be used once.

"The world's oil fields are going to be completely exhausted in thirty years anyway, you know that. It's time to be reasonable. You don't want the war, okay! Let's make peace on developing non-polluting and free energy."

Kisshanger replied:

"We can't! Develop solar panels, windmills, geothermal energy, etc. You are already good at that. You will be good at anything for that matter. Yet developing free energy is too dangerous. How do you want to control people if they have devices that give them free energy?"

"Solar panels, windmills, geothermal energy already give people energy autonomy and it's free when installed."

"Okay, but if you centralize those sources of energy, as we do with windmills, you keep the control. The problem with free energy, or over-the-unity apparatus, which produces more electricity than it consumes, is not only that the energy is free, but also that you can't construct large plants. Until now, and I don't know why, only small devices could deliver electricity. With big ones, there is too much of a loss of energy and the efficiency is not worth it."

"You can't advise us to save energy when your country has a 2/3 loss of power in its electricity grid distribution. You would lose less energy by having small units distributing electricity all over the country, as we are going to do anyway with the development of free energy devices. The Chinese people are fed up with all of these secret rules that limit their freedom."

Lee Chang Su stopped talking, then a malicious smile started to form on his face and he continued: "In fact, if you are not happy with that, wage war against us! Oh! I forgot! You don't want to do that! So… we can go to Taiwan without risk if you are not ready for waging war and defending your ally. I'm kidding. I like making fun of the Americans, and in their language! Okay! I am sorry! A bit of humor to relax everyone is sometimes necessary."

APHROMIS stopped the Akashic images from appearing on the screen and said: "Guys, I think you've got the picture. Who wants to comment on this?"

Li Pen raised his hand and said: "I didn't know that there were people in the higher levels of government who really put the well-being of our people ahead of everything else."

APHROMIS: "In high positions, you have people who care for others. And it's the case in any country, also in America. However, it's true that the Asian countries recently raised their concerns about being freer from America and taking better care of their people through mastering their economies more efficiently. But people like this Kisshanger reacted to that ultimatum after this meeting by using a secret weapon they have in Alaska called HAARP, using high frequency resonance to provoke an earthquake in response to the Chinese daring to be free from US power. The perfect weapon! For if it looks like a natural disaster, who can you blame but MOTHER EARTH?"

Li Pen: "The last earthquake was not natural? Was the big tsunami in the Indian Ocean a few years ago also triggered by the Americans?"

APHROMIS: "I don't know but the one at the beginning of 2008 in Japan was also in reprisal for the Japanese willing to be more independent from the US."

"I can't believe it," said Charles, the American from Seattle. "Our government has such a weapon and uses it to secretly force other nations to comply. Unbelievable!"

"Cunning, isn't it!" George X. Bush exclaimed. "No necessity to wage wars anymore! My namesake can withdraw our troops from Iraq and if the Iraqis don't give us the oil we need, a little sound of a harp and they comply."

APHROMIS intervened: "HAARP means High Atmosphere Activity Resonance Project. The first set of vibrations sent from the antennas in Alaska acts on the ionosphere to change it into a mirror-like surface, which reflects the second set to the ground and triggers an earthquake or disturbs the atmosphere wherever you want it to. It's enough to target the right part of the ionosphere. Hurricane Katrina was directed by HAARP to go to New Orleans. You even had the evidence of it: photographs on the Internet showing those waves, recorded by chance by a meteorological satellite. But presumably someone forced those images to be removed, for they are not there anymore."

Li Pen: "We really are like lab rats!"

APHROMIS: "It certainly appears you are, and don't count on Barack Obama, who will probably be the next President, or even on this Lee Chang Su, to really change things. They both look like nicer guys than George W. or Kisshanger, but they are both manipulated by the higher secret shadow powers. Count only on your deep relation to the Divine Within."

MATRIX: "Unlike rats, we can meditate and send good vibes to counteract the bad waves sent by the elite who effectively consider everyone else to be their personal lab rats."

APHROMIS: "The most paradoxical thing on planet Earth lies in the elite promoting their capitalist society as allowing you to live 'almost in a Paradise' compared to the so-called dark ages of the past, which had none of the comforts that technology provides now. It's the opposite that is actually true: the closer to MOTHER EARTH you are, the closer you are to Paradise. The more you trust in technology to provide you Paradise, the further away from it you are, as paradoxical as that may seem at first.

"I think we should stop this debate. As MATRIX said, everything lies in our relationship to the Divine Within through meditation. It is the only way to be aware of how things truly work on Earth, for there are more things on Earth and in Heaven than our brain can ever understand. Only our connection to the Heavens can help us absorb this understanding. Tomorrow, we'll try to comprehend the Heavens through how life exists on other planets all around the galaxy.

"However, beforehand, I want to tell you two stories. The first one is like a myth, a modern myth, actually, it is 'the' modern myth. Even if myths sometimes have a historical basis, they generally try to explain still unexplained phenomena or they try to justify certain customs or practices. They usually involve gods and heroes. Nowadays, they are considered imaginary and fictitious. Nonetheless, I'm going to tell you this modern true myth of your society that came out of my own imagination. Yet, you'll see that it fits with what we've talked about and what we've seen in the Akashic Records. It's my very own mixture of the myths of Prometheus and Sisyphus.

"The heroes are Rockefallen and Rottenchild.

"Like Prometheus stealing fire from Zeus, Rockefallen stole a precious liquid from MOTHER EARTH and used it to make fire. Then he used this fire to power vehicles that polluted people and MOTHER EARTH so much that She decided to intervene. She inspired lawmakers to put a heavy burden on him. They brought in laws that forced him to separate his assets into independent companies. Just like Sisyphus had to every day carry up a hill a huge rock that fell back down again every night, Rockefallen also had to carry up his fallen rock, that is, to rebuild his business empire, and each time he rebuilt it even more solid than the previous rock.

"After a while, he was fed up with the burden imposed on him. So he bought a super glue to stick his rock to the summit: he discovered the trick of inventing the so-called philanthropic foundation to subtly and better spread his business empire. He actually had opportunities to even make money with his foundations.

"He was helped by Rottenchild, who had made his business empire by also tricking people. With a few other friends, they decided that they were the gods. They fathered other gods: Big Business, Big Pharma, Big Agro, Big Brother, and Big Bang, the supreme god who fathered all of them. By behaving with immorality, but hiding it by controlling the media, they reached immortality. Between immorality and immortality there is only one letter T, like a cross that crucifies all other Humans.

"They thought: 'Humans accept our myths, like the Triumphant Science, the Never-Ending Progress, the Consuming-Makes-You-Happy, Freedom-but-under-our-control, Democracy-but-with-only-our-candidates, etc. Therefore, compared to us, other Humans are really stupid. So we are their gods, we are gods. Finally, we can do with them as the gods of mythology did: play with them as we wish!'

"Their final statement was: 'There is no God above us; otherwise we wouldn't be so successful at controlling people. Really, we are the only gods.'

"Actually they behaved, and are still behaving, like in the myth of Lucifer. He was the Light of God Bearer, but he finally pretended he was God, and that triggered his Fall. By being honest and true bearers of God's light, you can expose these gods and make them fall too, or better yet: don't make anyone fall, help everyone rise to divinity; tell them to recognize you, as well as themselves, as gods. Proclaim to everyone what the Bible truly says in Psalm 82:6, which Jesus quoted in John 10:34: 'Ye are gods'. I prefer to say, modernizing the claim: Ye are clones of God."

Many in the audience nodded their assent.

"The second story I would like to tell you is about secrecy, about what has been done behind your back that people generally don't believe, like man-made flying saucers or the free energy devices that have been developed and used secretly since World War II.

"In 1950, someone said: 'It won't be possible to make computers that weigh less than five tons.' Of course, with their thousands of vacuum tubes, crystal diodes, relays, resistors, capacitors and millions of hand-soldered joints, those early monster computers took up entire rooms. Now, suppose that the transistor, the micro-processor and all of the digital revolution would have been kept secret, like anti-gravity and free energy were! If somebody told you now: 'I overheard a CIA operative I know say that they have computers weighing just one pound', you would have replied: 'You were fooled, that's impossible!' It's exactly the same with Human anti-gravity saucers and over-the-unity energy producing devices!

"See you tomorrow!" APHROMIS concluded.

5- LIVING ALL AROUND THE GALAXY

APHROMIS introduced the second debate as follows:

"MATRIX and WITNESS agreed to talk about life on their planet Witma and on others they have visited. A few of us, who are living permanently at the Door of Heavens, including myself, have also lived on other planets and can give testimony about life there. We will start by asking questions of MATRIX and WITNESS."

"First," said WITNESS, "I would like to explain why we call our planet Witma. It's obvious that it comes from the contraction of WITNESS and MATRIX. It's actually in the English language. When we learned this language through our New Conditioning room, our central computer, communicating with the vibrations stored within the Spirit of Earth, translated it like that. In fact, in our language, Witma is SHISHAK because the WITNESS of the Universe is called SHI-VA and its MATRIX is called SHAKTI. Accordingly, the SUPREME WITNESS and the SUPREME MATRIX are SADA SHIVA and ADI SHAKTI from the Earth's East Indian tradition. MOTHER EARTH told me that when the three kilometer thick glaciers of the Last Glaciation started to melt 17,000 years ago, the Witmans came to Earth and were received as gods by the East Indian civilization of that time because they protected the people from massive floods. The lakes found inside glaciers in the Himalayas grew bigger and bigger, exerting so much pressure on the natural dams that they suddenly ruptured."

"Yes," APHROMIS said. "In the sacred texts of India, there are gods and goddesses traveling in 'vimanas'. The Ramayana describes a vimana as a circular aircraft with portholes and a dome, just like your spaceship is WITNESS!"

"Perhaps!" WITNESS replied. "Our present technological civilization is only a few centuries ahead of yours. However, in the past, on both Witma and Earth, there were advanced civilizations that collapsed. Probably my ancestors came here, but we lost that ancient part of our history just as you lost that part of the Golden Age that included the Atlantis civilization: it only remained for you as for us in mythological lore, for us as the Gods Age, when we were the gods of other civilizations in the galaxy. I assume the shape of our past spaceships were registered in our collective unconscious and came back into our minds when we again started to build anti-gravity devices, but I think their shape is also due to the nature of space, as the shape of cars on Earth are aerodynamic due to the penetration in the air. The 'lying saucer' shape is universal."

Jenya started the questions: "I would like to know: how many solar systems have you personally been to? And how many planets have you landed on?"

"Around thirty solar systems, maybe more, and around fifty planets," WITNESS answered. "What do you think of my numbers, MATRIX?"

"I traveled alone to two solar systems before meeting you WITNESS, and yes, we have traveled to approximately thirty solar systems and fifty planets."

"Therefore," replied Jenya, "you have lots of experiences with how people live on other planets. Can you tell us about the diversity of ways of living in the places you visited?"

"We only stayed a few local days on some planets," WITNESS answered. "So it's not the same as living a few weeks or a few months or even a few years as we now have on planet Earth. You form a different opinion when you are in a country for a vacation or for work. Nevertheless, on Witma we developed a system for learning about a planet and her inhabitants by contacting the Spirit of the planet and the Spirit of her Sun, or Suns, when there are two or three."

"And the life of people in a binary Sun or star system," added MATRIX, "is completely different from the life of people with only one Sun, as is apparently the case here on Earth. Nonetheless, I learned from Earth that the Sun has a companion, a brown dwarf star that has a long orbit of 3600 years or so around the Sun, and it behaves as a planet because it's a small star that is at the end of its life. In fact more often than not, star systems are binary. And the Sun's companion is actually going to be visible between 2016 and 2017, as it was in the time of the Babylonians who recorded its passage in the sky.

"This difference between one simple star and binary star systems doesn't only lie in the cycle of day and doesn't only lie in the cycle of day and night, which is more complex, but also because it influences the psyche of the people. It's the same as the influence of language: Chinese don't think in the same way as Anglo-Saxons do, partly because of their way of speaking and writing, or when you speak several languages, your mind is more open than if you speak only one.

"The influence of the number of stars can also be more general. For example, on Witma, like it is in fact on Earth, we have one star. So we tend to have one dominating race, or one dominating gender at any one period of time. On a binary system of stars, two races generally lead the planet, or there's more balance between the two genders. On Earth, the Moon plays the role of a second star to a certain extent, but not sufficiently enough for both genders to be in balance all of the time. So at one time matriarchy dominated, at another time patriarchy ruled. It's still the case now, but it will become more and more balanced as the dialogue with the SUPREME BEING spreads throughout the world."

"Tell us more about the relationship between genders on your planet," APHROMIS asked. "Here at the Door of Heavens, some people come from different star systems, others from Earth, and this diversity has created a real balance in our relationships. What's your way of realizing balance on Witma?"

"Balance," answered WITNESS, "is triggered through many things. On Witma, we have had only one language since time immemorial, so that favors unity and balance. Between genders, I believe relationships are more harmonious because we don't marry like on Earth and the family is not the basis of social life as it is here. You might think that this situation would trigger difficult relationships, but the opposite is true. We are not attached to a spouse or to our children. On Earth, as far as we have experienced it, the possessive way of behaving makes relationships difficult, whereas you believe the opposite to be true. When nobody is attached to anything or to anyone, relationships are more balanced and harmonious. Your love for someone is unconditional. As soon as one makes conditions for loving, one doesn't really love. You say as it were: I love you but you must be a good wife, a good mother, a good cook, etc. You have to be good, but you have to be good in the way I choose! My way is the only way. With those types of conditions, you don't love, you possess…"

Tania interrupted WITNESS: "We are conditioned since our childhood to behave like that, so we think it's the only good way. In fact, how do you experience your life as a couple, and your family life? What does it mean that you're not attached to your spouse and children?"

MATRIX intervened before WITNESS could say anything: "You're attached in detachment or detached in attachment. I will explain, otherwise you will die not knowing the meaning of my conundrum. For example, I am attached to WITNESS because I love him and live with him, but I'm detached from him having what you call an affair. Sexual intercourse and love are separate in our culture. Of course, you can unite them when you have great sex but for us you can have great sex only when you feel one with everyone. Making love with one or another doesn't make any difference as long as you have the feeling of making love with the entire population of your planet. Loving someone with the feeling that you love all of the beings of your planet is true love. When your usual partner loves someone else, that's normal, for we are all one."

"We are a long way away from that on Earth!" Tania remarked.

"Only a few years away!" WITNESS exclaimed. "Continue to meditate and to introduce people to meditating, and in 2012 many of you could be at this level of true love."

"That will be wonderful!" Igor said. "But what about bringing up children without the family unit?"

"You have this structure on Earth too!" WITNESS exclaimed.

"Where?" Igor questioned incredulously.

"In so-called under-developed countries!" WITNESS replied. "Extended families allow children to grow up harmoniously with parents, grandparents, cousins, uncles and aunties, sometimes with friends living together in one big house or in houses close together in a village, as it is in NARANI's village. It appears primitive perhaps for people in so-called developed countries, but it's a balanced way to raise children. On Witma, it's a bit different for we don't necessarily live in close settings, but we have big extended family gatherings every so often, and children can be raised for a while by grandparents or uncles and aunties, as it is on Earth in India, in Africa and in some parts of China. Yet Western people do not see it as a harmonious way to live. So go to developing countries of the world and live with them and experience it for yourself!"

Li Pen intervened: "Finally, life is very similar everywhere in the galaxy. Even here, we marry only to please our parents or the society that likes to organize everything in a certain way, but in fact we have a love life as free from convention as is possible. I am not married and love two women, discreetly. But don't tell anyone or my career would be in jeopardy!"

The audience laughed. Li Pen continued: "Actually I think there are more differences between Earthlings and Witmans regarding scientific knowledge and technology than about social life. Tell us about your science and your technology."

"Yes," answered WITNESS, "it is like day and night but it's mainly connected to our biology. For example, we eat very little for we have a metabolism that very efficiently processes nutrients. Another difference lies in filling our atmosphere with vaporized nutrients. We also have crops in the soil, but people who train themselves to eat less and less from the soil and more and more from the atmosphere can live with only what they breathe in. We can do that because our atmosphere is special. I don't think it's possible here on Earth. Nevertheless, you have a story in the Bible of the "manna" coming down from the sky, but I don't know if that could ever be permanent. Do you know, MATRIX, if it's possible?"

"Nothing is impossible!" MATRIX added, "Everything is possible with faith in the SUPREME BEING. I have heard of people in places like Australia and Germany saying they survive only by feeding on light. They call it 'prana', meaning without solid food, only drinking water and juices.

"Another difference between Earth and Witma lies in our relation to science. It is studied and practiced by everyone as their main occupation. But we are not specialized. Everybody studies and develops technologies in every domain of science. When we don't know how to orientate our experiments, we ask the SUPREME BEINGS and they provide us clues so we can progress.

"Some civilizations on Earth, like the Egyptians, the Mayas or the Incas, built their monuments because of intuitions received from their Divine Within. Actually, it's what your very few greatest scientists are doing now when they listen within. That's the main reason why our technology is a few centuries ahead of yours, but if more scientists on Earth listened to their inner intuitions, your science would progress like crazy. However, I am confident, if Earthlings continue to meditate with the SUPREME BEING, they will quickly catch up with us, even before 2147, which is the year the Time Patrol came from when we arrived at the Door of Heavens in 2003. We have succeeded in time traveling, but only in a limited way, using portals. I believe Earthlings will have done better by the middle of the 22nd century, haven't they APHROMIS?"

"I don't think so," she replied. "Ram and his Time Patrol came here because the Door of Heavens is a portal that creates links between two places or two times but through the 4th dimension, and therefore that allows travel to other times or places of the 3rd dimension. MATRIX and WITNESS, you have undertaken such travel when you arrived here, and a few times since when you've gone home to your planet Witma.

Actually, you can go to any planet in this solar system through this portal and to some planets in a few other solar systems as well. You don't need the technology of a spaceship to do that."

"To go to one place at a time, yes, you're right," WITNESS intervened, "but we also need to travel on the planet, not just to it. For example, here, when we want to go to Mars, we can use the Door of Heavens' portals, but we can travel only with our bodies. We can't move our spaceship through that kind of portal. Then when we get to Mars, we have to walk, so we are better off going there with our spaceship so we can travel much more quickly on the surface of the planet."

"There are other portals scattered around Mars," replied APHROMIS, "but they are more limited and you also have to travel from one to another on Mars or on any planet, for some are very specific, taking you only from one particular place to another particular location. It's the same for time portals!

"I went to Mars once and I sensed that Mars was a very strange place with structures built by an ancient civilization. In some parts of Mars there are areas with such strong vibrations that it's almost impossible to travel to. I don't know why, I couldn't move with my 3-D body. I could only move with my 4-D capabilities, and there were some vibrations that stopped me from traveling to certain parts of the planet, like what happens at the Door of Heavens when people who are not spiritually ready for the 4-D world cannot enter into our domain. You are right WITNESS: to travel through portals, you must do it with your 3-D body. So I couldn't go from Mars to other planets because there were no appropriate portals to do that through. However, I have sensed portals in certain locations but I wasn't able to go through them because I was too far away from them. Actually, the Door of Heavens is, as its name indicates, a multi-portal where you can travel to many places. So you can travel to a specific place on a planet and then return here in order to then go to another location on the same planet."

"When we go there tomorrow," replied WITNESS, "we can further investigate Mars with our spaceship. Our travels in the solar system will also be a good excuse to show Earthlings the capabilities of our spaceship."

"JIVALA," added APHROMIS, "who has been living here with us for years, knows where the ancient civilization on Mars traveled to."

JIVALA, who was a tall, blond man, answered:

"Yes, APHROMIS! They moved to my planet of origin, which is in the 4th planet of the star system of Alpha Phoenicis in the Earth nomenclature, 80 light-years away. The people of my planet have a legend about traveling from another planet before a gigantic meteor hit it around 15,000 Earth years ago. After a long period of time of researching throughout the galaxy, we found that the planet Mars matches the description we have in this legend about our former planet. In fact, before this upheaval happened on Mars, some people of my race settled on Earth too, and founded the civilization called Atlantis. I initially entered this solar system to conduct more research on both Mars and on the Atlantis that once existed on Earth."

MATRIX intervened: "WITNESS, maybe we can invite JIVALA to come with us, if he wants to. He could help us on our trip."

"We can actually accommodate one more person," WITNESS replied. "Would you like to come with us, JIVALA?"

"I would be very happy to if I can help you navigate on Mars," JIVALA answered.

APHROMIS intervened: "We now must end this meeting. If some of you want to continue discussing this subject tomorrow, we can continue on without our favorite Witmans and the lucky guys who get to go with them."

Many people nodded.

Someone said: "APHROMIS, you have traveled all around the galaxy. Yesterday we enjoyed your mythological story and your way of deepening our imagination. Do you have an ET myth to tell us?"

She reflected for a few seconds and then replied: "Yes, I do have one!

"Once upon a time on planet APHRO, people lived with very few needs because they received their food from trees without having to work at growing anything themselves. There was such an abundance of everything that they just had to gather it in from around their homes. Nonetheless, they manufactured various objects with a mineral that had similar properties to the plastic made on Earth. This mineral had to be mined and then transformed. There were two main races of people on APHRO and one race decided that the other race was inferior and they therefore enslaved those people for the mining and manufacturing of this mineral.

"However, after some time and much misery and fighting for their rights, the enslaved race received its freedom and slavery was abolished. Slavery was basically a tool for the rich and powerful people to have a cheap means to become richer and richer. Later, some rich and crooked people designed a plan to reinstate slavery without the people of the planet even being aware of its return. They thought: our people like to live a comfortable life and have objects in their home for decoration or to make their lives supposedly easier, even if those objects do not last too long because they are designed to deteriorate quickly.

"So a few rich people decided to give everyone a certain amount of credit for their entire life, but they had to then commit to work for them. The amount of credit differed in relation to the responsibility the person had and, once in a while, their credit line was increased. These elite people of course also controlled the entire banking system. Without even knowing it, let alone agreeing to it, the people of APHRO again became slaves to the elite and their banking system."

Someone in the audience said: "APHRO is not very much different from Earth!"

APHROMIS then dryly added: "Actually, I was summarizing, allegorically and schematically, the story of the last 5000 years on planet Earth."

6- TRAVELING ALL AROUND THE SOLAR SYSTEM

The spaceship left the Door of Heavens. The passengers accompanying MATRIX and WITNESS were NARANI, JIVALA and four of the Russians, Jenya, Tania, Inna and Igor. Two hours later, they reached Mount Shasta to pick up NEW TESLA and NEW BUDDHA, who were the friends WITNESS had talked about, and a third person, a guest of NEW TESLA. MATRIX introduced everyone to everyone. Then NEW TESLA introduced his guest:

"This is David Wilwit. He's a person I've been communicating with since my enlightenment. His website was so enlightening for me that reading it was almost like experiencing a second enlightenment. Actually, when you start allowing the Divine Light to flow within you, the ability and desire to receive more and more light and understanding never ends. He has written such amazing things about the solar system being a living being, that I invited him to be part of this amazing trip, with the agreement of WITNESS and MATRIX of course. David is also a psychic who reads people's auras."

"Welcome aboard David. Enjoy!" said MATRIX.

WITNESS and MATRIX asked their nine guests to sit in the piloting room where they briefed them about the trip. WITNESS started:

"In order to travel on a planet, guys, we use the planet's gravity energy flow grid. Here, like animals following the magnetic field, we follow the current of the Earth's energy grid. You can compare it to a grid of rivers. The energy we use for traveling comes from what you call torsion fields of the vacuum, or Zero Point Energy, and that energy exists everywhere, in any volume, even as small as a particle, even in intergalactic space. Actually, what gives energy to particles, if not to the 'substance' of space, is in fact the energy of SUPREME MATRIX."

"How do you manage the friction of the spaceship with the air?" asked Jenya.

WITNESS replied: "We use the energy that is within the molecules of the atmosphere and convert it, leaving behind us the field of the vacuum that created matter."

"It's like the conversion of matter into energy in the equation $E=MC^2$, which also explains nuclear energy," added Jenya.

"Exactly," continued WITNESS, "yet it happens at another level. The nucleus of an atom of uranium liberates its energy while splitting. Four atoms of hydrogen gathering into a helium atom liberates energy too. Those reactions happen in the 3-D world. Mass only exists in the 3-D world. The liberation of energy we use for navigating around a planet happens in the 4-D world, where light overwhelmingly dominates matter. Around a solar system, we travel through the 5-D world, and use the vibrations of that world to get the energy we need to actually be able to travel in the 3-D world. Between stars we travel through the 6-D world, and between galaxies or around the whole Cosmos, we are in the 7-D world. This ultimate trip leads you to the very limits of the Cosmos, or shall I say to its center, where SUPREME WITNESS resides. The seven dimensions of the Cosmos are the structure of SUPREME MATRIX. Some think there could be an infinite number of dimensions in an infinity of universes."

"Have you already done this trip to the center of the Universe, our Universe, WITNESS?" Jenya asked, with immense curiosity showing in his eyes.

"Physically, not yet," answered WITNESS. "You need to be spiritually ready for that. However, you don't need to do this trip physically to go there. Next time you meditate, ask SUPREME WITNESS to carry you there, and if your Spirit is ready for the experience, as I have been a few different times, you will see the entire Cosmos from the center of it! Actually, the center is everywhere and nowhere. That's the Big Paradox of the Universe!"

"Wow! As Americans say!" Jenya exclaimed. "So, all of the dimensions are entangled all over the Universe, aren't they?"

"They are, as surely as all of the particles of your body are also entangled with the whole Cosmos!" MATRIX replied.

Jenya could not say another word. Neither could the others! Nobody was able to utter anything but express amazement and wonder through their silence and the light emitting from their faces.

After a few moments, David broke the silence:

"MATRIX and WITNESS, I am pleased with what you have just said, for you have strengthened my own research. Einstein's equation $E=MC^2$ is true in a 3-D world, but you can also say $E=C^3$, or $C \times C \times C$, where the energy E of one C, which mathematically corresponds to the speed of light, is completely transformed into matter M. So the equation can be both $E=C^3$ or $E=MC^2$. In a 4-D world, it's $E=C^4$, C to the power of 4, where there is only light. As you said WITNESS, in the 3-D world there is mass, but in the 4-D one, matter is as light as light is. Light was created by God at the beginning of all time. Actually, it is written in the Bible, Genesis 1:3 if I remember correctly: 'Elohim, God, said: May there be light! And light was.' The Universe is light!"

"That's true," said Jenya, "in the domain of the Door of Heavens, light is everywhere, even at night."

"You'll see during our trip," added WITNESS, "there is only light, even through a trip in the darkness of the 3-D world between planets. Actually, our first trip to Mars will only take a few hours of Earth's time. In fact, any traveling from one planet to any other planet anywhere in a solar system takes only a few hours of Earth's time. Traveling from one star to any other star in one galaxy takes a few days. Traveling from one galaxy to any other galaxy takes a few weeks. That's because each trip takes place in a different dimensional world, where photons of light are everywhere.

"Therefore, time doesn't mean anything anymore. In fact, each trip in any dimension above the third one is instantaneous for the travellers' Spirits, but their bodies must adjust and that takes time, but only the time corresponding to time in the 3-D world."

"And even in the 3-D world!" David exclaimed. "Photons are everywhere, traveling from any and all directions to any and all directions. Your eyes perceive light only when the photons focus right at them. If a beam of photons travels in front of you from right to left, you don't see them at all. You only see them if the beam is stopped by an obstacle and reflected to your eyes. An obstacle can be composed of any matter, it can be a wall, a planet, even molecules of air. You will see a strong beam of light that is not targeted at you because the photons are reflected toward you by the air, whereas in a weak beam of light, photons go through the molecules of air without being reflected to you."

Inna asked: "What's the difference between the light and the aether or the energy of the vacuum?"

"The aether and the light," said MATRIX quickly, so as to have a chance to speak before WITNESS, "are like male and female, two parts of the same entity. We could say, what you call aether is SUPREME WITNESS and light is SUPREME MATRIX. Our SUPREME BEINGS organized everything in their image. And each dimension is nested within the superior one, but at each dimensional level it's the same. It's like your Russian dolls, Inna."

"I know," said Inna, "this concept of the dolls being inside one another is very spiritual, because it's connected, as you said, to the deep structure of the Universe."

"To come back to the numbers," said WITNESS, taking the floor again, "the speed of light is different in each dimension and the energy you receive through harnessing the light and riding it is exponential. To come back to what David said, in the 3-D world $E=C^3$, in the 4-D one $E=C^4$, but it continues on: in 5-D it's $E=C^5$, 6-D is $E=C^6$, 7-D is $E=C^7$. That's why the time to go to the center of the galaxy at speed C^7 is not that much longer than to go to the other side of your planet through the 4-D reality."

"WITNESS!" added David enthusiastically, "I knew that my formula to directly equal E and C was right. Finally, it's so simple!"

•

They had already traveled past the orbit of the Moon when, all of a sudden, the stellar objects, including the Earth, the Moon and the Sun, became invisible.

"Now we are in the 4th dimension," said WITNESS. "We transform the energy given by the light around us and give it back to the vacuum, the aether. In two hours, we'll land on Mars."

"Cydonia!" David exclaimed. "It would be wonderful if we could land in the area called Cydonia, where there are what might be called pyramids".

"And the famous so-called 'face'!" added WITNESS.

"Yes! I brought the photos from the NASA Global Surveyor mission, which anyone can see at www.malin.com. Dr. Malin is charged by NASA to take care of the photographs of Mars. With such a name, which has the same root as 'malign', I wouldn't be surprised to hear that he falsified some of the pictures."

David took a file from a briefcase that was close by him.

"Look at these photos of the face! On the photo on the left, taken from quite a distance by the space probe Viking in 1976, there is clearly the image of a face. On the photo on the right, taken at a closer distance in 1998 by Surveyor, we see more details but there is no face at all. However, some people think that the photo on the right was reprocessed by NASA, or this Dr. Malin was ordered to reprocess it, to erase the design of a face before releasing it. In fact, in NASA's haste to erase the details of what appears to be a very large artificially made huge sculpture of a face, they forgot to transform the perfectly straight left side and the perfect round top and bottom of the mound that corresponds to the parietal bone and the chin."

Everyone, one after the other, peered closely at the photo. Inna asked:

"Where is JIVALA? He could probably give us some clues about this."

"I think he went to the bathroom," answered WITNESS.

Staring at the photo, Inna noticed:

"The right side of the mound looks natural whereas the left one seems artificial. Was there a computer check done to differentiate between natural and artificial configurations?"

"Precisely," answered David, "computers analyze images and can find differences between natural and artificial shapes, and this 'face' mound has both. Actually, it's possible that the original mound is natural and was carved by a civilization of, shall we say people, but when this civilization left or died off, different natural processes damaged the right side more than the left, returning the appearance of the right part of the mound back more closely to what the original rock formation would have looked like. In various places on Earth, there have been found not quite as large rocks that had been similarly sculpted in the distant past. In addition, there are hills that were recently discovered in Bosnia and China that seem to have been artificially transformed into pyramids many, many centuries back. I assume in years to come even more such pyramids will be discovered in other locations all over the Earth.

"On Mars, there are more artificial pyramid-like structures in this area of Cydonia, a few miles away from the so-called 'face'. Another formation is called 'the fort', another is 'the city square'. Soon we will know who is right: NASA or 'foolish dreamers' who see aliens everywhere?" David concluded, while making a silly looking face.

"So," said Tania, "will we get to see the real face and all of these structures?"

"Of course!" MATRIX exclaimed.

When JIVALA came back, he looked at the photos and said:

"Ah! The famous face, built by my ancestors! NASA worked on the photo to give it a natural look, but I assure you: it doesn't look like that when you see it on Mars!"

Tania, who was an inquisitive person, replied, "If it is artificial, why didn't NASA want to reveal this fantastic discovery to the whole world? It would have made-up for NASA's many failures and they would have received much money from the politicians who at times are so miserly when funding scientific research."

"All over the world, our dear politicians think," said Jenya, in a joking voice, "that the average Human being is not ready to know that we are not alone in the Universe."

"That's why," added NEW TESLA, "the scientists who examined the Reptilian Leptan Flower, didn't accept him as being alien, on orders from the politicians I assume. And I know where those types of orders come from, from the top of the Human pyramid. At one time, I was not too far from that top. I know how they work. Yet now, I feel I am at the base of it and I really want this Human pyramid cut down to a one-story building, where everyone is equal and has the same level of importance."

"So," continued Jenya, "even if we take photos, people from NASA won't recognize their authenticity, will they? Only NASA has the means to make photos of Mars. Yet, if they are not allowed to tell the truth, they will say it's a hoax, like the report of the scientists on this TV program about the Reptilian, which was also broadcast in Russia."

"I have an idea," said David, "that will trick them and take away any doubts on authenticity. We can provide photos and videos of the pyramids, the face as well as your spaceship and us. Back on Earth it would be sufficient to display your 'flying saucer' and then let people compare it with the ship they'd see in our photos and videos."

WITNESS replied: "We'd like to keep our spaceship out of the story because we don't want it examined. We could have done that a long time ago to prove without a doubt that we are Extraterrestrials, especially after the refusal of the world's scientists to recognize the Leptans as aliens. However, we want to keep that option open until after the big shift in consciousness that will occur in 2012. Furthermore, videos can now be made with so many special effects that appear to be so close to reality. Terrestrial technology can easily do that. Rumors were even spread not too long ago that the landing on the Moon was set up in a studio. Actually, that's absurd, because in the late sixties special effects were not nearly what they are now. However, if I check the knowledge that the Spirit of Earth gave me about it, it's not clear at all."

"It's clear for me," added NEW TESLA, "for I spread those rumors about the Apollo hoax for fun to see how people would react to disinformation. It was really absurd because at the end of the sixties, as you said WITNESS, special effects were not nearly as good as they are now. Yet, all of these years later, a few websites are still trying to prove my mischievous idea to be the truth, whereas the stones that came from the Apollo missions are incontrovertibly from the Moon and not from Earth. However, there was a lie, a masquerade, which has never been uncovered. The Apollo apparatus was equipped with anti-gravity technology provided by the Leptans. After the Saturn V take off, the Apollo ship could fly through the Van Allen Belt and land on the Moon without any problems, thanks to the anti-gravity system. The Lunar Module itself was in fact also an anti-gravity vessel. That's why no dust was seen flying away whenever it landed or took off.

"Nonetheless, some pictures released from some missions were actually mixed with others shot on Earth in order to satisfy an American public that had grown fond of watching the Apollo program's pictures. That's why if you look closely, there are some shadows going in different directions on some photos. The Apollo missions were full of failures, and NASA sometimes needed to cheat in order to compensate for them.

"Apollo 18 actually had a secret mission: to look at an apparently unidentified crashed vessel which a previous crew had found while flying over it before landing. But officially, its mission was canceled, as were Apollo 19 and 20's. I have wondered though if these two missions were also secretly undertaken. By that time, the anti-gravity Apollo vessel was perfected and didn't require a Saturn V rocket for take off. Its hybrid technology, combining an anti-gravity system and a classical rocket engine, was later used in the B-2 'stealth' fighter. The anti-gravity system had to stay secret due to its obvious capabilities: speed of flight, speed of landing and use for a quick take off in some missions. Everything was top secret, unknown, unexpected, stealth, and it all gave a supreme strategic advantage should there ever be a conflict."

"I knew it!" David said. "The Americans even went to other planets with those flying saucers! It's well known in some UFO circles, but nobody believes what the ufologists say because they are ridiculed by mainstream scientists and big name journalists. Some even say that there are two million people living on Mars. We have to be careful there, they may not welcome our arrival."

"Don't worry," replied WITNESS, "I know the capabilities of those spaceships, I've seen them flying over Earth. They are quite primitive compared to ours. To come back to the subject about bringing back physical evidence of our trip to Mars, it would be enough to bring back rocks from Mars and compare them with meteorites that have landed on Earth and that Humans are virtually certain came from Mars."

"If we could find some small artifacts," proposed NEW BUDDHA, "from the old civilization that once lived there, it would be even better! JIVALA had said his ancestors once lived there."

"We'll know soon enough if small artifacts can be picked up," replied MATRIX. "When we land on Mars, we'll connect with the Spirit of that planet and ask Him to tell us where we could find such artifacts."

"Him! Is Mars masculine?" asked Tania.

"Everything is masculine or feminine, in the image of the two SUPREME BEINGS," said MATRIX.

"The Greeks even assimilated Mars into being their God of war," said Jenya.

"And everyone knows that Venus is the Goddess of love," said Inna. "How do you determine if a planet is masculine or feminine, MATRIX?"

"Through Her or His behavior at a precise period of time," answered MATRIX. "However, nothing is absolute. A star is the Witness of his planets; each of them can be a Matrix of life. Yet, a star can be feminine, a Matrix, in relation to 'Her' birthing planets. In the same way, planets can be feminine when giving birth to moons or when producing life or when very active like Venus, but can be masculine if they are barren and sterile, like Mars."

"That's not very nice to say that men are barren and sterile," said Inna. "But how did the Greeks know Mars was barren?"

"They knew about Atlantis and inherited some of the knowledge of this civilization," replied David.

"That's stupid," said Igor, "JIVALA spoke yesterday about Atlantis. I am also an archaeologist. We know about Atlantis only through what Plato wrote. The evidence proving the existence of Atlantis is very minimal. We haven't found any artifacts from Atlantis yet."

"That's not true," replied David vehemently. "Off the coast of Cuba and the Bimini Islands, at the bottom of the shallow Atlantic Ocean, there are remnants of construction, blocks aligned as a road, but nobody has investigated those sites properly yet, especially on the Great Bahama Bank and around the Greater Antilles. The Greek civilization and certainly those before it, Sumer and Egypt, cherished and kept the knowledge of Atlantis that was given to them by people who escaped from the sinking continent. We still have Portulans, maps from the Middle Ages, which show the coast of Antarctica without ice, as it was before the Egyptian civilization started. We can now see this coast with infrared images from satellites."

"Stupid!" replied Igor, "Antarctica has always been under ice."

"There is evidence that it was not always the case!" David said loudly and a bit exasperated. "During the last Ice Age, Atlantis flourished for millennia because of its latitude. The climate changes over time throughout the planet. For example, during the Middle Ages, there was a warm period with considerably fewer icebergs which allowed the Vikings from Norway to discover the northern part of America. Even they called it Greenland. Have you not ever wondered why this white land is called Greenland?"

"Guys, stop fighting!" WITNESS shouted. "We can go to the bottom of the Atlantic Ocean when we return to Earth with our ship. Now we are out of the 4th dimension. We'll soon be close to Mars. Look! On the screen! That little spot is Mars."

Everyone stared at the little white disk on the big screen in front of them. On it the size of the planet was very quickly growing bigger and bigger.

The entire screen was soon completely taken over by the image of Mars.

The spaceship, after a descent of a few minutes toward the surface of the planet, was now on top of the famous 'face', in the Cydonia area.

"Wow!" exclaimed David, "You can tell it's a face, a hill sculpted as a face looking at the stars, even if some parts are damaged. The NASA photos were transformed on purpose to make it look like a normal hill. We were right!" he shouted excitedly, raising his fist above his head. He added: "There were really guys at NASA who had the guts to do that. One small lie for man, a giant, a gigantic shame for mankind! Unbelievable! They treated us like mud! But those guys, they are the mud that prevents mankind from seeing reality as it really is."

WITNESS said, "We are shooting videos of this man-made sculpted mound with cameras from Earth that we had brought on board for later broadcasting on the Earth's TV networks. We're filming with our cameras too because of their better definition."

Jenya was amazed and commented: "It's one small mound on Mars, but for Earthlings it's a gigantic proof of ET presence. Now nobody will be able to say that it's natural."

MATRIX, who had her eyes closed, said: "I asked the planet in my mind to give me data. I visualized an apparently uninhabited place with little artificial domes close to a pyramid. Maybe they are the dwellings of the people who sculpted this face."

"They are not," said JIVALA. "I know them; they are the dwellings of people who were temporarily inhabiting Mars not so very long ago."

"Let's go there," added WITNESS. "I'll leave the video cameras running. MATRIX, can you drive our spaceship to the place of your visions?"

"Let's go!"

The ship hovered on top of a plain full of little rocks. Then they saw three pyramids on the screen.

"The one on the right," said MATRIX.

When they were close by, they saw the little domes. They landed as close as possible. Inna and Igor asked if they could investigate the closest pyramid while the others checked out the domes. WITNESS thought it was a good idea. They all put special suits on before leaving the spaceship. On their heads, they each wore a little light bubble made of some sort of transparent flexible plastic.

"Will we survive outside of the spaceship with just these light spacesuits on?" asked Inna.

"Yes," said MATRIX, "the textile isolates you completely from the hostile environment and atmosphere of Mars, giving you enough heat. The bubble lets the molecules of oxygen enter and then concentrates them for you so you have enough air to breathe. Mars' atmosphere is not rich in oxygen, but it's sufficient when concentrated by the bubble, which is actually a little plant for concentration of the oxygen and rejection of the carbon dioxide. It works basically with the same principle as fish use in the water.

As well, in each of these spacesuits, there is a device to let us communicate between each other."

"That's incredible," said David, "and these suits are so light!"

They went down in a little elevator to the ground. Then they walked over to the six domes, which were each five meters (seventeen feet) high and ten meters (thirty five feet) in diameter, made of a transparent material similar to Plexiglass.

NEW TESLA, trying to open one door said: "They're locked."

"Yes," replied MATRIX, "they're electronically locked, but watch this!"

She pressed a button on a little device she had in her hand and the door slid open on the side of the dome.

"It's a smart device that can decrypt any code," she added. "Let's look inside."

There was almost nothing in the interior of the dome, only a few objects on the floor.

"It's abandoned," said Jenya.

They gathered as many objects of different shapes and sizes as they could grab and held them in front of WITNESS' camera, to prove they were collected in this place.

"I am sure," said MATRIX, looking at something she held in her hand, "that this object is made of an alloy Humans are unable to make yet. We must test it in our spaceship."

"That could be a great piece of evidence!" exclaimed David.

While they were collecting these objects, a spacecraft landed close to theirs. Through the transparent dome, they saw the round-shaped spaceship with Humanoids exiting it by the bottom.

"Let me take the lead in our meeting with them," said WITNESS with a reassuring voice.

They walked out of the dome with their objects in their hands. When they were close enough to the other Humanoids, who also wore spacesuits, they could see Human faces as well as a few with Reptilian skin. WITNESS guessed that they were all in fact Reptilian-Human Hybrids, or skin-shifters. The ones having Reptilian skin faces were actually scared and their fear was triggering a shifting of their skin from Human to Reptilian. He also assumed that they had used the Reptilian technology to travel to Mars.

One person with a Human skin face, thus proving he was either not scared or that he was really Human, stepped forward in his bulky heavy suit.

WITNESS thought that their suits were quite primitive and that confirmed his earlier suspicions that the Leptans were less advanced technologically than the Witmans.

He then communicated with the on-board computer, with which he had been in constant contact, to learn the frequency of the communication system of these people. He received it and adjusted his partners' frequencies, as well as his own, to theirs.

He thought that it always gave you a psychological advantage to crack the technology of a potential adversary. He began to talk in English:

"Hello, I am the leader of this group, WITNESS OF THE SPLENDOR OF THE STARS, from planet Witma. What's your name?" And he pointed with his forefinger toward the person he thought was the leader of the other group, since that person was standing in front of all of them.

The perceived leader spoke back in English:

"I am Martin Aurora and I am in charge of the security in this section of Mars."

NEW TESLA intervened: "You are Hybrid; I know you Martin. I didn't know you were sent here from Earth. I am Meroveus."

The Hybrid replied: "Meroveus! I heard that you call yourself NEW TESLA now. In fact my Hybrid name given to me by the Leptans is Martin 54344 Aurora."

"You may call me as you wish. I will call you Martin. So they sent you here."

"Yes, I made a mistake on Earth, security-wise, and I was sent to this planet devoid of life as some form of punishment. Actually, there was life in the past here, but since a meteor landed on it 12,000 years ago, all life disappeared and the civilization that was living here vanished too. A few ET civilizations came from time to time, as you can see by the abandoned domes. But for now, my team and I are to guard this Cydonia area, and I have orders to allow nobody to take anything from it. So, I must ask you to put these objects back inside of the domes and I will inspect your ship and erase any video shooting you may have done of this area."

"That's a pity," said WITNESS, "because we need them. What would happen if we refuse?"

Slowly, Martin shifted to a Reptilian skin face, showing that he was scared by what WITNESS had just said.

"I know your reputation WITNESS! We receive all of the news from Earth here. I know you can overtake us with your technology. Yet, if you return to Earth with these artifacts and pictures of Cydonia, it will be evidence of my failure. So I'll again be in trouble."

"And you'll be sent to Lepta, won't you?" replied WITNESS.

"For sure! And I don't want that. I was born on Earth. I am not Leptan, but Hybrid. Facing a danger, being scared or risking a failure, I instantly take on my Reptilian appearance, as happened right now."

MATRIX intervened:

"WITNESS, on Earth we offered the Hybrids, who skin-shift like him, the opportunity to use our New Bodies room. Alas, not too many tried it on Earth. We can make the same proposition here."

"Marvelous idea, my darling MATRIX! Come to our spaceship with the other skin-shifters of your crew, and our technology will fix your problem within a few hours, giving you a permanent Human appearance."

"I can't force my soldiers, who are all Hybrids like me," replied Martin, "but I am willing to try out your technology."

The other skin-shifters were very happy with the news, for they too were fed up with their status of being caught between two species, and they also chose to try out the New Bodies room.

MATRIX and WITNESS organized everyone's turn in the special room. It took throughout the night on Mars for everyone to be changed. The next day, the six Hybrids were all done, definitely and permanently only Human. Everyone was happily chatting away while sitting in the on-board living room, all Humans now.

"Nobody will be scared by our Reptilian skin anymore!" exclaimed one of them.

Martin added: "We will now experience fear without being scared of scaring people."

Everyone laughed.

WITNESS said: "In a few years MOTHER EARTH will also skin-shift through Her magnetism and we must be prepared spiritually for that event. It will definitely solve your Hybrid psychological problems if you choose to evolve through meditation to a new awareness in order to be in harmony with this change in Earth's magnetism. Tell your still-Hybrid fellows of your physical transformation and of this spiritual shift they can also experience through the meditation we can teach you." He stopped, then added, addressing their chief, "Martin, I think we'll make you our prisoners and bring you back to Earth, so your leaders won't blame you, for they know that our technology is superior to the Leptan's. Do you agree?"

"We are so thankful for what you did, I think we'd agree to anything," replied Martin.

"How many spaceships do you have under your command for the surveillance of this area?" asked WITNESS.

"Only one!"

"Okay! I'll come with you while MATRIX will pilot ours. On the way back, we'll stop on the Moon. We also have to make video recordings of the constructions there."

"There are constructions on Europe too," said Martin.

"Europe, one of the moons of Jupiter!" David exclaimed. "So we were right! There are artifacts there too!"

"Yes! It's like these buildings on Mars," added Martin. "There are only a few abandoned buildings. We go there at times to police if somebody lands from outer space. There are a lot of other artificial constructions on Mars too, made by both Humans and Leptans. The Human ones are as recent as a few decades ago when the Leptans helped the Human race to develop anti-gravity devices."

"I have heard of that," said NEW TESLA, "but it came from the CIA, so I thought it was disinformation. The Leptans who worked with me in my base at Mount Shasta didn't tell me about that, the rascals! I even asked Flower a few times if I could travel in their flying saucers but he always refused, saying that radiation found inside their spaceships would damage the Human body."

"It's true," replied Martin. "That's why the Leptans helped to develop spaceships safe for Human physiology. However, it had to remain secret. I think it's like the ET presence: the U.S government said Humans were not ready to know the truth. However, I think the real reason was, and it still is: asserting their control of the Human population, as was the case for hiding the presence of the Leptans for millennia. You more easily control people by being secretive about your real agenda. And when secrecy is required, the more compartmentalized the information is, the better. You knew about the ET presence because you worked with them, NEW TESLA, but you didn't know about the anti-gravity devices built by the USA. Others know about the presence of Humans on Mars, but not about collaboration with the Leptans. Some know about the Apollo landing cover-up, but not about the Hybrid half-Human half-Leptan like me, etc."

David intervened, "I was completely mesmerized when I saw your skin-shifting yesterday, Martin! I suspected the presence of Humans on Mars, but there were no obvious clues."

"I didn't know anything about what all you've said, Martin, before this trip!" Jenya added. "Why did you say that the Apollo program was a cover-up? NEW TESLA told us it was half a hoax because the Americans landed on the Moon, but only with the help of the Leptan anti-gravity technology."

Martin answered: "I agree, but since its beginning, the USA organized the entire Apollo program as a cover-up for their anti-gravity spaceships."

"It's very expensive for a cover-up!" Jenya exclaimed.

"When you need to cover up a lie, you do all that is needed and spend all that is necessary to make it as perfect as possible. Yet, perfection is impossible. There are always flaws and leaks, but all the same, it was kept secret for a long time. Actually, it was not as expensive as it was said to be. A lot of the money, instead of going to NASA, went secretly and illegally to the anti-gravity space exploration program. The Apollo program consisted of building the Saturn V rockets and the Apollo apparatus, which was actually fake, for this material didn't go to the Moon on its own, but went in the anti-gravity spaceships. They set up the Apollo material on the landing sites and orchestrated the unfolding of the missions. Some tapes were already filmed on Earth. That's why a few shots look more fake than others."

"NEW TESLA had already explained that, although a bit differently!" Jenya exclaimed, "But organizing the landing on the Moon to cover up the anti-gravity program! Incredible!"

WITNESS said: "There are more things on Earth and in Heaven than you could ever imagine, Jenya! Okay, guys! We'll shoot all of the Apollo landing sites on the Moon. We can also have a little detour by Europe. A few more hours! Martin, how do you travel through the solar system? Is it by the 4th dimension?"

"Yes, of course," answered Martin. "Do you also want to shoot some secret Human and Leptan bases on Mars?"

"I have seen them on my trips on Mars," JIVALA intervened, "I have even seen an American flag at the entrance to one of the bases. Pictures of it could be part of the proof of a terrestrial presence on Mars."

"Okay! Let's go and take pictures of these places!" concluded WITNESS.

They took videos of the pyramids from many different angles so as to show their artificiality, and they especially focused on the entrance of the one that Inna and Igor had visited. Then the two vessels flew over the American base JIVALA had told them about and they used the video cameras to zoom in on the American flag but escaped quickly for an American flying saucer had already been scrambled to pursue them. However, the Witman spaceship disappeared into the 4th dimension to head to Europe.

Those constructions, which they shot, were also like little domes. Finally, they traveled to the Moon to shoot the Apollo landing sites and they were not surprised at all to again see the same kind of housing as existed on Mars and Europe. When they were walking among those constructions on Earth's natural satellite, Jenya asked:

"What is this civilization that built these domes throughout the solar system?"

Martin answered: "I was told it's an ET civilization that came a few centuries ago from the star you call Sirius, but lost contact with their mother home planet and then disappeared from the solar system because of a powerful virus they were sensitive to that killed them all."

Later, before heading back to Earth, David dared to ask: "WITNESS, or MATRIX, do you know where exactly the remnants of Atlantis are, from your contacts with MOTHER EARTH?"

MATRIX was the first to answer: "Of course, She gave us everything in one transfer."

David continued: "You said it is possible to go there with your spaceship. If we find some remnants of Atlantis, we'd be able to also show Humans that there are older, developed civilizations that succeeded on Earth before our own, as we did regarding the alien presence in the solar system." WITNESS agreed, then he said:

"Martin, can your ship go into water?"

"Yes, it is built for that too," he answered.

"Okay, let's go to Atlantis!"

"Hurray!" David exploded.

•

On top of the Atlantic Ocean, and more precisely off the coast of the Bahamas, MATRIX showed her guests lines and circles at the bottom of the shallow sea through a screen connected to the on-board computer and a device that had the capacity to see through two hundred meters (650 feet) of water like a much more sophisticated version of a man-made sonar would.

The two flying saucers dived slowly into the calm waters off of the Bimini Islands. Through their windows, they marveled at the colorful fish and plants in this tropical area. When they were fifty meters (160 feet) deep, they started to view through the video screen what seemed to be stairs.

"That's a pyramid," said David. "I have already seen photos of the same kind of steps under the Pacific Ocean near the Ryukyu Islands between Japan and Taiwan. This one must be a minimum of forty meters (130 feet) high."

The video system of MATRIX's ship could even see through the plants and corals to focus in on the stones that the pyramid was constructed of. They saw other smaller buildings, arches, columns, basically an entire city spread out over approximately four square kilometers (one square mile and a half).

JIVALA, wondered:

"Our buildings had exactly the same shapes 15,000 years ago. Our ancestors really did come here. Until now I only had contact with Atlantis through my meditations. Thank you WITNESS and MATRIX for allowing me to see these marvels of my civilization."

"You're welcome!" MATRIX and WITNESS said in unison, the voice of WITNESS coming from Martin's vessel.

Jenya asked innocently:

"If this civilization was so advanced, as Plato said, why do we only see buildings, and only buildings made of natural stones?"

David answered: "If our civilization suddenly disappeared, do you think after ten millennia you would see cars, electric poles and power plants. You would see only the remains of the concrete of our buildings; all of the rest would be decomposed and broken down. Even the concrete and the metal beams of our skyscrapers, of which we are so proud, would be broken up!

"MATRIX, can you tell with your technology the age of these buildings?"

"Yes," answered MATRIX, "but I can also determine their age by focusing on the Earth memory that is recorded in my mind. You can also do it David. You practice readings on people. You can do the same with buildings. Everyone can try it too, actually. I'll ask WITNESS and the guys of the other ship to do the same."

So everyone on both ships tried to concentrate on the age of the buildings while meditating. They received very close answers: between 12,000 and 15,000 years old.

"That's very old," exclaimed Inna.

"Yes," said David, "but it corresponds to the estimations other researchers and I made. It is said that Atlantis sank around 10,000 years B.C., or 12,000 years ago. So those buildings were at that time already perhaps three millennia old, and that corroborates with what JIVALA said about a group of his people moving from Mars to Earth."

"But, I can't believe it," said Jenya, "that period corresponds to the last Ice Age, when glaciers covered most of the continents!"

"Atlantis," David replied, "had a technology advanced enough to survive that cold period. Furthermore, at this latitude of the Bahamas, there were no glaciers."

"We must return and study this city in a much more thorough manner," said Tania.

"Our ship is at your service. I have already been taking videos for the last ten minutes," intervened MATRIX.

"MATRIX!" WITNESS said through the sound system of the ships, "we must now leave this place and go to NEW TESLA's quarters."

The Mars security team was under the control of the faction of the Leptans that was still in favor of supplanting the Humans in the long term, even after the vote on planet Lepta. Some of their leaders were still working in NEW TESLA's base. The latter convinced them not to sanction the six members of the Mars team.

This encounter with the security team on Mars was beneficial, NEW TESLA thought afterward, 'because now there are hybrid people who agreed to try to convince their fellow beings that to cooperate overtly with all of the Humans would be a more harmonious way of living than by acting secretly with only certain groups of them.'

This Mars team that benefited from the New Bodies room also agreed to use NEW TESLA's enlightenment machine.

Then, little by little, they persuaded other Hybrids to go through the same process. The snowballing effect among members of their community would convince more than half of them in just a few years. Of course, the hybrid Humans who were the highest in the hierarchy of government and Big Business were more reluctant to be "fixed" for fear of losing their power. However, their anxiety around skin-shifting spontaneously in public, even for just half a second, was so strong that some agreed to be "healed" more readily than if they only shifted in private. Yet, because they first had to go through NEW TESLA's machine for their enlightenment before fixing this physical problem, they could not go back to their cunning habits afterward.

However, in the multidimensional world of the SUPREME BEINGS, everything is as simple as the number one and as complex as infinity. Therefore, it was as simple to convert approximately half of the skin-shifters, who numbered only a few hundred thousand, and a large part of the Leptans, who numbered only several thousand, as it was infinitely complex to convince the remainder of them to convert.

As for the refusal to accept Flower as an Extraterrestrial, those people in power were more in the mood to continue the cover-ups, the secret operations and the manipulation of public opinion than the ones living in a simple and open-minded way.

In fact, they were caught up in their own trap of refusing the light. The SUPREME BEINGS couldn't help it: for creating duality they had to allow Light to have its opposite, Darkness. So beings were free to choose this other side of reality. The Human myth of Lucifer, the bearer of light, symbolizes this choice. Lucifer, within the Human psyche since time immemorial on Earth, represents the individual, the one that wants to keep the light for one's own use. However, nobody can keep the light so as to individually profit from it without sharing it. Light is for everyone.

By extension, people who keep others away from knowing Light as the working principle of the Universe, which is the body of the SUPREME BEING, act as Lucifer does and are Lucifer's disciples. It's why they created throughout the history of the Earth all of those religions with individual gods, jealous gods, vengeful gods, gods as egoistic as Humans could ever be. And when they act in this way, they reinforce the power of Darkness over Light.

They even had, throughout the centuries, practiced so-called satanic rituals, which are also based on the myth of Lucifer because they are based on the praise of those who are worthy of bearing the light while the masses are not. These practices had increased their power onto the world.

MATRIX and WITNESS knew all of this and they tried to counterbalance the power of darkness in three ways:

- First, by clowning around with the elite and their control of the world, through the Witmans' superior technological capabilities.

- Second, by telling the members of their meditation groups not to feed the bearers of the forces of darkness through the uncontrolled consumption of material goods.

- Third, by telling them to focus on the light during their meditation so as to spread light in a subtle way all over the world.

Three events in particular demonstrated in much more detail the implementation of these three ways of enlightening the world.

CHAPTER 10

CLOWNING AROUND, CONSUMING LESS AND WISER, FEEDING THE LIGHT

1- CLOWNING AROUND

A few weeks after their travels through the solar system and to Atlantis, MATRIX and WITNESS wanted to organize a television broadcast of the pictures and film taken during those travels, coupled with a live chat between the people who had been on board for the trip.

From the Door of Heavens, the team had spent three weeks contacting the major TV networks around the world to offer them the broadcast rights to the program.

The proposition was:

Are you interested in broadcasting a program for free about ET and terrestrial presence in the solar system, and about Atlantis, with pictures taken by MATRIX and WITNESS during a trip with Earthlings aboard their spaceship? Afterward, there will be a dialogue between them and several scientists. It will be a live broadcast but you cannot preview the pictures of the trip in advance except for those we'll incorporate into our advertisements.

The main US TV networks first refused for one of two reasons or both: It can't be real; it's a hoax! Or: We are not interested if we can't see the pictures beforehand. Furthermore, TV channels were so used to paying for exclusive scoops that they didn't want to air a program at the same time as the other networks, even if it was for free.

Nonetheless, they soon realized that many smaller TV channels all over the world had accepted the Witmans' offer and that they couldn't propose a program on the chosen day and time which would attract a greater audience. On the day of the first Human landing on the Moon, two-thirds of the world's population watched it. Therefore, a program about landing on Mars, on the Moon again, and then on diving beneath the ocean to the mythological Atlantis would attract even more viewers: nobody could beat that!

So, finally, some station executives changed their mind, for MATRIX and WITNESS were becoming more and more well known, and their sudden appearances on top of a lake, as if coming from nowhere, were at times being broadcast along with their meditation sessions, mainly on the Internet.

MATRIX and WITNESS' spaceship computer went to work printing fake American dollars, indistinguishable from the real ones, and they then opened a bank account with this money so that they could advertise the event in the media. The TV channels that had chosen to broadcast the program also promoted it and, as expected, the news about it snowballed.

It was decided to air the program live all over the world at the same time, 20:00 GMT, so as to create a unifying event as great as the landing on the Moon. Of course, it had to be viewed at different times of the day depending on where one was living, even at night, but for such an unexpected program, people felt it was worth staying up for. Of course, recording was an option for those who couldn't stay awake much past midnight.

MATRIX and WITNESS even clowned around and interfered with some programs, pirating, hacking into a few TV broadcasting systems, and interrupting other advertisements with their clip, where one could watch MATRIX and WITNESS saying:

"Hello everyone on planet Earth! I am MATRIX, and here is my companion WITNESS. We are from planet Witma. On September 11th, at 8 pm Greenwich time, we're going to broadcast a video of our travels around the solar system with several Earthlings. We will show pictures of the presence of Extraterrestrials and terrestrials on other planetary bodies like Mars and the Moon as well as on Jupiter's satellite, called Europe, and we'll also show pictures of Atlantis taken in the area of the Great Bahama Bank between the Bimini Islands and Cuba. This program is called "Truth Disclosed". Now here's some footage of Mars."

There then followed some short extracts of shots of the 'face', the pyramids at the Cydonia site and the domes, as well as some of Atlantis. To wrap up the clip, WITNESS said that on September 11th he'd display devices that had been found in these domes and which can make things invisible.

Finally, WITNESS concluded: "See you on September 11th! We'll be broadcasting at 8 pm, or 20:00 hours, Greenwich Time. Check your TV schedule for your own local viewing time."

Then MATRIX added: "Sorry for hacking into your favorite commercials. We now return to them but, nevertheless, don't be too influenced by them and try to buy wisely! Bye!" And as a last gift, she offered to the astounded audiences sitting in front of their TV screens a clownish smile and flutters of eyelashes.

On September 11th, their spaceship was on a geostationary orbit around the Earth, and at the scheduled time their broadcasting took over television satellites, voluntarily or by force, by imposing their own much more technologically advanced television signal. However, to avoid being located by the military and possibly destroyed, they changed their position every few minutes, while maintaining contact with the television satellite transmissions.

MATRIX was the 'mistress of ceremonies'.

"Hello everyone, I am MATRIX from planet Witma, which is a few dozen light-years away from Earth. I arrived on your planet a few years ago when my partner WITNESS and I came here for a vacation but were then enticed to stay permanently. We changed our appearance somewhat so as to appear Human. We are on board our spaceship with a few Earthlings who had joined us for a trip around your solar system. I'm going to succinctly introduce them to you and then they'll elaborate.

"First, here is my life partner, WITNESS. I met WITNESS approximately ten of your years ago on a trip to another planet in our own Witman solar system."

"And if you wish to know more about us and our planet," WITNESS added, "we wrote a book called 'Clones of God' where we explain life on our planet and our way of being and seeing the Universe as a means for the SUPREME BEING to divide ITSELF into the clones that we all are, in much the same way as your Bible says you're created in the image of God. Males on Witma, but on Earth and everywhere else too, are the witnesses of the Universe and are the clones of SUPREME WITNESS, and females are the matrices of the Cosmos and the clones of SUPREME MATRIX. Simple, isn't it!"

"Thank you WITNESS for your explanation and for the free advertisement about our book! Now here is Meroveus, who we also call NEW TESLA since he applied Tesla's ideas about energy in a very interesting fashion."

"Both of my nicknames are much too much! My real name doesn't matter. I am a simple servant of the Divine Light. Meroveus, which can also be written as Merovaeus, with an a, is the Latin name of Merowig, the grandfather of Clovis the First, who started the Frankish line of kings in Gaul in the sixth century. The legend says that Merovaeus' mother was made pregnant by a serpent, the symbol of male energy. I used my own energy for a while in very materialistic ways until the Divine Light made me aware that I am but a simple clone of it. Everyone can experience this transformation through a machine for enlightenment that I created with my team of scientists."

"Everyone is taking advantage of this program to deliver their own self-promoting ad!" MATRIX replied. "Okay! I knew how bad of a guy Meroveus was before his transformation and I can tell you that NEW TESLA is the completely opposite person since he went through his own machine! Now I introduce David Wilwit, who is an Internet researcher. David, you can advertise your site if you wish."

"Okay, it's www.divine_universe.un. I try to post on this website articles and videos about people who are not necessarily mainstream scientists but are more importantly

181

open-minded ones. I am not a scientist myself but a seeker of the truth that lies underneath everything."

Reader, you will find a reference to the website of the real person who inspired the character of David Wilwit under the 'About mixing spirituality and science' section of the Biblio-web-graphy appendix at the back of this book. His name is David Wilcock.

"Now, I introduce Jenya Mendeleev from Russia. Are you related to Dmitri Ivanovich Mendeleev, who classified the chemical elements in the famous periodic table?"

"No, MATRIX, I am not. I would like to be! He is one of my favorite scientists. With his Periodic Table of the Elements, he opened up so many doors to chemists as well as to physicists like me. I mainly study the nature of space, time, magnetism, gravity and mass."

"Our next guest: Inna Vadoyeva, is also Russian and a geologist."

"I study Earth geology as well as the geology of other planets. For the latter it has been so far through photographs but this trip throughout the solar system was infinitely more instructive for me and I thank you, MATRIX and WITNESS, for the incredible journey through the solar system that you offered us."

"You're welcome!" MATRIX continued: "There were two other Russian scientists, Tania and Igor, who joined us when we traveled through the solar system, but they couldn't be here with us today. Next, we have JIVALA, who lives in a place called the Door of Heavens in the Gobi desert."

"Originally, I am from a solar system that Earthlings call Alpha Phoenicis, about 80 light-years away. I came here to study the solar system, mainly Earth and Mars, because my ancestors had arrived on Earth at the time of Atlantis and had also lived for a while on Mars."

"Next we have Jeff or NEW BUDDHA, who went through NEW TESLA's machine and experienced a big spiritual transformation."

"Just as NEW TESLA said, my real name doesn't matter. As Buddha, I received enlightenment, but through a wonderful machine instead of through meditating under a tree. Now, as NEW TESLA told you, everyone can have this same kind of experience."

"Everyone can also experience that, as you said," MATRIX added, "through meditation, primarily by having a dialogue with the Divine Within. WITNESS and I teach the way to have that dialogue. You can also learn about it through our meditation groups located all over the world. See our Facebook page: Matrix and Witness."

"Another free ad," added WITNESS. "Yet it is free. To be connected to who you deeply are must be free. Our book can be downloaded for free too. And to finish with the introduction of our guests: here is NARANI, who showed us the way to the Door of Heavens."

"I have been living in the Gobi desert until now, and I guide people who have the desire to go further in their enlightenment experience to a special place effectively called the Door of Heavens. Yet now, I feel as if I am a girl of the world, a citizen of the Universe."

"Now," said WITNESS, "we will air the movie we made from the shots we took during our travels through the solar system and to Atlantis and we'll talk about it with our guests afterward. See you later."

•

Media sources estimated that 2.3 billion people watched the entire program live, including the movie, and subsequent polling indicated another billion people viewed recordings of it afterward. In total, half of the population of the world watched it. It was a ratings blockbuster!

The movie was fifty minutes long and included some of the discussions the team had on board the spaceship and when they were in their spacesuits on Mars. In order to make the film more interesting for the audience, MATRIX's voice-over provided commentary during the airing of the raw film footage.

Even members of the meditation groups, and those who knew through their dialogue with the SUPREME BEINGS that the world is so much more fantastic than one could ever imagine, were amazed by the pictures.

George and Felicity Thompson had organized an outside public screening in Vancouver's Stanley Park where the early miracles with the Witmans had occurred.

While viewing the pictures of the domes on Mars, Felicity said:

"The dome shape is so much easier for observing the sky with, especially with windows on the roof."

"It's why the Ancients built domes for observing the sky," added George, "and our astronomical observatories are of the same shape. In a dome-shaped structure, one can actually feel better as one is part and parcel of the heavenly spheres of the Universe."

"What amazes me is the pyramidal shape," said Ajay. "We see it on Mars as well as in Egypt and Central America. It's a shape that can create vibrating energy that benefits all living beings."

Nishi, Ajay's wife, intervened with a play on the word 'awe': "What an awesome movie, enticing people to be in awe of the Universe and to forget about the awful people of this world! I am awfully glad that they broadcast this movie!"

"Yes darling," concluded Ajay, "Awe-inspiring!"

Nonetheless, some Americans visiting Vancouver didn't share this amazement at all and tried to find flaws in the film or simply made fun of it:

"Those dudes mastered the special effects to perfection."

"Well done, but Hollywood would have made an even better movie."

"Extraterrestrials on Mars and on Earth! Why didn't Fox News tell us about that before?"

"Human beings are already living on Mars! Like hell! That's bullshit! Next episode they'll say that man visited a black hole?"

"If this is true, my grandma is ET!"

ETC! ETC!

•

"Now we can clown around with this documentary!" MATRIX said when the movie was over.

"To those who think this movie is fake, a fictional tale," added WITNESS, "we can say that some of the pictures of landings on the Moon were truly faked and it's very obvious when you view those photographs. The landings did happen, yet not with the Apollo mission's material but with anti-gravity devices that brought the Apollo material there. The American government has always wanted to keep secret that they mastered anti-gravity technology, probably in order to use it to surprise a potential attacker. So, exposing the American secretive elite, as well as other countries' secret practices, is part of the purpose of this program.

"However, I challenge anyone to find in our film the flaws that were found in some NASA pictures of the Apollo landings, especially shadows pointing in different directions."

"Especially my shadow and his!" MATRIX exclaimed, while pointing at him with one forefinger. She added, "They are like that," and she then moved her forefingers at arm's length from both sides, joining them in front of her, "going to the same point on the horizon."

"Like all shadows do, my clowning companion!" WITNESS concluded. "Now people at home, I understand that you can still be perplexed from decades of misleading or deceiving, or brainwashing I will say, by the so-called 'official' news media. However, our guests will try to show you why you must believe us. Jenya is going to show you right now the device we found inside of a dome on Mars and then he'll explain how it works."

Jenya took the device and pointed it toward his hand, and it disappeared.

"My hand just disappeared from the 3-D world but is still visible in the 4-D one. I experienced the 4-D world in the Gobi desert and I can tell you that a lot of things that seem impossible are possible there. Unless and until we change our way of thinking about the world, we'll have a limited way of grasping reality. You'll see now, when I turn the device off, my hand reappears."

"When I concentrated on these domes, where this device was found," added WITNESS, "I received information from the Spirit of Mars. Yes, all planets have a Spirit! I learned that the domes were left over from an Extraterrestrial civilization that visited

Mars a long time ago and constructed the face and the pyramids. Inna, our geologist, is going to expand on those artifacts."

"I found that the mound you saw in the pictures," said Inna, "and that is famously known as The Face, is natural, but was sculpted into a face to be seen from space. The right side is more damaged both because of erosion and because it was initially composed of more fragile rocks. This picture you now see on your screen is different from the NASA ones, which were probably tampered with prior to their release. Furthermore, you can see on this picture from NASA the straight line on the left side and the perfect curves above and below. Nature cannot make such perfect designs.

"Regarding the four pyramids, they also are too perfect to be natural. Yet, there is more to them. The scanning instruments on board our spaceship confirmed that their builders used mounds as the bases to construct them upon. They then added a material similar to concrete in order to shape each hill into a pyramid, and inside one of the pyramids we discovered halls and chambers. Here is a drawing I made of the cross section of the pyramid I ventured into."

She showed it to the camera.

"It's an approximate sketch, done with the help of the scanning device on the spaceship. We didn't have time to investigate more, but Igor and I spent half an hour in one chamber and had a wonderful experience: the concrete became transparent; we saw the entire sky above us and felt an incredible connection to it; we felt like we were part of it. These pyramids were no doubt built so that one could have a supernatural experience as we know one can experience on Earth inside of the chambers of the Great Pyramid of Egypt. However, the ones we explored on Mars are several times higher than the Egyptian pyramids. And recently, in Bosnia, a hill was discovered in the shape of a pyramid. A preliminary investigation proved that, as on Mars, this Bosnian hill was artificially transformed into a pyramid. So it's very clear, the ancient construction of pyramids is quite common everywhere."

"Thank you for your unbelievable testimony, Inna!" MATRIX enthusiastically said. "Another incredible proof of ET presence on Mars is the shot you saw in the documentary of a few Hybrids, for they are half Human and half Reptilians. Some of you will remember seeing Flower in a previous TV program. Many people didn't believe he was a full Reptilian and said it was a hoax. They will probably say the same thing about this shot! But that will be their attitude toward this entire program!

"Now, we will speak about a Human presence on Mars. JIVALA, who visited this planet several times, will tell you more about that."

"As you have seen in the movie," started JIVALA, "the Americans proudly put their flags on top of their underground bases because they assumed nobody would come there and the photos taken by NASA do not have sufficient definition to see fine details. Nonetheless, I will now show you a picture we have taken that you didn't see in the movie. In this photo you can clearly see the layout of the base. Again, nature can't create this kind of a design. You can also see the photo of the same Mars site on the Internet: 'Iwonderproduction.com', taken by NASA, but with considerably less definition."

"Thank you JIVALA," WITNESS said. "Now David will talk about the pictures you saw of Atlantis."

"They can be confirmed by virtually any team of scientists with the proper equipment that permits them to travel underneath the ocean near Bimini, a group of islands in the Bahamas, close to the Florida peninsula. Actually, a thorough investigation could have been done many years ago since it has been known for some three decades that there were blocks of some sort aligned together in the water near one of these islands. The same can be said about the unnatural shapes discovered with sonar between Cuba and Yucatan: after their discovery, nothing further was done! Yet, we dived into the Great Bahama Bank and found ruins of a city that was probably part of Atlantis and you saw in the movie. The powers that be are afraid of the implications of these types of discoveries.

"All over the world underwater cities have been found. In the ocean between Japan and Taiwan there are also remains of an old civilization, probably the Jomon, who were said to be hunter-gatherers. However, they made distinct pottery as far back as 15,000 years ago which has been found in archaeological sites not just throughout Japan, but also amazingly in South America!

"In the Gulf of Cambay, or Khambhat, in India, between Mumbai and the Kathiawar peninsula, sonar investigations again located a city, this time under the Arabian Sea.

"Specialists say that before the glaciers of the Last Glaciation melted, considerable land was part of continents or islands but is now underwater because the sea level rose 120 meters (400 feet) in but a few millennia, between 17,000 and 9,000 years ago, due to the melting of the ice. Presumably enormous lakes formed in the three kilometer-high glaciers of this time and when the natural dams that retained the water collapsed, massive floods inundated those cities. The so-called 'myth' of a Big Flood is universal and probably developed from this period of time.

"We are not the first advanced civilization to develop on Earth, but the media want us to believe that we are. However, to know about those earlier civilizations would empower us, and the elite people of the world want only to control us and to suppress any news that would make us believe, or even consider believing, that there are more wonders under the sky than we had ever dreamed possible."

"Thank you David!" MATRIX said. "Concerning wonders, NARANI is going to tell us now about the wonders of the 4th dimension."

"In the movie you just watched," started NARANI, "you didn't see any pictures of the place called the Door of Heavens, yet it's a place where people from other solar systems as well as highly spiritual Humans live in harmony, helping on a subtle level all of Humanity, and also on a more material level, for when you're spiritually ready, they welcome you there and you can then experience more about the wonders of the Spiritual World. I guide people who travel to China, my country, to find the way to this place."

"You can experience the spiritual path through many ways," added MATRIX, "and then you can find the material way to meet NARANI in China. WITNESS and I offer one spiritual way by initiating you to the dialogue with the SUPREME BEING within you, through meditation. NEW TESLA proposes another way through the use of his device."

"That's true, MATRIX!" NEW TESLA exclaimed. "And you can use it without any danger whatsoever! It's harmless! Thousands of people have already tried it, and as I was, have been transformed. You are not this body, you are not this mind, you are the reflection of the Divine Light, and this machine, which many different scientists helped me to conceive and design, emits special photons that free many other photons of light that are detained within all of your electrons. Those newly freed electrons enlighten you, as efficiently as Buddha was under his tree.

"Please look on the website the team that made this machine and I created, and find the locations in your country where centers offer for free the use of this Free-Light-Delight-Com machine. Delight for detained light and also for the delight of enlightenment. It's www.free-light-delight.com. Nonetheless, this enlightenment doesn't last too long, following it you must meditate in order to continue on with your journey of enlightenment, and MATRIX and WITNESS' programs help teach you how to go about doing that."

"So," concluded MATRIX, "we're at the end of this program, folks, and you have everything at hand to choose enlightenment or to stay in the darkness. Grab a pen and paper. You will see a listing of all of the websites we told you about on your screen at the end of this program. See you later!"

•

The next day, the media reported on this program in two main ways: ridiculing all of the impossible stuff shown in it, or marveling at it. Journalists were as keen as mustard about reporting on the event, in one way or the other. Nobody was half-warmhearted. Here are two samples from two different newspapers of those two ways of reporting about the show.

•

From the New York Sun, by Leigh Redman
WE WERE WITNESSES OF THE MATRIX: WERE YOU FOOLED?

As in the movie "The Matrix", were you fooled by the virtual reality the so-called Extraterrestrials MATRIX and WITNESS showed you? Wasn't that a good science fiction movie? How is it possible that we, Americans, have already settled on Mars

187

whereas recently it was so very difficult for NASA to escape from Earth's gravity and return with the Shuttle without any problems? If we had anti-gravity ships, we would certainly be aware of them! We would proclaim to the world how great America is!

The military didn't make any official statement. However, one of our informers from the military told us that such a program couldn't have been kept secret for two reasons. First, "Anti-gravity R & D is expensive and such a huge sum of money couldn't have been diverted without Congressional knowledge." Second, "Such a technology would have so many economic repercussions on industry that we would be crazy not to use it to improve our daily life." We of course don't see anything on the market today that uses this anti-gravity principle.

Our informer "hoped that soon we'll master anti-gravity technology, but for now the research is in its infancy."

What about the ET presence among us and on Mars? Ridiculous! They delivered us the same subterfuge as they did with Flower, the so-called Reptilian Humanoid. Well done as a hoax! But nobody believes that Extraterrestrials could be in the solar system, let alone here on Earth. Where do they hide? However, most people do quite like the notion that Extraterrestrials exist.

NASA issued a statement daring anyone to prove through the photos taken on Mars by their missions that there are incontrovertible artifacts. Anybody can see those photos by going to pds.nasa.gov, scrolling down and selecting "Planetary Photojournal" and then on that page doing "Photojournal Search" of "Cydonia".

The people who organized this fanciful and unorthodox program have a great ability to fool reasonable people like you and I, but it does not compute as a documentary. It's a good science fiction movie. That's all it is!

•

From the French newspaper, Liberté d'informer (Liberty of information), by Jean Paul Petit, who is a scientist and writer (translation by the author).

FINALLY AN INFORMATIVE PROGRAM
ABOUT DECADES OF COVER-UPS

The TV program, "Truth Disclosed", surprised many people with its information about primarily US, but also other international, government and military cover-ups.

The US has always denied having any knowledge about UFOs and there being an Extraterrestrial presence on Earth. So if MATRIX and WITNESS, the two presenters of the program, who say they are ET themselves, are right, why have the leaders of the US always wanted to hide this fact? After all, their anti-gravity technology alone would benefit the economy and the daily life of people.

My interviews with American scientists have provided me with some clues to this riddle. The military, and to a lesser degree the so-called elite, figured out that it would be more beneficial for them – but not necessarily for you – to have secret technologies available to either surprise a potential enemy or to be used only for their own private benefit. Imagine if you're one of these elite. You can travel anywhere in the world in less than two hours. And if you are a military leader and wish to secretly have troops in any country in any part of the world, the anti-gravity ship is silent and so quick that it is gone in no time. You don't risk any exposure whatsoever, for people reporting the sighting of such a UFO will be treated by the media, which you control, as crazy, or perhaps as naive, for having mistaken the object for, let's say, the planet Venus.

As for the money to finance these secret technologies, the US has lost track of billions of dollars for projects that their Congress has never even voted for. The Vice President of the USA, a few days before September 11th, 2001, was embarrassed when asked by Congress how $200 billion of the national budget didn't appear in the spending estimates. The so-called attacks on September 11th, 2001 distracted everyone from any further investigations, and at just the right time! Those billions of dollars financed secret projects, including the plan to attack the World Trade Center towers and the Pentagon and to cover it all up with scapegoats: nineteen Muslims full of hatred for America!

Through my research in Magneto Hydro Dynamics (MHD), I know that creating an anti-gravity device is possible, especially when you have a few billion dollars at your disposal. The Americans took advantage of a few more or less well documented UFO crashes to reverse-engineer their technology. They are fifty years ahead of other countries, except Russia, which during the Cold War provided money to fund their own secret military projects. China is now also catching up.

After the crash of the Soviet Union in 1991, many disillusioned Russian scientists gave information to the West about their past projects, including AJAX, which was an aircraft capable of flying at Mach 10 with rocket engines powered by MHD technology. Please read my books for more information about this project.

The Americans, through their Aurora project, did much the same. However, they accomplished so much more with their anti-gravity ships that are able to secretly travel throughout the solar system. The program "Truth Disclosed" delivered an accurate message about many of the secretive practices of the US intelligence community and their military, who even organized, according to the English language website www.serpo.org, a mission in an alien spaceship between 1965 and 1978 to another solar system, Zeta Reticuli. To this day, it remains controversial whether this program actually existed or was revealed for some sort of misleading, "disinformation" purpose.

The movie, "Close Encounters of the Third Kind", could very well have related a true story, for at the end of the film we see Earthlings boarding an alien spaceship! Hollywood has been a great vehicle for the American elite to misinform the world's population. Movies are fiction and not documentaries. If Hollywood creates a fictional story about improbable real events, in the minds of people they then can't be real events but only fictitious or science fiction! It's easy to ignore what Teilhard de Chardin said: "At the scale of the Universe, only the fantastic has a chance to be true!"

Misleading the population is the right arm of propaganda, and the US campaign of "intentional misinformation" that has been going on for decades now, since the end of World War II, equals that of the Nazi regime. It is even more cunning, for American propaganda also boldly states: "The US is the country of freedom and democracy." Those two principles cannot be further away from the truth in this country of freedom lovers who have no choice but to elect freedom controllers who are from the so-called left wing or right wing of Congress. Republicans and Democrats both favor the big corporations that finance their respective parties and then control everything. What a democracy when one can only choose between two ways of controlling and lying! Yet, make no mistake; other Western countries act in the same way, the US is only the worst! That's why more and more people are disclosing what they claim to be secret projects.

Dr. Steven Greer, who has led the "Disclosure Project" for a long time, was true in his claims. You can study his website: www.DisclosureProject.org (in English). In 2006 he published a famous book: "Hidden Truth: Forbidden Knowledge", which tells the story of his spiritual journey, his relationships with ETs, his meetings with people trying to keep the ET/UFO files secret, as well as his work on free energy issues. Dr. Greer was interviewed by the Project Camelot team and his interview, along with many others, is available on their website, www.ProjectCamelot.org, which specializes in publicizing interviews with whistle-blowers.

One can also study the website of Jean-Pierre Petit (in French), my namesake colleague, who has done research into the previously referenced MHD, among other disciplines (www.jp-petit.org) and the website of Jean-Louis Naudin (in French and in English), who is eclectic, but well known in the 'lifter' domain (www.jnaudin.free.fr). For those readers not familiar with what a 'lifter' is, it is an asymmetrical capacitor that uses high voltage to produce a thrust that will fly a light drone.

2- CONSUMING LESS AND WISER

APHROMIS had talked during the debate at the Door of Heavens about what must happen in the world if people "Consume less and wiser", and a group of people present at this meeting combined their energies to contact all of the organizations they could find, public or private, acting on that slogan. First, they created a non-profit organization called Ecoloco-op for ecol-friendly consuming, locally sharing, as a co-op. At the beginning of their efforts, they created a central website and then searched the Internet for other similar websites. To their surprise, they discovered that many existed all over the world, but primarily in isolation to each other, and so they created a list of links to them on their own website.

Of course, in the first decade of the 21st century, when one used a search engine in English, one only received a listing of English language websites. They desired to create an international website to connect together people in countries all over the world. Since the people in this group were already from all of the corners of the world, they translated their home page into an incredible sixty different languages! They then contacted the other websites and offered to work with them collectively, united against "United Big Business". And of course, when no non-profit organization existed in a locale, a local Ecoloco-op co-op was created.

At this time, when one typed into a search engine "consume less and wiser", one received links to the web pages of many companies that wanted to attract you or your business by offering their products for less and then having the audacity to say that by buying from them, you were making a wise choice. However, the Spirit of consuming less is truly about buying less in general and shopping only when you need to buy something. At its heart, it's about taking the time to wonder whether you really need the product or not. If the answer is yes, the next step is searching for the best quality of product and of course the most ecol-friendly choice. That's the "wiser" part of the process.

In fact, the Ecoloco-op co-ops started to create opportunities for people to share things rather than to buy things, locally, and also internationally. "Why buy when you can borrow?" was their motto. For a long time, many items had already been acquired like that on the basis of a rent, but not so much through sharing. Their fliers contained a message like: "Why keep books, DVDs, CDs, magazines and such on your shelves after only being used once?" One could argue that libraries and video rental shops already offered that service and the former often for free. However, when you couldn't find what you wanted at the library, and when it took months to convince the library to purchase a certain item, you bought it yourself. That's why, despite libraries existing in even small towns and villages, people still purchased many of these kinds of items.

To become a member, one could purchase a share in their local Ecoloco-op co-op for $15 (refundable like any share is if you leave the co-op) and then pay a $10 annual fee.

The co-ops offered so much more than just these kinds of items and services. They offered an opportunity to share all sorts of cultural "products", like paintings, sculptures, ornaments and other types of home decoration, all on the basis of a free rent. When you wanted to change the paintings on your walls, for example, you simply called your local co-op and received new artwork owned by other members to hang on your walls.

The central Ecoloco-op even offered to publish or release the works of author-members: books, CDs, DVDs and magazines. The authors were rewarded in an unusual way for those items were neither sold, nor lent, but something in between. Indeed, they were not sold as a book or as a DVD or CD or magazine. They were posted to a website and each time a member wanted to access them, he or she simply went to the website and downloaded them. That was it! The Ecoloco-op people had to find a way though to give the authors some sort of remuneration. That was accomplished by giving the author one dollar each time the work was accessed for the first time by a member. The funding was realized through membership fees, and the fee was higher if you wanted to use this kind of service than as a simple member of Ecoloco-op, either as an author or as a borrower. Of course, you also needed to be connected to the Internet in one way or another, and for that privilege you paid fees, whereas connecting to the world could be as free as breathing the air.

In this library there was a special section called "Inner dialogues of clones of God". Members who wrote down their dialogues with the SUPREME BEING could publish them either as e-books or audio-e-books or as extracts in e-magazines or even as videos to be downloaded. The latter were plays or stories where the characters were talking with God, **as in this novel you are reading, dear reader.**

Some local co-ops also offered meetings and workshops for members to help each other do all sorts of things like fix one's car, get information on how to improve the efficiency of one's engine, how to pollute less, how to transform a car with an internal combustion engine into an electrical one, and so much more.

George and Felicity Thompson, who were very active in the Vancouver area, even offered carpooling with an original modus operandi: once you were a member of their co-op, you received a membership card, a fluorescent green jacket with Ecoloco-op written on it to wear when you were a pedestrian on walkways, wanting a ride, and a flag on a little flexible metal bar to hook to your car window when you were driving to indicate you were available to pick up someone walking and wearing a green jacket. The rules were that the driver must be able to stop safely for picking up people and the person being picked up of course had the right to refuse to get into any car if she or he felt uncomfortable about the situation. Simple!

Of course, at the beginning there were not too many members, but after two years, thanks to the "snowball effect", they reached a membership of 20,000, one percent of the Metro Vancouver area. So statistically, you had to watch 100 cars on average drive by you before you saw a co-op member with a green flagged car. On a busy street, you normally waited some five to ten minutes. In the municipality of Surrey, in the Vancouver suburbs, the city council even helped with the promotion of the co-op's car-pooling program.

Other decentralized Ecoloco-op groups picked up on the idea, which then spread like wildfire throughout the world. Stealing, or shall we say "sharing" or "borrowing", the ideas of other local sections of Ecoloco-op was encouraged. Nothing was patented, as the GMO business had tried to do with life. How with any integrity can you patent ideas that save the planet?

In some co-ops, people helped each other grow their own fruits and vegetables by sharing seeds and also their knowledge of gardening, from working the soil to composting, from knowing the correct time to sow to knowing which plants thrive being planted close together, and of course by sharing their harvest.

Sharing everything was the motto of Ecoloco-ops.

When you give free rein to your imagination, to your natural ingenuity, to your intuitive inventiveness, they will run like wild and crazy horses.

At the beginning, a few co-ops even tried to compete with Big Pharma, promoting natural cures, but not homeopathy, which had been exploited by some pharmaceutical companies for profit above all, even if this type of healing demanded more responsibility from their users. They brought together all of the little known but effective ways of curing all sorts of diseases and ailments including cancer, malaria, arthritis, even obesity. Yet, when a cure is simple, natural and can't be patented, Big Pharma has no interest. Curing is actually considered bad for business!

Here is but one incredible story that co-op members wanted to make widely known to assist in the distribution of a miraculous healing product.

Jim Humble discovered solely by chance a way to cure malaria and many other diseases through what he called Miracle Mineral Supplement (MMS), which simply is $NaClO_2$ (sodium chlorite dioxide, not to be confused with $NaCl$, which is sodium chloride, better known as table salt). This product had been used for ages by adding an acid to remove the sodium, thus making ClO_2 (chlorine dioxide). It was used to disinfect water by killing the bad germs without producing any of the side effects of chlorine/bleach (the solution of $NaClO$, sodium hypochlorite).

However, Big Pharma never tested it on people. Jim did, and successfully. Most likely, Big Pharma did test ClO_2 (chlorine dioxide) on people but didn't publish the results because: How can they make money with a product everyone can either buy or easily make themselves? It's like wanting to make a considerable profit on natural products such as sodium hypochlorite. Impossible!

ClO_2 is made with $NaClO_2$ (sodium chlorite, with two atoms of oxygen instead of the one atom in $NaClO$), to which one adds a mild acid like acetic acid (naturally diluted in vinegar) or citric acid (naturally diluted in lemon) in order to remove the sodium (Na). It is that second atom of oxygen that is the difference between sodium chlorite and sodium hypochlorite, because it is in an ionized form that attracts electrons. But guess what? Pathogens (bad bacterium, viruses, protozoa, bad yeasts and fungi) have by their very nature free electrons on their peripheral molecules. Therefore, the chlorine dioxide ion catches them (up to five electrons per ion) and thus destroys those molecules that are essential for the germs, like a mini explosion. Luckily by nature, only the pathogens have free electrons to give, not the "good" cells.

As time passed, more and more co-ops also offered this MMS, which cost $20 for a 4 Oz bottle that would last one year or more. This Miracle Mineral Supplement was truly the panacea for it cured so many different diseases effectively and, unlike pharmaceutical drugs, without side effects. When co-op members offered their services, they would also promote this product, although it had not been approved by various national drug administrations. It was actually sold as a water purification solution of 22.4% sodium chlorite.

It was so easy to use! And at the beginning of the 21st century, who didn't know someone sick among their acquaintances? Alas, following decade after decade of people consuming more and more processed junk food and taking drugs with so many complicated side effects, combined with the Food Industry Giants making life miserable for organic producers and Big Pharma fighting against virtually any type of natural healing, how could healthy people be in the majority? Accordingly, these bottles sold like crazy. Members of co-ops even taught people how to make sodium chlorite at home. Jim Humble generously gave permission for people to make their own MMS and use the formula/recipe in his book "Breakthrough: the Miracle Mineral Supplement of the 21st Century". Foreseeing his own possible death or a threat to his person, he wrote in his book:

"Possible Cancellation of Copyright: In the event of the death of the Author for any reason, or detention of the author for any reason for more than 60 days during any 6 month period, or if the Author is missing for a period of more than 60 days after reported as missing to a police station in the state of Nevada, the copyright 2006 by the Author, Jim V. Humble, is canceled and this book becomes public domain. In addition, the Author grants permission to any person, or group, or entity to distribute this book free or for profit throughout the world should any of the conditions mentioned in this paragraph come about."

•

Actually, reader, the first 130 pages of this 280 page book along with an index corresponding to those pages can be downloaded from this website: www.miraclemineral.org/part1.php.

Jim Humble and his team had to be officially registered as a religious entity to prevent problems with the health authorities in different countries and the official name is Genesis II, Church of Health & Healing. Please read the critical article of CBC News at: http://www.cbc.ca/news/world/fifth-estate-mms-1.3474474 and compare it to what is written above.

One can find a non-exhaustive list of other useful websites about how to heal naturally and how to consume less and wiser, as well as different ways of cooperation, at the end of the book you are reading.

3- FEEDING THE LIGHT

You are perhaps wondering why I, as the writer, intervened in bold above and now here, as I do once in a while. I could give my opinion about anything within the story of the novel, indirectly, as I have been doing all along, in the dialogues or in the wandering adventures of the characters. Nevertheless, that's not the same. And here is where I would like to clarify.

You may have wondered: "Does Jim Humble, or any other character in the novel, actually exist in 'real life'?" Or was I inspired by someone real and transformed that person into a character? Or does s/he completely come from my imagination? Where does fiction start and where does "reality" end? Stop wondering! Stop the wanderings of your thoughts! Nothing in life is clear-cut. In fact, everything is clear-cut within your mind, as a clone of God, for everything is within God's Mind, and a clone is identical to the original.

However, I will provide you with a clear and drastic statement: Jim Humble is 100% real, as are Jasmuheen, Vladimir Megré and Michael Werner, all of whom you will read about in the next sub-chapter. David Wilwit was inspired by a real person, as well as Dennis Muccinich, who you will also read about in the next chapter. Other people are from my imagination, but you will never know if more or less unconsciously I was inspired by real people. The same can be said for the events and realities of our world that are described in this novel.

The following story about feeding the light has much to do with real people, let's say: 95%!

•

How can one feed the light?

By focusing on enlightening thoughts and deeds!

Therefore, MATRIX and WITNESS helped people do just that, for when you have an inner dialogue with the SUPREME SELF within yourself, you feed the light within but also indirectly the UNIVERSAL LIGHT without, which is everywhere. You thus help other people feel and then feed their own Light, especially when you send enlightened thoughts to other people. Actually, you feed yourself from the DIVINE LIGHT and return it. You reflect it. As a Human being, as a clone of the SUPREME LIGHT, you are a reflector, a mirror, yet a special one, especially when you reflect the Light by adding your own personal 'touch'.

There already were, in the beginning of the 21st century, many people feeding the Light through different means, whether through Yoga, mystic religious practices, meditation or charismatic devotion to a cause. Yet, there were also more and more people who physically fed themselves from Light. There have always been mystics among us who eat nothing, but, at the beginning of the 21st century, apparently because of the positioning of our solar system in the galaxy, more and more ordinary Human beings could also so exist. And when you physically feed yourself from the Light, you effectively reflect this Light toward others around you and you also make a significant impact throughout your world.

An Australian lady named Jasmuheen received inspiration to feed herself through the energy emitted by the Light that is within everything. For Light does not only come primarily from the Sun, with a little from the other stars, but It also is found within the particles of atoms, and in fact this subtle Light, as we have already seen, gives energy to particles, allowing particles to simply "exist". This lady followed her inspiration. She stopped eating, and instead, only drank water and juices. She experienced being fed by this Light, this energy that is in the air you breathe, the smell you smell, the sounds you hear, the things you see, the people you touch, the thoughts you have, the deeds you do and that the Yoga tradition calls Prana or Param-Chaitanya. The Chinese have named it Tao, the Greeks Eather, and some modern physicists Zero Point Energy.

It has always been known through those traditions, and many others, that simply focusing on this energy within everything feeds you and allows you to be able to stop eating. Of course, our Human addiction to food and the judgment of people ("he has a craze but he will get over it") are the principle obstacles to receiving life and nourishment from Light alone. Many Australians began experimenting with this experience in the 1990s through a three week protocol and in time people from all over the world latched onto Jasmuheen's idea. In particular, a German chemist named Michael Werner, was even monitored for ten days by a scientific team in a hospital that was completely isolated from the outside world in order to confirm that he was only feeding himself with fruit juices. Nonetheless, although eating no solid foods, he regularly exercised inside his hospital room.

The medical team obviously couldn't believe their eyes. For them, it was impossible to not lose weight while daily feeding yourself with only a liter or two of water and pure fruit juices and exercising half an hour per day on a bodybuilding device. Michael lost much weight at the beginning of his experiment, several years before his hospital stay, but after some time his weight stabilized and remained constant for many years.

If it is impossible for scientists to understand or explain, it is often discarded into the garbage called "para-science". Nevertheless, Nicholas von der Flüe, a Swiss national of the 15th century, lived as a hermit and didn't take any nourishment between the ages of 50 and 70. More recently, Therese Neumann of Konnersreuth, Bavaria, born in 1898, stopped eating and drinking, except for the daily swallowing of one small consecrated wafer, from 1926 until her death in 1962. In 2003, Prahlad Jani, an East Indian, was monitored by a hospital also for ten days. He did not eat or drink anything. He did not pass any urine. He claims that he has neither eaten nor drunk for the last 65 years.

Nevertheless, at the beginning of the 21st century, there were 'natural forces' at work that allowed 'ordinary' people to stop eating and instead be sustained with life from the energy of Light. Michael Werner, in his book 'Life from Light', gave reports from people who had undertaken to live from Light. He even coached some of them during the three-week protocol that one should begin with. Some failed to continue and for a variety of reasons started eating again, but they affirmed that they were certain they would practice this protocol again at a later date.

•

I twice attempted to stop eating and to only drink water and juices through this protocol. Twice I failed. Nonetheless, I feel that I will try again as many times as is necessary and that at last I will succeed too.

I am going to share now another way to feed yourself from the Light without ceasing to eat and which is therefore considerably easier. Actually, this practice is connected to the inner dialogue with the Divine and it is even a good way to begin such a dialogue.

This simple way helps you to stop thinking. Meditation is the way to do that, that is, to be in a thoughtless awareness that permits you to then be in the right state to allow the expression of Divine Thoughts and therefore the start of a dialogue. In fact, you do not stop thinking but you do stop the wandering of your thoughts and that in itself is not an easy accomplishment at the start, for it does not last long: the thoughts will start again, I mean, the ego's thoughts, the thoughts of this part of you that feels separate from the Whole, from the Divine Ego That Is Everything. And one thought leads to another and to another until you don't know why you are thinking of something; you don't know what triggered this succession of thoughts that led to that precise thought: one idea leading to another without your conscious knowledge.

The general principle lies in being aware of the wandering of your thoughts, and then in deciding to stop this wandering and to focus on something else and sticking with it.

For example, you can decide to know what the previous thought was, the one that led to the thought you had when you decided to stop the wandering, and the previous one, and the one before that, etc. However, when your thoughts start to again wander, you must decide to stop thinking again.

Another example: when you wake up, you begin automatically to think. When you are aware of that, you can decide to stop your last thought and focus on your body for a few seconds or for a few minutes. You can even make your attention "wander" along your body from your feet to your head. Then, when you feel "bored" by that, focus on something else, for example, the light coming from outside, or the air you breathe. The trick lies in diverting your attention from the wandering thoughts of your ego and to focus first on something simple but that you have decided, at that moment, to focus on. I very often simply focus on the top of my head, on the "Sahasrara chakra", or on the palms of my hands, which this chakra has a connection to. A cool breeze can be felt there. However, one can also focus on something outside of oneself, but do be aware of one's connection with it.

In this state of your awareness, diverted from your wandering thoughts, you can begin to focus on what the Divine Within has to say. It might simply be: "What a Divine Day today, Michael!" or "Look, Michael, there is a spot free over there to park your car!" or "Do you realize that the most important person is the person in front of you now?" or "What a special moment, now!" or "You are not of this mind, you are the Spirit." Etc. Then, when you become used to it, you can start a dialogue within the Self, this deeper Self of yourself, which can be called: God, or the "Clone of God" part of you, if you are not yet ready to call yourself God.

However, to be successful in stopping the wandering of your thoughts, starting this inner dialogue, and shifting your attention from your ego to God's, the trick lies in:

Counting the times you stop the wandering of your thoughts during the day.

You may ask: What does counting have to do with spiritual awareness? I have already told you, it's a trick, only a trick, and when your whole day becomes one inner dialogue, it won't be necessary to count anymore.

Until you're at this point, you will have to practice and count. I bet you that the first day, you won't go over twenty. If you do, you would have done better than my first day, and why not? However, before getting over fifty, you will have to progress bit by bit, day by day.

Then you can commence a separate counting: the number of times you stay in this thoughtless awareness for more than five minutes. If you extend it more it could become a time for a real meditation when you are deep in thoughtless awareness. If you don't already have a set meditation time when you can be in this state for around twenty to thirty minutes, morning and evening, decide to practice it: meditate, that is, stop the wanderings of your thoughts and start a dialogue within. The best method lies in practicing it as often as possible all day long, even if for just a few seconds at a time.

Yet, don't make me wrong: as it was said before in this novel, you don't hear God in your mind as though you were having a telephone conversation. You secrete both parts of the dialogue. You are both a clone of God and God at the same time. Remember: a clone is identical to its original. If you feel it's like a multiple-personality disorder or schizophrenia to be yourself speaking with your Self, forget this silly way of putting pejorative stickers on practices that are not following the mainstream of society: you are not only this body or this mind, you are the Spirit before all, a clone of God.

Again, another trick:

You can start the conversation doing both parts of the dialogue: yours and God's. The less you think, the more spontaneous the words will be and the greater the dialogue will be too…

…Until you are really convinced you are speaking with God. Really, God takes Her turn 'instead' of your pretending that you speak for Her, don't You GOD, SUPREME BEING?

…

I like when My clones play pretend Me talking with them. For, as you said, after a little while I like to surreptitiously 'enter' into the play and act as MySelf instead of your pretend acting as Me. The Universe is actually a gigantic stage and everything is a giant play! Furthermore, 'enter' and 'instead' mean nothing, for I am the Play, I am also your pretending, I am everyone and everything! And before all, I am the Light that feeds everything that I am. By being My talking with Me, you are the Light too. You feed your being with the Divine Light and you beam with light all around and feed others with your Light!

CHAPTER 11
SPIRITUAL ODYSSEY

1- REAL DEMOCRACY ODYSSEY

The years prior to 2012 were really an odyssey and spiritual journey for the whole of Human kind. The forecast reversal of the magnetic poles and the spiritual shift in Human consciousness that it would trigger appeared to be a marvelous prophecy. However, this upheaval in Human awareness could not be automatic. People had to be prepared through an inner dialogue, one way or another. MATRIX and WITNESS had offered one. NEW TESLA proposed another and even if his method looked easier, people still had to make the effort to travel to where one of his devices was located. But then, they were advised to go to meditation groups and practice the dialogue with the SUPREME BEING so as to continue feeding their inner light, because NEW BUDDHA and NEW TESLA had experienced that if they didn't meditate, their inner light would progressively recede and the enlightening device couldn't do anything to recharge them again. Going within and having an inner dialogue was necessary!

At times, this inner dialogue had to specifically be with MOTHER EARTH. She reminded people during their meditations that, in the past, magnetic shifts had triggered violent physical upheavals and killed many people. She told them that if they listened carefully to Her, she would tell them, individually, where to be so as to avoid being killed or injured when the rough times came.

MATRIX and WITNESS also had to be successful in converting as many people as possible to this inner dialogue in order to succeed in uniting the dimensions of space with time. They sensed deep inside themselves that the destinies of Human Kind and theirs were intricately connected.

However, the vast majority of people in 2008 refused to believe that this big shift was coming in 2012. Their arguments were simple: It's not the first time that prophets have announced the imminent end of times, or end of the world, complete with many apocalyptic catastrophes. At the time of Christ, or before the year 1000, and at plenty of other times that are lesser known, the end was deemed near. And even Hollywood and her movies will not have the final word in predicting when bad times will come. Yet, fiction is fiction!

The reality was that the Apocalypse of Saint John, the Mayan calendar, Nostradamus' prophecies, and many lesser known traditions, all pointed to the same time: the beginning of the 21st century. The Mayas were even more precise: on the 21st day of December, 2012. However, according to the non-believers, all of these predictions were only feeding the believers.

Natural disasters, tsunamis, hurricanes and earthquakes were presented as mini apocalypses forewarning of the big one. Yet, with good insurance and a good weather forecast, everything was fine for the non-believers. Even earthquakes were now predicted accurately by simply better observing the warning signs displayed in the behavior of animals. They advertised that "Science and Insurance are the two nipples of life".

The debate was fierce.

However, one political event did tell the world that the spiritual shift was on its way. This spiritual and political upheaval was embodied in a person who was already one of the candidates at the Democratic Party Convention for the 2004 American Presidential election: Dennis Muccinich. For his first campaign for President, he learned much although he was unsuccessful at winning the Democratic nomination. This first try for the Oval Office taught him not to make the same mistakes again. The main one being that he didn't make himself known enough. Of course, money is the first key to being elected. A broad base of supporters is the second one. However, if you don't have an esoteric, underground support network, you can't win any election in any country, and especially not in America.

In this most powerful country of the world since the dismantlement of the USSR, most of the Presidents and their opponents, since George Washington, were either Free Masons or descendants of a royal family or heir to a major corporation or two or even all three of them. Dennis was none of them, and that was a significant handicap and an impossible challenge.

However, Dennis became aware of that "handicap" during his first campaign for the Democratic Party nomination for President. As a spiritual person himself, he found that the only esoteric or spiritual support he could get was from people in organizations that were not entrenched in the past, but open-minded people who could help him at a subtle level with meditation, prayer, or any spiritual practice that respects the personality of the others. Free Masons were once like that in centuries past, but when they succeeded in gaining power during two revolutions, the French and the American, they did not want to lose it. So instead they lost their open-mindedness and their listening to people at the base of society; they only pretended to be open-minded and to care.

These influential people were entrenched at every level of leadership in society. It was difficult for any candidate of the Democrats or the Republicans to escape from their seizure of everything in society, especially on the wheels of the primary system of designating the candidate of each party. If you were independent of both parties, trying to win the presidency was virtually impossible.

However, Dennis Muccinich got so much popular support, including financially, that he continued his campaign after not being designated as the Democratic candidate. He primarily addressed many spiritual organizations. They responded positively to him both domestically in the United States and internationally in nations around the world. People who lived outside of the States realized that if they could help an open-minded person counterbalance the twisted political power of the most powerful nation on Earth, it would have a huge influence upon the entire world as it journeys on the way to more harmony.

Barack Obama's charisma overshadowed Dennis' underground campaign, financially and philosophically. People at the base of society didn't know that Obama was also backed up by the elite, and many sent his campaign small donations. Yet, very quickly after his election, they were disappointed by the President's handling of politics in the exact same fashion of his predecessors: follow the elite's agenda!

Dennis also received little amounts of money from so-called 'simple' people, whereas money for election campaigns usually comes from big companies with a big interest in having a President or a member of Congress, either in the House or Senate, favoring Big Business. For the elite at the top of the financial pyramid, people at the base are only good for gluing posters on lamp posts!

Yet those simple people supported Dennis in many ways. Not only were they giving money, but they were also talking to people, meditating in little groups to send positive vibes, forwarding campaign emails to friends and relatives, etc.

However, after the evidence of an Extraterrestrial presence on Earth and in the solar system, and of the secret American presence on Mars and the Moon, the cunning elite had to reduce their ambitions. The American people liked Dennis Muccinich for his support of the evidence produced by MATRIX and WITNESS about these secret operations. He took advantage of the general public's indignation at these cover-ups. He exposed people working in secrecy and then forgave them at the same time.

He was not the official candidate of any party or even an official independent candidate. However, he was campaigning as if he were a candidate. The official candidates tried to ignore him but people were paying so much attention to him on TV and Internet programs and at public meetings that he was difficult to ignore. He was firm and open-minded in his talks but he waited until the last day of the Presidential campaign of

2008 to kill the "Beast" in the way Native Indians did when they killed an animal: asking for its forgiveness. It was a real performance, what would become a talk as historical as the Founding Fathers' Declaration of Independence or Kennedy's 'The President and the Press' talk or Martin Luther King's 'I have a dream' or Michael Moore's chapter entitled 'A Liberal Paradise' in his book "Dude, Where's My Country?" In fact, Dennis plagiarized them all a bit! The talk was known as 'My dream for Americans'.

He bought time for his own TV broadcast on an independent US channel. You perhaps haven't heard of it because the mainstream media, owned by the elite, were ordered not to rebroadcast it or to even report on it. Here is a transcript of his address:

"I was not nominated as the candidate of the Democrats in 2008, as in 2004, because I am not financed by Big Business. I literally had no chance. However, I am fortunate because I have a dream for Americans. But who would like to finance a dream? You would, and you have done it, you, the people!

"My dream for Americans lies in Jesus' dream: love your enemies. I would like this dream to be realized, and not just be words that disappear into the night following this broadcast.

"My dream for Americans lies in reconciling everyone.

"My dream for Americans lies in loving the enemies of the past and of the present, for it is the only way to have no enemies in the future. For two centuries, Presidents have made you believe in enemies, for they thought it was the best way to unite you, even if they had to lie to you. The bigger the lie, the more we believed in it.

"My dream for Americans lies in recognizing the lies and forgiving the liar.

"My dream for Americans lies in recognizing the lies about our so-called enemies, and forgiving everyone: liars and enemies.

"Forgive those who lied to you about Pearl Harbor. They knew we were going to be attacked. They let the enemy do it in order to force us, the people, to accept our country going to war. Forgive the liars and forgive the enemies.

"Forgive those who lied to you about Hiroshima and Nagasaki, telling you that the atomic bomb would prevent thousands of Americans from dying on a foreign land. They didn't tell you that the enemy was ready to surrender. They wanted to experiment with their bomb on civilians in a so-called 'real' war situation. When kids or warmongers have a toy, they want to play with it, and for the Generals, the cities of our enemies are no more than anthills are for kids to hit with their sticks."

At this time in his talk, the sound suddenly stopped. One could no longer hear Dennis' voice. It was interrupted for 'security reasons' the TV channel said later. The elite was certainly scared and they intervened for they 'somehow' controlled all of the TV channels. Nevertheless, people were able to watch – and listen to – the entire talk on the Internet. So here is the continuation of Dennis' talk:

"I am sorry for the interruption of the airing of my talk that happened two weeks ago. It was done on purpose. That shows you how powerful the control of the elite is and how scared they become when someone tells the truth. I ask you to forgive them. Fortunately, MATRIX and WITNESS, the two ETs everyone now knows, hacked into the Internet and allowed me to finish my speech. Here it is:

"Forgive those who lied to you about John F. Kennedy's assassination. It was a plot: several bullets from different directions entered the President's body and also hit Texas governor John Connally. More bullets hit the car, the concrete and the public, which you have never heard of: thirteen in total! All fired by one person, Lee Harvey Oswald, and all fired in a very few seconds! It was already difficult for him to fire the official three, according to the Official Commission. But only one, the so-called Magic Bullet, entered John F. Kennedy's body then exited and hit the governor's.

"Forgive the liars and forgive the plotters-assassins.

"Forgive those who lied to you about 9/11, Osama bin Laden had nothing to do with September 11th, 2001. Open your eyes. Look at the videos of the twin towers that collapsed. Look at them with a controlled demolition expert. Show him the collapse of World Trade Center tower 7, without telling him it is that tower, and he will tell you it's a controlled demolition. Yet, no plane crashed into it. Even the owner of the tower said the next day in an interview that on September 11th it was decided for security reasons to pull it down. He blundered, for it takes weeks to organize a controlled demolition of a 47-story building.

"Forgive that liar and all of the others. However, he probably knew that it was done with powerful vibrations sent by a secret apparatus and not through explosives. Dr. Judy Wood, physicist, wrote a book pointing to that kind of evidence in 'Where Did the Towers Go?'

"Forgive the lies about the Pentagon, which had no wreckage of a plane on its lawn and too small of a hole in its exterior wall. It couldn't have been made by an airliner, whose pilot would have had to execute, in relation to the approach of the building, a maneuver that would be considered difficult for even an experienced pilot.

"Forgive those who lied to you about the crash into the Pentagon: some people believe the Pentagon was probably hit by a missile.

"Forgive the lies about the crash in Pennsylvania. There were only a few small pieces of wreckage and a little hole at that site. See the pictures on the Internet. There is nothing there that is similar to other accidental plane crashes.

"Forgive the lies and forgive the liars. Nobody would like to believe it! It can't be true! The people who rule us can't have planned 9/11! Therefore it's impossible! It was impossible that they lied to us about the ET presence, about our use of anti-gravity spaceships and about our colonization of Mars. The two people from planet Witma gave us the incontrovertible evidence about all of that. As our rulers did with the Witmans'

TV program, tomorrow they will tell you other lies regarding this talk I am delivering tonight, trying to escape from their previous lies.

"Forgive them for they don't know, for now, another way of being, and one day they will ask to be forgiven because of your power of forgiveness and compassion.

"I could stay here the whole night telling you about the lies of Americans lying to other Americans for two entire centuries. They lied for your wellness of course! They lied when what they said was good for you or for the whole world, but it was really only good for their own well-being and mainly to make their wallets bigger and bigger! The most antidemocratic nation is the one that permits a few to impose their rule over all of the others in secret ways, making the average citizen believe they are in a democratic country and that everything is under the people's control. Let us now be the light of democracy to the world, not by showing off like the so-called elite has been doing for ages, but by showing forgiveness as only the people at the base of a society can do.

"My dream for Americans lies in their being proud of their citizenship, and not being afraid to go abroad to countries where a very few people from our country did so much harm.

"My dream for Americans lies in being welcomed by people all over the world, people who will recognize the light of forgiveness in our eyes: by us forgiving those who abused our trust and by us asking the citizens of other nations to forgive the American people for what our liars have done in the past.

"Forgive those who demanded increased security, secrecy, censorship and concealment as a means to expand their power and control.

"My dream for Americans lies in more security through less secrecy.

"My dream for Americans lies in the freedom of information, but not that of pretending to be free to say anything only if it serves your own interest and then denying this right to all others that do not share your values.

"My dream for Americans lies in the plurality of information, even that of our previous so-called enemies. Through the Internet, we have that plurality: our military generously gave their older network of satellites to create it, yet it was created in order to better control everyone by spying on the information being conveyed through this incredible medium. Forgive the people who use it for spying, or for planning conspiracies with coded messages, or for practicing immoral activities.

"However, what exactly is moral? What exactly is immoral? Is it moral to kill people little by little through the sale of cancer-giving cigarettes or the sale of junk food or the polluting of the air they breathe?

"Is it moral to kill because you have the permission of your government in warfare and then immoral to practice compassionate euthanasia or therapeutic abortion?

"My dream for Americans lies in reconciling the desires of 99% of my fellow Americans with those of the 1% so-called elite.

"If 99% of us are worried about the air we breathe, the water we drink, the food we eat, the greenhouse gas effect we produce, the waste of natural resources we create when we don't recycle, or worried about the way the corporate elite act when they choose to forget the collective good for their own benefit, our duty lies in reconciling both parties. Our duty lies in reconciling the means with the purposes, the individual needs with the collective ones.

"My dream for Americans lies in the harmonious relationship between the people and their leaders. As John F. Kennedy said of his dream relationship with the press, quote: 'The duties of the Americans and their President, in a mutual way, are to inform, to arouse, to reflect, to state our dangers and our opportunities, to indicate our crisis and our choices, to lead, mold, educate and sometimes even anger public opinion.'

"Indeed, communication and dialogue work both ways! Forgive those who didn't listen to you or pretended that they did but then went and only fulfilled their own agenda. In many ways democracy has never really existed, but we can dream it will in the future.

"My dream for Americans lies in the leaders of corporations acting as responsible citizens, willing to have an honest conversation with you, the base of our society, just as I am now, without lawmakers forcing them to do so. Forgive the past misbehavior of corporate CEOs and be open to having a more harmonious relationship with them.

"My dream for America lies in Americans communicating and informing all others, through word of mouth and the Internet, about their deepest feelings. That way, we'll end the one-way information system of the media over these last two centuries, selecting what they wanted you to hear and see. Forgive those who did that selecting and censoring.

"My dream for America lies in asking you to do the impossible: not to believe that tomorrow you will elect a President who will realize the material promises he made to you. All of the Presidential candidates in elections past have always made considerable promises and none of them have been able to realize those promises in the end. I ask you to have the almost impossible awareness of being the Light of the world that Americans have always wanted to be but that our previous leaders have always extinguished, not letting you be what you are.

"My dream for Americans lies in letting you express your spiritual nature. Then and only then will you be able to receive the material life you deserve. But first you must forgive the liars. Then I promise that a great era of spirituality will follow, my fellow Americans.

"As you know, I did not win the primaries of my party, Barack Obama did. You believed that with him our dreams could be fulfilled. Yes we can, you say. I know you believe in him and will elect him. So many of you gave him small amounts of money to finance his campaign, but he also received huge sums of money from the elite who reign, whether in politics or in business. You probably felt at the beginning of his candidacy as I did: it seemed unbelievable that this first term senator, apparently coming from nowhere, dared to compete with the obviously more well known candidates.

"Then I learned that he was a 3rd cousin with James Madison, a 4th cousin with Lyndon Johnson, a 7th with Harry Truman and a 10th with Gerald Ford, That means: three, four, seven or ten generations back they share a common ancestor. You can check it out for yourself on Wikipedia, search for 'genealogy of US Presidents'. Most of them are from the same families.

"Barack Obama didn't focus on that during his campaign of course. John McCain didn't either! They both have King Edward the First of England as a common ancestor.

"The same can be said of most of the elected Presidents as well as of the unsuccessful contenders for the White House. Some geneticists say that we all come from the same Eve (300,000 years ago). For once they agree with the Bible, but how many people can claim to descend from Edward the First? Not too many, especially since so many of those people tend to intermarry in the same bloodlines. After my research on the Internet about that, I knew Obama and McCain were like all of the other candidates and elected Presidents since the foundation of the USA: backed up by the elite!

"People of the elite, after two centuries of lies and secrecy, believe they are like gods and we are their creatures. Really, we are. They created this society and we are their puppets if we don't wake up. But first, forgive them.

"I offer you more than any President can: a way to fulfill your dreams. You cannot expect the outside world to fulfill them. You must start by looking within yourself, each of you, individually.

"If the dreams of Americans are great and deep, within themselves, how gigantic America's dream will be, and how extraordinary will be the achievements of us as a society and as a people.

"My dream is to inform you through my website and to air videos of my fellow Americans interviewing me. Thanks to my two favorite ETs, this dream will be realized as they will protect this website from being removed or interfered with. Together, we will be able to check on what is being done and what more we can do together.

"Good evening and see you again."

•

Dennis started working with co-ops and non-profit organizations to begin to implement the dreams he spoke of in his famous talk: cooperation with neighboring communities; favoring small businesses who create innovative and environmentally-friendly products; developing private schools that favor an education centered on life instead of on strictly the accumulation of knowledge; Promoting natural health care, helping people to get loans without interest, especially people with low wages, as John F. Kennedy had wanted.

However, Kennedy was assassinated in November 1963 in part because he was beginning to have a 'social conscience' which conflicted with the Big Business money that had bankrolled his election campaign.

To complicate matters, due to his father's connections, his 1960 Presidential campaign was also probably bought and paid for with money from the Mafia. It was too much for all of them. There was no need to respect the people who elected him. The only appropriate sentence was: death!

Trying to make the elite forget the past and focus on the future, Dennis embarked on a New Frontier, as Kennedy had done, but through cooperative actions, establishing a 'parallel stock market' with people giving their money to co-ops and not to banks.

In doing so, they opened up the economy to new inventions such as free energy and anti-gravity devices. People thus became more energy independent and less reliant on giving money to the companies who produced power. Unfortunately, those devices were not mass-produced and were only sold in these parallel markets.

In 2009, Dennis, who had become surprisingly influential in China, helped the Chinese people to force their government to take significant steps toward real democracy, but the American news media propaganda chose not to report on that success.

Chinese people at the base of their society claimed more freedom. They took advantage of the summer Olympics being held in Beijing to increase their demands. Previous US leaders couldn't really propose anything 'democratic' to Beijing, for how can one ask other countries to be more democratic if one's own way of governing is based on hypocrisy, deception and cunning?

How can one tell people elsewhere to embrace democracy if one's own President was 'elected' by five Supreme Court judges in 2000 and then 'reelected' in 2004 by a manipulation of electronic voting machines?

Dennis' way was an open-minded way, opposed to the usual narrow-minded and cunning ways of most politicians. Chinese people even considered him as the real President of the USA. They held a collective attitude resembling Gandhi's nonviolent way of responding. However, they also remembered the violent reaction of their government in Tiananmen Square. So their actions and activities were primarily conducted underground, oriented to consuming wisely and boycotting products that were made by polluting plants. When their government wanted to impose new taxes on some products, they then boycotted those products.

Communism had prospered in China because of the sense of collectivity of the Chinese people. That tradition led them to be collective in a civic manner, with organizations that were very inventive and flexible.

Then, when their government tried to dismantle a few of these organizations, new, even smaller ones appeared that were even less controllable by the authorities.

Dennis Muccinich, with his growing popularity among the Chinese people from continental China, didn't hesitate to speak about democracy there and everywhere on Earth.

He knew that the two established parties in the USA didn't obligatorily result in a democracy when both of them were financed by the same Big Business. He also realized that having too many political parties, as in some countries, makes it impossible to either elect a majority or to form a coalition that can effectively govern. Nonetheless, either option is better than having just one party that does not tolerate any dissent whatsoever. He once said when lecturing in Beijing: "The ideal democracy hasn't existed yet, even in the USA, especially in the USA. Each country has the right to experience democracy in its own way, for all people are different."

He also traveled to Russia, mainly to attend a lecture given by Vladimir Megré, an incredible entrepreneur who became a writer after meeting a recluse called Anastasia who lived in the Siberian taiga.

This Russian lady had extraordinary powers, but did not appear in public, except on a few occasions to assist Megré when he was in difficult situations. Generally, she came from nowhere and disappeared in an instant. Dennis suspected she was like MATRIX or WITNESS: an ET.

Actually, we are all ETs, for ETs came to Earth over millions of years and interfered with our evolution, giving us bits of their DNA, as we were doing with Genetically Modified Organisms at the end of the 20th century and even into the beginning of the 21st.

However, those ETs were scientifically more advanced than Humans and also more cautious in their manipulations.

Therefore, Anastasia, the Siberian recluse, presumably reactivated ET genes that were dormant within her. Despite her incredible ability to materialize and dematerialize and travel through dimensions, like people at the Door of Heavens, Anastasia promoted, through Megré's writings, a way of living that existed in the Vedic time a few millennia ago: a way of living in harmony with nature through the taking care of one hectare of land (about 2.5 acres). Millions of Russians, as well as people from other countries, started to implement the ideas she initiated. Millions of books in many different languages were sold worldwide by Megré at the end of the 90s and into the first decade of the 21st century.

There were so many people who became enlightened that it would take an impossible number of pages to tell all of their stories here. Nonetheless, there is one man worth noting who was significantly helping the world to change.

His name was Benjamin Guildford. He was a Canadian who had been living in Japan for the last twenty years and had become acquainted with many different politicians through his work as a financial journalist. He had written books about how to reform the global economy and had suggested improvements that would benefit everyone rather than just the chosen few.

This journalist was contacted by a secret Asian society and told that he would be given the opportunity to implement his ideas. Asian countries were fed up with American imperialism and the ever-increasing domination of their economies.

As we saw with APHROMIS remote viewing system, this secret Asian society sent, through Benjamin Guildford, an ultimatum to the Western elite: "Reform the economic system in a more equitable way or else we will use our Ninjas to kill your leaders one by one."

The American shadow government, which controlled the Federal Reserve, the military, the spy communities, and most of the big corporations, had taken the exact same approach for decades: kill any leader who opposes the status quo.

They knew very well that the Asian countries had the means to skillfully poison or 'suicide' people, or even kill their targets in a so-called 'accident'.

Therefore, they took this ultimatum seriously, but did not change their cunning practices. They instead tightened their security. Three different times without success they even tried to kill Benjamin, who then decided to call on people to stop feeding the system by working less and buying less, and as many heeded his call, the power of the elite decreased. Life for most people in the world was going smoother than it ever had and that was mainly because of the subtle action of people meditating while having a dialogue with the SUPREME BEING within, also called the Intelligence of the Nature of the Universe.

Even the so-called atheists or free-thinkers, who couldn't have a conversation with God because they couldn't believe in Her/Him, could believe in the Intelligence of the Universe and have a conversation with this Intelligence, which in reality is the only real entity, as all of the others, including Humans, are illusory individualizations of that one, the only One we all are, the Whole of All.

These changes were preparing the world for the Big Shift of 2012. Nonetheless, the most significant shift in the consciousness of people and their awareness of being only one entity, came through the simple but extraordinary evidence provided by the video taken of Mars, Earth's Moon and one of Jupiter's moons called Europe: "We are not alone in the Universe."

Before this ET evidence, more and more people were convinced that Intelligence similar to that of Humans could emerge within beings throughout the Universe as soon as certain favorable conditions existed, as had been the case on Earth. Nevertheless, this assumption was insufficient to cause the average person to accept that Life and Intelligence probably existed throughout the Cosmos, especially after decades of disinformation about the ET reality.

However, the photos and videos of ET artifacts on Mars and on the Moon, taken by MATRIX and WITNESS, were so tremendously well done and incontrovertible, that even the most skeptical Human had no choice but to surrender. Some tried to contest the evidence but were so challenged by the majority that they ceased their arguments.

People very often believe in what they see. Of course, some media refused to see the evidence, as was the case with the Leptans. They contested the pictures and the artifacts that made things disappear, even though several experts said that some of the artifacts were made from such a complex alloy that existing Human technology could not have constructed them. Some objects were made from isotopes of titanium that Humans had yet to develop a method to produce.

Nevertheless, in some experiments that at the beginning of the 21st century were known only to a select number of experts, it was discovered that certain metals from the titanium group disappeared from view when heated, and then reappeared when cooled. In fact, when something seems impossible, it doesn't exist to those people who refuse to acknowledge the evidence.

However, people like to see even the impossible, but when a metal object disappears right in front of their eyes, that's too much for them to comprehend! Things like that are absolutely impossible, or it must be a trick like in magic. They cannot acknowledge that the Universe is one gigantic magic trick. Our science is so upside down!

It was the same scientific response as with an ore David Hudson had found on his property: it also had the propensity to lose its complete weight and disappear from view when heated. Despite this evidence, the vast majority of scientists refused to believe in the possibility of objects disappearing from view. In fact, scientists refuse what doesn't fit the narrow-minded paradigm of their time.

At the beginning of the 20th century, Einstein turned Newton's laws of physics upside down with his own theory of relativity, yet it was a much more complete paradigm, for Newton's laws of physics still held true, but only at a certain level of reality.

At the end of the 20th century, the same situation existed, but this time it was Einstein's physics that were turned upside down. However, Einstein would have embraced the Grand Unified Field theory, which many scientists refined, clarified and perfected for decades and which provided the reasoning he was searching for to expand upon his own laws of relativity.

Nonetheless, he would have admitted that the Cosmos is composed of Zero Point Energy, which can be compared to the intelligent substance of God. He was already convinced that "God doesn't play dice with the Universe." We can now better say: "God plays with 'Her' body, the Universe."

Dennis Muccinich's way of practicing politics, Meroveus' way of doing business, and MATRIX and WITNESS' way of meditating, among many others, were like day and night compared to the cunning manners of the classical politicians, old capitalist businessmen and money-oriented gurus of the past.

Concerning their lies, cover-ups, wars and 'dividing to better rule' principles, people at the base of society were behaving much less like 'sheep following the herd' and instead were more open-minded, more open to dialogue, more acting overtly and more applying the 'divulging to better rouse' principle than they ever had been in the past. Rousing others to do their best and to be their best was more and more the people's way of doing in life, instead of allowing themselves to be ruled through fear.

Those few years before 2012 will be remembered as the time Humanity finally began to embrace true democracy!

2- SPIRIT ODYSSEY

WRITER: You surely wonder how I know so many things about the world, even about the future in volumes 2 and 3. Actually, future doesn't exist, only the eternal present. Furthermore, I am more than this present incarnation that types these words. As everyone is, I am the Spirit. Therefore, my real life is everywhere, at any time, not only in this body at this precise period of time. The journey in space and time I am having now, here, is linked to my Spirit odyssey.

You'll see in volume 2 if my so-called previsions, or premonitions, or prophecies, or readings of the future, will occur or not. In one space-time, they have already occurred, but that is in the one of my imagination. Therefore, within the imagination of the Spirit of the Universe, they have already happened too, haven't they, SUPREME MATRIX?

SUPREME MATRIX: Yes, everything has already occurred, in My mind.

WRITER: That's logical! You're out of time, experiencing everything at the same time.

SUPREME MATRIX: Being everything at the same time would be more accurate, wouldn't it, SUPREME WITNESS?

SUPREME WITNESS: My witnessing also makes everything occur. How can something exist without a spectator to watch it?

WRITER: SUPREME WITNESS and SUPREME MATRIX, you both look like an old couple, having a smooth conversation. Do You quarrel sometimes, like people You created in Your image?

SUPREME WITNESS: If quarreling Humans looked more like the image of the Divine Reality we are, they'd behave more nicely, as we do.

WRITER: Yes, I understand. However, if we fight and are in Your image, that means You quarrel sometimes, as we do. Am I right?

SUPREME MATRIX: Fights and quarrels can be done only when you're more than one. How can you battle against yourself?

WRITER: There are people who are good at that. They don't like their image or their nature, and they do all they can to change it, physically and psychologically. I mean, people enhancing their breasts, lifting their face, changing their sex, or playing roles to better fit with what others expect from them.

SUPREME WITNESS: Duality and unity can exist at the same time. It's why we never quarrel in our conversations SUPREME MATRIX and I. Each of you can behave in the same way, for you are dual beings, yet you're one unity at the same time. As Our clone Carl Jung said: You all have a feminine part and a masculine one, anima and animus, matrix and witness. When you forget to be the witness of a situation, you get too much involved and start fighting with the other. When you forget to be the matrix of a situation, you don't get involved enough into a relationship with another and forget that you're one with him/her.

WRITER: That's a wise and universal answer to my narrow-minded and down-to-earth question. So, what do You think of this novel so far? Of the characters, of the topics, of Your presence in it? Tell me everything!

SUPREME MATRIX: *So, what do you think of Our inspiring you in everything you have written so far about the characters, the topics and of the great idea we whispered in you about Our presence and participation in it? Tell us everything!*

WRITER: Funny! That's not fair to answer back to me with the same kind of question!

SUPREME WITNESS: That's because there are no questions, no problems. There is only one answer, one solution: We are one with everyone, everything. This novel is a good way of telling that.

WRITER: Thank You for Your help.

SUPREME WITNESS: You're welcome! Thank yourself actually, your Self, which We are! Your odyssey is Ours. We are on the same ship called 'Cosmos Reality'.

SUPREME MATRIX: *And the substance of the Cosmos is My flesh. It's through it that I influence the life of Humans and their civilizations.*

WRITER: However, in 2012, Your flesh in the Milky Way is going to shiver, and Your flesh as Earth is going to sneeze, reversing the magnetic field, making the tectonic plates move quickly and kill millions of people, maybe billions!

SUPREME MATRIX: *Maybe, maybe not! This reversal of the magnetic field will be so beneficial to the billions of survivors!*

WRITER: You've always the last word to say.

SUPREME MATRIX: *I am the Word…*

SUPREME WITNESS: And I am the Light…

…*FOLLOW US!*

WRITER: I am aware of being a clone of You, therefore I can only follow You. I am Grandly and Oddly Divine. I am GOD, even if I am also mud.

SUPREME WITNESS: Yes, you're MUD, Merely and Ultimately Divine. You are US, the Ultimate Supreme. Cloning is just a way of doing. Saying you're a Clone of US is a way of speech. Being US is the only way.

3- THE WAY TO 2012 AS A SPIRITUAL ODYSSEY

The closer the world came to the year 2012, the more passionate the debates became in the media, as well as in local communities and around the dinner tables in people's homes. One TV debate in 2011 was particularly memorable. It was broadcast around the world and included some very well known scientists, a few politicians such as Dennis Muccinich, but also MATRIX and WITNESS, and the heroes of the videos showing ET construction in the solar system: Jenya Mendeleev and David Wilwit.

Before the debate, a fifteen minute-video was shown, explaining what was happening to the world. By that time, the magnetic North Pole was moving so dramatically that the landing systems at airports, which were based on the orientation of the magnetic field of the Earth, as shown by a simple compass, had to be constantly adjusted. There had also been a dramatic increase in hurricanes, floods and earthquakes. Solar activity was so much greater that scientists even had to readjust the scale of measurements.

At the beginning of the debate, classical scientists said that they didn't know what the reasons were for this solar and Earth activity, and that they did not know if there would be a major upheaval the following year.

David and other guests stated that a massive upheaval had been predicted by the Mayan calendar that finishes up on the 21st day of December, 2012, the end of a cycle of 5125 years. It had also been predicted through the famous Constant of Nineveh found in Ashurbanipal's library in what was then Assyria. The scientists laughed at these predictions and David got pissed off because his books were so well researched and they so well documented this pending reality. On television though, to be convincing, one had to be so concise. It wasn't just politicians who had to master thirty second sound bites!

"How can one explain in a few words what took ten years of my life to research and then write and document over seven different books?" he exclaimed.

MATRIX, who had studied all of his books and appreciated his excellent work, flew to his aid without even asking for permission to speak:

"The problem isn't so much the precise date or how it was determined. Don't be too picky! You've all seen the recent dramatic movement of the poles. That has not happened for millennia. Data from satellites show that the magnetic field of the Earth is so tilted in relation to the geographic poles that its axis will soon come to a turning point within the telluric grid. Then, following along these lines of force within the Earth and her atmosphere, it will reverse. That is a fact. It may take a few days. It actually may only take a few hours. That reversal will probably activate the tectonic plates, which will then slide on the core of the Earth at the same pace, triggering considerable earthquakes and floods. We believe that the probable date for this phenomenon will be the 21st day of December, 2012, a Friday. Therefore, with the proper preparations, we will have a much better chance to avoid as many casualties as possible. And, if nothing has occurred by the end of December 2012, we can begin to progressively reduce the threat level. I believe Dennis Muccinich can explain to us what the international community has thus far planned for this period of time."

"Thank you for introducing my speech, MATRIX. First, I would like to express to you and your companion my gratitude for making Human beings aware of this shift of the magnetic field. As my entire political life has been dedicated to shining light and bringing openness into the dark corners of society and government, it's taken some time to get used to being referred to by some as the shadow President of the United States. I promise you I will never work in the shadows. Lately, what I have been doing is working with many different people around the world to prepare for this magnetic shift. The evidence is so strong that we cannot run the risk of being unprepared. It would be the epitome of irresponsibility. The United Nations has been preparing for this eventuality for the past two years, even though some countries sadly remain reluctant to participate in this international effort to save as many lives as possible."

The 'shadow' President stopped for a few moments to review his notes.

"The plan being prepared will help people to move away from zones at risk of destruction. Hundreds of zones have been mapped out all over the world because of their potential vulnerability to earthquakes or volcanic activity. Thousands of inhabited areas, close to bodies of water with a high potential for flooding from tsunamis, will also have evacuation plans. They will not be obligatory, but they will be proposals, that individual nations can review and amend as they see fit.

"People will not be moved far distances but to safer, higher elevations, as near to their current homes as possible. Strong, inflatable, heated domes will be available for people to move into, beginning the 15th day of December, 2012. If the shift does occur on the 21st, and if damages are not too severe, people will be able to return home quite quickly, within a week of evacuating. If damage is severe, people will be able to remain in these domes for several weeks. 99% of all natural disasters that devastate our planet happen so suddenly there is no time to prepare for them and to save lives. They come without warning. We are so blessed to have such a precise date to prepare for and work toward. To still be alive after Christmas will be the best gift Christians could receive. However, I proposed to the UN that people who won't have to move be encouraged to send gifts to the Blue Berets, who will play Santa and distribute them on Boxing Day to people temporarily removed, Christian or not.

"I would like to again thank MATRIX and WITNESS for the use of their technology and the invaluable data it provided us to locate the places on our planet that are at risk. As you know, WITNESS and MATRIX traveled here from outer space and they have made us Humans aware of this infinite Universe that we all share together. The people of their planet Witma, light-years away from ours, are centuries more advanced than Earthlings are, in every way, including spiritually.

"MATRIX and WITNESS have helped us to develop our technology, including the anti-gravity devices used to transport people. We had been working on that for several decades, primarily by studying the few flying saucers from outer space that had crashed on Earth.

"However, it was all being done in secrecy, in the shadows and in the darkness, and we lacked so much knowledge, including a method to focus on our Earth as a source of navigation through the telluric grid.

"Finally, their most significant assistance came through helping us all to be more aware of our own source of power, the Spirit within us, and I can never thank them enough for that."

He started clapping and the public in the TV studio followed him. Then WITNESS raised his hand in order to ask Larry Queen, the journalist leading the show, if he could speak. The latter nodded and stated WITNESS' name.

"We are glad to have helped you believe in yourself and thus find your Self, the Spirit of the Universe, the Supreme Being we all are. I must add something to our discussion about the magnetic shift. We've learned from our contacts with the SUPREME BEING that it will also be a dimensional shift. Planet Earth, through the reversal of the magnetic poles, will now shift into a reality with four dimensions."

There were whisperings amongst the public.

"Earthlings will live in a completely different world. Some enclaves already exist on Earth which for ages have been in the 4-D reality. I have traveled to a few of them, mainly in the Gobi desert and in Tibet at a place called Shambhala. Other Humans have traveled there too, and I can tell you that the spiritual transformation the 4th dimension will give you is unbelievable. Before you've experienced it, you can't imagine how it is, can you, Jenya?"

"I experienced it with a team of Russian scientists. Words are insufficient to express what happened to me. It was like I was in heaven; everything was possible. I am still in heaven in my mind."

The public laughed.

WITNESS continued:

"Human beings, prepare your people in a spiritual way for this event. Meditate and try to dialogue with the Spirit, the SUPREME BEING within you, who is everything in an 8 dimensional reality. Sooner or later, whether in a few centuries or in a few millennia, your world on Earth will become a 5-D reality. And then it will reach the 6-D and 7-D ones. The next ultimate step is fusion with the Great Whole in the 8-D reality.

"Our planet Witma also remains at this moment in the 3-D reality because we have lived too much, as you have, on an individualistic level. To travel, we go to the 4-D reality, but our presence there can only be temporary. I know from the Supreme Being that our planet Witma is going to proceed directly to the 5-D world because of recent and significant progress on a spiritual level of our people. In fact, we actually progressed too quickly and were not in a part of the galaxy with enough dense 'energy of the vacuum', as some scientists on Earth call it. This so-called 'energy of the vacuum' is the Divine Energy of SUPREME MATRIX, the feminine aspect of the SUPREME BEING. The insufficiently dense energy we found ourselves in was the reason why the shift had yet to occur. But now, the density of this substance of SUPREME MATRIX in the part of the galaxy where our planet is, is so massive and our spiritual evolution has been so quick, we will soon be able to make an incredible shift of two dimensions all at once."

Larry Queen interrupted WITNESS in order to ask him a question that he felt was of great importance:

"Why don't Human scientists know about these other dimensions that some call densities of the vacuum? We have some great scientists and it's amazing that we haven't heard anything from them about this."

"Some do know about other dimensions, but they are not in the mainstream. Their theories are too controversial or too damaging to the status quo. Einstein's law of relativity is too sacred to mainstream scientists. It dare not be violated, even if experiments on Earth demonstrate that without a doubt the speed of light is not the maximum speed.

"It is true for the 3-D world, but as soon as you're in another dimension, the speed of light increases dramatically. The other dimensions are better understood if you think of them as different densities of space. Each point of space has a different energy; it's why some call it Zero Point Energy. Some scientists prefer Vacuum Field. The Ancients called it Aether. The latter intuitively recognized it as the flesh of the Divine. Some priests also knew it through previous technological civilizations like Atlantis.

"Atlantis hid that knowledge after their land was submerged in the Atlantic Ocean. Mayas, Sumerians, Greeks, Hindus, Egyptians, they all expressed this knowledge in either their monuments, their mathematics, such as in the sacred geometry of the Greeks, or in their holy texts. Everything is in vibrational harmony with the Divine Energy, the subtle substance of the Universe.

"I also want to thank you all for the extraordinary odyssey we have had on your planet. I feel that this event in December 2012 will also result in a big shift for MATRIX and I. I don't know how or what yet, but I can feel it within my flesh, my mind, my Spirit, my entire being!"

WITNESS stopped talking and the audience, so moved by his words, clapped profusely.

Following this TV program, many more people started meditating and because the media are always quick to promote the latest trends, they were more inclined than ever before to report on meditation, on the magnetic inversion, and on the existence of other dimensions. Even if there was a bias because so many journalists were so conditioned to view the world in only one particular black and white way, it was interesting to notice the difference in the reporting. Of course the media didn't want to miss such an event, even if it was only to mock it! There was only one more year to go, and if nothing happened, they said, it would be easy to make fun of it. Yet, when in doubt, you'd better address the subject from both sides. In this case, once as 'the magnetic inversion is the best prophecy ever' and the next time as 'the biggest hoax ever'.

The media, for the most part, was still in the hands of Big Business, which also still controlled the global economy. A few masterminds at the top were still trying to tell people what to think, what to buy and how to behave. In fact, the preparations for this worldwide catastrophe, ever since the United Nations recognized the seriousness of it, fueled the economy better than any war had in the past. Many different sectors of industry benefited both from the preparations to orderly evacuate people from the zones at risk and from the huge construction projects being built to prevent damage and death from floods.

Nobody could do anything to stop the trend that the active spiritual minority started by simply expressing the Spirit they are. More and more people meditated in one fashion or another, becoming more and more aware of the incredible spiritual change the event would bring for the benefit of mankind. The first decade of the 21st century, especially after 2008, was a tremendous opening for spirituality. André Malraux, the French writer and minister of President Charles de Gaulle, had said in the sixties: "The 21st century will be spiritual or won't be."

In the last year before the big shift, the world became such an overflowing cornucopia of spiritual awareness that people who were used to hiding the truth –Free Masons, multinational CEOs, politicians, the spying community, and the skin-shifting Reptilian-Humans–-all started to act more transparently and more willingly. However, it was not obvious to them, for they were so used to hiding and working in secrecy.

Some acted transparently because they were caught and exposed and under the circumstances could not avoid telling the truth, just like the exposure of the intentionally hidden artifacts in the solar system revealed truths long hidden. However, beforehand, they would have denied this type of evidence.

Meroveus-NEW EINSTEIN-NEW TESLA worked hard to convince his ex-friends in the world's secret governments to use his enlightenment machine and to then act transparently. His basic message to them was:

"What is the best and most effective way for you to lead Human beings and impose your dictates on the masses? Like farmers managing their cattle or like enlightened beings following the laws of the Spirit? If you choose the former, you will be seen as devils. If you choose the latter, you are in synchronicity with the Universe; you become the light of the world and are seen as Divine Beings. And the simplest way to achieve that goal lies first in going through my enlightenment machine."

The vast majority refused due to their long conditioned mindset. However, a few succumbed to his promise to become the lights of Human beings, almost like new saviors. NEW BUDDHA was helping them learn how to meditate afterward, especially teaching them how to have an enlightened communication with the SUPREME LIGHT of the Universe.

Then would come the day prophesied by so many different traditions, Judgment Day, the Apocalypse, the Shift of the Ages, the end of one era and the beginning of the new one.

It was Judgment Day, mainly for those who refused to see the Light of the Spirit in the world. However, they were provided one last chance to change their own judgment about how they viewed the world.

It was the Apocalypse, the disclosure, the bringing into view of those who had amassed material wealth that would have had no value after the big upheaval of December 2012, but now had no value in light of the law of loving and sharing.

It was the Big Shift that all civilizations since the fall of Atlantis were waiting for!

It was the end of the kingdom of Ego and the beginning of the Kingdom of God! Throughout the entire year 2012, there were many transformations occurring in the solar system as well. Solar activity, which had risen since the beginning of the 21st century, increased so dramatically that the so-called solar wind brought to Earth so many high energy particles that occasionally in some places electrical devices worked without being plugged in, including electrical appliances in houses, electric trains and cars. Nonetheless, this free electricity was only available from the 'gods' from time to time.

Astronomers calculated that the planets would all be aligned with the center of our Milky Way galaxy precisely on the 21st day of December, 2012, including the Earth but excepting Pluto (which had recently been declassified as a real planet and ranked among the asteroids).

Such a conjunction of all of the planets, from Neptune to Mercury in one straight line with the center of the galaxy, had not happened even once since the Humans of all of the world's civilizations had started gazing up at the sky and recording its wonders.

The solar system was traversing through the galactic plane in its slow waving journey above and below it. The whole solar system was like a being rearranging itself.

This intense astronomical activity also had an influence on the people who had already spiritually prepared themselves for the big shift of December 2012. More and more people stopped working and focused more on enjoying simple pleasures such as gardening, painting, playing music, biking, hiking, etc. They no longer worried about money but their bank accounts were always in the black and they worked only occasionally in order to pay the bare minimum of required expenses.

Paper money had been suppressed in a few countries in 2011 after Singapore had led the way in 2006. People were only making purchases and paying expenses with plastic cards or by direct withdrawals. However, these particular people had already decreased dramatically their buying appetite. They lived with little, often in a village, and exchanged goods with each other in the village's markets or did transactions through community currencies they had established. They moved to areas, away from big cities, where they sensed it would be safe during the shift of the magnetic field, and they lived in little communities where autarky was practiced as much as possible. However, they were very well organized, as autarky certainly does not mean anarchy. Most of these people followed principles described by Anastasia and Vladimir Megré in the Ringing Cedars series, mainly the deep relationship one has with nature, where you give to Her instead of only taking from Her as happens in industrialized farms.

Through the dialogue with the Divine SUPREME BEING, one could feel anything and one could live as one felt it. Nonetheless, these "Nature Birds", as they were called, were not completely removed from the technological society. Because they were not connected to companies and their biases and conditioning, they were not afraid of losing markets as the local one was sufficient, of losing money in a crash of the stock exchange as only the exchange of products was important, or of competing with new products that made theirs obsolete as their new inventions were innovative and sustainable.

Therefore, creativity, unencumbered with the weight of narrow-minded views of life, allowed people in these little communities to invent new products that were more respectful of nature, more long-lasting, more useful, and more revolutionary.

In spite of their lack of finances to invest into their projects, they conducted research in anti-gravity and produced devices that worked wonderfully, as paradoxical as that appeared.

Although they lacked an industrial structure to develop vehicles for Humans, they did create two to three foot-long devices that flew all over the community where they were living to control and provide automatic surveillance of everything within it, in a way that gas-propelled devices could never have done. But this surveillance was not in a Big Brother way: small surveillance at a community level is for preventing outside intrusion, controlling pests and checking if everything is working smoothly in production.

This kind of machine was more manageable and more silent, needing no refueling as its energy came from its interference with the magnetism of the Earth. The more it moved, the more energy it produced. This principle was also used by Nature Birds to make electricity and to thus be energy independent.

These little communities were proving that one does not need a complex society in order to produce cutting edge technological devices. And it was certainly the choice of Big Business to have not earlier circulated anti-gravity devices, for the elite preferred to keep these types of things secret and to use them for only their own benefit. In fact, the elite developed their anti-gravity research because they had the opportunity to study Extraterrestrial crashed 'flying saucers' with taxpayers' money in secret government sites such as the 'infamous' Area 51 in Nevada. It's easier to work in secret, for you can't be checked up on by those nosy taxpayers.

Some alien species like the Reptilians also helped the governments to build flying saucers. This alien technology helped researchers to understand and use the energy of the vacuum to suppress the effects of gravity. And it was the Nazis who had prepared the way before the war with ETs who helped them build anti-gravity disks. Following World War II, 'Operation Paperclip' allowed the Americans to, shall we say, acquire German scientists, who then worked for them. America's Cold War Russian enemies also undertook this same sort of acquiring.

However, these communities of Nature Birds invented anti-gravity devices without any ET help by simply applying the laws of Electromagnetism and Zero Point Energy to annihilate the Earth's gravity field.

A simple gyroscope also generates this anti-gravity effect, albeit a very weak generation. A flying anti-gravity device is only slightly more complex, yet it has an incredibly stronger effect on gravity. These laws were also used to produce free electricity.

The secrecy principle of much of 20th century society certainly also flourished in its patenting process, which had the perverse effect of freezing inventions when a company bought a patent from an inventor, then put it into a drawer and forgot about it so as to better protect their own inferior products that made more profit.

Nikola Tesla, who definitely allowed the Alternating Current to prevail, suffered the most from this 'invention suppression' because, at the beginning of the 20th century, he wanted to give people access to free energy: and that was of course unacceptable to almighty Big Business!

In fact, patents are kept by bodies that are more or less controlled by governments that can classify them for security reasons and then use them secretly. Presumably John Keely got his classified! He invented an anti-gravity device seven years before the first flight of the Wright brothers. After his death, his patented inventions were no doubt developed secretly and with great difficulty over a long period of time and this was due to the fact that an inventor can't put all of what he has in his head into a patent application.

He was a genius who could only be equaled by Tesla himself.

Nature Birds revealed the plans for their inventions on the Internet for the benefit of everyone, as Paul Pantone did in the 90s with his carburetor, which produced such a complete combustion in engines that exhaust fume pollution was dramatically reduced and in some circumstances even suppressed. The fact he made his invention available on the web allowed handymen all over the world to build upon and even perfect his original invention.

These inventors were not money oriented, but in fact benefited indirectly from this transparency, opposed to secrecy, feeding each other and perfecting their own inventions in a snowball effect. Real inventors are rich with the Spirit of invention. Patents are good for making money, but not for being inventive.

However, the real happiness of these Nature Birds was based in their confidence that the "Shift of the Ages" would transform automatically all of the others who had not yet made the initial significant spiritual step forward in their minds; even the simple thought of the pending shift was sufficient for the Nature Birds to enter into a trance-like state where they felt one with everyone.

CHAPTER 12

THE SEVEN DAYS OF THE END

1- DECEMBER 18th TO 24th, 2012

Seven days! The end of time took only seven days, as in the Book of Genesis it also took only seven days for the Creation of the world to be realized. Actually, the Bible was right about this creation in seven days, yet seven days in God's time, and even one of God's days can stretch to eternity. It's really worth having a look at those seven days-eras of Genesis, for the days of the Shift of the Ages, Earth days, were pretty similar to the Divine Days of the Creation, though in a reverse way. The end is like the beginning, reversed.

In fact, the days comprising the real genesis of Earth differ slightly from the ones recorded at the beginning of the Bible, as SUPREME MATRIX will tell you if you ask Her. Only by a bit though! They also differ from what the mainstream scientists of the 21st century say. Seven days correspond to the first seven numbers and their symbolic meanings in the Divine's Mind. Everything is symbolic. Always has been, always will be!

Let's see that in the Eternal Present of Now!

•

In the beginning, there is nothing, Zero, the vacuum,
Yet, potentially, full of everything!
The first day, the Zero becomes the One Spirit of the Universe, the Aether.
Yet, the Zero still exists.
The second day, a dialogue begins between these two: Zero and One.
Binary reality, fruitful duality!
Zero, the Vacuum, the Witness, fathers Darkness.
One, the Aether, the Matrix, mothers Light.

He is the Spectator; She is the Dancer.
The third day, She dances around Him, and sings,
Emitting flows of light, which create space in three dimensions,
Producing flows of sounds, which model geometry in three dimensions.
Light and sound, spiraling, model musical spheres,
Which create particles and atoms,
Then organize the beautiful Cosmos, the first galaxy.
The fourth day, the musical spheres start moving,
And create Time and the 4th dimension in space.
The first galaxy mothers baby galaxies.
The fifth day, galaxies mother stars, myriads of stars,
And the 5th dimension!
The sixth day, stars mother planets, one by one,
And settle them at harmonic distances, orbiting around.
The 6th dimension is created.
The seventh day, light continues dancing, spiraling,
Making spheres of energy that organize the atoms into spiraling molecules.
Those molecules organize light as a source of memorizing,
Storing information.
The light, spiraling one way or the other within molecules, works like a computer.
The Divine Light never rests, even on the seventh day.
The 7th dimension is created.
The eighth day is now, the eternal now.
At the end of this big cycle,
The Divine Light recollects and recaps the beginning of times,
During the seven days of December 2012.

•

December 18th, 2012,
Day Zero,
The day before the first day,
Nothing really happens.
Yet, sensitive people feel that the beginning of the end is for the next day.

•

December 19th, 2012,
The first day,
Sunspots increase to the point of becoming one.
Solar winds are so dense that they make auroras over both of the polar caps,
And emit sounds.

•

December 20th, 2012,
The second day,
Light emits note A, the Earth replies with note C.
A dialogue starts between the light of the Sun and the substance of planet Earth.

•

December 21st, 2012,
The third day,
With A and C, a third tone is heard: E.
A-C-E, ace harmony!
The auroras organize colors like in a rainbow, in the atmosphere.
Each color of the aurora-rainbows starts following the Earth's magnetic field,
Like filings of iron, in the upper atmosphere.
Each color separates from the others, in thin filaments,
Then they break into individual dots that follow each other.
And electric plasmas are created all along.
Light, Electricity and Magnetism are like one.
It is like the whole atmosphere wants to participate
In a Christmas symphony of light!
At noon exactly, everything stops.
It is like the clock of time has stopped.
Then, one filament of light following the magnetic field of Earth
Starts moving in the reverse way,
Then another and another and so on,
While half of the filaments continue in the same way as before!
Fifty-fifty!
Therefore, there is no massive Earth upheaval, no move of the tectonic plates.
Smooth event!
Nobody notices anything.

•

December 22nd, 2012,
The fourth day,
A fourth tone is heard: B.
The natural force field at the Door of Heavens stops to operate,
And in the other spots of the 4-D world on Earth!
Then the whole planet becomes a 4-D world.
The faces of people are like glowing with light from within.
They are very often outside, watching, silent, communing with these wonders.
At night, the phenomenon continues.

Yet, the enlightened magnetic field gives light all over,
Like just after a bright sunset.

•

December 23rd, 2012,
The fifth day,
A fifth tone is heard: D.
The site of the Door of Heavens becomes a 5-D world.
It is the same in other places where the 4-D world has already existed before.
At the pass of the Door of Heavens, MATRIX, WITNESS, people living there,
And thousands of meditating people coming from all throughout the world,
Thank the SUPREME BEING.

•

December 24th, 2012,
The sixth day,
The three visitors from the 22nd century materialize again at the site.
They are sitting together in meditation like everyone else.
All of the people meditating know they are present, without opening their eyes.
Everyone starts to hear this dialogue within between
RAM, the Time Patrol leader, and APHROMIS:
On a subtle level, within:

RAM: "We already came here in 2003, for we knew that the time between 2003 and 2012 was critical to making the shift in consciousness. Enough spiritual people have started the dialogue with the SUPREME BEING.

"So you made it! Congratulations!"

APHROMIS: "Thank you! So, what were you worried about? What exactly triggered your trip to the year 2003, nine years ago, and what happens in 2147?"

RAM: "You're our past, so we already knew that you would be successful. However, we didn't know if the initial boost of the Spiritual World, yours and ours, would receive enough momentum to win over the Materialistic World that exists in a parallel dimension at the same time between 2012 and 2147."

APHROMIS: "A parallel world! What do you mean?"

RAM: "Even though what you are living in this present time is strong and decisive, I didn't tell you something in 2003 so as to not scare you at that time. The SUPREME BEINGS permitted a time split to be created on December 22nd, 2012. You experienced it two days ago. On Earth between 2012 and 2147, the Materialistic World still exists at the same time in a separate way, in the 3-D reality. This type of split has previously occurred several times on Earth, especially at the time of Atlantis and during the Pyramid civilizations of the Egyptians and the Maya. A 4-D world has already existed on Earth, but the 3-D world always triumphed over it. We expect this time that the 4-D world will stay forever, but it's still not 100% certain.

"I know that people have a hard time even imagining that time is flexible and that you can travel through it or have two civilizations existing on the same planet at the same time in two different dimensions. Nonetheless, at the Door of Heavens' domain, you and your people are more open-minded and can therefore have a glimpse of this possibility of a space-time split.

"I think the SUPREME BEING is the best to explain that. Now we can continue on meditating and concentrating within in order to listen collectively to the Supreme Reality."

"*SUPREME MATRIX speaking! Time is an illusion I allow My Self to create while turning around SUPREME WITNESS.*"

"SUPREME WITNESS speaking! That's why everything turns around everything, galaxies, stars, planets, particles and people. Hands of clocks turn too."

SUPREME MATRIX: "*However, everything can turn clockwise or anticlockwise at different times. I can dance clockwise and anticlockwise at the same time. Earth's magnetic field after the 21st day of December, 2012, turns both ways at the same time, as you have noticed, allowing a 4-D world and a 3-D world, and two civilizations, to coexist without interfering with each other. Actually, they don't interfere too much, do they, RAM?*"

RAM: "In 2147, there is a significant interference. That's why we came in 2003 to check if everything was on the right track to give enough momentum to our Spiritual 4-D World to overcome the other one, the Materialistic 3-D World, and not to be submerged by it. In 2147, we can travel through the past but not through the future as we have already done before. Something prevents us from doing that. Therefore, we can't see what happens after the year 2147. Maybe one day we will overcome that impossibility.

"In our present, we have at times a surge of the materialistic 3-D civilization into ours in some parts of the Earth. Even though each time it doesn't last long, it's scary and annoying. Imagine a wild beast once in a while suddenly invading your living room. When you're used to it, you know that it's not going to last long and that it's like an illusion, a 3-D movie projected in front of you. Nevertheless, when it happens more and more often, you wonder if it will cease to be illusory, becoming real, and thus, forever."

SUPREME WITNESS: "Be the witness of it, as I have told everyone for ages! The more you are scared and annoyed, the more the other civilization will come to you. They live on fear. Your fear attracts them like magnets. The more you aspire to be in the 5-D world, the quicker you will be in it and permanently out of reach from the 3-D world."

MATRIX: "Nevertheless, can we do something to help them, SUPREME WITNESS?"

SUPREME WITNESS: "To help them will be part of your job tomorrow, MATRIX and WITNESS. That's all we can say about it for today."

SUPREME MATRIX: "This shift in consciousness is tremendous because you both gave this planet so much of your energy and that raised the vibrations of people and motivated them to speak with us. The critical mass of Human beings meditating and speaking with us was reached in just a few years.

"Of course, spiritual people in the 20th century had already prepared the way. More and more people talking with us made Our energy in this part of the Universe beneficial and thus triggered this shift of dimension of planet Earth. It will definitively help the 4-D world of planet Earth in 2147 to shift to the 5-D one. Even though for us, these years from 2012 to 2147 correspond to the time of a sneeze, it's a long time for Humans, but it's a very, very short time for Humanity as a species. MATRIX and WITNESS, this great achievement of yours, helping Humans to speak with US, increased your own vibrations tremendously, and we must tell you that tomorrow you'll have an experience that will conclude your stay on Earth. Be prepared for that."

"See you tomorrow!" SUPREME WITNESS adds in the Eternal Moment of Now to His partner's talk and to conclude it before anyone can reply.

There are a few long seconds of silence in this present moment and everyone is surprised at this sudden conclusion and the withdrawal of the SUPREME BEINGS from the dialogue. Then, RAM says:

"Now, we must tell you, APHROMIS, that your son in our time is the leader of this site of the Door of Heavens and is preparing it for the shift to the 6-D reality, and for the Earth to the 5-D. As SUPREME MATRIX said, we hope that it will happen before the end of 2147, helping us to definitively get rid of the 3-D Materialistic World that sticks to us!"

APHROMIS: "I'm glad that the Door of Heavens is being prepared for the next dimensional shift, but I have no son yet. How old is he in 2147?"

RAM: "He was born in 2013, and is virtually immortal. When one reaches the 6th dimension, one lives a few thousand years or more, we don't know yet. Actually, APHROMIS, you'll probably live a few hundred years in the 5-D world. In 2147, you're still living and in good health.

"Our travel to your time is now concluded. We must immediately depart."

APHROMIS: "Okay! See you in 2147!"

RAM: "As the SUPREME BEING said: See you tomorrow! 2012 to 2147, it's like the time of a Divine Sneeze!"

This conversation is heard by everyone meditating. Then Ram speaks a few moments privately with APHROMIS before disappearing. The members of the Time Patrol then vanish too.

2- MORE ABOUT DECEMBER 24th, IN THE ETERNAL PRESENT OF NOW

My reader, you are now privy to a second and private conversation, this time between *APHROMIS* and WITNESS, *italic for her,* regular for him.

"*WITNESS, tomorrow you're going to leave Earth with your companion MATRIX.*"

"Yes, SUPREME WITNESS said it during the collective meditation we had with the Time Patrol: tomorrow, MATRIX and I will have an experience that will conclude our stay on Earth."

"*Tomorrow is the seventh day after the beginning of the events of the transformation of planet Earth and of Her people. I feel there will be a significant event to conclude this cycle of seven days. Intuitively, I know you'll be, MATRIX and you, the heroes of this day, with some kind of ascension, your ascension!*"

"You mean, physically, is it like Jesus Christ's ascension, as told by Luke? In fact, only Luke wrote about it!"

"*Yes! Jesus came back to Earth after this event. He disappeared into the other dimensional worlds. He appears to people in the 3-D world, periodically, as does his mother Mary from time to time. Actually, during those apparitions, SUPREME MATRIX projects Herself on Earth as the Feminine Principle and SUPREME WITNESS projects Himself as Christ the Masculine Principle. There are still people in 2012 who say that they saw them.*

"*However for you, I feel that your ascension will be forever, but maybe you will have the possibility to project yourself to Earth's 4-D world from the upper worlds where you will go. The spiritual ascension of the whole of Human kind occurred two days ago, and the 4-D world of this land at the Door of Heavens ascended to the 5th dimension. Yet for you and MATRIX, it will be the ascension to the 6th dimension, or maybe to the 7th, I can feel it!*"

"Wow! Why?"

"*I believe it's because, through your devotion to your mission, you raised your level of being worthy of this ultimate dimension. Yet you know, after the 7th dimension, there is still the very ultimate one, the 8th, the octave; like with music, you reach the same note, but on the octave. The 8-D world is the SUPREME BEING's domain.*"

"When I see the vibration of light in the 5-D world here at the Door of Heavens, I imagine that at the 8th level of reality, there is only light."

"*Probably!*"

"When one ascends individually, is it physical, like Christ's? I am confused, because in the information MOTHER EARTH gave me, he ascended from Her to the

Heavens, in fact, from the 3-D world to the 8-D one, passing through all of the other dimensions at the same time.

"However, I also have in my implanted memory from MOTHER EARTH that Christ also lived after his crucifixion and resurrection and went to India to finish his life there, in Kashmir more precisely, where his tomb is said to be. I further have in my memory that he lived there with Mary Magdalene and had children. There is also another myth, about Mary Magdalene living in France. In addition, recent archaeological findings locate the tomb of Jesus and his family in Jerusalem. The Mormons even say that he went to the Americas. Therefore, I don't know what's true and what's legendary or mythological. All is so intricately complicated in Human history! I don't exactly know how Earth stores events in what the East Indian tradition calls the Akasha and sorts through the real and the imaginary."

"Akasha stores everything. It stores events like a librarian stores printed material, from books to personal manuscripts and diaries and everything in between, but Akasha also stores all of the thoughts that have ever been emitted. Sometimes it's difficult to sort through all of that! I experienced this difficulty too, from here, at the Door of Heavens.

"Actually, Christ is a symbol. Jesus was Human, and as every Human can do, he became Christ through his spiritual experience in the 3-D world. He became aware that all dimensions are interconnected. When he walked on the water, he was in the 4-D world. When he multiplied the bread and the fish, he brought their substance from the 4-D reality. He said that everyone in the future will do the miracles he did, for he knew that this period of time Earthlings are living in now would project everyone into the 4-D Universe.

"Mary Magdalene and Jesus lived together in India because it was too dangerous for them in Palestine and throughout the Roman Empire. He impressed his disciples by ascending to Heaven with his spiritual body, but came back into his material body and left Palestine. He moved with Mary to India and Thomas, the most spiritual disciple of them all, accompanied them. When Jesus' Spirit eventually and definitely left the Earth, his body was indeed buried in Kashmir.

"Mary then moved westward with one of the caravans traveling across the Euro-Asian continent and finally arrived by boat with Jesus' mother in France, where they then initiated people to the teaching of Jesus. A city in Provence region, south of France, is even called 'Saintes Maries de la Mer'. 'De la mer' means 'from or of the sea', and Maries is Mary in plural. When they died, their bodies were brought back to Palestine and later some bones of Jesus were also repatriated into Jerusalem.

"So, you see, all of the legends are true, except for the Catholic Church, as the remains of Jesus are nowhere to be found since he left the Earth with his physical body after his resurrection. It's the material ascension that the Gospel of Luke records, and only this one Gospel of the four official Christian ones does so, and there is no ascension recorded either in the other Gospels that Humans called 'apocryphal', which means from the Greek: 'obscure',

'secret', 'non-canonical', or 'hidden away'. Obviously, those writings didn't correspond to the doctrine the first Christian bishops at the beginning of the 4th century wanted to propagate."

She stops; then slowly begins:

"WITNESS, I would like to now ask you for a big, a really big favor."

He suddenly feels the gravity of the favor in her voice. He feels it even in his bones, physically, yet full of good vibrations. Then she smiles and he suddenly feels completely light, in fact as light as light is, he is reassured and knows that he will grant her favor. She continues:

"RAM said I would have a son next year. However, I dedicated my life to this mission of bringing the Door of Heavens to the 5-D vibration and the rest of the world to the 4-D vibration. That is now accomplished, but I've never had the opportunity to develop a relationship with a male partner. I have to say that I had never before found someone with vibrations that fit mine, until I felt yours."

She stops so as to feel his reaction.

"Yes, I have felt these vibrations between us since we first met and I was quite surprised, but also moved at the same time."

"It's your destiny to leave Earth with MATRIX tomorrow and both have this transcendental experience that I feel will happen. However, I would like to have a baby with you, this son that RAM spoke of. Because the Door of Heavens is now in the 5th dimension, I know that it's enough for a male and a female to wish to have a baby together for the female to get pregnant without physical intercourse but through what we can call love-meditating. I am in the right period of my cycle to be fertilized. Yet, to be honest with MATRIX, she'll have to agree; otherwise we won't have this baby together. Of course, you must agree too!"

After a moment of silence, he answers her proposal:

"I don't know what to say, APHROMIS."

"So, don't say anything!" she replies, while touching his mouth with her index finger.

They look at each other intensely. Silently. She then continues softly:

"Would you agree if MATRIX agrees?"

"I would be pleased to sire you a son that will continue your mission in this land at the Door of Heavens. If MATRIX agrees, I agree, but it won't be easy to make her say yes, even if the baby is conceived without physical intercourse! Actually, how is that even possible?"

"Tell her that you and I won't have any physical sexual union. We'll only need to meditate and ask the SUPREME BEING to conceive a child within me, who is full of your vibrations. It won't be the first time that the Holy Spirit has done that."

"If we do leave Earth tomorrow, MATRIX and I, this baby won't have a father. Don't you feel it will be difficult to raise a child alone?"

"I will have other children and live with a companion, RAM told me so in private. He didn't tell me who he will be, but I do have an idea. Nevertheless, I would like my first child to be from you, as a meaningful remembrance of our mission together for Humanity!"

In reply he only smiles and raises one hand to her chin and touches it, delicately. She smiles back.

"I will wait for you," she concludes. Then she leaves.

•

WITNESS is now with MATRIX:

"I knew it! I knew it!" MATRIX shouts. *"I knew you would both fall in love,"* she adds, while quickly banging WITNESS' chest with her fists, one after the other. Then, with her anger subsiding, she starts to slow down the hammering, and then finally stops, rests her head on the same chest, and starts to uncontrollably sob and cry.

"My baby," he says, putting one hand on her head.

"Don't you dare call me baby!" she replies while pulling her head away from his chest.

"It was not the appropriate word, I know."

"Why does she want to be inseminated with your sperm? Can't it be done with any other sperm if she so much wants this baby who was prophesied?"

"I've already told you: there won't be any physical intercourse!"

"Will this baby be yours or will it not?"

"It will be done in a spiritual way through the SUPREME BEING, I've already told you! Okay! She wanted your approval. You don't agree. So, I'll tell her and that's it!"

"Try to feel as I feel! Wouldn't you be jealous if I told you that I was going to make love, even in a spiritual way, with…NEW BUDDHA for example?"

"If it's for a good cause and if you feel great vibrations flowing between both of you, why not?"

"Nevertheless, wouldn't you feel jealous?"

"If I make spiritual love with APHROMIS at the same time, probably not," he says half seriously and half humorously. Instantly though, he again realizes that they were not the best words to use to make his companion more cooperative. So he quickly adds:

"Okay! Forget it!" And he starts to turn around. But she replies, grasping his shoulder:

"Wait a minute! Okay! I would like to experience how to make love, spiritually, with a Human, as an experiment, in a scientific way."

"So, for the sake of science, that's a good cause!"

"I won't make love, even in a so-called spiritual way, with someone other than you for a so-called good cause. I'll make love only to have a new experience of love. Hey! If APHROMIS gets pregnant from you, or from the Holy Spirit through your vibrations, I also can have a baby! But I don't want to be pregnant from NEW BUDDHA's vibrations, even if it is in Spirit! I just want to try this new experience without getting pregnant in the end, like using contraception while making love."

"It's a spiritual experience, MATRIX! You and NEW BUDDHA can ask the SUPREME BEING during the love-meditation not to create a baby. If S/He can make APHROMIS pregnant, S/He can do the opposite. So far we haven't wanted to have a baby when we were making love, and we haven't had one. Desires and thoughts are powerful and allow us to create the lives we choose. Anyway, we're going to leave Earth tomorrow."

"To leave Earth! I had thought we were stuck here forever! SUPREME MATRIX mentioned the conclusion of our stay on Earth, but I didn't know what to make of it."

"We were stuck here because we had a mission to accomplish. Now it's over. Everything is complete: planet Earth rose to the 4-D world. APHROMIS feels that you and I are going to go to the 6-D or even the 7-D reality. I don't exactly know where those realities are, but we'll see tomorrow."

"So, maybe the time has arrived for our dream to become reality! We'll finally discover this Trinity. However, three is still far from six or seven! I didn't understand what SUPREME MATRIX told me about uniting with the third SUPREME BEING."

"If it's related to our dream, we'll experience it tomorrow. So, for today, what do we do?"

She comes close to him and caresses his chest, saying:

"I love you unconditionally my WITNESS, so you can do anything you wish. Even if we are separate, I'll still love you. Hey! I hope this Trinity business and those other dimensions don't mean that we're going to be separate!"

He laughs, "Maybe we'll form a Trinity with APHROMIS!"

"Naughty boy! Why not a quaternary with NEW BUDDHA?"

"Because in our dreams, it's only a Trinity!"

"So, I will make love, spiritually, with NEW BUDDHA, while you do the same with APHROMIS."

"If he agrees!"

"He has no partner and he's already shown me that he would like to go further with me on a spiritual level."

"Further! Do you think he would like to go further even if he knew it would be the first and the last time he makes love with you, even though it is only on a spiritual level?"

"Maybe we'll be able to travel from this 6th dimension to the 4th on Earth and stay in touch with the people here. Anyway! The goal of every being is to feel one with everyone. Therefore, I am certain we'll somehow be able to stay in contact with all of the Human beings on Earth."

"We'll see tomorrow," WITNESS concludes.

·

NEW BUDDHA accepts MATRIX's proposition because she tells him she is going to leave Earth the following day to go to the 6th dimension and he desires the opportunity to have a final spiritual experience with her.

Knowing MATRIX's intention to have a love-meditation with NEW BUDDHA, APHROMIS says:

"Great idea! Why don't we love-meditate together at the same time and in the same room?"

MATRIX and WITNESS are reluctant. NEW BUDDHA is shy and reluctant too. Nonetheless, they eventually all agree to be in the same room for they sense their experience will be a spiritual one. It will be much more than a mere physical orgasm, more than ordinary pleasure: not a 'matter of fact' but a 'Spirit of Being'.

Furthermore, APHROMIS also feels a strong connection with NEW BUDDHA and intuitively knows that he will be the father of her other children that were prophesied by RAM.

In the late evening, they enter into a room with four cushions on which they sit. APHROMIS says:

"When we are in contact with the SUPREME BEINGS, we'll ask them to tell us how to practice this love-meditation since it's the first time for all of us, even though SUPREME MATRIX did tell me about it in one of my earlier meditations."

·

When they are all in deep meditation, they hear SUPREME MATRIX speak:

"Spiritual love-meditating is not that different from physical love-making: it's a union of two partners, except there is no physical involvement. We know what each of your purposes are, so don't speak, just follow our instructions."

SUPREME WITNESS then takes His turn:

"First breathe slowly and deeply like in the Yoga Pranayama you all know how to practice."

When the breathings of all four are at the same rhythm and they all feel connected at a subtle level, WITNESS has the feeling that he is not only in connection with APHROMIS in front of him, but also with MATRIX and NEW BUDDHA. After a while he feels he is all of the Male Humans and all of the Male Witmans. Similarly, MATRIX feels that she is the Female Gender, all of the Females of both planets.

NEW BUDDHA, although young, has already had several sexual partners and has previously had the feeling of being the Maleness incarnated in him, but not at the level of today's experience of being the Male Gender.

APHROMIS does not need to make love to have this feeling. In the 4th dimension, feeling one with everyone is a common experience.

MATRIX now feels she is the Female Gender of the entire Universe. WITNESS feels the same, he is the Male Gender. They know their partners have similar feelings.

Eventually, and ultimately, MATRIX feels she is SUPREME MATRIX and her partner, NEW BUDDHA, is SUPREME WITNESS. APHROMIS feels the same with WITNESS.

They spontaneously start chanting the 'AUM' of the Yoga tradition: A-U-M. The sounds begin to create a visible bubble of vibrations around each of them. Then the bubbles fuse into one with their partners' bubbles. Finally, their spiritual bodies separate from their physical ones and move toward their partners' bodies and mix with each other. Their physical bodies still chant the AUM but it grows higher and higher in pitch. They don't need to breathe again to emit sound; it's like the whole atmosphere is within them. Their spiritual bodies now vibrate at a higher and higher pace.

Eventually, they experience the orgasm SUPREME MATRIX and SUPREME WITNESS together had when they created the Universe.

Then, each spiritual body returns to its physical one.

3- DECEMBER 25th: CHRISTMAS DAY

Finally, the ultimate experience occurs. It is midnight. It is the seventh day: Christmas has dawned. The bodies of MATRIX and WITNESS become completely transparent, radiating and glowing light. They slowly, at the same time, begin to rise up, into the air, above their own cushions, and then move toward each other and join their lights together. The two become one. They are now in a sphere of light radiating above and between APHROMIS and NEW BUDDHA, who look up to them in amazement and wonderment.

Then the sphere, with the two translucent Witmans in it, rises slowly and departs through the ceiling. APHROMIS and NEW BUDDHA wave their hands, for they know it is the time of the Witmans' departure to another dimension, the time of the good bye, the time of the farewell. Nevertheless, they rush to exit the building and try to follow them.

Everyone at the pass is outside, meditating, for they know it is the last day of the Apocalypse, which means not the end of the world but the uncovering of the veil of illusion in order to reveal the reality underneath. They know that this very veil began to vaporize seven days ago. Now everything is clear! People do not want to miss even one second of this last day. So, at midnight, everyone is outside. They are glad to be there and to participate in what they feel is the main event of the day, of the week, of the year, of all of the ages of all of the times.

APHROMIS states loudly enough for everyone to hear:

"WITNESS and MATRIX are in this sphere of light. They are this sphere of light. They will soon melt into the SUPREME BEING."

"Into the SUPREME BEING!" NEW BUDDHA exclaims. "MATRIX told me they would go to the 6-D world."

APHROMIS answers him and tells everyone at the same time:

"I feel they'll even go to the 8-D world. NEW BUDDHA and me, we participated in their travel through the 7-D world, for we were like in 7th Heaven when we were but love and light within them. Now they are going to blend with all of the other individual souls that are already in the 8th dimension, the one of the SUPREME BEING. In fact, they'll be within the third part of the SUPREME BEING. However, all three are but one! The third part of the Trinity is where Christ resides, as the son of Humanity, the son of all intelligent beings, the prototype of all conscious beings. We're all destined to travel there, one day, and experience the entire Cosmos as one being. That is the cosmological reality."

While speaking, APHROMIS senses that it is not her saying these words but that SUPREME MATRIX is directly inspiring them from within her.

NEW BUDDHA slowly takes her hand and says:

"Now that they are gone, you are the only one with whom I can travel to the 7th Heaven."

"And give me other children?"

They smile at each other.

Everyone is flabbergasted to see this ball of light on top of the buildings, growing and growing, brighter and brighter, and then, suddenly, the last, remaining, visible, identifiable fragments of what once were MATRIX and WITNESS, Mr. and Mrs. Hennings, break to pieces as they explode, returning to the Heavens in a multitude of sparks.

APHROMIS continues, telling eveyone:

"We are all made of light. It is enough to vibrate with this substance of SUPREME MATRIX in order to feel it within. We are all love when we vibrate at the same pace as light. The sphere becomes our shape, the only supreme shape of light, of love. However, in the other dimensions, all of the shapes must dissolve."

She pauses a moment to see what effect her words trigger on people's faces, and then she continues:

"We'll miss them! However, because of the time we have all spent with them, we'll forever have a special connection with them. During your meditations, you may also speak with them as the Third Person of the Trinity, the Intelligence of the Universe. SUPREME

MATRIX is its substance. SUPREME WITNESS is the spectator. The Third Person of the Trinity is the SUPREME INTELLIGENCE.

"MATRIX and WITNESS will still exist and give the intelligent meaning of the Cosmos to you, as they have done when they were living amongst us. When you're lost, ask them for direction and for the meaning of your life, and they will answer you."

NARANI comes up to APHROMIS and says:

"They could have nonetheless said good bye."

"There is no good bye to say," she replies to her, in a lower voice, slightly stepping away from the rest of the people, and then continues on, louder, so everyone can hear: "We will be with them for ever and ever, for we all are the children or the clones of our two SUPREME BEINGS. I would rather say we all are the results of their love. She is the energy that attracts everything to Him, the center of the Cosmos. He is the energy that pushes everything away from Him to Her. We all are the results of those moves. We are the balance between attraction and repulsion, drawing and pushing, centripetal and centrifugal force. We are the fruits of their actions and reactions, the fruits of their love. We can say the same with our children, for as parents, they are the fruits of our love.

"NEW BUDDHA and I, we have just now chosen to create those fruits together. However, before leaving, WITNESS gave me the fruit of his love, the baby I am expecting and that RAM and his travellers from the future told me will be my successor to lead this land and her inhabitants to the 6-D world and to help planet Earth and Her children to move to the 5-D one in less than two centuries from now. Planet Earth has just moved to the 4-D world and the whole of mankind has moved with Her. The Door of Heavens has moved to the 5th dimension in order to prepare for this next dimensional shift.

"However, this next shift will again be as a result of the work of everyone; otherwise it will not happen, as was the case for the general shift to the 4-D reality: it wouldn't have happened without your working on yourselves. Leaders can't do anything without the masses, and reciprocally.

"MATRIX and WITNESS are now with Jesus Christ and Mary Magdalene, Radha and Krishna, Isis and Osiris, Eurydice and Orpheus, Niukua-Yin and Fuhi-Yang, and all of the other great couples that have led Humanity to the consciousness of being One with the SUPREME BEINGS."

4- EVERY ODYSSEY MUST HAVE AN ENDING

This story is finished.
I die to the existence, to being its author,
To better be reborn as the author of my next novel, and the one following…
Eternally!
My characters stop their existence too,
To better live again as the heroes of:

2017-2047: DIVINE CLONES OF TRANSPARENCY

"Knowing that secrecy is not Divine, choose transparency!"

The printed version will soon be published.

The first two chapters will be available for free online.

Then,

2047-2147: A DIVINE COSMOS OF CLONES

"Nothing is evil in the Divine Cosmos, clone of God!"

This third volume will be published one year after the second.

The first two chapters will again be available for free online.

Ask for them at divinecosmos@yahoo.com.

As we await these sequels,

Let's stay with our heroes for an ultimate moment!

Enjoy the epilogues on the following pages!

Last words to the readers who read this novel after December 2012:

You may say,

"I didn't see those events happening!

I didn't experience what is described in the seven days of the end:

The magnetic field becoming a symphony of sound and light in the sky,

Its split into two fields, one still flowing in the previous way, the other in reverse."

That's because your awareness of the 3-D world is still stronger.

Only people who are also aware of the 4-D world experienced those phenomena.

However, be reassured:

One part of you translated to the other dimension, to the other density:

Your double, your 4-D clone.

You are in both worlds!

And we'll see how doubles communicate in the sequels, volumes 2 and 3,

With our preferred heroes and with many new people too!

See you there and then!

EPILOGUES

1- SUPREME DIALOGUE BETWEEN MATRIX AND WITNESS, WHO NONETHELESS NOW TRULY FEEL AS ONE!

(That's why there is no separation, no line, in between their sayings,
Only italic for *MATRIX* and regular for WITNESS)

WITNESS, where are we?
I don't know where you are, MATRIX, but I am in the center of the Universe.
I feel it.
I feel I am the whole Universe itself.
I am in the center, like you, but I am also the sphere of the Cosmos.
I have billions of arms, billions of legs.
They connect me to the galaxies that are within this sphere.
The stars are like my fingers, the planets are like my fingertips.
I have the whole Universe at my fingertips! Wow!
And I witness that, MATRIX, from the center of it.
Through you, I also have the Cosmos at my fingertips!
Including all of the intelligent beings!
So, we became SUPREME MATRIX and SUPREME WITNESS!
We are not in either the 6-D or in the 7-D world!
But we are in the ultimate, the 8-D reality, the octave!
Yes! We are at the harmonic octave of reality.
However, I feel we are in between the two SUPREME BEINGS.
We are a third reality together within their reality, together altogether.
We're the third part of the Trinity that we dreamed of.

I felt like I would fall down when we traveled to this nowhere-everywhere.
Yet, it was instantaneous and we are without time for we are the whole space.
Being the whole space, for us, it's like there is no space.
And no space means no time!
So, our individuality died and we are reborn to this collective state.
Yes! But where are the SUPREME BEINGS?
We are them at the same time, MATRIX!
Yet, I have the impression that we're in a different Universe,
But that which is also the same.
It's the Third One!
There is a Trinity of universes, all similar and different at the same time.
More! I feel there are billions of universes like this one.
They are similar to the Universe where we were, with billions of galaxies.
Actually, we are somehow still living in that Universe too.
Vertigo!
So, we'll start again to be individuals?
We'll have relationships with the other BEINGS that the other universes are?
Am I right?
You know DIVINE MATRIX that you are right.
You are SUPREME, the SUPREME INTELLIGENCE of this Universe.
So first, you talk with me in order to organize everything.
Then, we talk with all of our clones over all of our Universe.
Then, we both talk with the SUPREME BEINGS.
Then, we talk with the other DIVINE COUPLES in charge of the other universes!
Then, it's never finished!
When you're eternal, yes! It's never finished!
And everything happens all at once in the eternal present of now.

2- SUPREME DIALOGUE

MATRIX:
I feel I am all people who are living everywhere!
Including those of the past and of the future!
And of all planets!
And of all of the souls of all of the planets, of all of the stars, of all of the galaxies!
WITNESS:
Me too! I am Christ and Judas,
Hitler and Gandhi!

George W. Bush and the thousands who died on September 11th, 2001!
Ravanasaraswati and Lucifarchangel!

MATRIX:

Who are those last ones?

WITNESS:

They live in planet Lucirava in the Milky Way.
I received that in my universal memory.

SUPREME MATRIX:

You are as we are: Everything!

MATRIX:

Yet, we're not completely both of You, SUPREME BEINGS! Are we?

SUPREME MATRIX:

Yes you are. Why not?

MATRIX:

We feel we are the Third Person of Your Trinity.

SUPREME WITNESS:

Trinity is but One!

WITNESS:

If we have a dialogue, that means we are not completely You!

SUPREME WITNESS:

For under-standing and upper-standing and in-between-standing, we tell you:
All of our clones are destined to be the third SUPREME BEING, at last!
In the eternal first and last moment!

SUPREME MATRIX:

I am the first and the last.

SUPREME WITNESS:

I am the beginning and the end.
You are everything in-between.
However, you are completely melted within us.
You are also within all of the Divine Couples you felt existed in other universes.
Separation is illusion!
A necessary illusion!
The Truth is:
We are One.

MATRIX:

Did we really deserve to be here?

SUPREME MATRIX:

Where? You are everywhere!

MATRIX:
When I was jealous of WITNESS wanting to make APHROMIS pregnant,
I showed that separation was my awareness, far away from the union with You.
SUPREME MATRIX:
You don't need to deserve anything!
You only need to be who you are in any situation created for you, by your Self!
You created yourself in the eternal present!
Particularly, you chose to help Humanity reach the threshold of awareness!
That allowed the 2012 shift to the 4-D world to happen on Earth!
Clones of God, before all, you are created from US.
So you come back to US.
Everyone can come back to US at any moment of the eternal present.
You are Consciousness, God, the SUPREME BEING, the Cosmos Intelligence.
This awareness is enough in order to be what and who you really are!
So be That!
MATRIX:
What's our role now?
SUPREME MATRIX:
In the Eternal Now, you are Consciousness; you are Me.
No other role for you other than being Me.
As it has ever been the role of each clone of US!
MATRIX:
And all of these beings I feel at my fingertips,
What do I do with them?
SUPREME MATRIX:
As we do now:
Have a dialogue with them!
Be their guardian angel, the one who takes care of them!
By talking with them and advising them!
As we did with you!
MATRIX:
So many people to talk to at the same time!
SUPREME MATRIX:
You now have the ability to talk to everyone at the same time,
For time does not exist for you anymore.
It is a little difficult at the beginning of eternity!
But you will get used to eternity in the split of a second.
WITNESS:
Yes, in fact, if time is an illusion, there is no beginning.

SUPREME MATRIX:
Right!
I used a way of speech.
Speech is good for dialogues.
And I am The Speech!
MATRIX:
And so, I also am The Speech!
SUPREME WITNESS:
And I am The Word!
WITNESS:
And so, I also am The Word!
SUPREME MATRIX:
So prove it, and talk to the materialistic people on Earth,
Guide them to join with the spiritual people before the end of 2147!
That's your first "job" as The Supreme Third Being of Our Trinity.
MATRIX:
That will take too long.
2147 will be over long before we can influence everyone, within them, on Earth.
SUPREME MATRIX:
You are the Speech!
Say: On Earth, May the light enlighten everyone in 2147!
And it will be done!
MATRIX:
Is it really that easy?
I thought you had to talk for ages within people before they evolve!
Wait a minute!
If I don't say it, Earth's 3-D and 4-D worlds will continue to interfere, as RAM said!
APHROMIS' son, who My WITNESS fathered, will suffer from that for ages!
No shift to the next dimension in 2147!
That reminds me of what Einstein said:
God doesn't play dice with the Universe.
But it's like playing dice if I wonder: to say or not to say!
That is the question!
If I don't say the magic words:
'May the light... etc.', the 3-D and 4-D worlds will crash into each other!
More and more!
May the dice be on 6-6-6, and Earthlings will be saved!
Hell! The number 666 is considered on Earth to be the mark of the Devil!
You want me to play the role of the devil's advocate or what?

WITNESS:
MATRIX! Cool! You're the Great Goddess now.
You have to behave as a Divine Being.
MATRIX:
How can I be Divine whereas I came directly to the 8th Heaven,
Without testing, or tasting, all of the others below?
I have just experienced the 4-D world for a bit on Earth,
And the 5-D one at the Door of Heavens for a little!
I tasted vaguely and quickly the 7th Heaven!
This fantastic yet bizarre experience of spiritual light, while love-meditating!
And not even with you, WITNESS, at the beginning!
Say the magic words, WITNESS!
I can't help it but not say them!
WITNESS:
MATRIX, stop being a prisoner of time!
At the beginning, I was also love-meditating with you, through NEW BUDDHA.
You were love-meditating with me, through APHROMIS.
At the end, we came to the 8th Heaven together.
Stop being a prisoner of limitations!
You are everyone, everything!
Actually, I feel we have always been everything, everyone.
Our lives as MATRIX and WITNESS were only dreams.
Okay! I say the so-called magic words:
Let there be light!
I now am SUPREME WITNESS OF THE SPLENDOR OF THE LIGHT!
I enlighten everyone on Earth in 2147!
MATRIX:
Okay darling!
I will stop being a prisoner of time!
I now am SUPREME MATRIX OF THE DAWN OF THE SPIRIT!
I inspirit Humans on Earth!
FOREVER!
FROM THE BEGINNING... TO THE END... OF THE ETERNAL NOW!

3- DIALOGUE BETWEEN THE READER AND THE AUTHOR OF THIS DIVINE FICTION

This story must unfortunately fit in between a beginning and an end,
Within your eternal present, reader!
However, a story is never finished.
Is the Creation ever finished in the eternal present?
Was the Cosmos ever actually created?
No it wasn't!
There is no beginning, no creation, only an ongoing process.
This novel is an ongoing process as well,
Like interminable TV series,
Like life itself!
Wait for the next episode of the adventures of MATRIX and WITNESS…
Excuse me, SUPREME MATRIX and SUPREME WITNESS of the Divine Trinity!
While waiting, you can have a dialogue with me, the author,
Through the Divine Internet:
Divinecosmos@yahoo.com.
You can also go to Clones of God's Facebook page,
In order to check the recent writings in my journal.

•

How can I narrate the next episode of this novel?
How can one tell the story of two Gods stuck in the Divine Trinity?
Lost in the middle of everywhere?
Is that what you're wondering, reader?
"Gods can eventually talk, but can they have adventures?" You wonder.
"That was okay with those of the mythologies!" You add.
"But not with the Divinity being everywhere and thus nowhere!" You conclude.
Justly, the SUPREME BEING, inspiring my mind,
Always has a trick in His/Her Universal Bag in order to solve this riddle.
And I can tell the adventures of all of those beings that are at Her/His fingertips!
Finally, the only difference in this novel from other novels lies in
The Extra-Ordinary and Supreme Relationships between beings and
The SUPREME BEING!

•

For those who don't believe the scientific assertions of this book,
I further provide a non-exhaustive list of websites and books.
Through them, maybe, you'll be astonished at discovering

That reality overruns, overtakes, oversteps and overshoots fiction.
Most of these assertions are controversial or crap for mainstream science.
Anyway, Copernicus, Newton and Einstein were at first controversial.
And the Grand Unified Field Theory through the Zero Point Energy principle,
Which Einstein was searching for during his entire life, in vain,
Will only be accepted when its detractors are dead.
It will become the new absolute,
As the law of relativity was an absolute during the 20th century!
However, only the Supreme Relativity is Absolute.
A so-called absolute is outmoded by the next one.
There was an 'absolute' limit of speed, in the law of 'relativity'.
Ironically!
However, experiments showed that information can go much faster than light,
In certain conditions!

•

What about the Reptilians?
Some websites are devoted to them.
Even a Supreme Matrix of the Universe is on the verge of being demonstrated,
On the Internet!

•

Finally,
A fiction is not only about plot;
A story is not only about people's lives;
A novel is not only about fiction.
Ultimately,
A fiction-story-novel is about expressing who one is.
Like the story of the Cosmos is an excuse for The One to express
What Unity is, through Diversity!
Diversity in all of our lives and throughout the whole Universe exists
In order for us to discover and enjoy the
One expressing what and who the One is.
Call it GOD, or SUPREME BEING, or The SUPREME MATRIX of Everything!
Or otherwise!
It doesn't matter!
It does Spirit!
Expressing the One Spirit gives Spirit to everything you experience.
Spirit is even within everything you have not experienced yet.

•

AND THE SPIRIT SEES THAT EXPERIENCING IS GOOD!

•

A final scene to reconnect with the trivial reality on Earth before the final curtain.

4- INTERVIEW OF TWO FRENCH PHILOSOPHERS

Hello everyone watching Spirit TV channel, on this Sunday, December 30th, 2012!
My name is Felicity Thompson.
My husband and I were the first Humans to see MATRIX and WITNESS.
Our two ETs are now gone and we miss them.
We miss their wisdom, their wit, their sense of humor.
We really miss their presence among us.
They taught us so much during their time on Earth.
Today, I am joined by two French philosophers:
Michel Hughes Lonfray or MHL and Benjamin Hector Levite or BHL.
They will share their insights on what has been happening in these past two weeks.
Michel and Benjamin, welcome to Spirit TV channel!
Let's start with how you feel after what happened to the magnetic field of the Earth?

MHL:
I feel dual: one part of me is with you here.
I feel another part of me is somewhere else.
For a few days now, I have heard people who followed those 2 ETs saying:
"There are now two dimensional worlds existing simultaneously on Earth."

BHL:
That's a subject for science fiction.
It can't be true: what the two ETs' followers said influenced you to feel that.
It's like hypnotism: one can suggest you sleep and you then fall asleep.

MHL:
But I really feel it deep inside:
My double still struggles with the Materialistic World we had before.
The two ETs' adepts say it's still a three dimensional world there.

BHL:
And we are now talking in the 4th dimensional one?

MHL:
I really feel that reality is different here and now.

249

BHL:

I don't feel it. I don't believe it.

Do you feel like we are in the good world?

And that our so-called doubles are still in the bad one?

MHL:

Don't make a Manichean interpretation of the situation.

BHL:

But the Universe only exists through the opposition between:

Light and darkness, movement and stillness, negative and positive, etc.

Even both of us: we are opposed in our philosophical view of reality.

Some even joke about our similar initials, MHL and BHL.

The only difference, they say, is that B is for Bien, Good, and M is for Mal, Evil.

Felicity Thompson:

Gentlemen! I am interviewing you today, but I also am a philosopher.

Please! Let's remain polite and be fair to each other!

SUPREME MATRIX said: the poles' reversal allowed for two parallel worlds to exist.

And the people of our meditation groups have a dialogue within with Her or Him.

What do you think about that inner dialogue?

And another complementary question:

As philosophers, what do you think about the SUPREME BEINGS?

I mean: about SUPREME MATRIX and SUPREME WITNESS?

Michel?

MHL:

As for everything, all is dual and there are also two kinds of philosophers:

Those who follow Plato, and who say, roughly, everything is God.

And those who follow Nietzsche, who say, God is dead.

The Platonist people say they live with the Divine Inspiration.

They say that it gives them access to higher insights about reality.

The Nietzschean people live with the perspective their reason allows them to.

And one thousand different minds elaborate one thousand values of reality.

I feel you, Felicity, are Platonist, through this inner inspired dialogue.

BHL is more Nietzschean, but his perspectives and values are his and only his.

For me, a philosopher must be universal, but he can also be an atheist.

I try to be universal and I don't believe in a SUPREME BEING.

So I have a dialogue with myself; I don't believe in an inspired dialogue with God.

BHL:
I believe in God but I also don't believe in an inner dialogue with God.
My perspective about the reality of the world is only mine, I agree.
And I agree with Nietzsche that each Human has his or her own vision of reality.
Nonetheless, we all try during our lives to agree on a few things.
That's the main challenge of this world.

Felicity:
So, both of you, what do you think of the saying:
'I am the God of the Universe of my cells;
I am as well a cell of the Body of God, which the Universe is?'
Is it a definition you could agree with, even as an atheist?
If so, as we have a dialogue with our cells, why not also having a dialogue with God?

BHL:
I am not an atheist, but the dialogue with God is not possible.
The dialogue with your cells is not possible either.
Actually, the dialogue between Humans is also quite impossible.
We are all isolated in our ivory towers, like islands separated by the sea.
And as I said, a dialogue in life is so difficult.
All of our life, we try to agree on even but a few things, but most of the time we fail.

Felicity:
But love is when the dialogue is crystal clear between two beings.
And we have a constant dialogue with our cells:
When your tongue cells are not happy with what you eat, they tell you: that's bad!
You listen or not.
When you don't and you eat the food anyway, you tell them: too bad!
So your stomach cells reply: feel bad!
This dialogue can be way more complex, and also way more positive:
You say: I love when the mouth of this person and mine are united.
And your lips' cells send you a message of pleasure when both salivas mix.
Same with God; you can say:
Thank you, God, for this love between my partner and I!
God replies: You are welcome in the Universe of happiness that love carries you to.
More complex dialogues are also possible between Humans and God.
MATRIX and WITNESS taught us how through meditation.

MHL:
I like your philosophy, Felicity, but no philosophy is better than another.
If that one works for you: great!
Mine is more hedonist, as you know.
And it can be summarized thus: enjoy what the present gives you.
If you don't like it, ask for help, even from the person that bothers you.
People can so suddenly receive an instant of grace and change their minds!
You could say it's the Divine Grace, maybe, why not!
It doesn't matter from where it comes.
Its greatness lies in the efficiency of the dialogue.
Even if, as BHL said, to dialogue between people is not always easy:
Grace is always here.
It is always ready to make the present moment enjoyable.

BHL:
I agree completely with you, for once, and ultimately, as Lao Tzu said:
If rape is inevitable, enjoy!

Felicity:
You have to be a man to agree with that philosophy.
All women of course disagree, and some men too.

BHL:
Rape can also be understood in a figurative way.

Felicity:
Give me an example!

BHL:
Any abuse is a good example:
Parents who force their children to do something against their will;
Children who control their weak parents for egoistic gains;
People who blackmail friends and ask them to lie for them thanks to their friendship.

MHL:
It can also be a boss giving his employees no other choice than to work for peanuts.
It is also a scientist finding a way that will make money for his or her company,
However it will be to the detriment of nature.

It is someone who knows he can save people from death but doesn't do anything.
Not saving people from death could be seen as being even worse than rape.

Felicity:
I think we understand what figurative rape means.
However, we can add: 'If you can't fight or fly, yes, enjoy!'
But most of the time, for children, none of these are possible choices.

MHL:
Lao Tzu said 'inevitable', it means 'inescapable'.
Only very strong-minded people can fight or even fly from the devil's rape.
And I am not its advocate!

Felicity:
I prefer being the Divine's advocate.
Gentlemen! We will conclude with that.
I thank you for your participation in this program.

BHL and MHL together:
You're welcome!

APPENDICES

APPENDIX-1: BIBLIO-WEB-GRAPHY

There are a plethora of books and websites dedicated to the subjects dealt with in this novel-essay. Below, sorted by themes, is a non-exhaustive list of resources I have found useful and that you can refer to in order to confirm what is written in this book.

However, there is no real way to finding the truth. Truth comes to you when you are ready to receive it. Each person/author receives part of what is the Truth not through random searches but primarily through intuition received from within. Therefore, first ask within for the Supreme Intuition to inspire you. The more books you read, the more websites you visit, the more chances you will have to get closer to the Truth, but it is important to remember though that no one will ever completely reach the Ultimate Truth, only the Divine Internet will send it within you, sometimes, in rare illuminating intuitions, which will alas only last a few seconds and then vanish like a rainbow when the rain stops or when the clouds hide the Sun.

So, the truth is within each of us, at different degrees depending on how many layers of lies are on top of it (lies from others or lies from yourself), preventing the connection with the Divine Within. When you feel a sense of coolness on the top of your head while you are doing something: reading, watching TV, meditating, doing virtually any activity, you will know that you are close to the Truth, for it is only within your deepest feelings that you will find it. This "Cool Breeze of the Divine" has been described throughout the ages in many different traditions, including as the Holy Spirit in Christianity, Ruh in Islam, Shekinah in Jewish lore, and as Kundalini in Hinduism.

There are more websites listed than books because they are free, easily accessible, and provide infinite possibilities of finding information through texts, pictures, videos and links.

The first web page you can access concerns the dialogue between the Oracle and Neo in The Matrix Reloaded, which inspired me to write the dialogue between MATRIX and SUPREME MATRIX in the novel, chapter 6 # 3. Go to: http://thematrixtruth.remoteviewinglight.com/html/reloaded-transcript-4.html

(In each section, books are listed first and then websites)

About cutting edge science, generally non-mainstream:

- Physics of the Impossible by Michio Kaku (A scientific exploration into the world of force fields and time travel)
- The Divine Matrix: Bridging Time, Space, Miracles, and Belief by Gregg Braden
- The Unknown Spirit by Jean Charon (This is one of the best books I know of that connects matter and Spirit, science and spirituality. For the author, a physicist, the Spirit is located within all of the electrons of the Cosmos, so it is within everything)

http://blog.hasslberger.com (Physics, Economy, New Energy)
http://cheniere.org (Scientist Tom Bearden's website)
http://divinecosmos.com (David Wilcock's website; a must see site to understand the world differently from the mainstream view)
http://electric-cosmos.org (The Electric Sky)
http://gravitycontrol.org (Anti-gravity research and technology)
http://hado.com/ihm/ (Masaru Emoto's website on water crystals photographs; how water reacts to the environment, including to music and words: each crystal is different)
http://holoscience.com (The Electric Universe)
http://keelynet.com (Free energy, gravity control, alternative science)
http://life-enthusiast.com/twilight/research_emoto.htm (Masaru Emoto's messages from water)
http://medicine-of-sickness.blogspot.com (Conspiracy, manipulation, repression, fascism, scientific deception, scandals, disinformation, alternative medicine)
http://non-newtonianphysics.com (Physicist William Day's site; the unity of space, motion and the structure of matter)
http://pureenergysystems.com (Grouping of sites with practical and innovative systems)
http://subtleenergies.com (Orme / Ormus / White Gold / Manna)
http://theresonanceproject.org (Physicist Nassim Haramein's website)

About the magnetic field reversal and 2012:

2012 has come and gone and apparently was not as catastrophic as some people foresaw or predicted. Most of the following books and websites are nonetheless interesting because of what they predict for the times following 2012, especially on subtle levels of reality, as described at the end of this novel, where many ethereal events occurred that most people did not see or feel, but which will influence the future, as we will see in volumes 2 and 3.

- 2013: The End of Days or a New Beginning? by Marie D. Jones
- Fractal Time: The Secret of 2012 and a New World Age by Gregg Braden
- Maya Cosmogenesis 2012 by John Major Jenkins
- The Mayan Code: Time Acceleration and Awakening the World Mind by Barbara Hand Clow (The Mayan calendar matches important periods of the evolutionary data banks of Earth and the Milky Way)
- The Mystery of 2012: Predictions, Prophecies & Possibilities (Articles by dozens of prominent thinkers)
- Toward 2012: Perspectives on the Next Age edited by Daniel Pinchbeck and Ken Jordan (36 articles by different authors)

http://alignment2012.com/ (John Major Jenkins' site)
http://calleman.com (The Mayan Calendar; Carl Johan Calleman's site)
http://www.diagnosis2012.co.uk/oldindex.htm (2012: dire gnosis; Beyond 2012; Geoff Stray's site)
http://pureenergysystems.com/news/2005/02/27/6900064_Magnet_Pole_Shift/index.html
http://survive2012.com (Robert Bast's site)

About the elite's control:

- Dark Mission: The Secret History of NASA by Richard Hoagland and Mike Bara
- Infinite Love is the Only Truth: Everything Else is Illusion by David Icke
- The David Icke Guide to the Global Conspiracy (and how to end it)
- The New Pearl Harbor by David R. Griffin (One of the best books about 9/11 being an inside job)

http://911truth.org (Investigation, Education, Accountability, Reform)
http://abovetopsecret.com (Alternative topics, videos and forum)

http://brasschecktv.com/ (Short videos on diverse subjects connected to the elite's control)
http://davidicke.com (Exposing the dream world we believe to be real)
http://historycommons.org (Information about past and present events and entities with timelines)
http://projectcamelot.org (Video interviews of whistle-blowers and transcripts of their evidence. One of the best sites to free one's mind from the Matrix we live in. It's like taking the red pill to see what our Matrix is)
http://serpo.org (About a top secret project à la "Close Encounters of the Third Kind")
http://wanttoknow.info (Reliable, verifiable information on major cover-ups and a call to work together for the good of all)
http://whatreallyhappened.com (Alternative topics, videos and forum)

About healthy living and environmental issues:

http://care2.com (Causes and news, health and green living, taking action, community)
http://earthhour.org (Focusing on special events and actions we can take)
http://www.edf.org (Climate change, land, water and wildlife, oceans, health)
http://thedailygreen.com (The consumer's guide to the green revolution)
http://vergemagazine.ca (Travel with purpose)

Magazines and websites that provide news that one can't find in the mainstream media:

http://www.namastepublishing.com/ (Wider view / Hidden news / Cutting edge information / Health)
http://nexusmagazine.com (Alternative news / Health / Future science / The Unexplained)
http://projectcensored.org (Media Democracy in Action / The news that didn't make the news)
http://ufodigest.com (UFO and paranormal news from around the world)
http://welcomethelight.com/ (UFO, channeling and ethereal information)
http://wired.com

About mixing spirituality and science:

- Shift of the Ages by David Wilcock (Free e-book: Earth is already undergoing a dimensional change)

- Science of Oneness by David Wilcock (Free e-book: A compelling case to illuminate the full cosmological mystery of God's existence)
- The God Code: The Secret of Our Past, the Promise of Our Future by Gregg Braden
To get these first two listed books:

http://divinecosmos.com
http://glcoherence.org (Global Coherence Initiative, uniting people in heart-focused care)
http://health-science-spirit.com (Natural, holistic and spiritual healing, spiritual science)
http://hiddenmysteries.org (Articles) and **http://hiddenmysteries.net** (Videos)
http://llresearch.org (Site of the 'Law of One' material; difficult to read at times but so very deep; about a collective consciousness from the 6th dimension communicating through a medium)
http://salvation-of-humans.com/English/ (Toward a meaning of life)
https://www.youtube.com/watch?v=dJdxwQtv6cc (Extraordinary videos with physicist and spiritualist Nassim Haramein)

About people named in the novel:

- Life from Light by Michael Werner and Thomas Stöckli (How to stop eating and live only on light and juices; see a few lines below, visit the website 'books.google.com' for free extracts of the book)
- "The Ringing Cedars" series of nine books by Vladimir Megré (Website information is provided just a few lines below this reference to the books)

http://books.google.com (Insert "Life from Light" by Michael Werner in the 'search' function to retrieve lengthy extracts from this book)
http://benjaminfulford.com (Benjamin Guildford, real name: Benjamin Fulford; He wants to change the world by changing our economic practices)
http://divinecosmos.com (David Wilwit, real name: David Wilcock; Some say he is the reincarnation of Edgar Cayce, the sleeping prophet)
http://jasmuheen.com (Living on light and peace)
http://jimhumble.com (Directory of Jim Humble's websites and MMS (Miracle Mineral Supplement, also called Miracle Mineral Solution or Master Mineral Solution)
http://projectcamelot.org (Project Camelot; video interviews of whistle-blowers)
http://ringingcedars.com/ (Vladimir Megré and Anastasia: The series of books can be read as novels, yet they're true, the author says, as extraordinary as that appears)
http://zeitgeistmovie.com ("The Spirit of the Age"; the end of old ages and the beginning of a new one, video documentary by Peter Joseph)

http://thezeitgeistmovement.com (Reforming society through an in-depth study of how it works)

About websites selling material on what to do to live freer:

http://life-enthusiast.com/ (Natural health solutions from this co-op)
http://toolsforfreedom.com (I haven't purchased anything yet from this website, but everything is certainly very tempting!)

About civilizations of the past:

- 1491 by Charles C. Mann (A new view of the "New World" before Christopher Columbus discovered it. Not surprisingly, it was much more civilized than the conquistadors and historians said it was)
- Supernatural by Graham Hancock (A journey into the other dimensional world that shamans in many different ancient civilizations explored with the use of drugs, which may very well explain the incredibly creative artistic expression of these ancient peoples through painting, monument construction and all kinds of uncovered artifacts)
- The Mayan Code by Barbara Hand Clow (Time acceleration and awakening the world mind)
- Underworld by Graham Hancock (The author shows how major floods inundated coastal lands when the Ice Age ended. Graham himself has dived to some of these antediluvian civilizations and their cities that are now 120 meters (400 feet) underwater)

http://atlantisrising.com (Magazine of ancient mysteries, unexplained anomalies and future science)
http://calleman.com (The Mayan calendar)
http://world-mysteries.com (Lost civilizations, ancient ruins, sacred writings, unexplained artifacts, science mysteries)

About ETs and the solar system:

- Dark Mission: The Secret History of NASA by Richard Hoagland
- The Divine Cosmos by David Wilcock (Free e-book: http://www.divinecosmos.com. It's about the energetic transformation of the entire solar system and the most recent ideas surrounding a cosmology that connects everything from the quantum level to the whole Universe)

http://enterprisemission.com (Richard Hoagland's site about artifacts on Mars and the Moon)

http://www.themarsrecords.com/wp/ (Much evidence of an intelligent presence on Mars, including the Relfes' account)

About spirituality:

- Remember, Be Here Now by Ram Dass (The author shares how he journeyed from being "an ordinary man" to becoming a spiritual being through experiencing the "here and now" of the Eastern tradition)
- Ringing Cedars series by Vladimir Megré (Anastasia; The Ringing Cedars of Russia; The Dimension of Love; Co-creation; Who are We?; The Family Book; The Energy of Life; The New Civilization; The New Civilization II - Rites of Love. A series of nine books telling the story of the author's encounter with the shaman Anastasia in the deep forests of Siberia. His different brief stays with her turned his materialistic view of the world upside down and into a spiritual adventure; nine incredible books! And to be continued! There is a tenth one in Russian. For more, see: **http://vmegre.com/en/titles/836/**)
- Spirit Matters by Michael Lerner (Only two words in the title but they say everything about everything)
- The Power of Now by Eckhart Tolle (To live in the present is the key to the inner Self)
- The Secret Teachings of All Ages by Manly P. Hall (First published in 1928 and constantly republished ever since. It's about mythology, ritual, symbolism and hidden wisdom)
- "…With God" series (Conversations… Friendship…Communion… Home…) by Neale D. Walsch (He was the one who inspired me to start my own inner dialogue with God)

http://sahajayoga.org (the official site of Sahaja yoga and its founder Shri Mataji Nirmala Devi. If there is only one site worth to see, it is this one)
http://bestspirituality.com (To inspire and change seekers through a deeper understanding of who they are and what this life is all about)
http://crystalinks.com (The site of psychic Ellie Crystal; lots of articles)
http://new-age-spirituality.com (A site to explore, through various channels, the idea that this life, this world, are not the totality of our existence. In fact, it might be just one small part of something much bigger, just one tiny step along an infinite journey)
http://practical-spirituality.com (The site of Dr. Chris Tong with introductions to his 25 books, which cover such key topics as: why do we suffer; does God exist; the nature

of death and after-death; the secrets of Human transformation; belief in God vs. experience of God; and the happiness of genuine spiritual awakening in God)

http://sacred-texts.com (Sacred texts from all of the traditions: the encyclopedia of sacred texts)

A few other sites devoted to helping you to both change yourself and to change the world:

http://care2.com
http://www.change.org/
http://www.globalcitizen.org/en/
http://secure.avaaz.org/en/
http://theshiftnetwork.com

APPENDIX-2: SUMMARY OF CONTENTS

CHAPTER 0
VACATION ON THE BLUE PLANET OF STAR # 1996

PHASE A: ARRIVAL (p 1)
Two ETs come to Earth for a vacation.
MATRIX OF THE DAWN OF THE GALAXIES, shortened to MATRIX;
And WITNESS OF THE SPLENDOR OF THE STARS, shortened to WITNESS.
MATRIX: "It's time to work, darling!"
WITNESS: "Are we going to work, or be on vacation?"

PHASE B: MEDITATION (p 2)
The SUPREME BEING gives them the choice of staying on Earth for a mission:
Helping the intelligent beings of this planet to evolve.

PHASE C: ETERNAL CHOICE (p 3)
"To land or not to land?"
"Experiencing and remembering are the purposes of life!"

PHASE D: YOUR CHOICE (p 3)
Reader's choice to read a short story or a novel.

CHAPTER 1
NEW WORLD

PHASE A: NEW CONDITIONING (p 5)

Receiving the entire memory of the Spirits of this star and of this planet

PHASE B: NEW REFLECTION (p 5)

"Such primitive intelligent beings, who are so convinced they have an advanced society!"

PHASE C: NEW BODIES (p 7)

"Worth becoming Human! To be primitive is not so bad after all!"

PHASE D: NEW WORLD (p 7)

Landing in the Gobi desert in China:
"I have the impression of knowing this land as if I had been living here all of my life!"

CHAPTER 2
POLARITY

1- KNOWLEDGE AND EXPERIENCE (p 11)

"Stop giving your opinion WITNESS! And continue experiencing the dance around this big fire!"

2- REALITY AND ILLUSION (p 13)

SUPREME BEINGS: "You are each a clone of us. That is the only reality. The rest is illusion."

CHAPTER 3
BEYOND THE ILLUSORY REALITY: THE CONNECTION

1- BEYOND THE ILLUSION OF REALITY (p 19)

"They are running and at the same time they are already at the pass. It's impossible! What's reality? What's illusion?"

2- THE SUPREME REALITY (p 27)

The more one raises one's awareness, the more one can see the upper worlds!
Until being completely united with the supreme level where the One resides.

3- TIME AND SPACE REALITY (p 27)

It's enough to enter the 4th dimension, which corresponds to time within the 3-D world,
In order to travel through time!

4- CONNECTION BETWEEN ILLUSORY REALITY AND SUPREME REALITY (p 29)

The SUPREME BEING in fact exists in two parts:
SUPREME MATRIX and SUPREME WITNESS.

They say, as one:
"And remember that you, each of you, can contact US at any moment!
Within your mind, even without meditating!
Where your attention goes, we are.

We are always where your attention goes!
Or in other words, when you are aware of US, we are here.
We are where you are aware of US."

CHAPTER 4
EXTRATERRESTRIAL AND TERRESTRIAL EXPERIENCE

1- LIVING IN THE HEAVENS AND LEAVING THE HEAVENS (p 31)
In this Paradise, it was enough to think of something and it appeared in front of you,
Physically!
APHROMIS:
"When you are away from the Door of Heavens,
We'll still be able to be physically in contact,
As soon as we concentrate on each other."
2- AS TRIVIAL TERRESTRIALS (p 33)
MATRIX:
"Thank you God, SUPREME BEING,
For making us, Your clones, laugh so much!"
3- ENCOUNTER WITH TRIVIAL URBAN TERRESTRIALS (p 35)
Or, from the terrestrials' side:
**ENCOUNTER OF THE THIRD KIND WITH THREE ALIENS,
INCLUDING TWO REAL EXTRATERRESTRIALS**
Our heroes meet with Felicity and George.
WITNESS:
"We can give so many explanations about what we see, or what we think we see.
But what is real? What is illusion? Who knows?"
4- SPIRITUAL GROUP (p 39)
The ways of communicating were subtle.
Subtle ways for making spiritual connections!
Spiritual connections for making the words flow between the Spirit of
Humans and The Spirit of the Universe!
**5- ENCOUNTER OF AN UNCOMMON TYPE
WITH THE SUPREME WRITER**
(p 43)
Reading your destiny, through speaking with the SUPREME WRITER:
What a great pleasure for you!
So begin the SUPREME DIALOGUE, within!

CHAPTER 5
READING PAST, PRESENT AND FUTURE

1- READING THE PAST (p 47)
Article in a newspaper.
When you believe in the "Source of Everything", everything is believable!

2- COMMENTS ON THAT ARTICLE BY THE WRITER OF THIS NOVEL, AND MORE (p 48)
For this is the story of who we are, you and I, reader!
For we are one within the SUPREME BEING, remember!

3- READING THE PRESENT (p 49)
Ajay:
"My dialogue with the SUPREME BEING taught me so far that,
Within Her gigantic body, which the Universe is,
Only the fantastic has a chance to be true."
WITNESS:
"You will have the most incredible spiritual experience you can have.
You will go through it in an apparently desert place."

4- READING THE FUTURE (p 55)
SUPREME WITNESS:
"WITNESS, you will have a difficult experience tomorrow.
Don't worry about that! It will be fine, at the end.
At the end of anything, everything is fine."

CHAPTER 6
ABOUT PERFORMING MIRACLES

1- EXACT DIVINE PROPHECY (p 59)
"What made you think that I will be the only one in trouble tomorrow, dear goofy wife?"

2- WRITER'S INTERVENTION AGAIN (p 61)
I couldn't help plagiarizing "The Matrix", the movie.
Any resemblance of the following dialogue
With a dialogue you have already heard is no coincidence.
It's voluntary!

3- DIALOGUE BETWEEN SUPREME MATRIX AND MATRIX (p 61)
SUPREME MATRIX:
"I am always here and everywhere, but especially within you now,
To help you remember who you really are."

4- DID YOU RECOGNIZE IT? (p 64)

Did you recognize the structure of the dialogue of the movie?
"The Matrix, Reloaded"?
For the fans of The Matrix, the movie:
The reference of the dialogue between Neo and the Oracle is on page 256.

5- WAIT AND SEE: GOOD FORTUNE WILL KNOCK AT YOUR DOOR (p 64)

"MATRIX, we didn't wait long for good fortune to knock at our door,
Showing the son Keymaker, announcing the father."
"WITNESS you are a genius!"
"You too MATRIX! We have everything within us.
It's enough to use the Spirit within us in order to be a genius."

6- EVERYTHING IS WITHIN US (p 68)

In each atom, the nucleus is the matrix, the substance of reality, its gravity,
And the electron is the witness, the spectator, the awareness of matter, the Spirit of it,
Like a female is the matrix of a baby's body,
And the male the witness of this miracle of creation!
However reversely, for everything is in everything,
The nucleus is the witness of what the frenetic electron does around it,
As the female witnesses what the hectic male does around her.

7- ARTICLES ABOUT MIRACLES (p 70)

At a certain level of being only what is fantastic has a chance to be true!

CHAPTER 7
BEING ONE WITH EVERYONE

1- BEING ONE THROUGH MEDITATION (p 75)

SUPREME MATRIX:
"I am everyone! I am the One! And everyone is Me!
Everyone is the One! Everyone is One within Me! That's it!"
MATRIX:
"I am glad to hear that!
Why don't You blow what You have just said in everyone's mind?"

2- BEING ONE WITH YOUR ENEMY (p 79)

It's always better to cooperate with the enemy than to fight with him, whenever possible! To feel one even temporarily with a so-called enemy is a way to be one with everyone.

3- BEING ONE THROUGH EXCHANGING IDEAS (p 84)

Once upon a time, there was only light.
In the beginning there was Einstein.

4- BEING ONE THROUGH SPEAKING WITH THE SUPREME BEINGS (p 90)

Where Jeff Connors becomes JEFF THE NEW BUDDHA OF THE EARTH,
And Arnold Keymaker, ARNOLD THE ONE WHO OPENED DOORS AND MINDS.

5- BEING ONE THROUGH ENLIGHTENMENT (p 92)

At present, people are really enslaved: slaves of money, drugs, work,
And in general of their narrow-minded way of living!
The enlightenment will make them free from people taking advantage of them,
People who make them consumption addicts, workaholics,
And more and more debtors of the bankers!

6- BEING ONE WITH EVERYONE (p 94)

Meroveus becomes NEW EINSTEIN OF THE ENLIGHTENMENT.
SUPREME MATRIX:
"The others are here and there to help you grow
In the awareness of being one with everyone, no more, no less!"

CHAPTER 8
SO OBVIOUS, SO SIMPLE

1- SIMPLE AND OBVIOUS COMMENTS FROM THE WRITER (p 97)

Actually, the whole Universe is already within you,
From the light atoms of hydrogen to the heavy iron ones.
It's enough to communicate with them to know the story of this Universe.
That's not only the theme of a novel; it's also the reality,
Which is within you and within each particle as well, as incredible as it is!

2- SIMPLE AND OBVIOUS AWARENESS (p 98)

Awareness of names:
Flower 0732 Innocence, Valley 57146 Optimism, Elephant 4674 Integrity,
Star 2132 Courage and Diamond 1432 Liberty are five Leptans.
Meroveus/NEW EINSTEIN becomes NEW TESLA.
Awareness of communicating through infinite space and voting telepathically

3- OBVIOUS REALITY, SIMPLE ILLUSION (p 109)

Check-up of Flower the Reptilian Leptan: pure and simple illusion of true science.
Meeting in Berkeley: obvious reality of open-mindedness.

4- SIMPLE AND OBVIOUS DIALOGUE BETWEEN THE SUPREME BEINGS (p 120)

Through dialogue, everything is obvious and simple,
Save when one doesn't believe in the power of duality to make unity,
Of diversity to make oneness,
Of communication to reconcile all of the parts of the One,
Of being Divine to heal one's Humanity.

CHAPTER 9
…ALL AROUND…

1- MEDITATING ALL AROUND THE EARTH (p 123)
"Let's meditate with all of those around the world!
We concentrate on our Mother the Earth and all of the beings living on Her.
We feel that we are One with Her.
We feel we are One with all living beings.
We send vibrations of love and harmony to everyone.
We are separate from no one."

2- DANCING ALL AROUND THE COSMOS (p 130)
SUPREME MATRIX's dance in this part of the Cosmos
Will soon create an inversion of the magnetic poles of the planets of the solar system,
Which will even more accelerate the spiritual transformation of Human beings on Earth.

3- SEEKING ALL AROUND THE WORLD (p 131)
Seekers from the whole world are gathering at the Door of Heavens.
Russians come there to study the expected magnetic shift in 2012.

4- LIVING ALL AROUND THE EARTH (p 141)
Through the Akashic Records, APHROMIS shows different Human ways of behaving.
How people in power lead the world, considering basic people as cattle.

5- LIVING ALL AROUND THE GALAXY (p 156)
MATRIX:
"Nothing is impossible!
Everything is possible with the faith in the SUPREME BEING."

6- TRAVELING ALL AROUND THE SOLAR SYSTEM (p 163)
About Einstein's equation and traveling through upper dimensions
About the Moon, Mars, the planets, and Atlantis

CHAPTER 10
CLOWNING AROUND, CONSUMING LESS AND WISER, FEEDING THE LIGHT

1- CLOWNING AROUND (p 179)
Truth Disclosed about the solar system being secretly colonized for ages by ETs,
And by Earthlings after WW II through anti-gravity technology.

2- CONSUMING LESS AND WISER (p 190)
Ecoloco-op, eco-friendly consuming, locally sharing, through co-ops.
Jim Humble and the Miracle Mineral Supplement.

3- FEEDING THE LIGHT (p 195)

Jasmuheen and Michael Werner fed through light.
Starting the dialogue with the Divine within.

CHAPTER 11
SPIRITUAL ODYSSEY

1- REAL DEMOCRACY ODYSSEY (p 201)
Dennis Muccinich was supported by communities and simple people,
He addressed everyone in his famous talk:
"My dream for Americans"
Then he started to really do what he said he would do in co-ops, favoring:
Neighboring communities, Small businesses,
Balanced parallel education, Natural health care, and
Loans without interest for people with low wages!

2- SPIRIT ODYSSEY (p 213)
WRITER: You've always the last word to say.
SUPREME MATRIX: I am the Word…
SUPREME WITNESS: And I am the Light…
…FOLLOW US!

3- THE WAY TO 2012 AS A SPIRITUAL ODYSSEY (p 215)
For it was the last judgment! For it was the Apocalypse!
For it was the shift that all of the civilizations after the fall of Atlantis were waiting for!
For it was the end of the kingdom of Ego and the beginning of the Kingdom of God!

CHAPTER 12
THE SEVEN DAYS OF THE END

1- DECEMBER 18th TO 24th, 2012 (p 225)
The beginning is like the end, reversed. Everything is symbolic, actually.

2- MORE ABOUT DECEMBER 24th, IN THE ETERNAL PRESENT OF NOW
(p 231)
About love meditating and spiritual conception
How MATRIX and WITNESS become a sphere of light and explode to pieces,
So as to fulfill the prophecy of their becoming the Third SUPREME BEING.

3- DECEMBER 25th: CHRISTMAS DAY (p 237)
MATRIX and WITNESS are now with Christ and Mary Magdalene,
Radha and Krishna, Isis and Osiris, Eurydice and Orpheus, Niukua-Yin and Fuhi-Yang, And all of the great couples that led Humanity
To the consciousness of being One with the SUPREME BEING.

4- EVERY ODYSSEY MUST HAVE AN ENDING (p 239)
This story is finished: I die to the existence, to being this author,
To better be reborn as the author of my next novel, and the following one…

EPILOGUES

**1- SUPREME DIALOGUE BETWEEN MATRIX AND WITNESS,
WHO NONETHELESS NOW TRULY FEEL AS ONE!** (p 241)
I have the whole Universe at my fingertips!
2- SUPREME DIALOGUE (p 242)
Unity, Duality, Trinity! Oneness, Dialogue, Clownery!
Everyone, as a clone of God, can clown with the SUPREME BEING
At any moment of the eternal present!
**3- DIALOGUE BETWEEN THE READER
AND THE AUTHOR OF THIS DIVINE FICTION** (p 247)
Like this novel, Life is an ongoing process.
The relationship between beings and the SUPREME BEING is Life: Dialogue is Life.
The Divine Internet allows all of the dialogues possible,
Including between reader and author.
And the SUPREME BEING always sees that the experience of dialogue is good!
4- INTERVIEW OF TWO FRENCH PHILOSOPHERS (p 249)
Felicity interviews MHL and BHL.

APPENDICES (p 255)

1- BIBLIO-WEB-GRAPHY (p 255)
2- SUMMARY OF CONTENTS (p 262)

THE AUTHOR (p 271)
THREE APPETIZING TEASERS (p 272)

THE AUTHOR

As Intelligence of the Nature of the Universe,
I chose to incarnate on Earth through Michael INUIT, born in 1947.
As Universal Biographer of Life,
I am experiencing who I am through Michael, yogi, artist, teacher…
…It does not matter what I did, nor what I do; for I am a clone of God:
The Intelligence of the Nature of the Universe Incarnated Terrestrially.
I am **INUIT**.
We are all INUITs.

A TRINITY OF TANTALIZING TEASERS: THE THREE ARE TRULY ONE

CHANGE YOURSELF!
CHANGE THE WORLD!
All masters of wisdom, one way or another, said:
If you want to change the world, first change yourself.
And it's still true in modern times.
Actually, there have always been so many who live applying that saying.
Yet, we have still not reached the critical mass required to really change the world.
For each of us lives it their own way and do not necessarily tell others about it,
Because we feel our contribution is small.
Actually, there are neither small changes nor big changes.
However, some changes do look more difficult than others.
But it's very subjective, depending on what you have in mind.
Start with what looks easy for you, and then go forward.
Yet you could tell me: What personal change is sufficient for changing the world?
There is a simple rule for knowing that:
If everyone does it, would it be hell in the world, or would it be heaven?
With an example that is not a supposition but is real, you'll understand better:
If everyone drives a vehicle with an internal combustion engine,
Does that lead to hell or to heaven?
Obvious answer: It is hell now on Earth because of carbon dioxide pollution.
What if everyone as often as possible rides a bike instead of a car?
Again obvious: We would be on the way to heaven.
You can ask the same kind of question for everything.
And start building heaven on Earth!
At this point you could ask me:
What if I feel I am the only one to have changed and everyone else still lives in hell?
And I answer: The most important thing lies in your living in heaven!
For heaven is within you, first!
Second, what if people see you happy in heaven?
They will ask you how to be in heaven, as you are.
And to welcome someone in heaven will make you even more heavenly happy.
If that's possible!
Actually, nothing is impossible!
Is riding your bike as often as possible, impossible?
Is recycling your kitchen waste into compost, if you have a garden, impossible?
Is opening your mind to the not obvious and the marvelous, impossible?
Is choosing each of your words as wisely as possible, impossible?

Is stopping watching TV and having more fun while doing family things, impossible?
Is sustaining life only with fruit juices, impossible?
Is inventing an anti-gravity device, impossible?
Is producing free energy from the Divine Substance of the Cosmos, impossible?
Is stopping hellish things from happening in the world, impossible?
Is making heavenly events occur, impossible?
Are miracles impossible?

WHAT IS FOR YOU THE MOST IMPOSSIBLE THING TO ACCOMPLISH? SPEAKING WITH GOD?
That's one of the easiest! Easier than inventing an anti-gravity device!
"CLONES OF GOD" is evidence of that!
Isn't speaking with You, God, easy?
Yes it is!
I am within everything, so I am thus within everyone.
Therefore, it's enough to establish the communication!
And the dialogue starts.
It's not as easy as in a phone conversation, but actually it's not too far off.
The trick lies in listening.
How can two people have a dialogue if one person speaks all of the time?
The dialogue with Me happens within the Human mind,
Human beings have to shut up! To stop thinking!
Then, to listen to My thoughts!
I inspire you all of the time!
Call them the thoughts of:
Your Consciousness,
Your Guardian Angel,
Your Spiritual Intelligence,
The Divine Within,
The Individualized Infinity,
The Self of Yourself,
The Connection to the Divine Internet,
God Clowning with Her Clone.
ETC!
Extra Terrestrial Clone you are!
Extra Cosmic Clown I am!
Yes, I can be funny!

And yes, you're a clone of the Divine Primordial Cell.
It developed thanks to My Intra-Uterine Universe!
You are My cells, divided from the Original One.
Any of your cells has the same genetic code as the fertilized ovum of your birth.
It takes just one cell for geneticists of genius to make the whole of you.
Geneticist of Genesis I am!
Human beings are all clones of the Whole I am.
"Ye are all gods!"
Even the Bible, which is very often boring, has moments of genius!
I inspired those moments.
For the others passages, their writers wouldn't shut up:
Then they wrote their own thoughts.
Sometimes, when God inspires me within, I have no words to say!
Yet, when you start having this dialogue within,
All of the rest becomes possible!
Divinely certified and true!

"CLONES OF GOD" IS FICTION.
BUT MANY PASSAGES ARE IN FACT OUR REALITY.
IT CAN BE READ AS A NOVEL OR AS AN ANALYSIS OF OUR SOCIETY.
Two ETs come to Earth for a vacation.
However, they choose to stay for a mission:
To help Earthlings to have a dialogue with the Divine Self Within.
They help Humans to change the world before an event happens in 2012.
"Now, come, join together with these ETs and Humans on this journey, this odyssey!"
Read about the disclosure of the deceitful reality the elite would like to hold us in!
Learn how to escape from this cunning reality by this inner dialogue!
Truth is within, isn't it, God?
Truth is everywhere, within, without, within your imagination.
Within what you imagine to be without!
However everything is within Me; without Me, nothing exists!
This material world is of worth and of value, indeed.
But only if it is connected to the Whole Eternity of the Spirit!
That which I am! That which you are. That which everyone is.
It is true in a way that through You I have access to the whole Cosmos.
My imagination is Your making images within me about everything, everyone.

For sure!
With Your prompting me within, my words can be the Word, can't they?
Chances are that you are right if you are 100% connected to Me.
But alas it is rare.
How can I be 100% connected to You and be the Word of God?
Shut down your thoughts and listen to Mine.
You do it now: you stopped thinking on your own and let Me open My mind.
The Divine Imagination that makes the world exist is yours if you listen to Me.
Then we can let our imagination express itself freely.
And start clowning with the world, My clone!
That is true for sure!
Now about clowning: for those who are interested, there is another book I wrote:
"GOD AND I, CLOwNING, Dialogue with the Divine Within".
In it we are clowning, God and I, in a journal about:
My life, my dreams, my writings to people.
God is also clowning with Her creation.
The two last chapters include a play and a short story.
The latter is actually the beginning of "CLONES OF GOD".
Have fun with your reading of it.
Have fun with everything, clown-clone of Me, God!
Promote it once you have read it!
You can email me at divinecosmos@yahoo.com to get it.
And then you can read volume 2 and 3 of the Divine Cosmos Trilogy:
Volume 2: 2017-2047: DIVINE CLONES OF TRANSPARENCY
"Knowing that secrecy is not Divine, choose transparency!"
Volume 3: 2047-2147: A DIVINE COSMOS OF CLONES
"Nothing is evil in the Divine Cosmos, clone of God!"

275